T5-ANZ-500

Dear Romance Reader:

This year Avon Books is celebrating the sixth anniversary of "The Avon Romance"—six years of historical romances of the highest quality by both new and established writers. Thanks to our terrific authors, our "ribbon books" are stronger and more exciting than ever before. And thanks to you, our loyal readers, our books continue to be a spectacular success!

"The Avon Romances" are just some of the fabulous novels in Avon Books' dazzling *Year of Romance,* bringing you month after month of top-notch romantic entertainment. How wonderful it is to escape for a few hours with romances by your favorite "leading ladies"—Shirlee Busbee, Karen Robards, and Johanna Lindsey. And how satisfying it is to discover in a new writer the talent that will make her a rising star.

Every month in 1988, Avon Books' *Year of Romance,* will be special because Avon Books believes that romance—the readers, the writers, and the books—deserves it!

Sweet Reading,

Susanne Jaffe
Editor-in-Chief

Ellen Edwards
Senior Editor

Other Books in
THE AVON ROMANCE Series

DREAMSONG *by Linda Ladd*
FORBIDDEN FIRES *by Elizabeth Turner*
HEART'S FOLLY *by Jane Feather*
INNOCENT FIRE *by Brenda Joyce*
PASSION STAR *by Mallory Burgess*
PRIMROSE *by Deborah Camp*
WINDS OF GLORY *by Susan Wiggs*

Coming Soon

DESPERATE DECEPTION *by Maria Greene*
WILD SPLENDOR *by Leta Tegler*

Avon Books are available at special quantity discounts for bulk purchases for sales promotions, premiums, fund raising or educational use. Special books, or book excerpts, can also be created to fit specific needs.

For details write or telephone the office of the Director of Special Markets, Avon Books, Dept. FP, 105 Madison Avenue, New York, New York 10016, 212-481-5653.

Temptation's Darling

Joanna Jordan

AVON BOOKS NEW YORK

TEMPTATION'S DARLING is an original publication of Avon Books. This work has never before appeared in book form. This work is a novel. Any similarity to actual persons or events is purely coincidental.

AVON BOOKS
A division of
The Hearst Corporation
105 Madison Avenue
New York, New York 10016

Copyright © 1988 by Debrah Morris and Pat Shaver
Published by arrangement with the authors
Library of Congress Catalog Card Number: 88-91524
ISBN: 0-380-75527-0

All rights reserved, which includes the right to reproduce this book or portions thereof in any form whatsoever except as provided by the U.S. Copyright Law. For information address Anita Diamant, Literary Agent, 310 Madison Avenue, New York, New York 10017.

First Avon Books Printing: September 1988

AVON TRADEMARK REG. U.S. PAT. OFF. AND IN OTHER COUNTRIES, MARCA REGISTRADA, HECHO EN U.S.A.

Printed in the U.S.A.

K-R 10 9 8 7 6 5 4 3 2 1

IN MEMORY
THIS BOOK IS DEDICATED
TO OUR BELOVED OZARK GRANDMOTHERS

Willie Bell Mitchell Dugan
(1897–1982)
and
Bessie Texanna Cannon Murray
(1907–1975)

Chapter 1

Hot Springs, Arkansas, 1889

Stealing out of town under cover of darkness went against Case Latimer's principles. He didn't like running from trouble and would've preferred to disentangle himself from this knotty situation in his usual manner—by talking himself out of it. But having met the Buscus brothers, he knew there would be no rational discussion tonight. Those boys were full-grown in body only, the impulsive type who shot first and did their talking after the smoke settled.

"Sorry to spoil your rest, old boy," he murmured as he tied the saddlebags containing all his worldly goods onto his sleek, black Morgan stallion. Long ago he'd decided that if he ever died and someone felt the urge to inscribe an epitaph on his tombstone, he wanted it to read: *He traveled light, lived fast, and died happy.* The problem was, he wasn't ready to die. Not by a long shot.

He led Shadow out of the livery stable, closing the heavy door behind him. A stiff wind shook the new leaves on the trees and the scent of coming rain was as strong outside as the scent of animals had been inside.

"I don't like traveling on a stormy night any better than you do." He spoke quietly to gentle the high-strung horse. "But we have to make tracks before the wedding party shows up." Wishing he had a slicker, Case pulled on his long dust coat and was preparing to mount when the sound of dissension rumbled from the stable.

"You wait here for Latimer. The skunk might try to sneak out of town." Case recognized the voice of the eldest Buscus brother but he couldn't remember his name.

"That means I'll miss all the excitement." The whiny tenor, stuck somewhere between boy and man, had to belong to the youngest of the three.

"That's right," said another, obviously the middle brother. "It also means you won't be around to get in our way when we catch the sorry sonuvabitch who did our poor sister wrong."

"Would that be the same poor sister what blacked your eye last night?" Youngest goaded.

There was a scuffle inside the barn and Case knew it was now or never. He swung onto the saddle and turned Shadow toward the main road. The animal snorted and tossed his head as if excited at the prospect of a midnight run. He'd gone only a few yards when three men charged out of the stable.

"You get on back here, Latimer," Youngest squeaked. "You gotta do right by Ardetta."

Case reined in his prancing horse and called over an ominous roll of thunder, "I understand your wrath even if it is misguided. I'm a gentleman and if I were guilty of any wrongdoing, I'd do the honorable thing."

"That why you're hauling yourself out of town in the middle of the night, like a drag-belly cur, 'cause you're so honorable?" Eldest's fingers twitched near his gun belt.

Case had no desire for the confrontation to result in gunplay. He didn't want the death of one of those boys on his conscience and he sure as hell didn't want his demise on one of theirs.

"Nothing untoward happened between your lovely sister and myself."

"That ain't the way Ardetta tells it." Middle hoisted an ancient shotgun and sighted down its length.

"But that's the way it happened." A lot of good it did Case to have right on his side. They had might on theirs.

"You're a bald-faced liar!" Youngest waved a pistol in

what was meant to be a menacing manner. He could use a lesson or two in concealing his emotions, Case thought. Anyone who cared to look could see the kid was as nervy as a sore tooth. And he didn't like being on the business end of a nervous man's gun.

"I never touched her." There was no need to tell them that the girl whose honor they were ready to die for had practically begged him to make a woman of her. They were riled up enough as it was. More than likely they weren't crack shots, but Case didn't want to risk a wild bullet hitting him or his horse. Shadow meant more to him than anyone he knew.

Middle spoke up. "Ardetta's set on marrying up with you, fancy man, and we're duty bound to keep you from leaving."

"That's what I figured." Case shrugged and, touching one finger to the brim of his black hat in salute, he nudged the restless horse away from the men. "Sorry to disappoint the young lady, but I've got places to go and things to do. No hard feelings, boys," he called magnanimously over his shoulder.

"You come on back here, Latimer, or we'll make buzzard bait outta you," Youngest screamed.

"If you don't stop, we'll shoot," Middle yelled.

He didn't and they did. Shadow interpreted the shots as a starting gun and took off as if his own money were on the race.

Scarcely a mile out of town, Case heard the riders galloping behind him. The night-shrouded trail was as dark as the inside of a snuffbox and roiling clouds blanketed the high-riding moon. A bullet cut the ground just ahead of him and he leaned low over Shadow's neck. Only inexperienced fools would fire at a target they couldn't see. More shots zinged past and he hoped there was no such thing as beginner's luck. It would be a sorry way to go, especially since his brief flirtation with Ardetta Buscus had been less than gratifying.

He didn't have much experience with respectable women

but knew that unless a man was ready to be hog-tied, he didn't dare take what they demurely offered. The Buscus gal had not only enticed him; she'd initiated a round of kissing that might have gotten out of hand had it not been for his well-exercised self-control.

A bullet zipped past his ear, so close he could smell the powder. Too damned close. Dammit to hell, was he going to have to plug one of the young idiots, after all?

Abruptly, he wheeled Shadow into a full turn, stopped, and yanked his rifle out of the sheath on his saddle. Hoping a taste of their own medicine would prove a deterrent, Case cradled the barrel on his arm, aimed carefully over his pursuers' heads, and popped back several shots. They cursed him but didn't slow down. He clicked a command which his well-trained mount recognized instantly and they were once again galloping full out.

In a crazy way, he was beholden to Ardetta, damned if he wasn't. If she hadn't come banging on his hotel room door, he never would've known her brothers were laying for him. He remembered her as he'd last seen her, snarling with rage and spitting like a she-cat. It hadn't been a pretty sight.

When he'd answered her knock, Ardetta had flung herself into his arms. "Case, we've got to get out of town fast."

"Calm down, Ardetta," he'd said. "Tell me what happened." He shrugged out of her grasp and pulled up a chair. "Sit down."

Temper flaring, she kicked the chair away. "I don't have time to sit down. My brothers are coming here and they've got guns. Don't you understand? They're aiming to get us hitched."

Case dropped into the chair himself. Being a gambler, he knew that for all the ones you won, there were some you lost. He didn't mind facing the music in most cases, but he wasn't partial to the wedding march. "I hope they'll understand if I decline."

"Decline all you want to, that won't stop my brothers.

You have to get out of here tonight. And you have to take me with you."

"I'm going all right, but I travel alone." Case gathered his few belongings and crammed them into his saddlebags. In his trade, a man didn't require much.

Card talent, good nerves, lively wits, and the ability to conceal emotion didn't need to be packed and unpacked in every town and mining camp, and he had little use for material possessions. His wardrobe wasn't extensive, but what he owned was of the highest quality. He prided himself on that much. Maybe he was what some folks would call a drifter, but he had standards.

"I want to go with you, Case," Ardetta screeched.

"I have no intention of being railroaded into marriage. I'm only twenty-six, not nearly ready to settle down. I may never be."

"If you take me with you, they'll leave us be. And you don't even have to marry me."

"Thanks for the offer, honey, but like I said, I travel alone."

Ardetta grabbed his arm, forcing him to look her in the eye. "They think I'm in the family way."

"Now, why would three marginally intelligent young men think something like that?" he asked tightly.

"Because I told them so, that's why," she said spitefully, her blond ringlets bobbing around her plump, reddened face.

"Well, well, what an interesting turn of events." But a turn he was hardly responsible for. "Congratulations."

Ardetta slapped him then. Hard. "If you leave without me, I'll make sure the rest of your life's a living hell."

He rubbed his cheek and maneuvered his jaw to make sure it was still in working order. "Why me, Ardetta? I'd make a lousy father, hanging out in saloons and fancy houses like I do. Surely, there are more acceptable candidates. Or is it my rugged, manly appeal?" he asked wryly, consciously employing the boyish dimple he knew contrasted with his polished manner. "I'm not a newborn fool, you know."

"You are if you think you can lead me astray and get away with it." She jammed her hands on her ample hips and glowered at him with farmgirl hauteur.

"I led you astray? Hell, gal, it was run or get trampled."

She hauled back to slap him again, but he grasped her wrist and she spat out scornfully, "You won't be laughing when my brothers get done with you."

"They'll get over it. I can't believe your moderately upstanding folks are anxious to welcome a gambling man into the bosom of their family."

"They're not. But your way of life suits me fine. For years I've dreamed of getting out of this no-horse town, away from these mean-minded, dreary people. You're my ticket out."

Shrugging, he thoughtfully stroked his dark, well-tended mustache. His looks alone had endeared him to any number of females, and he was glad he hadn't fallen into this one's nasty trap. "Sorry, sweetheart, but this ticket isn't ready to be punched."

"I want some excitement and I need you to get started."

"One thing you've gotta learn, honey. In this old world, it's every man for himself. Every woman, too." He blew her a kiss from the doorway. His last glance at Ardetta Buscus, she was pitching the biggest, noisiest fit he'd ever witnessed.

Case knew he was innocent, but it was his word against the word of a maiden pure and fair. He didn't much cotton to being back-shot, nor was he fond of the idea of killing farmboys, but either one was a damned sight better than being married. Wedlock was a life sentence in a picket-fence prison from which there was no escape.

This was the worst mess he'd ever been in, but he had only himself to blame. He'd learned early to choose his female companions carefully from among the ranks of powdered and perfumed women he met in the gambling dens and saloons where he plied his trade. He avoided "nice" women who got the wrong idea when a man lavished a little attention on them. He'd found that paying in advance eliminated most wounded womanly feelings and almost all misplaced expectations.

Tugging at the wide brim of his black hat, he pulled it lower on his head as Shadow sped down the road. He cursed his bad luck, thinking he wasn't known as Hard Case Latimer for nothing, when blue-white lightning forked down and a heavy caisson of thunder rent the night with a sound like cannon fire. Perhaps the self-righteous Buscus family had enlisted the aid of God almighty himself.

"Hey, Lord," he yelled. "I'm innocent. Surely you wouldn't strike a man down in his prime for something he didn't do."

Lightning arced from heaven to earth and Case smelled the electricity in the air. Then suddenly rain hammered down, pouring so hard it was nearly impossible to see even a few feet in front of him. The faithful Shadow never faltered.

Rainwater cascaded off Case's hat brim and ran down the collar of his coat onto his back, making him cold and miserable. During the illumination of another lightning flash, he spotted a small wooded area alongside the road and guided the horse into it. The rain beat against him, penetrating his coat and stinging his face and hands like cactus needles. The harder it rained, the madder he got.

He should've known better than to get involved with a gal he met at a Kickapoo Indian Medicine Company show. But it had been over a year since he'd had any homemade apple pie and he'd gone there with plans to enter the pie-eating contest.

A gaggle of town girls was hanging around looking for excitement and he'd struck up a conversation with them. Ardetta Buscus had drawn him away from the others, acting so aggressively coy that he'd temporarily lost his good sense. When she squeezed his arm and told him she had two pies in her buggy, he thought he'd died and gone to heaven. He'd agreed to forego the contest and join her for a moonlight ride just as Dr. Laughing Dog began his patter about his wondrous dewormers, salves, and stomachics.

Coyness wasn't the only thing Ardetta had been aggressive about and he'd had to summon up all his southern chivalry to turn her down gently. When he'd relented and obliged her with a kiss, she'd been on him like ugly on an ape. He'd narrowly escaped her clutches with his honor intact.

Diligently, he swore to avoid all nice women in the future. Especially nice *young* women. The worst part was he never did get any of that damned apple pie.

Shadow skittered nervously as Case urged him up an embankment in search of a different road, any road that would get him as far away from Hot Springs and the peal of wedding bells as possible. Once he was out of the running in the in-law contest, the Buscus boys could turn their aggravating attention to locating the hapless man who'd been unable to resist their sister's charms. Damn women and their wiles anyway.

Surely he'd lost his pursuers by this time. He was anxious to find cover until the storm abated and, when he spotted a dense thicket, he dismounted and pulled his reluctant horse in behind him. The branches slapped at his face and clawed at his coat as he wound his way deeper and deeper. At last he was satisfied that he was safely hidden.

Shadow was breathing hard so he took a handkerchief from an inside pocket and held it over the animal's nostrils. Horse and man stood patiently for long moments. He heard voices nearby and groaned inwardly. Laying a hand on the horse's flanks, he willed him to remain quiet.

When they spoke, it was as though the men were right on top of him. "I coulda swore he come this way." It was Youngest.

"Where'd he get off to then?" Middle challenged.

"If you ask me, that damned Latimer's got his ass snugged up in some woman's bed, all dry and happy, while we're out here like a bunch of drowned possums," Eldest groused. "We'd best head on back to the nearest farm until this god-awful rain lets up."

"If we go back without him, Ardetta will take a strip off our butts," Youngest whined.

"Well, I for one ain't afraid of our sister, li'l brother," said Middle.

Since Case had been subjected to the girl's fury, he had to wonder if the young man was bluffing.

"I'll be sure and tell her when we get home," Youngest sneered.

"You do," Middle growled, "and I'll send you straight to hell."

"Shut up, or I'll skin the both of you," Eldest promised.

"He started it," Youngest accused.

"Me! You started it!"

"Good God a-mighty!" Eldest swore. "Do I have to end it?"

"Ardetta'll be madder than a sore-tailed bear if we come home without that no-count gambler man," Youngest pointed out unnecessarily.

"I don't care! I'll be damned if I'm spending what little's left of this miserable night listening to the two of you bitch," Eldest ground out. "I'm heading for shelter."

"I don't know," Youngest complained. "If we go back without him, we'll have to face Ardetta. If we stay out here we'll get shot or end up with the miseries."

As far as Case could tell, it was a toss-up as to which would be the worse fate. They argued so violently, he began to hope they might end up shooting each other. No such luck, but they did finally agree to stop for the night. Their bickering eventually became inaudible as they headed back the way they'd come.

To get a good head start and be as far away as possible by morning, Case would have to keep moving. Shadow trudged on all night while he dozed in the saddle. When daybreak finally came, the rain had tapered off to a bone-chilling mizzle.

They might have given up the chase last night, but Case knew the Buscuses would be searching for him this morning. Though normally not the optimistic sort, he found something good about the miserable rain; it had surely washed out his trail. Fortunately for him, the brothers were sodbusters, not skilled trackers. He had every right to assume he'd seen and heard the last of the Buscus family. Lady Luck was fickle, but she'd never deserted him for long.

His most cherished possession, his freedom, was out of imminent danger and he made a vow to whatever gods were watching. Never again would he get himself in a position where a woman, any woman, could threaten it.

Butler County, Missouri

"Hellfire!" January Jones shaded her eyes from the bright April sun and glared at the unwanted visitor in the yard. Of all the critters who might have turned up on her doorstep, Mose Cleek, with his sly grin and ravaging eyes, was only slightly more welcome than a fluxy hog.

If she hadn't been expecting her father home for the midday meal, she never would've opened the door. "If my pa knew you was here, he'd knock you plumb into next week."

"I think ole Jubal's too lazy to knock anybody anywheres, but I 'spect he mought take a whip to you fer cussin' at comp'ny." Mose leveled his gaze on her chest. Just thinking about January being in that shack all alone made him swell up fit to bust his britches.

"You ain't company and you're about as welcome as typhoid." She scowled as Mose's stubby fingers plowed through his dusty brown hair. The action was slow and deliberate, like everything he did, as if he had to ponder even the simplest of gestures. All seven of the Cleek boys were tetched in some way, and the girls had their own problems, as was apt to happen when mother and father were double cousins.

It wouldn't bear close inspection, but as far as she could tell, Mose had the correct number of limbs and digits, though they were long and gangly. She reckoned he was lucky not to be whomper-jawed; not all the Cleek offspring had been so fortunate.

He also had more sense than the rest, especially that spooky Yarnell who claimed to have seen something so scarifying that his hair had turned white overnight. He wasn't too clear on what the something had been and it changed considerably from telling to telling. Yarnell called it a bog-stalker, said it looked like a man but was too big and ugly and hairy to be a human being.

Though January guessed the creature was some long-lost Cleek foundling, it had become a local legend. Parents used it to threaten their unruly children. She wasn't sure which would be more frightening—encountering the bog-stalker on a moonless night, or running into poor, pale Yarnell himself.

As a result of his ravings, he'd become an even greater object of ridicule in the community than merely being a Cleek would've justified. Yarnell was determined to trap the bog-stalker and prove once and for all he wasn't as crazy as everyone said. But it'd take more than a hairy, inhuman creature to convince most folks. The bogs and woods were so full of Yarnell's clumsy snares that a body had to be careful not to get caught up in one.

"You better be nice to me, January. Real nice, else me and Toad mought git insulted an' leave." Mose scratched the ugly dog's ears, but his stare remained on her breasts and she shivered as if he'd touched her.

Toad was aptly named, but he was the best hogdog in the holler and Mose was rightfully proud of him. The dingy, mud-colored cur bared his teeth and growled as menacingly as an animal his size could. "Now, wouldn't that be a pure dee shame," she scoffed.

Mose laughed, a sound like a hoe striking rock. He was narrow between the eyes and his leering look made her feel like she had the time she'd stepped barefoot into the middle of a dead-ripe possum.

Mose had been sniffing around after her since they were young'uns and more than once she'd had to wallop him good. But he was no longer a skinny adolescent to be bested with a well-placed kick. He was a crude clod of a man who was becoming more open about his threatening intentions.

Mose was barely tolerable, but Old Man Cleek was the landlord and Pa had made January quit chucking rocks at Mose for fear they'd get kicked off the sorry farm they sharecropped. She'd obeyed, but the way Mose was staring at her now made her fingers itch for a good-sized stone.

Mose's gaze roamed over her slim body. The gal was finally getting some meat on her. She always was a wasp-tongued hellion and that hadn't changed, but her hair had toned down some and he liked the looks of the mahogany curls better than the red fuzz she'd sported as a kid. He hankered to bury his nose in that long stuff.

It'd smell purty. January was right regular about her bathing habits—he knew because he'd peeped through the window plenty of Saturday nights and watched. He'd seen her pale skin, glowing like a ripe peach in the flickering light of the kerosene lamps, and the sight had left him with a bad case of the horn colic. He imagined what it would be like to have his way with her, to touch her all over and render her weak and helpless. The thought was enough to turn a man inside out and Mose knew it wouldn't be much longer before he could quit dreaming about it and just do it.

"Yer finally a-curvin' out some, gal," he said. "Yer face is changin', too. Why, yer pert near the finest gal in the holler." Mose was going to enjoy bringing her down a few pegs. He was handy at putting women in their place—on their backs beneath him. This one wielded her tongue as well as she did a skinning knife, but a good skirt-tossing would knock the pepper out of her.

It stuck in his craw that she acted so high and mighty around him, and her no better than the white trash she claimed him to be. Her pa was a no-good and always would be. When Mose was done with her, she'd get down on her knees and beg forgiveness for her high-handed ways.

"Comin' from a damned squee-jawed stinkbird like you, that ain't much of a compliment."

"I orter take a whip to yer butt fer talkin' to me like that." He leered at the pleasurable prospect. "An' I mought jest do that, once yer my woman."

"I ain't your woman and I never will be," January informed him vehemently. "So climb on your mule and git on out of here, Mose. I ain't got time to waste on the likes of you. I got chores to do." For emphasis she curled her fingers around the barrel of the Winchester propped by the door.

"That ain't a very friendly way of talkin', January June. An' I reckon we orter start cozyin' up since yer pa tole me he wouldn't be agin' you an' me a-jumpin' the broomstick, if we was a mind to."

"That'll be the day." She swung the rifle to her shoulder, leveling it at his chest. "Don't take another step, Mose." She glared at him, so mad she could spit nails. The very thought of Pa agreeing to such a thing made her want to run behind the cabin and retch. He'd often accused her of doing unseemly things with Mose, that overgrown horny toad, but she hadn't believed he meant it. She'd thought it was the moonshine talking.

If Pa came home in one of his moods and caught her alone with a man, she was liable to get another hiding. She was grown, nearly eighteen, and she'd be damned if she'd take a whipping over the likes of Mose Cleek.

The Cleeks were a lazy, shiftless bunch. None of them believed in doing an honest day's work and they had acquired their questionable assets not through industry, but by thieving and cheating other folks. All they were good for was drinking, gambling, whoring, and mistreating their women. Shameful as it was, her own father wasn't much better.

As a youngster, January had promised never to leave Pa. At the time, she'd needed him more than he needed her, but as the years passed, that promise grew harder to keep. If Jubal Jones wasn't mighty careful, he'd soon be shifting for his own lazy self.

January worked harder than a stump-tailed cow during fly time, only to have him drink and gamble away what pitiful profits she managed to make. Only stubbornness and determination made her work so hard for so little. That and the hope of someday owning her own place. A place where she could prosper by her efforts and not have to forfeit half of everything to a landlord.

She'd been thinking a lot about that lately, seemed she couldn't get the crazy notion out of her head. Pa always likened her to a snapping turtle; once she latched on to an idea, it was hard to shake it loose. She brandished the rifle and ignored the snarling dog. "Git, Mose, you've worn out your welcome."

"We'll jest have to see about that." Mose stood his ground.

Her gaze narrowed on him. He was a dang sight worse than Pa, who at least claimed to be sorry when he sobered up and found out what he'd done. Being worthless was about the kindest thing a body could say of Mose Cleek. He was cruel and sneaky and had the morals of a razor-back hog. He didn't know it, but she'd seen what he'd once tried to do to his little sister.

Poor Almafae hadn't been quite right since the time she'd stuck her head in a gnat ball at the age of two. Mose ought to be strung up and thrashed for what he'd tried to do to that pitiful child.

January usually avoided the Cleek place, but one day she'd stalked a deer into the bottom. When she heard Almafae's frightened cry, she crept up the hill, quiet as a panther. A body with any sense just didn't blunder into a swarm of Cleeks; it wasn't healthy. Hidden by the crookedy barn, she'd witnessed his would-be attack on the twelve-year-old child. January had been poised to shoot Mose, right in the privates if need be, but Old Man Cleek had come out of the barn and saved the girl. His action had kept January from wasting a perfectly good bullet.

She'd stayed hell and away from the Cleek place ever since. Because she avoided Mose at every turn, she couldn't figure out why he was so determined to attach his unwanted attentions on her. Most likely it was her attitude and ability that appealed to him. He probably figured to get a woman who'd work so he wouldn't have to. It was common knowledge around the holler that her sweat and ingenuity had acquired for the Jones family a cow, two shoats, and a swayback mule. The ornery horse didn't really count for much, since he was worthless to a fault.

It was also well-known that Jubal was do-less by nature, either drinking up or gambling away every penny he got his hands on. As a skilled hunter, January did more than her share of providing for the two of them, in addition to doing most of the farm work.

"Didn't you hear me?" Mose hated the way January ignored his proposal and didn't much care for where she was pointing that rifle, either, not when he'd come courting. "I'm a-thinkin' it's time fer us to get hitched."

"If you think I'd leave one shiftless no-account for another, you got nothin' but slop for brains," she said coldly.

Mose stared at the gun she held, then shrugged. "I been waitin' a long time, but I kin wait some more, I reckon. You got the drop on me this time, but you'll be sorry of it. Ain't nobody kin say I ain't give you fair warnin'." Taking his own sweet time, he swung his lanky frame onto his mule.

"Someday soon, I'm gonna catch you alone, without no gun nor knife, without a door to lock or a pappy within shoutin' distance. Then we'll see who does what to who. You could make things a mite easier fer yerself, gal," he threatened. "Sure ya don't wanna sit and talk a spell?"

In answer she cocked the rifle and watched as he kneed the mule and rode away. She probably hadn't heard the last of him.

She slammed the door with a bang and threw the flimsy bolt. Her heart thudded with rage at Pa for leaving her alone and at Mose for what he'd suggested. Did he honestly think she'd ever bed down with him? There'd be many a wet and dry day before that happened.

Sometimes, when Pa was liquored-up crazy and took out his rage and frustrations on her, January almost hated her mother, Daisy, for not taking her when she'd left and for not coming back to rescue her since then. But truth to tell, she remembered her pa holding this same Winchester on Mama, ordering her off the place.

After that, Pa's drinking had gotten worse, and through the years he'd gradually left more and more of the work for her. At first, she'd dreamed up excuses for his failures, attributing his bad temper to loneliness and Mama's absence. He must've been sorry for sending her away because sometimes he called Daisy's name in his sleep.

As she got older, January realized his drinking was a sickness that took over its victim's heart and soul. During his "bad spells" Jubal gambled foolishly with money they could ill afford to lose. Then he'd come home and accuse her of every sin in the Bible, and a few that weren't. When he got in a bad way, he reminded her that she was beginning to look just like her mother, and she'd better be careful she didn't start acting like her, too. He declared he'd countenance no more trollops in his house.

Sometimes, January worried he might be right. Like mother, like daughter? If her mother really was as bad as Pa said, would she turn bad, too? She swore it'd never happen and was extra tidy in her habits, keeping herself above reproach.

Someone banged on the door and January nearly jumped out of her skin. "Git out of here, Mose Cleek, before I mallyhack you!"

"Open the danged door, gal!" her father commanded.

Relieved, she flung it open and threw her arms around his neck, wrinkling her nose at the sour smell of corn liquor on his breath. "Oh, Pa. Where've you been so long?"

Jubal was in no mood for shenanigans. He scowled at January's display of emotion and drew away. The gal didn't show him proper respect. "That's none of yer business. Mose been here a'ready?"

"He has." She faced her father, who wasn't much taller than her own five foot two. "If that polecat don't quit coming around here, I'll—"

Jubal stumbled across the room. "You'll start actin' like a gal what's bein' courted, that's what you'll do." He was cursed with this child. He couldn't figure out how she'd turned out so hardheaded. He'd done everything he knew to break her spirit. It was a wonder any man would have her, even a man like Mose.

"Courted? By Mose Cleek? You can't mean that, Pa!"

His look was cold, his eyes reddened by his indulgence. His head hurt and he wasn't putting up with no back talk. He'd just take what he'd come for and get on back to Dorville's for that big poker game. He glanced at the mess of greens and fatback on the table, but he had no appetite. He didn't need food when spirits were available.

"Oh, cain't I jest?" Pushing her, he staggered past and slammed his fist against the table, rattling the chipped dishes. "He swore he'd do things proper, courtin', weddin', and all." It'd be just like Mose to go back on his promise. "He do anythin' he shouldn't?"

"Nothin' Pa, I swear." January was torn between anger and the fear her father's drinking engendered. "I don't like him, he scares me. He's bad, Pa, clean through, and I don't want nothing to do with him. We don't need the Cleeks or this broken-down farm."

She went to him. "Lets you and me pack up and get out of the holler. This ain't no way to live. If we owned our own land, we'd do right well by ourselves." She didn't add that she hoped getting away might restore some of her father's long-lost self-respect.

Jubal thrust her aside. ''The day the Joneses become landed gentry is the day they start givin' it away,'' he scoffed as he searched the larder. He emptied a tin of precious sugar on the floor, then dumped coffee on the table.

''They *are* givin' it away, Pa.'' She ran across the room and dug beneath her cornhusk mattress. ''Looky here.'' She waved a crumpled piece of paper like a banner. To her, that's what it was: a flag of freedom. ''Let's head on out to the Oklahoma Land Run and get us some of this here free land.'' She rushed to him, hoping to stop any further destruction.

Jubal slung her away, laughing derisively. ''Yer jest like yer ma! Always dreamin', always wantin' what ya kin never have. Sharecroppin' ain't good enough fer ya. Gotta own yer own land.'' He grabbed the blue piece of paper she'd snitched from the window of Hibley's store. ''How do you know anythin'? You cain't even read.'' He wadded up the treasure and flung it across the room.

She retrieved it and stuffed it down the front of her dress. ''I don't have to read to know what it says. That land's free for the takin', the gover'ment says so, and I'm gonna get me some. With or without you.''

''You ain't goin' nowhere!'' He couldn't let the gal get any wild ideas, not when Mose had made him such a tempting offer.

''I'm goin' all right. I'm leaving here. I'm tired of workin' myself near to death for somebody else.''

He stared at his daughter, caught up in the flashing fury of her brown eyes. Some of her wild hair had slipped from the string that held it and high color stained her cheeks. She was the spit 'n' image of Daisy. It was hard to treat her good, to think right, when she grew more and more like her mama. She was a silent, daily reminder of the shameful way he'd treated his wife and he'd been thinking it was time to marry her off so he could have some peace.

In sober moments, it shamed him to think and act like he did. But he wasn't sober now.

"Jest like yer wicked mama, you want to go runnin' off 'cause you think it'll be better someplace else." He drew back his hand and smacked her, knocking her against the curtained crate in which she stored her possessions. She hit the floor hard.

"I know you got silver dollars stashed somewheres. The ones you been hordin' to git us to Arkansas City and that fool land run. You ain't goin' nowhere, so hand 'em over."

"I won't," she said calmly, picking up her scattered belongings.

Jubal stood over her, his fists clenched. "I'll beat ya within an inch of yer life, gal. Give 'em to me!"

"Over my dead body." January knew the look in his eyes, but she could take it; she had before. But it would be the last beating she'd ever suffer. That money was her start in Oklahoma. It was sewn into a secret pocket in her drawers to keep it safe from her father's drunken thievery. "I froze my tail off all last winter trappin' pelts to earn that money. I'm not about to let you gamble it away."

"Trappin'? Ha! How'd I know you didn't git it from Mose?"

"I wouldn't take a dipper of water from Mose if I was burnin' at the stake!"

"There's some reason he's got his eye on you. And there's only one thing men like him are after." He slapped her again. "I won't have you whorin' in my house. Hear me, gal?"

Ears ringing, January glared at him and something in her heart turned to cold, hard stone. She wouldn't defend herself against such false accusations. She raised her chin and looked him in the eye until his gaze fell away. He stalked over to her cot, ripping off the quilts. "You got some money and I want it."

"You took it all last time. You just don't remember because you was too damned drunk!"

"Don't you ever talk to me like that!" He grabbed her by the shoulders, shaking her. "I know you got more. Where the hell is it?"

"I won't give it to you and you'll never find it."

She was a muley wench. He could beat her till his arms fell off and she'd budge nary an inch. But there was one thing she feared more than a whipping. "You better start talkin', gal, or I'll lock you in that cellar again. A few days down there will loosen yer stubborn tongue."

January wrenched away from her father. Trembling, she stared him down, though his threat filled her with more real terror and revulsion than had the idea of coupling with Mose. "You'll have to kill me first."

Despite his drunken haze, Jubal knew she meant it and backed down. "Mose is of a mind to hitch up with ya. He offered a right smart sum to take ya off my hands." He spat a stream of tobacco juice on the floor. "I don't know why he'd want a sassy little piece like you, but I'm tired of puttin' up with ya." He stalked to the door.

January blanched. Pa would do anything for a few dollars; it was his biggest failing. "I won't do it! I'm not some critter you can barter off to the highest bidder."

"Yer a female and you'll do as I say until ya take a man. Then you'll do what yer man says."

Fury rose in her like a spring flood. Hellfire! She wasn't a pluckless, milk-livered rabbit who'd take being sold without a fight.

Jubal fumbled drunkenly for the latch. Now that his mind was made up, he was anxious to give Mose the good news. He'd have to skip the game tonight, but soon he'd be flush with money and could do whatever he wanted. Five hundred dollars for January. It was a steep price for a hateful thing like her. No telling how Mose was planning to come by such a sum, but Jubal didn't really care.

"It's time you was married, gal, yer ripe for the pickin'." He opened the door to leave. "And jest so's you'll know, Mose bought the cow and them pigs yer so partial to. Said he'd be by to collect everythin' later. Could be he's tryin' to do the right thing by ya. Mought even make ya a good husband."

"I need a husband like a frog needs spitcurls!" January yelled at his retreating back as he rode off on the mule. "Where you goin'?"

"After a jug. When I git back, we're goin' to the Cleeks' to celebrate the happy occasion of yer betrothin'. Get gussied up and start lookin' like a happy bride. I won't be gone long."

She stared after him, stricken by the unholy thought of trading vows with that scaly peckerwood, Mose. She'd suck pond scum first.

She rushed into the cabin, a hasty plan already forming in her mind. Looking around, she spotted the nearly empty flour sack, grabbed it up, shook it, and sent a cloud of white powder swirling in the still air. She ransacked their food supplies, taking only the necessities. She had money to buy more later; the important thing was to be far away before Pa returned. If need be, she'd live off the land. Heaven knew she'd done that often enough.

She dropped her slingshot, knife, and personal belongings into the sack. It was a pitiful collection. She hadn't much to show for her life in Possum Holler and if she stayed, it was all she'd ever have. That thought strengthened her resolve. Running away might be crazy, but the uncertainty of a questionable future in the Territory was far less frightening than the reality of a life of misery with Mose.

She had no qualms about escaping on Pa's horse or taking his prized Winchester, even if it was stealing. She figured she'd earned the twelve-year-old rifle and even older horse.

She tried to wrestle the ancient saddle onto Brownie, but he sidestepped. "Hellfire! Brownie, you chucklehead, I'm in a hurry. I don't have time for your pranks. I gotta be a piece from here before Pa and Mose find me gone." Too bad Pa had ridden the mule.

It took all her strength and agility and a fair amount of

cussing to get the job done. But there wasn't a contrary beast born that could best January Jones. She stepped around Brownie and untied the reins.

"Takin' a little trip, air ya, gal?" came a voice behind her.

She whirled around. "It's no business of yours what I do."

Mose leaned against the door and Toad snarled beside him. She lunged into the saddle, thinking to make a run for it. She kicked fiercely, but the stubborn beast wouldn't budge. "Hellfire, Brownie, giddap!"

Moving with unusual quickness, Mose dragged her from the saddle and slapped her. The action provoked Toad into a barking frenzy.

"Oh no, ya don't, ya little hellcat. What ya do is my bizness now. I passed ole Jubal on the road an' he said y'all was jest dee-lighted to accept my proposal."

"He's a damned liar. I wouldn't marry you if you was the last man in the holler." January winced as his fingers bit into her arm. "Let me go, you varmint."

"Don't reckon I kin do that. Not now there's a weddin' in the wind. I figger we don't gotta wait fer a parson to give us his blessin'. I'm plannin' to have you here an' now." He spun her around, trapping her. "Be still an' I won't hurt ya none. It'd be a shame to bruise up that purty face." Toad's yipping drew a fierce kick from his master. "Git outta here, you sumbitch!" The animal tucked its tail and backed off.

Mose's hot, evil breath assaulted January's senses when his mouth came down wetly on hers. She feared she'd be sick, but knew there wasn't time. She had to escape before he did something worse. She couldn't get to her weapons and she didn't have the strength to fight him off. She'd have to outwit him.

Forcing herself to relax in his arms, she pulled her mouth free and murmured, "That hurts. Is this how you treat women?" It was hard to keep the hatred from her voice, but she managed it.

''Not one that's ready to oblige me.''

He pressed the hard ridge of his manhood against her and she was filled with revulsion. Forcing a false smile, she felt his grip loosen. She chose that moment to draw back her knee and slam it up between his legs. He moaned and doubled over. She yanked away and made a dash for the door.

She didn't head for the house; the weak latch would never keep him out now. Instead she plunged into the woods, clutching her skirt up to her knees, hoping to put some distance between them.

Mose sounded like a wounded bull on the rampage, and he was right behind her. Toad bayed as though he were on the scent of a wild hog. January knew the woods intimately and prayed Mose wasn't so well acquainted. Eluding the dog would be another matter.

Her boots churned up the dead leaves left over from winter and she ducked limb after low-hanging limb, feeling them rip at her clothes, but she was beyond caring. Mose was gaining ground.

''I'll git ya, ya little bitch! Ya cain't run forever. I'll git ya,'' he puffed out. ''Shut up that infernal yappin', Toad!''

She had no intention of running forever, but she could outlast him. If she led him a merry enough chase, he'd soon fall down panting and she'd have time to double back to Brownie.

''Shee—it!'' The strangulated cry was bitten off as though Mose had swallowed his tongue. ''Goddammit,'' he raged. ''I'm caught! Sumbuddy help me!''

January ran on, fearing a trick. When she no longer heard crashing sounds behind her, she wheeled to a stop and slunk back through the dense bushes to see what had happened. She nearly laughed out loud when she caught sight of Mose hanging upside down by an ankle from one of his own brother's bog-stalker snares.

He was strangely silent and white-faced. It was possible his ankle had snapped when he'd been snatched up. He swung in a slow circle, his arms dangling, his fingers clawing air. Then Toad closed in and Mose had to bounce and squirm to avoid the animal's snapping jaws.

He spotted her and beseeched, "Git this addlepated varmint off'n me." He turned on his prize dog. "Dammit, Toad, I ain't no hog! Cut me down, January, I'm a-dyin'. My leg's busted an' I'll prob'ly be crippled fer life."

"Serves you right, you lowdown skunk. Maybe then you can't go chasing after poor girls what think you're lower than a step-ant."

"Stop yer sassin' an' cut me down. I ain't sure how much longer I kin stand the pain. I mought die up here."

Clamping her hands on her hips, she walked slowly around him, surveying the ingenious snare. Maybe Yarnell wasn't so simpleminded after all. "Good. It'd serve you right and spare me the trouble of doin' it myself."

Mose clenched his jaws against the pain. It felt like his bones and sinews were being ripped apart. "Please, cut me down."

"Refreshin' as it is to hear you beg, Mose, I'm not fool enough to do that." This was too good to be true and she owed Yarnell a debt of gratitude for giving her this head start. She raced for the shed and Brownie, pausing momentarily to yell back to her tormentor. "Keep hollerin', Mose. Someone will miss you sooner or later."

On impulse she called, "Toad!" When the animal's ears pricked up, she added with a smile, "Sic 'im, Toad!"

From the sound of his vicious snarls, she decided Toad was a well-trained hogdog. Mose cussed the dog first, then her. "You ever come back to this holler, gal, an' I'll make you sorry you was ever born. Ya hear me, gal? I'll rip off yer clothes an' I'll . . ."

Curses and threats of what he'd do to her if he ever got his hands on her stung her ears, but didn't scare her. She'd never return and Mose didn't have the wherewithal to chase after her. Circling back to the shed, she mounted Brownie and, with no remorse about leaving Mose strung up like a hog at butchering time, she headed west.

She was on her way to Arkansas City, Kansas, one of

the official starting points for the Oklahoma Land Run. She didn't know how long it'd take or how far it was, and she didn't much care. January urged the reluctant Brownie into a loping gait and forced all thoughts of Pa and Mosé from her mind. Suddenly she was filled with excitement.

She was free!

She'd claim herself a homestead and have the home and security she'd always longed for.

It wouldn't be easy, but she knew what it would take to make her dreams come true. Gumption, but she had a whole batch of that. Hard work, something she was uncommonly familiar with and not opposed to doing on a regular basis.

For once, Brownie didn't balk but pounded down the trail as if glad of the chance to make things up to her. January grinned in spite of the bone-jarring ride. She'd take care of herself from here on out. Hellfire! That wouldn't be anything new.

January Jones was through with men who wanted to boss her. In fact, she was through with men of any kind. God help the next one who got in her way!

Chapter 2

It had rained off and on for five days and, though the downpour had finally stopped, the sky was filled with clouds to match Case's temper—dark and dangerous. He'd pushed north out of Hot Springs with the notion of heading for points west after putting a couple of state lines between his pursuers and himself. Pursuers who should have given up the chase long ago.

He hadn't counted on the Buscus brothers being so infernally tenacious. Not only had they found a trail where none existed, but they'd dogged it like simpleminded hounds. No matter how many times he'd doubled back or circled around to throw them off, they'd managed to stay just beyond heel-snapping distance. He'd been forced to avoid settlements, and the loss of small comforts such as beds and hot meals had unkindly disposed him toward those responsible.

The fools had to be operating on dumb luck. If they had a lick of sense, they'd have figured his destination was the no-man's-land of Indian Territory and never would have followed him into Missouri. But since they had, he was just about mad enough to take them on. If he had to spend one more night sleeping on the ground, maiming those boys wouldn't seem quite so reprehensible.

"If it's a showdown they want, a showdown they'll get," Case told Shadow, turning him away from the road and into a copse of trees. No doubt they'd be along soon. He waited.

* * *

January stood in the stirrups to ease the pain of the hard ride and massaged her backside.

"Hellfire, Brownie, giddap now." Nudging the horse with her heels, she glanced at the sun riding low in the west. Its position added to her determination to get moving. When darkness fell, it would come quickly and completely to the oak and pine woods.

It was a good thing she wasn't planning to take up horse thieving on a permanent basis. "No real horse thief would've made a getaway on a mulligrubbing critter like you." She punctuated her disparaging remark with a firm kick. "Come on, you flat-footed old bonebag, I'm not planning to lose out on free land on account of a cross-grained horse whose only purpose in life is to give me saddle sores and eat whenever he's a mind to."

The animal snorted, yanked on the reins to get his head down, then chewed the bit, trying to reach the new spring grass growing along the muddy road. Yanking back in a stubborn contest of wills, she slapped him with her hat, but the beast ignored her.

"At the rate we're going, the run will be over before we get to Oklahoma," she yelled.

The horse glanced back at her, his rheumy eyes conveying that he didn't really care. Once more he jerked at the reins—the movement sent a flicker of pain through her raw hands—and promptly returned his attention to his single-minded chomping.

January sighed in frustration and hoped she'd make a better homesteader than she did a horse wrangler. She'd spent plenty of time staring at a mule's rump as she plowed the fields, but she'd never had much occasion to ride for pleasure. Not that riding Brownie was any pleasure; from the moment she'd hauled him out of the shed, sheer determination and fear had made her fight him every step of the way.

January wasn't afraid of the unknown, of starting over alone in Oklahoma, or of the hardships she would have to endure. But she *was* afraid of being caught and returned to Possum Holler. To Mose. She choked back a giggle and wondered how long he'd swung in that trap before someone had cut him down. He'd be laid up awhile and madder than a whole nest of hornets. One thing was for certain sure: she could never go back.

Pa was too lazy to chase after her, but she wouldn't put it past the old reprobate to turn her in to the sheriff for taking his horse and rifle. January knew horse thieves were at the bottom of the outlaw barrel, undeserving of much justice. Hellfire, out west people still hanged them.

That's why she'd hacked off her hair with her hunting knife and dressed in poorly fitting boy's clothes. Adding to her growing list of crimes, she'd snatched the garments off a bush while an unsuspecting housewife was busy at her laundry tubs. She was pleased with her disguise because, if the law was after her, they wouldn't be looking for a runty little feller, which was exactly what she looked like.

The cold rain had stopped, but January had yet to warm up or dry out clear to the skin, despite the sun which had peeked in and out among the clouds all day. To add to her discomfort, a brisk breeze had caked on the mud until she thought she'd never come clean.

As if being muddy and saddle sore weren't enough to make a body cranky, she was also hungry. The snitched supplies had run out, and though she'd gathered a few wild greens, the rain had ruined any chances of hunting. It seemed critters with sense just naturally holed up somewhere dry when it stormed.

Her rumbling stomach made her consider eating Brownie. She soon discarded the notion—no doubt the wheybelly would prove too tough for consumption.

The world was turning out to be a much bigger place than she'd ever imagined and for the first time in her life, January worried about getting lost. Even more annoying was the fact that she might not even know it if she were. The run was scheduled for April twenty-second, so she couldn't afford to waste valuable time. Each morning when the sun rose, she set her sights in the opposite direction. Heading due west, she was bound to come to Kansas sooner or later.

Brownie's head jerked up as his flared nostrils sensed something in the air. "All right, you win. Again," she added with a grudging sigh. It was discouraging, indeed, to think that anything so vital as making the run hinged on the dim-witted navigations and voracious appetite of such an uncharming animal as Brownie.

Since she wasn't going anywhere, she decided to rest. She draped the reins loosely over Brownie's neck and removed her right foot from the stirrup. Hooking her knee around the pommel afforded her aching muscles a little relief. Naïvely, she'd expected to get used to riding all day and had waited for the soreness to work itself out. So far she was still waiting.

She pressed her fists into the small of her back and cussed Brownie some more. "Durn you, you old piece of crowbait. I could make better time afoot."

Brownie snorted and nibbled the wet grass.

From his vantage point in the thicket, Case spotted a rider sitting carelessly atop a grazing horse. The reins slack, one leg slung over his saddle horn, the man sat his saddle like a rocking chair. But Case wouldn't hold such lack of horse sense against him. The man wasn't a Buscus and that fact alone was enough to endear him to Case.

The stranger was no doubt a pilgrim going west, he thought with disgust. Probably headed for Oklahoma like so many others he'd encountered. It seemed half the country was hell-bent for the Promised Land, where they all planned to make their fortunes the first week out. Case urged Shadow back onto the road and drew his revolver. If his fellow traveler was the get-rich-quick type with robbery on his mind, it wouldn't hurt to be prepared.

"Hold up there, stranger," Case called out.

Brownie whinnied and sidestepped, turning in awkward

circles. Clinging tenuously to the saddle, January didn't know whether to comply with the would-be bandit's instructions or to hang on for dear life. Gauging the distance to the ground against the relative size of the man's pistol, she made a snap decision. To hell with it, she was going to hold on.

As Case drew near, two facts registered simultaneously: the man was no more than a boy and the source of the horse's fear was a very large snake. He fired instinctively, severing the reptile's head. The bloody length flipped once in the air, then slithered in a circle, curling into itself before it finally lay motionless in the mud.

When the shot ripped through the dusky quiet, January grappled to retrieve the reins she'd dropped when the snake first writhed into Brownie's line of vision. But the horse reared, tumbling her backward from the saddle. She landed heavily, her tongue between her teeth, sprawled and cussing in the muddy ditch. She struggled to regain the breath that had been knocked out of her.

In an uncharacteristic and unexpected show of spirit, Brownie bolted off into the woods as though he were two jumps ahead of a grass fire.

Stunned, January sprang up and took after him, momentarily forgetting the man who'd fired the shot. "Come back here, you misbegotten, boneheaded, old puddin' foot!" she screamed at the rapidly retreating horse. "Hellfire, Brownie! I didn't mean that about hoofing it. Come on back here, ya hear!" She screamed deprecations until her throat was raw from the effort, but the horse didn't even slow down.

She watched in helpless frustration as he disappeared through the shadowy timber, then pounded her thighs and yelled, "Just for that, I'm going to Oklahoma without you!"

Looking for her hat, she limped back to the spot where she'd been thrown. Now that she was without food, water, blankets, and transportation, she had a sudden affectionate attachment to the battered piece of felt. Angry tears threatened, but she refused to indulge in a bawling fit. Clapping the hat on her head, she tugged on the brim and scoured the woods for another glimpse of the now-distant Brownie.

"You'd better run, you mossback, 'cause when I catch you, I'm gonna kill you." Whirling around, she confronted the man who'd fired the shot and caused all her troubles. The damned fool had the nerve to sit there on his fine black horse and grin. "What's so damned funny, mister?" she shouted.

"You, boy." Urging Shadow closer, Case added, "That was quite a show. You must be a professional trick rider."

"And you must be a professional pistoleer. I reckon there's not a snake in the state what ain't heard of you and your fast draw." She was so mad she didn't stop to consider the man a potential threat.

"Hey now, that's no way to talk, kid. Show some gratitude."

"For what?" she shrieked. "For scaring my horse and making him dump me in the mud?" She paused to wipe her dirty face with an even dirtier sleeve. "He's gone to hell and breakfast by now and I'm in a pretty fix. All on account of you." An unfamiliar weakness that had nothing to do with being horse-throwed and hungry threatened her bravado when she gazed up at him.

The stranger had rich brown hair and a thick mustache to match. He wore a long, open dust coat over a fine suit of dark clothing, complete with a fancy vest. A shiny gold watch chain looped across his flat middle and, though muddy, his boots were of high quality.

His wide-brimmed black hat sported a silver band and shadowed his face, but she could still see his eyes. They were the color of mountain skies brooding up a summer storm. No doubt about it, he was the handsomest, dandiest, cleanest man she'd ever seen.

One look at the grimy face staring up at him and Case's gambler instincts flashed him a quick warning. He'd do well to ride on as soon as possible. This wretched young wayfarer had "Help me" written all over his mud-caked face. And right below that inscription was "Trouble."

Ordinarily, he'd be willing to help the boy, but the slight prickling of hairs on the back of his neck cautioned him against exercising his philanthropic tendencies. Case had a superstitious belief that contradicted the sobriquet he'd earned in gambling dens and parlor houses along the Mississippi. Hard Case Latimer believed an opportunity to render service to others was fortuitous and should not be taken lightly.

He was convinced his penchant for helping people brought him luck at the gaming tables. He was equally sure it wouldn't be held against him if he lit out in a hurry, just this once.

Still, looking down into the kid's wide brown eyes, he saw not only anger, but distress and unveiled hope, so he ignored the warnings of his survival instincts. "Don't be so fast to condemn. I saved you and your horse from a fatal snakebite, didn't I?" Case was proud of the fact that he'd nailed the reptile from such a distance.

"Not hardly," she snorted as she poked at the snake with the toe of her boot. "That there ain't exactly a deadly viper. That's a bull snake and harmless as a kitten."

"I hate all snakes," he said in a quiet voice. "Where I come from, there's no such thing as a harmless snake."

She was about to ask him did he come from some jungle on the dark continent, but decided there were more pressing matters to attend to. "You going to sit there jawing all day or are you going to help me find my horse?"

"I'd like to help you, but I don't have time. That bag of bones was really picking them up and putting them down, and is probably long gone by now."

"Hellfire! He picked a fine time to go and get fleet-footed on me." January was tired, dirty, and embarrassed by her fall in front of this stranger, who surely must think her a fool.

She stroked his horse's neck. The stallion was high-blooded and black as sin. Judging by the long legs clamped to its sides, she decided the rider was tall. He didn't slouch; his back was ramrod straight. He leaned forward, crossing his forearms on the pommel, and this new position gave her an even better view of him. A tingle began deep in her belly and she attributed it to hunger. She pure dee admired his finely made face.

Though she'd never encountered one in her seventeen years back in Possum Holler, January was convinced that this beautiful man was a true gentleman.

The gentleman eyed her speculatively. "What's the matter, boy? Did you hit your head when you fell?"

Furious at herself for such a moon-eyed appraisal, she barked back in what she hoped was a fair imitation of a cocky male adolescent. "Course not, mister. I was just thinking about that lumbering pea brain of a horse. He's got about as much sense as a goose in a hailstorm."

That apt description could also be applied to its rider, but Case held his tongue. The kid obviously had enough trouble. The bald-faced way he'd been staring made him wonder if the youth wasn't simpleminded into the bargain.

Normally, Case had no patience with weakness in any form, but his sympathy stirred involuntarily in response to the pathetic little fellow who was, after all, scarcely more than a child. Beneath all that mud were smooth cheeks bearing not even the slightest hint of peach fuzz.

The stripling showed no signs of the man he'd eventually become. In fact, in his long-lashed eyes and soft-looking lips you could still see the babe he'd been. His longish, rusty-colored hair looked as if it had been sawed off by a blind barber. His baggy, dirty pants and coat hung on his scrawny frame. Case didn't think the poor kid's belly would chamber a liver pill.

"Is your horse always that spooky?" he asked conversationally.

"Only when he's being shot at."

"I told you—"

"I know," she said with a snort of derision. "You was saving me from certain death."

He glared at the sassy brat. "If you'd been sitting your horse properly, you wouldn't have been thrown."

"If you hadn't been so danged trigger-happy, you mean."

Hoping good fortune would repay him double for aiding one so ungrateful, Case made an impulsive decision. "Well, come on. I can't just ride off and leave you here." He shook his left foot from the stirrup and extended his hand. "Grab hold and I'll pull you up."

January backed off a few steps. "Exactly what's the plan, mister?"

Case sighed and searched the sky, noting it was growing darker by the minute. "I thought I might sell you off to some Kiowas over in the Territory. You're pretty scrawny, but I might be able to get a few rabbit skins for you." He was teasing, but the look on the boy's face said he believed the story. That's what came from years of plying the green cloth—a convincing bluff.

"Look, I'm willing to take you to look for your horse. I reckon I owe you that much. So do you want to climb up or walk the rest of the way to wherever you're headed?"

"Oklahoma." She resented having to accept the handsome stranger's offer of help, but since it was his fault she was in such a predicament, she did. Grudgingly.

Oklahoma. "Figures somehow," he mumbled as he hoisted her onto the back of his saddle.

Once aboard the high-stepping animal, January sat stiffly, her arms dangling at her sides. She gripped the horse's flanks with her knees, anticipating movement, but the man held him in check with expert ease.

"You like falling off horses, do you, boy?"

"Course not," she shot back. "That's a fool thing to ask." She grew increasingly uncomfortable. Aside from those horrible moments in the shed with Mose, she'd never been so close to a man before. Pa had many failings as a parent, but letting men near his daughter hadn't been one of them.

"If you don't hold on, you're going to end up on your

butt again." Case was beginning to wish he'd heeded those earlier instinctive warnings of his.

January obliged, not entirely unwillingly, by wrapping her arms around the man's narrow middle and scooting closer. He smelled manly and nice, like sunshine and leather. She checked the unbidden impulse to rest her cheek against the reassuring warmth of his wide back. That would be entirely too familiar since she didn't even know his name.

"I'm J.J. Jones." Hoping to keep her femininity a secret as long as possible, she used the initials for her real name. Although vague about details, her pa had cried havoc about the awful things that could befall lone females. Until she had Brownie back and could make a clean getaway, she was at this man's mercy.

"Case Latimer," he said unenthusiastically as he headed in the direction Brownie had fled.

Case Latimer. January mulled the name over in her mind and decided it fit him. Case sounded dangerous yet unthreatening, like the man. Latimer suited him, too; it rolled easily off the tongue and was not only strong but genteel as well. Without knowing a thing about him, she decided the man around whom her arms were fastened so tightly could be trusted. She hoped to high heaven she was right, because as vulnerable as she was now, her life might very well depend on it.

"You from around here?" she ventured.

"Nope."

"Just passing through?"

"Yeah."

"Where you headed?"

"West." He chuckled at the idea of sending the Buscus boys on another wild-goose chase, then amended, "Then north."

"Going to Oklahoma for the run?" January was growing impatient with his tight-lipped answers, but clamped down on the temper that had gotten her into so much trouble in the past. She admired the strength of his voice, its softly refined drawl.

"Nope."

"Why not?"

"Look, kid, I figure my business is my business and your business is yours."

Stung by the rebuff, she was silent for a while as the man followed Brownie's tracks across the muddy ground. She soon grew tired of biting her tongue. "Can I call you Case, mister?"

"No. You can call me Mr. Latimer. Didn't anyone ever teach you to respect your elders?"

January stiffened at the slur on her upbringing. Maybe she had been raised by a hardscrabble, sharecropping moonshiner, but she had manners. Besides, he wasn't that old. He couldn't be a day over twenty-five. "Where I come from, respect has to be earned."

"And where's that?"

"A place called Possum Holler, in Butler County, Mizzoura."

"Well, if you're headed for the frontier, you'd better learn something about the code of the West. The first thing is, you never ask a stranger his name or his business. If he wants you to know, he'll tell you." Young Jones's destination was a lawless territory and he wouldn't last as long as a paper shirt in a bear fight.

Oklahoma was already filled with outlaws of the worst stripe, not to mention the desperate boomers who had entered the land illegally and would fight anyone who questioned their claim to it. Add to that volatile mixture the thousands of hungry souls looking to grab some of the bounty and the outlook for a kid like Jones grew even bleaker.

Case had reconsidered his theory that the boy was simple, but a strong mind was no compensation for a weak body. Case had been amazed at how light the lad was when he'd pulled him onto Shadow. The horse scarcely noticed the extra weight. Maybe he was a late bloomer and would be more substantial when his voice changed and he filled out a bit.

"What's the second thing?" January asked.

"Second thing?"

"The second rule in the code of the West."

"Let me think," he stalled, inventing further details. "The second rule is to help others without expecting anything in return."

"That's good, 'cause I ain't got nothin' to pay you with."

She wouldn't consider parting with the silver dollars sewed in her drawers. She'd worked too hard for them and had hoarded them too long to let them go now. The small sum had to see her through the first hard year of homesteading. Besides, why should she deprive the dandy-looking stranger of doing his duty and feeling good about himself?

"How do you expect to get to Oklahoma, boy? You've got no money and less brains." Case tested the kid's grit. If he'd let another take advantage of him easily, he'd never last on his own.

"You must be right. I'm with you, ain't I?"

"You've got a sassy mouth, son. It's going to get you into big trouble one of these days."

January let the comment pass. Hadn't she heard the same thing from Pa and Mose for years? Case's nearness had a leavening effect on her spirit and she had no intention of being cast aside just because she always had to have the last word. The sky was fading from rose to indigo and the sound of a meadowlark's song filled the fresh, rainwashed evening air. She was suddenly happier than she'd been in a month of Sundays.

"There ain't nothin' sweeter than springtime in the Ozarks," she mused. "The woods are plumb purty when the oaks bud pink and dogwood blossoms speckle the hillsides." She lost herself to her surroundings. Adding even more color to the green woods were the delicate traceries of redbuds and clustered blossoms of hawthorns. Flowers bloomed in shadowy, secret places beneath the tall trees—trillium, oxalis, and dogtooth violets.

Case shook his head in amazement. Not one to rhapsodize about Mother Nature, he rarely gave a thought to flora or fauna. His idea of beauty was a good card game, a talented woman, clean sheets, and smudgeless shot glasses. "Wait till you get a glimpse of the Territory, boy. It isn't called no-man's land for nothing."

Since she wasn't even sure where she was, January only hoped she'd get the chance. But she could hardly admit that. "You ever been there? To Oklahoma?"

"Yeah," he clipped, thinking he should tell the kid to skedaddle back to Pumpkin Holler or wherever it was he came from. Any boy who talked so longingly of springtime and lovely things had no business in the barren, untamed world of Oklahoma.

"It can't be so different from the Ozarks. Land is land. And if it's mine, that's all the better. I aim to lay claim to one hundred and sixty acres of prime farmland."

"I wouldn't set my expectations too high if I were you," he warned, trying to let the boy down easily. "You'll need a good horse if you want to make the run. You planning to ride that nag you were cussing earlier?"

"Like I told you, Brownie can run if he sets his mind to it," January said defensively. "Good or bad, he's all I got."

Which wasn't much, Case thought, lapsing into silence. But it wasn't his place to worry about J.J. Jones. It was no business of his if the kid made it or not. He refused to take on that kind of responsibility. He'd find that damned horse and send them on their way.

January knew Latimer considered her situation hopeless. Hadn't she thought the same thing? But she had to try. Never in her life had she had anything she could truly call her own. Never had she gone to sleep without the fear that she might wake up and find out Pa had lost what little they did possess. She'd lived in terror that the land, which she worked so hard but could never hold the deed to, would somehow be taken away from her.

Long ago she'd decided that owning property was the only real security a body could ever have. The government's scheduled giveaway of Indian lands was a godsend, the first time in the nation's history that public lands would be opened up in such a way. Rich or poor, everyone would be lined up to await the firing of a pistol. All would have an equal chance at claiming a homestead, the determining factor being one's own resourcefulness. She had to believe she would be one of the lucky ones.

"Mr. Latimer?"

"Hmmm?"

"I saw something over there." She pointed to a thick stand of hickory and oak trees off to the east.

He urged his horse closer and began to laugh, a deep-hearted rumble. "I do believe that is the redoubtable Brownie. What do you think? Must we sneak up on his blind side or will he let you take him peaceably?"

Before she could answer, Brownie's head jerked up and he came crashing through the thicket, dragging the reins through the mud. He drew up beside Shadow and Case leaned over to retrieve them.

"No doubt he's had time to regret his rash actions. He seems plumb glad to see you."

January said nothing. Brownie's turning up so quickly was yet another mark against him. Now Latimer was bound to part company with her and in a little while it would be as dark as the inside of a pitch bucket. She slipped off his horse and mounted her own. "Even though it was your fault he took off, I appreciate you helping me catch up to him."

Case bit back a smile. That was as grudging a thank-you as he'd ever heard. "Don't mention it. I'm just happy to be part of the touching reunion." The kid didn't seem exactly thrilled to find his horse. "So long, Jones. Good luck in Oklahoma." He didn't add that he'd need it.

"So long."

Forlorn as a motherless child, that's how the kid sounded, Case thought. He knew he should urge Shadow on, but he couldn't bring himself to ride off and leave the boy. Dammit, he looked scrawnier than ever sitting atop the big horse and gave every indication he might even start bawling.

Case sighed. Weren't the Buscus brothers enough to have to worry about without getting mixed up with a backwoods kid who was sure to be nothing but trouble? Still . . . he wouldn't leave a three-legged hound in such straits.

"Hey, Jones!"

"Yessir?" January tried to keep the hope out of her voice.

"You got any grub?"

"I was planning to hunt me some supper, once I made camp."

"You a good shot?"

"Yessir, I'm a fair shot." She wasn't bragging since it was true.

"Do you think you could get a rabbit to go with the beans I've got in my pack?"

"Yessir!" January didn't know why, but the idea of shooting any critter for Case Latimer filled her with elation.

"All right, we'll throw in together for tonight. But just for tonight," he warned in case the kid got any big ideas. "Tomorrow you go your way and I'll go mine."

It was difficult to think that far ahead. All she could conjure up was a strong vision of hot food, a fire to dry out by, and Case's comforting companionship. "Sounds good to me."

"I see you've got a nice Winchester there."

"Course, I do. A body needs a rifle in the Territory. Why, I wouldn't be caught dead without one." Stroking the polished wood, she wondered if Pa would ever forgive her for taking it.

Discretion dictated Case not mention the fact that when they'd met, Brownie had been in possession of the weapon.

"That's a pretty big firearm. Can you hold it, aim it, and fire it, all at the same time?"

January felt heat rise in her face. She didn't much cotton to the airy Mr. Latimer holding her in such low regard, as if she weren't no smarter than a Cleek. But it wasn't really her he was funning, she reminded herself. It was J.J. Jones, sorry young orphaned pup. She was happy her disguise had fooled him, but it wounded her female vanity that it had been so easy.

"I reckon I can manage," she said in a voice heavy with sarcasm. "That's where my trained horse comes into the act."

The detour they'd taken to find Brownie led them to a perfect camping spot. A running creek had widened and formed a small pool a few hundred yards from a clearing where, judging from the evidence of old fires, others had camped before them. Past caring if the Buscuses saw it, Case gathered windfall wood and built a fire. Breaking out his supplies, he boiled coffee in a small, blackened pot.

The kid had left on foot to rustle up some meat, but Case didn't hold out much hope for his success. It was nearly nightfall and even a fair shot couldn't see in the dark. He hoped the boy got back soon, because he didn't relish the idea of hunting him up later. He was looking forward to a hot supper, his first in several days. He was also looking forward to the cheroot and flask of whiskey he'd enjoy afterward.

Case jerked up when a shot reverberated through the silent woods, his hand instinctively finding the reassuring weight of his holstered Colt. A few minutes later the boy stepped into the clearing swinging two white-tailed jackrabbits by the ears.

Wordlessly, he slung them down on a flat rock, withdrew a deadly-looking knife from under his coat, and fell to skinning and eviscerating the luckless creatures. Case's eyes widened and he made a mental note not to aggravate the brat in the future. He wouldn't care to be on the receiving end of that much skill.

Chapter 3

"I only heard one shot, boy."

"That's right." January didn't look up from her task and made quick work of readying the rabbits for the fire spit. It was amazing what hunger could do for a body's concentration.

Case stared at the kid. He obviously knew his way around a rabbit's insides. "But you've got two rabbits there."

"That's right. One for you and one for me. I don't know about you, but I'm hungry enough to eat buzzard bait."

"The point I was trying to make is that I've never heard of anybody getting two rabbits with one shot."

"Until now." January smiled sweetly and brought the carcasses to the fire where she soon had them browning nicely on the spit, the juices dripping and hissing in the dancing flames. She wasn't about to tell Mr. Thinks-He's-So-Smart Latimer how she'd come to bring down two rabbits with one shot.

Truth to tell, she'd gotten the first one with her slingshot. The critter had sat stock-still, flat dab in front of her, begging for a stone between his eyes. The second one she'd shot on the run when she flushed him out of a blackberry bramble.

Case didn't ask any more questions about the two-for-one rabbit special, but his estimation of the boy eased upward a notch or two. After they'd consumed the rabbits and beans, and started in on a tin of peaches, he ventured a question.

"What exactly are your plans when you get to Oklahoma, J.J.?"

"Seems to me that question is in clear violation of the code of the West, *Mr.* Latimer." January grinned at Case as she polished off the last of her share of the peaches and licked the juice from her fingers.

"I reckon you can call me Case, boy, so don't be so fresh and just answer my question." He spat a peach pit into the fire.

January reached inside her coat pocket and pulled out the crumpled flyer, which she passed to him. She'd kept it because it hadn't seemed right to go to Oklahoma without it.

"I'm planning to claim me a place of my own."

"Homesteader, huh?" Case didn't need to read the paper to know what it said; he'd seen enough of them. Thousands had found their way into the hands of land-hungry people who were at this moment surging to one of the designated starting points, hoping to grab land that had once been promised faithfully to the Indians.

"It was a sad day for America when Grover Cleveland signed that Indian appropriations bill into law," he said.

"Sad?" January was amazed by his attitude. "How can it be sad to give poor folks a chance to build a home for themselves, for their future kin? To take those two million acres and make it into something grand?"

"Do you think the only participants in the run will be God-fearing 'poor folks' looking to civilize the wilderness?"

"Well, who else would want a homestead?"

Case smiled at the boy's naïveté. "Homesteads aren't the only thing of value in the new territory, J.J. Towns will spring up overnight and when that happens, you can bet the lawless, the corrupt, and the just plain greedy will swarm in like horseflies."

"It's a big place. I reckon there's room for everybody."

"Not quite. Doesn't it bother you that our government promised that land to the Indians forever?"

January hadn't considered previous claims to the land, but now that she did, she decided what Case said didn't change the law. "Maybe it's wrong, but it's gonna happen and I want to get a share of it."

"You and fifty thousand others." The paper he held was wrinkled and thin, as though it had been folded and refolded hundreds of times. He eyed the boy speculatively; it seemed he'd missed one important point. "Can you read this paper?"

"I know what it says." January's eyes didn't meet his. It was a point of shame that she couldn't read or write, but Pa hadn't let her go to school after Mama left. He claimed girls didn't need education; it only put wicked ideas into their heads. She'd wanted to learn, but there had always been too much work to do and never enough money for books and such.

"Are you planning to meet up with your father or older brother in Oklahoma?"

"I ain't got no brother and my Pa's so lazy he wouldn't say sooey if the hogs had him. Poverty suits him just fine, so I'm making the run my own self."

"How are you going to do that when it says here that only the heads of households over the age of twenty-one are eligible?"

January snatched the paper and pored over it with a feeling of dread. Was he telling the truth? Did a body really have to be twenty-one to file for land? She saw the figures "2" and "1" in the middle of the page and knew he hadn't lied. She was a single woman, and only seventeen.

She couldn't make the run and she'd never have a place of her own. Suddenly the tiny, drafty cabin and her pa's no-account ways didn't seem so bad. Still, there *was* Mose. She could never return, not after the threats he'd made. She'd heard of people burning their bridges behind them, but up until now she hadn't known what that meant.

The paper fluttered from her lifeless hands and was swept into the campfire. January watched it, and her dreams, go up in smoke.

"You aren't twenty-one, are you, J.J.?" Case asked gently.

"No."

"Will you be going back home now?"

Her head snapped up and her eyes flashed. "I don't have a home to go back to. I ran away from my pa and stole his horse and his rifle. He's probably got the law looking for me right now." She refrained from mentioning Mose. Relating that story wouldn't do her disguise any good.

Case fished a square-ended cigar from a leather case in his saddlebags and lit it with a long stick from the campfire. He drew deeply and sent a few smoke rings spiraling upward. "I'm sure your father is worried sick by now and has reported you missing," he said in an effort to reassure the boy.

January laughed mirthlessly. "You don't know my pa. The only thing Jubal Jones is worried about is his property and that don't include no indentured children. Thank goodness he's too shiftless to come after me or he'd probably have me hung for a horse thief."

The boy's words were vehement enough, but Case had a hard time accepting that the father had so little parental concern for the lad. "Surely you exaggerate. I imagine all children feel misunderstood by their parents."

January glared at him, mad enough to chew splinters and spit logs. What made him think he knew so much about it? "Well, I ain't no child and feeling misunderstood is just about the least of my worries."

He puffed on the cigar, smoke wreathing his head. Squinting against it, he said, "I'm sure things aren't really as bad as they seem right now. Why, in the morning you can head home and I'm willing to bet your father will forgive and forget."

"Pardon my lack of respect," January said coldly, "but you don't know nothin' about nothin'. Pa ran Mama off for a hussy when I was only six years old. A few weeks later, he laid down the law. There'd be no more schoolin' on account of it being wicked. According to Pa, work cleansed the soul. He wasn't worried about his own, but he made sure mine was lily white and had a guaranteed seat in heaven.

"When I got big enough to do a full day's work, Pa went back to his primary occupation, which happens to be moonshining." She smiled wryly. "No, truth is, moonshining ain't really his primary occupation. Drinkin' the vile stuff, and gambling away every cent we ever get, is what he does best. Sharecropping is just something he does when he's sober enough to think about it."

Case heard the anger and hurt in the boy's words and knew he wasn't just making a bid for sympathy. On close inspection, some of the dirt on his face might turn out to be bruises. The kid had been dealt a very bad hand in life.

"So, to make a long story short, I've been killing myself working land so poor that two redheaded women couldn't raise a ruckus on it. Every fall when the crops are sold, Otis Cleek, the landlord, gets half and my pa gets half. All I get is wore out."

Case had a much better understanding of the boy now. He was obviously tougher than he looked. If J.J. had survived such a brutal childhood, he might stand a chance on the frontier, after all.

"You must be disappointed that you can't make the run."

Disappointed? She was devastated. "You could say that. I told Pa once I wasn't going to work all my life for nothing, that President Lincoln had freed the slaves and I was going to have me a place of my own someday."

"What did he say to that?"

"He laughed in my face and said the day a Jones became landed gentry would be the day they started giving it away."

Case chuckled. "It must have seemed like an act of fate when you heard about Oklahoma."

"I don't know nothing about fate but it sounded like the answer to my prayers."

"So what will you do now?"

More than anything else, January hated to quit. She'd never been one to give up or give in, no matter how bad things got. She clung stubbornly to the idea that had given her the courage to try for a new life. "Go on, I suppose. It'd be my word against theirs. How would anybody know I *wasn't* the legal age?"

"The same way I knew," Case said gently. "Son, you can't be a day over thirteen and it'd be foolish to try and deceive the land registry office."

January was glad she'd been able to fool him about her true identity, but it was insulting for a man like Case Latimer to think she was a thirteen-year-old boy. Something crumbled inside her when she realized she was unwomanly enough to pull off such a masquerade so easily.

She'd never had any pretty clothes, had never even owned a store-bought dress. Her curling auburn hair had been her only glory and she'd had to chop it off to ensure her disguise. What few curves she possessed were covered by the raggedy clothes she'd stolen. Dried mud covered the lot and she knew how she must look to a fine gentleman like him.

"I guess it would be foolish," she agreed reluctantly. With a look of defiance, she added, "But I'm going to Oklahoma and I'll figure out what to do when I get there."

Case had to admire the boy's determination, even if his logic left something to be desired. He poked at the fire and placed a few more wet logs on it. It sputtered, but the added brightness gave him a clear view of J.J., who huddled dejectedly across from him. He gestured at the mud-caked clothing. "You got any clean clothes in your saddlebags?"

"Maybe. What's it to you?"

"Don't be so damned suspicious all the time. I just thought you might want to go down to the creek and wash up. Once you get the road dirt off you and get into some clean clothes, the world is apt to look a little less frightening."

"Who said I was frightened?"

"Just a figure of speech, boy. I'll clean up around here since you provided the main course. You go on and have your bath." Case dug around in his saddlebags until he found what he was looking for. "Here."

January caught the tossed object—a cake of fancy soap. All she'd ever used was smelly homemade lye and the thought of washing her filthy hair and skin with this sweet-smelling stuff brought a smile to her face. "Thanks, I believe I'll do just that." She felt like whistling as she walked to the pool, so she did.

Away from the campfire, it wasn't as dark as she'd thought it would be. Stars sparkled in the black satin sky like newly minted silver dollars, and a half moon gave off its own pale light. When she reached the pool, its waters seemed mysterious and murky, but having seen it in the daylight, she knew it was clear, the bottom filled with small, rounded stones.

She stripped off her clothes quickly and the brisk night air raised gooseflesh on her skin. Testing the water with her toe, she found it to be as cold as she'd expected. It was wonderful.

She felt warmer when submerged in the water so she waded out and sat on the bottom, scrubbing her face and arms, then lathering her hair. The slowly moving water lapped just above her breasts and, as she washed away the dirt, she washed away some of her cares as well.

When she heard someone moving through the woods, she panicked, struggling to rinse the lather out of her eyes and hair. It was Case! He was singing the words to the tune she'd been whistling earlier and he was headed for the creek. She splashed water frantically at her face, but succeeded only in blinding herself more.

" 'Buffalo gals, won't you come out tonight? Come out tonight, Come out tonight?' " he beseeched in a pleasant bass that would serve him well if he decided to take to the stage. " 'Oh, buffalo gals, won't you come out tonight, and dance by the light of the moon?' "

He'd almost reached the water's edge when January got the bright idea of how to rid herself of the irritating soap. She simply ducked completely under the surface.

"J.J., you'd better come up for air. How's the water?"

Unable to hold her breath any longer, she broke the surface in a fury of coughing and sputtering. "Hellfire! It's cold. You'd better not come in." What did anyone as clean as him need to take a bath for anyhow?

"Nonsense. A good, bracing dip stimulates the circulation," he said, removing his shirt without so much as a by-your-leave. The moonlight revealed a strong muscled chest with a mat of dark hair curling in its center. She was shocked when she realized her wanton fingers fairly itched to find out if his hair was as soft and springy as it looked. Was she destined to become a hussy like her mama? No, she wasn't like that, no matter what Pa said.

She didn't know what to do. Her arms and legs were starting to turn numb in the cold thigh-deep water, but she couldn't stand up and she couldn't escape. Hellfire, she couldn't even swim.

"Really, Case, it's damned cold. I'm freezing," she said in a voice she knew was much too high to belong to a man, even a young one.

"Then get out, you little fool. I wanted you to wash, not catch pneumonia." Case longed to tease the youth about his falsetto pitch, but the lad took everything too seriously.

"No!" She didn't know if her strangled cry was a refusal to walk naked out of the water or shocked realization that, having removed his boots and socks, Case was now stepping out of his pants.

"What's the matter with you, J.J.? You'd better get out. I think the chill has affected your brain."

She whirled around, but not before laying eyes on the only naked male body she'd ever seen. She yearned to sneak another peek, but didn't dare. She'd had no idea a man's body could be so beautiful. She'd thought it would be coarse and covered with hair, but the brief glimpse she'd had of Case told her differently.

His skin was smooth and pale and there was a light dusting of dark hair on his forearms and legs. It grew thicker on his chest and . . . and that other place.

Hellfire! She *was* on the road to ruin.

Case moved steadily toward her, splashing noisily and griping about the icy temperature. Cautiously, she scooted out further, hoping he wouldn't follow. He did.

"Hey, where's that soap?" he said from right behind her.

"Here." January's heart was beating so hard it fairly hurt. She tossed the soap backward over her shoulder and wiggled away from him. The ground beneath her feet sloped and she was able to walk out until she was visible only from her mouth up.

"You all right, kid? Where're you going anyway? It's a little late for swimming, so why don't you come over here and soap my back for me, then I'll soap yours and we can get out." The boy sure was acting strangely, but Case attributed his modesty to the awkwardness of adolescence. He'd been self-conscious himself at that age.

At his suggestion, January whirled around, her eyes wide with the fear of total damnation. Soap his back? Actually put her hands on a man's bare skin? She couldn't imagine doing such an unseemly thing, or having it done to her. But even those frightening thoughts weren't what scared her most. She'd suddenly stepped into a deep hole and was now in over her head.

She struggled to regain her former footing, but her movements only carried her further out into the murky depths. Arms flailing, she hoped to get her head up long enough to cry for help, but whenever she opened her mouth, it filled with water.

Case listened to the boy's thrashing and splashing and thought how wonderful it was to be a child. Not long ago, J.J.'s most cherished dreams had been dashed, but the tragedy was soon forgotten in his enthusiasm for a midnight swim. Case was glad he'd suggested it.

January kicked her feet, not sure how much longer she could survive. Her lungs were hurting and her body felt leaden in the water. With one last supreme effort, kicking like a mule, she crested the water and screamed. "Case, help me! I'm a-drownin'!"

At the boy's cry for help, Case dropped the precious cake of soap and plunged in after him. He dove beneath the surface and, quite by accident, grabbed the boy as he sank to the bottom. He scrabbled for a secure hold, but J.J. was slicker than a greased pig and fought him with the strength of a full-grown man. For a moment, Case wondered if he was actually going to effect the rescue, or die trying. Finally, he clutched the boy beneath the arms and struck out for shallow water.

Despite J.J.'s efforts to thwart him, Case finally touched bottom. When he felt the earth firmly beneath his feet, he pulled the struggling boy close in a vain effort to calm him. That's when his hand closed over a mound of soft flesh that couldn't possibly belong to an adolescent male.

"Good God! You're a female!" In his surprise, he let go of her and she promptly slipped beneath the surface once more. Being a foot taller, he'd forgotten the kid couldn't touch bottom. He quickly corrected his error by grabbing a handful of hair and pulling her above water.

She came up choking and swinging. "So what if I am, you damned idiot. It's no reason to drown me." She'd been mortified when Case's hand had grasped her breast. For a moment she'd actually pondered whether a quick death by drowning wasn't preferable to the degradation she was bound to experience now that her true sex had been discovered. She couldn't bear a repeat of what had happened with Mose in the shed. Or possibly worse.

Those horrid thoughts lent her renewed strength and she pounded Case's chest with her fists. He was a strong man and she had as much chance fighting him off as a grasshopper had hopping across a chicken yard. But she didn't let that stop her. The next thing she knew, he'd grabbed her around her knees and flung her over his shoulder as if she were no more than a rag doll.

She dug her elbows into his shoulder blades, lifting her breasts away from his warm, naked back, but the rest of her was clasped tightly against his hard body as he slowly made his way toward the bank. Oh, the shame of it!

"You're gonna pay for this, you bastard!"

"You keep calling me names, you little wretch, and we'll see who pays." Already angered beyond reason that he'd been deceived by a child who had nearly drowned them both, Case gave her rounded bare bottom an open-handed slap for good measure.

She gasped with humiliation, remembering Pa's warnings that all men were after only one thing, the same thing Mose had been after. It didn't matter that Case had been her friend; now that her femaleness was apparent, he'd be certain sure to display his true rapacious male colors. "Let me go, you damned snake."

Somehow he managed to hold on to his self-control and her, no easy task since she fought like a wildcat. His fury grew with every little scratch and kick. It might take all his nearly depleted strength, but he was determined to get her to the water's edge before anything else happened. He was still shocked. Not once during the time they'd spent together had he suspected J.J. was anything but the scruffy boy she'd appeared to be.

She struck out blindly, but the blows she delivered were ineffectual, he held her so tight. "Dammit, J.J. It's useless to fight me. I'm not going to let you go until we get back to camp. You owe me an explanation and I intend to collect."

"I owe you nothing, you sneaky jackass. And don't think for one minute I don't know exactly what your intentions are!" she yelled in a vain attempt to spare her dignity. But it was nearly impossible to fight the wildfire of confusing emotions that blazed inside when so much of their mutually bare flesh was in intimate contact. She was mortally embarrassed that he'd beheld her nakedness, and totally shamed that he had his hands all over her.

Mostly, she was frightened because his touch gave her such wrongful pleasure. The warmth of his skin next to hers was surely the sweetest pain she'd ever known, nothing at all like what she'd felt in Mose's slimy clutches. Surely hers was the heart of a harlot. She liked it too much to be decent.

He grasped her hips, sliding her all the way down his length until she stood before him, shivering. She was almost sorry to be separated from him until she reminded herself of the indignities she'd already suffered at his hands. Before he could disgrace her further, she ran to her bedroll and grabbed the Winchester. But Case was quicker and his running dive knocked her backward before she could take proper aim.

He flung the gun away and wrestled her to the ground beside the campfire. She kicked out at him but missed and he straddled her, making her humiliatingly aware of his maleness against her thigh. She pushed against his chest, trying to wriggle away, but one of his big hands clamped both of hers above her head, leaving her helpless and vulnerable.

"You would've shot me," he exclaimed incredulously, his nostrils flaring. God, no wonder his instincts had tried to warn him when he'd first stumbled across J.J., or whatever her name was. Being saddled with a kid was bad enough, but a female child intent on dealing him death was completely out of the question.

"That's for damned certain! Low-down polecats like you don't deserve no better! Let go of me," she yelled, her chest heaving.

She wasn't *exactly* a child, he corrected, watching the rise and fall of her nubile young breasts. Her wet-dark hair gleamed in the light from the fire. He leaned closer, taking note of how very large her eyes were. Filled with fright and excitement, they captivated him with their indignant innocence.

As he watched, her small white teeth clamped down on her bottom lip and an all too familiar ache swelled in his groin. Holy hell! he thought, slackening his hold on her wrists, I'm lusting after a child!

His face loomed closer and January gasped, recognizing the feral glint in his blue eyes. The sinful feelings churning up her insides could only be caused by the devil himself and she feared desperately for her mortal soul. She had to get away from him before she succumbed to whatever he was about to do to her.

She noticed his grip had slackened. Ever so slowly, she inched one of her hands from his, over to the edge of the blanket and the knife hidden beneath it.

Miss Jones, Case decided with a roving gaze, though reed-slender, was a well-developed young woman and that made matters worse. He felt drawn to her. He wanted to kiss her, that's all, just one little kiss to still her quivering lips. No, it was insane even to think it.

There'd be the devil to pay if he got mixed up with this innocent backwoods girl. Look what had happened when he'd allowed Ardetta Buscus to practice some of her wiles on him. He already had three enraged brothers on his tail and he'd be crazy to incite the wrath of a moonshining father as well.

But fool that he was, Case didn't offer much resistance as his lips were pulled irresistibly to hers.

January's hand encountered the cold steel blade of her knife just as his head swooped down. She clasped the handle at the same instant his mouth brushed lightly, then covered hers with such sweet tenderness that her fears began to evaporate. Her senses reeled, her ears roared, and her heart began to hammer. She tingled all over and waited, resigned, for whatever happened between men and women to start happening.

Case moaned deep in his throat, surprised and delighted that a simple kiss could induce so much pleasure. All her obvious shortcomings aside, the girl wriggling beneath him excited him beyond reason. A new, inexplicable hunger raced through his veins, taking control of his better sense, robbing him of good judgment. He wanted more, so much more.

January felt as well as heard his low, throaty growl and shock rippled through her body. She'd never been kissed by a man in that way and the delightful beauty of it made her want to cry. The shock went away, replaced by feelings she couldn't name. Then something rock-hard and hot touched her . . . down there, frightening her even more.

"Stop!" She wrenched her lips from his and shoved the knife point against his warm skin.

"Holy hell," Case whispered, not daring to move a muscle. What a mess he'd gotten into. Here he was, naked as the day he was born, compromising a mere slip of a girl who now held a knife at his gut. He hoped to hell no one ever heard this story; it wouldn't do his reputation a damned bit of good.

"You're just an eyeblink away from bein' a gelding," January said breathlessly.

Case's desire wilted as suddenly as it had begun and he stopped dead-still. "Okay, okay. Now don't do anything foolish, I'm just going to get up. I'm not going to hurt you," he said soothingly, as though talking his way out of a den full of mountain lions. Putting words into hurried action, he rolled off her and onto his feet.

Hoping against hope that he could settle her down, he kept up a steady stream of stupid, yet cajoling statements. "It was just a kiss, honey. Nothing to get excited about. People do it every day. Just a harmless little kiss."

January, still gripping the knife, dressed quickly. She didn't believe that for a minute, nor did she trust him to keep his distance, so she kept him in her sight at all times. She commanded her eyes to stay above his waist, but they kept betraying her. Much to her disgrace, her gaze made several forays up and down his tall body, drinking in the male beauty of him against her will.

His legs were straight and slender, his belly flat and

hard, his manhood very much in evidence. Never had she guessed men could conceal such enormous things on their persons. And it wasn't nearly as unsightly as she'd always imagined.

"Get dressed," she snapped, collecting her weapons and hoping she wouldn't have to resort to violence. If he tried to take any more liberties, she wouldn't hesitate to bean him with a rock from her slingshot. To that end, she crouched down and stuffed a handful of large pebbles in her pocket.

She hoped that wouldn't be necessary because she really didn't want to hurt him. In fact, just thinking about what they'd been doing stirred up those harloty feelings all over again.

It was crazy to think about such things. A man like Case Latimer wouldn't be interested in an illiterate country girl like herself, outside of that one thing her pa said all men were interested in. She scooped up her bedroll and stalked away.

"J.J., I'm sorry." Case stared at her retreating back. "I promise not to touch you again. There's no excuse for what I did and I'm truly sorry I frightened you. I guess I just lost my head." He breathed a relieved sigh when she halted her steps.

"I ain't no soiled dove and I don't expect to be treated like one." January lifted her chin and cocked the rifle she held. "I'm leaving and you'd better not try to stop me."

"I don't like to think of you heading out in the dead of night. Please don't go. I swear I won't touch you again." And he wouldn't, he vowed silently, no matter how badly he wanted to. He feared for her safety because the fact that J.J. Jones was a girl cast a whole new light on things.

During the past few hours, he'd come to feel a grudging respect for the kid who'd endured a life of hardship and struck out on his own to improve it. However misguided those actions had been, they'd required spunk and spirit. To think a slip of a girl had done so made the accomplishments even more admirable. He'd never heard of a girl who could take two rabbits with one shot, who was as proficient with a flaying knife as a mule skinner, and who could outcuss one to boot.

He didn't know much about females aside from the nameless professional women he'd eased himself with over the years. He'd always maintained a personal policy that limited intercourse, social or otherwise, to those females who didn't get big ideas when you spent a few hours with them. The one time he'd broken his own rule had proved disastrous and he had the Buscus boys hot on his trail to show for it. Why was it respectable women always had a lot of nasty-tempered menfolk?

But he couldn't worry about that problem just now. There was the more immediate issue of Miss J.J. Jones. She stared him down and he felt obligated to drop his gaze first.

"I swear to you, if I'd known you were a girl, I never would've gone down there to bathe. It sort of took me by surprise. You nearly drowned yourself and then the both of us with all that kicking and squirming. Then you tried to shoot me and . . . I suppose I just became over-excited." In truth, he felt as low-down as a snake's belly for what he'd done. His carefully cultivated control and ability to hide his emotions had failed him.

January decided Case didn't seem like the type of man to force himself on a woman and he sounded sincere. "I'll stay till it's light," she conceded. "But you stick to the other side of the fire. I'll sleep over here." She dropped her bedroll on the ground and spread it out with the toe of her boot, keeping the rifle within easy striking distance.

"Okay, kid," Case said, dropping more wood on the fire before he climbed between his blankets. "I'm glad that's settled. Now, I think it's way past the time for you and me to have a little talk."

His voice was edged with anger, although what he had to be mad about she couldn't guess. "About what?"

"About what?" he repeated incredulously. "About a slight discrepancy in anatomy, that's what. Why'd you let me think you were a scrawny backwoods boy when you're really a scrawny backwoods girl?"

"You're so smart, why'd you think?"

Case considered that for a moment. An unescorted girl *was* easy prey for anyone she encountered on the road. "All right. That was a stupid question, but . . . dammit, you rile me. And you're going to freeze over there so far from the fire."

He eyes narrowed and she glared suspiciously at him.

"Suit yourself," he said, "but you're gonna be colder than a well digger's butt before morning."

January *was* cold. She tightened her grip on the knife handle and crawled out of her bedroll. Cautiously, she moved a little closer into the fire-lit circle.

"Jesus! What are you planning to do with that thing?" he yelled when he saw what she had in her hand. "Scalp me?" The memory of those skinned rabbits was still fresh in his mind and it had only been moments ago that he'd felt the cold steel against his own belly.

"Only if I have to. But I aim to protect myself."

"I gave you my word not to harm you."

"Yes, you did," she agreed. "And this will see that you keep it."

He was unaccountably indignant. "I'm the same man who saved your ass when you lost your horse. I shared my food with you and my last cake of soap, which sunk to the bottom of the creek because I rescued your fool neck from drowning not twenty minutes ago. Didn't I, J.J.?"

"Yeah, maybe so. But you didn't know I was a girl when you did all them things. When you found out, you jumped on me quicker than a duck on a June bug."

Case sighed in frustration. "How long will I have to pay for that mistake?"

She eyed him skeptically, tossing the knife from hand to hand in what she hoped was a menacing manner.

"For Chrissakes, pocket that frog-sticker, will you? You're beginning to make me nervous. And sit down. I won't bite you."

Pa hadn't said a word about biting, but she couldn't rule out the possibility—he hadn't said anything about how a man could make a woman feel, neither. "What do you want, mister?"

"Mister, is it? A while back you were begging to call me Case."

"That was when—"

"I thought you were a boy. Yeah, yeah, I know. What's your name anyway? Your real name?"

"January June Jones."

"January June, huh? When's your birthday?"

"April thirteenth," she replied defensively, wondering what that had to do with anything.

"I see," he said, rolling his eyes heavenward. Two to one she'd been born on a Friday. "Tell me what else you lied to me about."

"I ain't no liar, mister. Everything else I told you was the gospel truth." She hadn't put the knife away and gestured with it as though challenging him to make something of it.

"I believe you, kid. Just calm down before somebody gets hurt."

"Ain't nobody going to get hurt, except maybe you if you make a false move."

He pulled the whiskey flask from his saddlebags, thinking he'd never needed a drink so badly. When he made a move toward the coffeepot, January flinched and he felt like a louse. He hoped he hadn't scared the poor girl off men forever. "Want some coffee?"

"I don't care to," she answered, thinking how delicious the hot brew would taste. She was still chilled from her swim.

"Suit yourself," he replied.

January realized he'd misunderstood. Anybody from the hills would've known she was really saying, "Thank you, I'll be delighted to have some coffee." But he was obviously *not* from the hills.

She spoke quickly, before he had a chance to withdraw the offer. "I reckon I will have some of that there coffee."

Regarding her as if she'd lost her mind, Case handed her a tin cup of the strong black brew, then poured a generous amount of whiskey into his own cup. He topped it off with coffee.

The man was a drinker, she noted with alarm when she saw him tilt the spirits into his cup. She tightened her grip on her knife. A man who imbibed drink was capable of anything.

"Are you still afraid of me?" he asked.

"Shouldn't I be?" She stared at him over the crackling fire, her hat pulled down on her head.

"No, and please don't be. At least not now."

"Why shouldn't I be afraid of you, after what you was trying to do? Besides, you're a man, ain't you?"

"I can't argue about that. But I swear on my mother's grave, it will never happen again." Not unless you're willing, he didn't bother to add. "Do you believe me, January?"

She nodded. If a person swore on their dead mother's grave not to do a thing, it was likely they meant business.

"The fact that I'm a man doesn't mean I'm a threat to you. After what happened you may not believe it, but not all men are rampaging Turks, out to sack and pillage. And not all men take advantage of innocents, be they male or female. Some do, but I'm not one of them."

If she understood him correctly, his statement contradicted the ideas fostered by her pa's dire warnings, but January decided it was welcome information all the same. "I'll keep that in mind."

"Good. I've been thinking. Since we're both headed west anyway, you can travel along with me as far as Arkansas City. That way I can keep an eye out for you."

"What makes you think I'd want to travel with you anyhow or have your dadburned eyes on me?"

He squinted against the glare of the fire, trying to get a good look at the girl sitting across from him. He couldn't see much; she had that disreputable hat slouched down over her hair and face and her collar was turned up. "Well, you can't ride all that way alone. It's too dangerous."

"You was willing for me to ride alone when you thought I was a boy," she reminded him.

Case bit back the urge to tell her to just go ahead and get the hell out of his camp. But he wasn't a randy bull with no control over his bodily cravings and he intended to prove it, to her and to himself. Lady Luck wouldn't take too kindly to his abandoning the girl to her fate. The way his fortunes had been running lately, he couldn't afford to court further disaster.

He took another swig of the coffee-laced whiskey and cursed again the bad luck that had crossed his path with that of Miss J.J. Jones. "You aren't a boy, so that's out of the question now. What do you say?"

"I say, what's in it for you?"

"Nothing. Call it my good deed for the day."

"Good deed?" she scoffed. "Now, why'd you want to go and do somethin' like that?"

He was in no mood to explain his philosophy. "God, girl," he snapped, "whatever happened to give you such a sorry view of humanity? Maybe I'm just a good person willing to offer you my protection." Though he'd have to be crazy to think a gal like her needed anyone's protection.

"You protecting me?" Her snort of derision spoke volumes on that subject and Case's patience wore thin.

"Dammit, I apologized for that!"

His stormy blue eyes seemed to burn through her and once they held her in their grasp, she wasn't sure she could resist if he made further advances.

"I'm sorry I yelled," he said in a voice as caressing as a warm summer breeze. "Would you take that hat off so I can see your face?"

A tendril of excitement licked through her at the thought of Case Latimer wanting to look at her. She was about to snatch the hat off and toss it into the fire when it occurred to her that he might be disappointed. More than anything, she didn't want that. Despite her swagger and bravado, she was still just a scared girl who'd always longed for someone to love her. She knew it wasn't love, but Case had made her feel something thrilling a little while ago.

He watched as she hesitated, then slowly drew the stained hat away. She turned her face from him, stealing glances from under her fanlike lashes. She was a pretty little thing and for the first time since they'd met, she was washed and fragrant. Her skin was the color of ripe peaches and there were no freckles to blemish its creamy perfection, only a few fading bruises. He had a sudden impulse to find the man who'd put them there and thrash him.

She said nothing, not even when he stood and walked around the fire to sit down beside her. Gently, he crooked a forefinger under her chin and lifted her head, forcing her gaze to clash with his. Her doe eyes were dark with emotion, challenging, wary. She merely watched him, waiting for his next move.

She had a fine little nose, straight and sweet, and her lips had the color and lushness most women could obtain only by artificial means. His free hand reached out and finger-combed her still damp hair, which had formed springy curls around her face and neck.

Case expelled the breath he'd been holding and continued to gaze at her for long moments. Her looks weren't voluptuous in any erotic sense, but the girl's homespun prettiness was most engaging. With an experienced eye, he predicted she would mature into a real beauty. "How old are you, January Jones?"

"Seventeen. Eighteen in a few days." The words came out in a rush. She'd been holding her breath while Case peered at her, turning her face this way and that, inspecting her like a horse at auction. She'd thought he might kiss her again and the idea wasn't at all as loathsome as it should've been.

She'd never received a man's approval before, but somehow sensed she'd received his. She could tell he found her acceptable by the faint, appreciative upward turn of his lips. Lips that were so close to hers, she could feel his warm breath.

Shameless hussy that she was, she found herself leaning toward him expectantly, his nearness disturbing her in unheard of ways, stirring up all those strange and wondering feelings again. But Case wasn't going to kiss her and she was humiliated that she'd expected him to, so she quickly brushed his hand from her hair. "What's wrong? Ain't you gonna check my teeth?"

He snatched his hand away as though he'd been scalded, amazed he'd been so swept away by the sensations she aroused. What kind of man had libidinous thoughts about such a young girl anyway? "I wanted to see who I was bedding down with, that's all."

January's hand flew to the hilt of her knife. "Who said you were beddin' down with me?"

Mortified that she'd interpreted the thought behind his words, he flushed. "That was just a figure of speech," he lied. "I didn't mean it literally."

"Seems like the only figure you're interested in is mine."

"For Chrissakes, woman, what makes you think I'd want you in the first place?"

January bristled. "You mean I ain't good enough for you, Mr. High-and-Mighty Latimer who thinks he's God's own cousin? I'm just as good as you are. And you sure had me bumfuzzled, if you call what you done earlier not wantin' me."

Exasperated and out of patience, he retraced his steps, gulped down the remaining coffee-flavored whiskey, and flung himself onto his bedroll. "There is simply no talking to you. First you're ready to castrate me because you think I've got ulterior motives, then you get up on your high horse because I don't. Just stay away from me. Shut up and go to sleep."

"Sure." January harrumphed. "You're the one who

wanted me to move closer,'' she added with mocking sarcasm.

''I *thought* you might like to be nearer the fire. But if you prefer to freeze tonight, be my guest.''

She kicked her bedroll further away from him. ''You know, Pa was right. All you men are a bunch of debauching horny toads who'd as soon seduce a girl as look at her.''

Case sat up and yelled back. ''Oh, is that so? And just what would a pindly little pup like you know of debauchery or seduction?''

''Enough to know that the only reason you want me closer to the fire is so it'll be easier for you to catch me unawares and crawl into my blankets with me.''

He flung himself back on the saddle he used for a pillow and yanked the covers close around him. ''Lady,'' he called over his shoulder, ''I'd as soon crawl down a rabid badger's hole as crawl into your bedroll.'' He was glad he sounded so convincing. ''Now kindly shut up and let me get some sleep.''

January had no reply to that remark. Was she really so undesirable? She didn't know exactly what went on between a man and woman at night when they were in bed together, but it made her miserable that whatever it was, Case didn't consider her a likely candidate.

After long moments of silence, she declared, ''Hellfire, Case Latimer, you're a blamed liar.''

''Don't bet your last dollar on that,'' came his muffled response.

''You mean to tell me you don't want to come over here right now and kiss me?'' She was shocked at her boldness, but she'd never forgive herself if she didn't have the last word.

Case sat up and glared at her across the fire. Never had a girl so needed to be kissed and that was exactly what he wanted to do. But he wouldn't tell her that. If they were to be traveling together, and it appeared that they were, at least temporarily, then he couldn't afford to let his feelings dictate his actions.

He'd always kept his emotions aloof from any encounters he'd had with women, but already he felt a protectiveness toward this one that he didn't want to feel. One look in those innocent eyes of hers had thrown a chink in the brick wall he'd built around his heart. If he didn't watch out, she'd have him roped and hog-tied before God could get the news.

No. He wasn't going to let her get to him and he was going to keep a safe distance, not only from her pouty little mouth but from her bedroll as well. "No, I do *not* want to come right over there and kiss you," he denied hotly, angry that she'd read his thoughts so accurately. "That mouth of yours is your most lethal weapon." Reminding himself he'd do well to remember that, Case settled uncomfortably in his bedroll and waited for the sleep he knew would be a long time coming.

Chapter 4

As was her habit, January arose before sunup the next morning. She built up the fire, sharpened a long stick with her knife, and went to the creek for breakfast. Her sudden appearance at water's edge startled a huge, noisy bullfrog into dilatory activity and he splashed away to croak his grievances from the opposite bank.

January exulted in the clean morning air and predawn chorus of birdsong, mingled with the raucous hum of insects. She waded barefoot into the cold water and waited for the ripples to subside. There was just enough light for her to wield her spear in the fashion taught her by an old Cherokee Indian back in the holler. While concentrating on spiking the glittering, thrashing fish from the water, she considered her situation.

She'd lain awake the night before, listening to the reassuring sound of Case's snoring and wondering what to do. Even knowing she wouldn't be allowed to make the run, she hadn't given up the idea of going on to Oklahoma.

As for traveling with Case as far as her destination, she felt she could trust him if last night was any indication. At first she'd been leery of even so much as closing her eyes for fear he might pounce on her, but he'd no more than covered up until he was snoring. Her bewildering curiosity had soon turned to smoldering anger. It seemed his own blood hadn't been as deeply stirred as hers if he could just hurl an insult at her, then roll over and fall asleep.

She'd finally dozed, uneasy with the grating awareness

that she wouldn't have fought too hard if he'd tried to touch her again.

It was now her heart-deep belief that he wasn't a threat to her safety or her virginity. There'd been plenty of opportunity, but he'd kept his distance. Any man as handsome and fast-talking as he was could have all the women he wanted and he wouldn't have to say boo to get them.

It would be wiser to travel with him than risk her safety with the outlaws that surely frequented the trail. Case sounded too smart and was too smooth to be a villain or robber.

When she had a meal-sized mess of fish, January returned to camp, expecting Case to be up and about. She was shocked to find him sleeping as soundly as ever. As she cleaned the fish and prepared them for the fire, she tried to wake him several times. "Get up, Latimer. You plannin' to sleep the day away?"

When he didn't respond, she stomped over to where he lay curled in his bedroll and gave him a not-so-gentle nudge with her foot. He slept on. When their meal of roasted fish was nearly done, she tried again. "Hurry up if you want some breakfast before we hit the trail," she called to the motionless, snoring form. "I want to make up for the time I lost during the storm."

Case opened one eye and saw her expertly turning something over the fire. His nose told him it was fish and that they would taste as delicious as they smelled. Evidently, she was as skilled with a fishing line as she was with a rifle and that damned knife of hers. It was maddening for any woman to be so self-sufficient. Grudgingly, he wondered if she'd taken all the fish with the same worm. "What do you mean, breakfast?" he muttered. "It's still night."

"Hogwash. Time's a-wastin'. The sooner I get to Arkansas City, the sooner I can escape your 'protection' and the sooner you can be shut of me. Get up!"

"Wake me again when the sun's a little higher." He wasn't accustomed to early rising. In his profession, this was just about the time he normally turned in for the night. He'd known there were good reasons why he disliked life on the run and this was one of them. He'd spent the last few years mostly indoors and roughing it paled considerably in comparison. Still . . . He sniffed involuntarily. The aroma of fresh fish and coffee was mighty tempting.

"I got me a canteen of cold creek water here and if you don't roll out of them blankets in five seconds, I'm goin' to empty it all over you, you lazy loafer." January sloshed the water around in the canteen for emphasis.

"All right, all right," he grumbled as he got to his feet. "No need to get testy." He glanced toward the campfire where she crouched, plate in hand. "Those fish do smell appetizing."

"Taste good, too," she elaborated as she forked a bite into her mouth. "I can tell you ain't no farmer, but what kind of work do you do that lets you laze around in bed all day?"

He found a tin plate and helped himself to the fish. All day, indeed. He watched the first rosy streaks of dawn light the eastern sky and was tempted to point out the irony of her question. Then he took one look at January, who was eating with the same energy she lavished on everything else, and thought better of it. Irony would be lost on a person who lived in such a literal world.

He was struck afresh by her unguarded beauty. She'd left off that awful hat and her chestnut hair caught fire as weak rays of sunlight played upon her head, reflecting deep gold and rich red. Her features were, indeed, artfully arranged and if memory served him, her form, though slight of build, was just as perfect. She was a bit thin, but a few weeks of good nourishment would round her out.

Case was appalled by the sudden realization that he'd enjoy force feeding her every bite, watching her grow even more beautiful and curvaceous by the mouthful. Those were dangerous thoughts.

"I do a little of this and a little of that," he finally answered, hiding his distressing thoughts.

January frowned. "This and that what? Do you make your living honestly or are you some kind of four-flusher?"

"There are those who might disagree," he said amiably between bites of savory bass, "but I happen to think mine is a noble profession. It requires not only iron nerves and quick wits, but an understanding of human nature as well. And it takes years of practice to perfect one's skill."

She chewed thoughtfully. "So what are you, a dad-burned tooth-jumper?"

"A dentist!" Case nearly choked on his fish. "Certainly not. I happen to be a professional gambler."

She couldn't have looked more shocked if he'd admitted he robbed banks and despoiled women for a living. He smiled at her consternation and prompted, "What's wrong, J.J.?"

She swallowed, continuing to stare at him. Not only did he drink, but he gambled. For a living! She'd have been better off throwing her lot in with the devil himself. "You mean you're one of them no-account, low-life cardsharps, what preys on the weaknesses of innocent folks?"

"Not exactly." He chuckled. "I gave up preying a long time ago. I belong to an exclusive fraternity open only to honest gamblers."

"I didn't know there was such a thing. Every time my pa gets in a game, he loses the shirt off his back."

"Perhaps your father is incredibly ungifted at cards. I happen to be so good, I don't have to cheat."

January found it hard to believe anyone could make an "honest" living gambling in dens of iniquity. Or that they'd want to. That explained why he wasn't sun-roughened and why his hands looked so clean and felt so good against her skin. "Ain't you never done no real work?" she asked incredulously.

He laughed. "If you think sitting in on a high-stakes poker game, sometimes for thirty-six hours at a stretch, in a smoky room filled with hot, smelly cowboys and miners, isn't work, then you should try it sometime."

"No thanks, I'd rather earn my living by the sweat of my brow."

"I guess that's where we're different, J.J., because I prefer to earn my living by the sweat of someone else's brow."

"It's sinful, that's what it is," she declared, with the sinking feeling that she'd nearly succumbed to such a sinner. "Those poor men lose the very money that would put food in their families' bellies." She should know; she'd been hungry too many times to count. "Don't it make you feel like a low-down cur to practically steal milk from outta the mouths of babes?"

"I can see you have a distorted view of the gambler's art," he answered with a devilish grin. "Allow me to explain. First of all, I find miners and cowboys make the most agreeable players since they tend to consider it their God-given right to whoop it up however they see fit. Most miners and cowboys are single men without kith or kin. Second, the primary reason they labor out on the range and down in holes in the ground is to make money to have a good time.

"Now, three things will assure them of having that good time. Getting drunk, finding whor— er . . . female companionship, and gambling. That's where I come in. Since I don't sell whiskey or women, I figure it'd be a real dereliction of duty not to oblige them in some modest fashion."

January sat quietly through his long-winded speech, shaking her head in disbelief. When he'd finished, she spoke up. "Pa done sold my cow, Latimer, so I don't reckon I need your bull."

He laughed again and set his empty plate on the ground. Pouring himself another cup of coffee, he said, "Maybe you have a point there. As long as we're going to be traveling together, let's adhere to a live and let live policy. What do you say?"

What could she say? Most of the time she didn't even know what he was talking about. She didn't think he'd learned all those high-dollar words in any saloon or gambling hall and she wondered where he'd come from. She was about to ask when he spoke again.

"I can see by your blank expression that you haven't the vaguest idea what I just suggested."

"Maybe not, but if you suggested it, it's probably something I wouldn't want to do."

"Must you be eternally suspicious? I'll make it simple. In an effort to make this journey as painless as possible for both of us, why don't we agree that you won't try to turn me into a dirt farmer as long as I promise not to corrupt you by turning you into a lady gambler." He grinned at the absurdity of that thought.

"That'd be the day," she snorted.

Case hooted with laughter. "Indeed, it would be. Now if you'll trot down to the creek and get these plates washed up, we can load up and be on our way." He stood and stretched, pressing his hands into the small of his back. He was disappointed she was so judgmental. But her disapproval would make it that much easier to keep his distance. "I know how you dislike burning daylight."

He watched her rise haughtily, delicately dust off the seat of her pants, and settle her battered hat on her head as though it were a piece of exquisite Parisian millinery. After tucking her errant curls under its wide brim, she turned to him. "I figure it's time we ad-here to another one of them policy things."

She wasn't about to take orders from no tinhorn gambler. "Since I'm the one what caught and cooked breakfast, you can be the one that cleans up and breaks camp. Like I told my pa, Lincoln done freed the slaves some time back. The work ought to be nippety-nip." The look she leveled at him said she wasn't open to argument.

"Nippety-what?" he asked, puzzlement arranging his features in a frown.

"Fifty-fifty. Don't you understand your mother tongue?"

He let the remark pass, in no mood to get into another argument. Since the girl was not only mule-headed and unpredictable, but subject to displays of violence as well, this was a time when there would be honor in retreat. With a pointed look in her direction, he gathered up the soiled utensils and headed for the creek, mumbling objections all the way.

When he returned, she had the horses saddled, loaded, and ready to ride. "What took you so long?"

He glared at her as he packed but didn't say a word. He wasn't about to defend himself for taking time to wash up and shave. She would never understand such a frivolous waste of time.

They traveled for several hours, mostly in silence. January didn't have much trouble with Brownie since he seemed pleased to be in the company of Case's sleek Morgan. He followed the black horse's lead with a tractability he'd never before displayed.

January wasn't so sure about her choice of human companions. When she'd made up her mind to travel with Case this morning, she hadn't known he was a fast-talking, low-life gambler. Now that she did, she wondered anew at what kind of trouble might befall her in such bad company.

She already suspected he was as slick as a wax snake, but the gleam he got in his eyes when they spotted a small house, set deep in a clearing away from the road, convinced her.

"How'd you like to save time and have a hot, home-cooked meal without having to kill it yourself?" he asked, watching smoke curl from the stone chimney.

"I'd like that fine, but since it's for sure you ain't going to kill it, just how do you propose we get one? I ain't no beggar."

"Nor am I. I'll stake my reputation on the fact that there's a plump little housewife in that shanty, one just dying for some male attention. By the time I get finished, she'll be begging me to take food off her hands."

January hooted with laughter. "Oh yeah? You're crazy as a coot. How do you know there's a woman in there?"

Case's head tipped to the rise behind the structure where the day's laundry was spread out to dry on bushes. Among the items were petticoats, shirtwaists, and several underdrawers, size ample.

"So what? How do you know she ain't got herself a big old wooly husband whose hobby is beating up on wise-ass gamblers?"

"You see anything on those bushes that might belong to a big old wooly husband? Now you stay here. You hear?"

"I hear you." She didn't know if her aggravation stemmed from being left behind or from not knowing what was about to take place inside the house. "I hope you get a tail full of buckshot."

"That'll never happen, I assure you."

He sounded just as full of himself as ever and as she watched, he smoothed down his hair, which was as rich and brown as a prime beaver pelt. He slapped the road dust from his hat and suit, then polished his boots on the backs of his trouser legs. He rearranged his string tie and straightened his white cuffs. No doubt about it, Case Latimer was as handsome as the devil, red-hot from home.

She dismounted, tied Brownie to a fallen tree where he could graze at leisure, then heaved herself up on a stump, her legs dangling, and watched him lead Shadow up to the neat-looking place. Almost immediately the door opened and out stepped a wide-hipped, frizzy-haired young woman.

January couldn't hear what they were saying, but directly, the woman smiled and stepped aside, issuing a clear invitation for Case to enter.

January got a knotty feeling in her stomach as she watched him strut inside and she had to grip the side of the stump just to keep from flinging herself after him. What did she care what a tinhorn like him did, anyhow? He meant nothing to her and she meant even less to him. There could never be anything serious between her and a man who gambled for a living, not in a hundred years. Hadn't she seen firsthand what the vices of drinking and wagering did to a man and his family?

Yes, she had, and despite the way her stomach fluttered

when Case was in touching distance, she vowed to work harder at loathing him.

If Pa hadn't taken to drinking, he'd have provided a better life for her and her mother. It was the moonshine that made him so jealous and angry, that had driven him the day he'd run Daisy off. If he hadn't resorted to drinking, maybe he wouldn't have lost what little dignity he'd had left. There'd have been no agreement with Mose and maybe she and Pa could have gone to Oklahoma together. If . . . if . . . if! If a frog had wings, he wouldn't have to hop. The day she'd declared her independence from servitude and whippings, January had also vowed she was through with drinking men.

She wasn't without her own faults, being the daughter of a drunk and a hussy. Pa said she couldn't be trusted and accused her of having sinful feelings in her heart. Now, for the first time, she understood what he'd meant. But they were sins she hadn't even come close to committing. Leastways, she hadn't until last night.

January studied the snug-looking little house. It was well-built of timber, painted white, and had a sturdy roof. It was hard to tell, but judging from the number and placement of the windows, she guessed it contained three or four rooms. A deep, railed porch, shaded by tall pines and squat cedars, ran the length of the front. It didn't take much imagination to know how cool and refreshing it'd be to sit there and rock on a warm summer's evening.

A garden was planted out back and she could see that it, too, was well-tended, with spring lettuce and radishes already in evidence. Fat speckled hens, some trailing chicks, scratched in the dirt yard. The well was near the back door and a discreet distance away stood the necessary, a half moon carved in the door.

Beyond that, the barn stood in the middle of cleared ground which had been left fallow for some time. While it was obvious the woman took pride in her place, she wasn't using it to its full potential. Those fields should be planted in wheat or corn, or some other cash crop. Already the woods had begun reclaiming that which had once been its own.

January longed for a place exactly like this one and hoped there were oak and pine forests in the Indian Territory. She wanted to find a shady little knoll with a stream nearby and put down roots. Roots would grow strong and deep in such fertile soil.

A bird trilled overhead and her head jerked up. She noted the position of the sun and wondered how much longer Case was going to be in there. She had half a mind to go on without him; she didn't want to waste any more time. Maybe she couldn't make the run herself, but if she got there in time, maybe she could meet up with some young feller who had everything he needed to take up homesteading, except a wife.

She was surprised at how easily her mind accepted the idea, though she knew she didn't have too many choices. Marriage wasn't the ideal solution to her problem and she balked at being under a man's dominance again, but it was the only one she could think of. Lost in a daydream, she tried to imagine what this future husband might look like. The only image her mind would send was of Case.

She laughed in the stillness of the woods. That'd be the day, when she got hitched up to a shiftless gambler. She'd gladly enter the frail sisterhood before she'd let such a revolting thing happen.

January lost track of how much time she spent on that stump, kicking bark off with the heel of her boot and chasing tiny red ants with a sharp stick. He'd had plenty of time to sweet-talk the woman out of some grub, so what was keeping him? She had a fair idea what it might be and tried unsuccessfully to force her thoughts in a different direction. What kind of man would stoop to such methods just to get a free meal? Hellfire! What were the two of them doing in there all this time?

Glancing up, she noticed the sun had reached its zenith and had begun to sink westward. She could've shot a whole brace of wild critters, skinned them, cooked them, and eaten them in the time he was taking to save time. She was startled out of her musings by Case's voice behind her.

"I'm glad to see you didn't get tired of waiting."

"Well, I did. I was fixing to go off without you. You'd sure be in a pickle then. Without me to hunt for you, you'd starve looking for lonely women."

Case laughed. "Now, don't be cruel. The Widow Green was right neighborly." He pulled a dishcloth-wrapped bundle from under his coat. "She even sent this along for the road. I thought you might be getting hungry."

"Thanks for remembering me. A body could keel over with the miss-meal colic, for all you'd care," she said icily before grabbing the package. She untied it eagerly, recognizing the fragrant aroma of biscuits and ham. Eating hungrily, she stared at him, trying to determine just how far he'd had to go to get it. "So she was a widder, huh?"

"That's right. A nicer, more genteel lady you'd never want to meet." Case sat on a nearby stump, watching January eye him.

"What'd you say that made her happy enough to feed you dinner?" she asked, curiosity getting the best of her.

He laughed and the sound rang through the woods around them. "You are an innocent if you think talking makes a lady happy."

She felt the color heat up her cheeks. "Tarnation, she weren't no lady then."

"Don't speak ill, J.J. Just enjoy the bounty." He reached inside his coat again and pulled out a canning jar full of fresh milk. "I thought you might enjoy this," he said, handing it to her.

"Thanks," she mumbled around a mouthful of biscuit. She watched him thoughtfully and wondered if he'd used the same brand of sweet-talk on the woman's cow. "Don't you feel no remorse at doing such a vile thing?"

"Such a vile thing as what?" he asked innocently.

"You know what I mean. Why, I bet that gal's got a bigger grin on her face right now than she had when she opened the door."

He howled, knowing what she was obviously thinking. What he didn't know was why she was suddenly acting like she cared. It was almost as if she'd been bitten by the green-eyed monster. "You're not jealous, are you?"

"Jealous?" she screeched, nearly choking on a swig of milk. "Me jealous of a sidewinder like you?"

He adopted an air of studied nonchalance. "Well, you do seem powerfully curious about what went on between that widow woman and me."

"That woman? Why should I care what you did with the likes of her?" She sniffed her disapproval. "She looked so bowlegged, I bet she couldn't pen a pig in a ditch."

"Oh, really? I didn't notice," he baited.

"She was so ugly she'd have to slap herself to sleep."

"Good thing we weren't sleeping, then."

She had a sudden, vague picture of Case with the frizzy-haired woman, touching, kissing, whispering things she'd never understand. The way he'd kissed her last night. The image burned through her and she wanted to strike him, to make him swear on a stack of Bibles he hadn't done those things.

Then she wanted him to do those things to her again. Only she didn't know how to make him want to.

"Well, you don't have to sit there grinning like a skunk eating cabbage!" she yelled, suddenly full of frustrated fury.

"Am I grinning?"

"You know you are," she said huffily.

"I guess I'm just feeling content," he teased. Actually, nothing had transpired in that tidy little house, outside of a friendly talk while the apple pie finished baking. The widow had been obliging when he'd confessed his weakness for apple pie. She was lonely and anxious to talk of the trouble she'd had since her husband had died, of how she longed to go home to her parents in Springfield, if only she could find a buyer for the place.

January stared at Case, feeling her claws coming out

and not knowing why. She didn't care what that low-down polecat did, so why was she acting like a jilted bride?

"If you're finished eating, let's get on down the road. I'd like to make a little time this evening," Case said.

After stuffing the dishtowel in her saddlebag and leaving the empty jar on the stump, January mounted Brownie. "That's a right good idea. We wasted a lot of time today saving time. Maybe you should remember that when next you get the urge to shine up to a widder woman." She yanked on the reins, startling the hapless Brownie, and kicked him into a trot. Not slowing down when she reached the road, she soon left Case behind to eat her dust.

He didn't know what to make of her behavior, but made up his mind not to let it bother him. If his suspicions were correct and the girl had taken a shine to him, all the more reason to keep a distance between them. He felt a familiar stirring in his loins each time he remembered holding her naked body close to his and he could see nothing but trouble at every turn.

The road had dried out some and they made good time that afternoon, most of it passed in silence. Case tried to talk to January, but she would do little more than answer his questions with a yes or no. Finally he gave up trying to draw her out and fell to thinking about his own problems.

With any luck, he'd thrown the Buscus brothers off his trail. If not, there was no telling when they would show up again. If he made it to Arkansas City without incident, he would hang around just long enough to collect a sizable stake. Any place where men gathered for something as risky as a land run should be rife with fools willing to gamble. Then he'd catch a train to Seattle. There, he'd have no trouble finding a ship to take him to his ultimate destination—Juneau, Alaska.

It was an extreme move, but he'd been thinking about the gold fields of that northern country for some time now. He had no intention of changing his trade to miner. Why dig it out of the ground when you could sit behind a deck of cards and wait for men to hand it to you? But he thrived on adventure and this part of the country was getting way too tame for his tastes.

Everywhere you turned, you could hear the ring of hammers building schools and churches and picket fences. As a rule, gamblers were not made welcome in places suffering the civilizing influence of women.

He could head west, to the gold and silver camps of Arizona and Nevada, but it wouldn't be long before the feminine tide washed over those as well. Alaska, being inhospitable in clime and inaccessible most of the year, was surely his best bet. Besides, when dealing with drastic individuals like the Buscus brothers, drastic measures were often the only solution.

Several hours passed before he turned to January. "Are you ready to stop for the night?"

"If you're too tired to go on, I reckon we could."

"I didn't say I was tired. I was thinking about you."

"So don't bother thinking about me. I can keep up. I can take anything you can take," she said defensively.

He rolled his eyes heavenward. January was the only woman he'd ever met who'd bite a man's head off for being considerate. He was growing extremely trail-weary, but in light of her last remark, he could scarcely say so now.

They rode into a thick stand of trees, the shade casting a twilight darkness upon them. His stomach rumbled, reminding him he was also hungry. "Dammit, do you want to stop or not?" he yelled in exasperation.

"I think that would be a plumb good idee, mister," twanged a voice from the shadows. "Now, don't do nothin' stupid like goin' fer yer guns, fellers, 'cause I believe we done got you'uns surrounded."

Chapter 5

Before Case had time to react, four horsemen appeared out of nowhere. They were, indeed, surrounded, and by as unsavory-looking a lot as he'd ever seen. He caught January's frantic expression, her eyes clearly commanding him to do something. Given the two-to-one odds, and the fact that the bushwhackers had the drop on them, he had no idea what that something might be.

The men quickly disarmed him and January, although for a moment Case feared she'd fight for possession of the Winchester. He thought briefly of the derringer in his saddle pack but dismissed any notions of heroism for the time being. Even if the derringer were tucked up his sleeve, as it usually was at the faro table, its accuracy and range left much to be desired. Besides, going for a gun would only get them both shot.

Sizing up the opposition, Case quickly determined his only real weapon was his wits.

"Unclimb those horses," commanded the apparent leader of the scruffy band.

January tightened her hold on Brownie's reins, trying to decide on a plan of action, weighing possible acts against possible outcomes. She had her knife, but she could only take out one of them with it. That would pare things down a mite, but three to two still wasn't real encouraging.

She could make a run for it, but Case was already dismounting and couldn't possibly get away. She told herself it was everyone for himself but she didn't want him to get a bullet in the back because of her. Besides, if Brownie had one of his stubborn spells, she'd be up a tree for sure.

"Get off'n that horse, Junior," ordered a red-haired fortress of a man. "Ain't nobody ever taught you to obey yer elders?" For emphasis, he raised his shotgun level with January's chest, leaving her no real choice in the matter.

"Now," the leader said amiably, "we're gonna take up a little collection." With his revolver, he motioned for Case and January to stand side by side. "Play like yer in church and dig real deep."

She stared at the man, sure she'd never forget him. He wasn't much taller than she was, and so thin his clothes hung on him. There was a spark of intelligence in his close-set eyes; just enough to set himself as leader among the brawnier, older men, enough to make him dangerous. For the first time since they'd been stopped, real dread quickened within her.

"Clink," he barked to the red-haired giant, "pass the hat. These good pilgrims are ready to offer up."

"Right, boss." Clink jumped to do the other man's bidding and, snatching off his hat, he held it out to Case. "Empty your pockets, mister."

Inwardly, Case was relieved. He and January were getting off easily; the men were only after money. He dumped his in the hat. Cash was expendable: there was always more to be had at the next saloon or gaming parlor. They might escape with their lives, after all. If the bandits were intent on murder, they'd have shot first and searched the bodies later.

He clenched his fists at his sides when the ham-handed thief relieved him of his gold pocket watch. That heirloom was definitely not expendable. He made a move to reclaim it, but Clink's shotgun talked him out of it.

"I ain't got no money," January told the big man when he thrust the hat at her. Her head was level with his chest and she had to look up to stare him in the eye. She couldn't allow them to discover her hidden cache of silver dollars. After turning her pockets inside out, she jabbed an elbow in Case's ribs. "*He* won't let me have none. Says I ain't reliable. Hard to believe we came out of the same womb, ain't it?"

Case glared at her, willing her to shut up. It would do no good to anger the thieves unnecessarily and his expression told her if she had money on her, it was time to ante up.

She glared back defiantly. "All the brothers in the world and I had to get this 'un. Just because he's older'n me, he thinks he knows everything. Our ma told me to watch my back and when a man's own dear mammy calls him a snake in the grass, then you know whose belly's dragging the ground, dontcha?"

The men were staring at her, a couple of them scratching their heads. She wasn't sure what she was doing, but it seemed to be working because the feller called Clink was passing her by.

"Don't take that snot-nosed kid's word for nothin'," the leader ordered. "Search him!"

Case stiffened and stepped between the two of them. A search was out of the question. If these ruffians discovered January's true identity, he'd be forced to go up against them all. And he'd do it somehow before he'd let them lay their filthy hands on her. "I'm the head of this family and I carry all our valuables."

"Hell, boss," Clink complained. "Look at him. You think a slicker like this here feller is gonna let a know-nothing like that keep anything on him? Dadgummit, you don't never let me have more'n a couple a bucks."

Clink turned away and Case hid his relief, just as he'd learned to mask all his emotions. A cool head was all that stood between them and an itchy trigger finger. He'd forgive January's show of temper on the basis of her youth, but if they got out of this alive, they'd have a little talk regarding her hotheaded impetuousness.

"We got ever'thin' they had, Willard," Clink insisted. "Let's get hell and gone away from here."

The leader seemed reluctant to heed that suggestion and glared hard at January, as if he doubted their story. She glared hard right back, determined to let him know she wasn't about to be cowed. It was bad enough Case seemed so all-fired eager to test the notion that the meek would inherit the earth.

"Tub, you and Lefty take their horses," Willard called to his silent accomplices. He turned around to Case and January. "Let's have them boots."

"No," she said evenly.

"What did you say, kid?"

"I said no. I ain't giving you my boots." She had to draw the line somewhere. The loss of material possessions was bad enough and, with Brownie gone, she was losing her chance to get to Oklahoma in time. She might never see her dreams come true. If she had to walk to Indian Territory, she'd be damned if she was going to do it barefooted. "You're taking our horses, all our money, spare clothes, and supplies. If you want my boots, you'll have to pry them off my cold, dead feet."

Case's curse, though silent, was nonetheless vehement. The stupid little hothead was practically begging the man to kill them. If the tables were turned, he'd be tempted to shoot her himself. Instead, he clenched his fists and geared himself for the fight that was sure to come.

Pointing his revolver at January's head, Willard smiled but didn't look amused. "Reckon that could be arranged."

Their chances of survival had been severely diminished because she had gone and gotten righteous, Case mentally lamented. Her stubbornness would be the end of them yet. "Give him the boots," he muttered under his breath, as he peeled off his own and handed them over.

Her look said she was disappointed in him. Hell, all he was trying to do was get them out of here alive. He wasn't that attached to his footgear and he'd learned from experience that right didn't make might and all the principles in the world wouldn't make them any less dead if there was a bullet between their eyes. "Give him the damned boots."

With a surge of recklessness, January adamantly shook her head and folded her arms across her chest. "I won't give them up, no matter what." She didn't mean for her words to sound like a challenge, but they were taken that way, because Case's eyes widened in shocked surprise and the outlaw's in derision. The other three hooted their amusement.

"You heard the kid, Willard. You're gonna have to fight him for 'em." Clink laughed so hard his beer belly shook.

Fight? January thought. He wasn't going to shoot her? Maybe it wasn't too late to pull the fat out of the fire.

"You're plumb crazy, kid," Willard said.

"I must be," she agreed.

She was tempted to express her indignation that Willard should even consider hitting a woman and waited for Case to call him out on it. His silence reminded her that, as far as the others were concerned, she was *not* a woman. Hellfire! She'd be in an even bigger fix if that fact were pointed out.

The one named Tub called, "Sic 'im, Willard. I think he's a little too big for his britches. Show 'im who's boss."

That did it. Her own big mouth and Tub's had just sealed her fate. Puffing out her chest, but not too much, she said, "He might be your boss, porkbelly, but he ain't mine."

Case drew his fists tight and thought it was too bad she couldn't do her fighting with her mouth. There wasn't a man alive who stood a chance against its rapier edge. But they weren't dead yet and before that happened, he intended to cram their insults back down their ignorant throats. With this turn of events, he was thankful he hadn't succeeded in seducing January last night. At least he wouldn't go to his grave with that on his conscience.

"He may be a snot-nose," Case said loudly, "but he's the only brother I've got. You'll have to go through me to get to him."

"The hell you say," mumbled Clink. A sharp blow to the temple with the butt of his gun effectively removed Case from the battle.

When she saw Case crumple to the ground, January

fought the guilt-ridden urge to gather him into her arms and kiss the hurt away. Instead, she gave a Rebel yell and crouched into a fighting stance. It was between her and Willard now. She circled the little man, a look of wild-eyed desperation in her eyes, murder in her heart. She'd licked Mose when they were younger and she didn't doubt her ability to give Willard a run for his money.

"Forget it, Willard," Clink said when he'd stopped laughing at the sight. "We ain't got time for you to square off with a fly spit like him. Let's just get out of here. Those boots of his'n don't look to be worth fightin' over. Why, jest lookit how them toes is all turned up!" The others unanimously agreed.

"Usually I don't fight children." Willard sneered and circled in the opposite direction. "But I'll make an exception in your case, you little bastard."

A shaking fury overcame January at the scurrilous slur on her parentage. Because of that remark and the attack on Case, she'd have some revenge. She might die trying, but she'd die with her boots on.

Willard kept circling, his fists poised to attack. "After I get through poundin' on ya, I'm gonna make a steer outta ya," he promised.

Since she had nothing to lose, she gave in to her blind rage. Head down, she lunged viciously at the thief, striking him just below the breastbone. He tumbled backward, but was soon scrambling to his feet, sucking in great quantities of air.

With a sudden eruption of violence, he sprang forward, his fist connecting with her cheek, and she staggered a step back, stalling while crazy noises rang in her head. Willard turned, bragging to his buddies, "He ain't so full of piss and vinegar now."

Attacking clumsily, but with the added power of surprise, she lit into him again. She raked her nails down the side of his face, then landed a quick, hard punch right on his nose. Although he struck out with both fists and feet, she was able to dodge each blow, infuriating him further.

The other men formed a rough circle, alternately urging on their leader and rooting for January.

Case stirred, but it was a few moments before he gained enough sense to understand why he couldn't move his arms and legs. He'd been trussed to a tree trunk! The blackness was receding, but the throbbing in his temple made movement painful and the ropes made it almost impossible. He was shocked to see the fight already in progress—a pale blur of butts, elbows, and boots—and knew he must put an end to it. But how?

He couldn't bear the thought of January suffering pain from Willard's slimy hands. On closer inspection, it appeared she was holding her own. That made it more imperative for him to intercede, before it was discovered that she was a female and before Willard got mad enough to draw his gun and end it himself.

As Case watched in stupefied fascination, January lashed out with her boot. Willard grabbed his shin, dancing away on one leg.

"J.J.!" Case yelled, wincing at the pain the sound initiated. He had an idea. It was a long shot and likely the result of the sudden scrambling of his brains, but what the hell, it might just work. "Back off, son, don't hurt him none. You know what happens when you get too mad."

The sparring continued, but Clink looked sharply at Case. "What does happen when he gits too mad?"

"He's liable to have a fit. It's a horrible sight."

"You mean . . . ?" Clink asked, obviously reviled by the loathsome picture his mind conjured up.

Case nodded gravely. "If J.J. bites him, your man is doomed. He could go blind if J.J. even so much as spits in his eye."

"Like hydrophoby or something?" Clink asked and there was a note of morbid fascination in his voice.

"It's somewhat similar. When a fit comes on him, J.J. goes plumb crazy. No one can hold him, wouldn't if they could. They don't dare try."

"Is he fixin' to have one of them fits now, do you reckon?" Clink asked eagerly, as if anxious to witness such a spectacle.

"Looks like it." Case added a repulsed shiver for emphasis.

"Willard," Clink yelled. "Guess what? The kid's got some kind of sickness. Get away from him afore you git it, too."

The two combatants lunged at each other and fell to the ground. Case saw January's hat fly off and wondered how long it'd be before she was found out. "We'd better do something to separate them," he warned. "One bite and . . ."

Case's words finally spurred Clink into action. He waved for Tub to join him and the two waded into the fray. Their timing was right, because it looked like Willard was in danger of being taken down. Tub grappled with a snarling Willard; Clink hung on to a swinging, hissing January.

The big man let out a bearish yowl as her sharp teeth clamped down on his forearm. "I'm bit!" he cried. "The little devil bit me!"

Willard had composed himself by this time, apparently deciding his fight with the kid had resulted from an unleaderlike loss of control. He was trying to resume authority.

But Clink's frenzied howling soon got the best of Willard. "Goddammit," he snapped. "What the hell's got into you?"

Clink was holding January by the scruff of the neck with one hand. Her feet barely touched the ground, but she was still swinging with both arms like the madman Case had claimed her to be.

"Pizen!" he screamed. "That's what's got into me. This here devil done went and pizened me."

Helplessly, Case held his breath and watched the proceedings, wondering why no one had yet noticed January's obvious femininity. Her golden-red hair, soft lips, and pale skin were a dead giveaway and if these men couldn't see how beautiful she was, they were blind as well as stupid. In her fury, she looked like an avenging angel.

He should have known old Willard was too sharp. "*She-devil*, you mean. Boys, looks like we done captured us a woman." He approached her with malice glittering in his eyes, the malice of a man who'd been shamed. With a quick movement, he ripped open her baggy coat. With both hands, he tore open her wool shirt, revealing the cotton chemise beneath.

Case strained against his bonds, unable to give in to the ecstasy of vented rage, for he knew her only chance was his ability to verbally dissuade Willard and the others. He fought against the terrible need to use brawn instead of brain as he watched the heaving motion of January's breasts under the thin fabric.

The light of revenge and lust glimmered in Willard's eyes and Case knew the man's humiliation was even more excruciating now that his men knew a girl had challenged, and nearly bested, him.

"You know, boys," Willard was saying, "we was heading for the nearest town and whatever bodily comfort our money could buy. I reckon we can all get comforted right here and now. And it won't cost us a red cent." He drew his pistol and pointed it between January's breasts.

She didn't feel so brave now. She knew she wouldn't fare well in this man's hands. She felt a sob tremble inside, quaking for release, but she bit it down, unwilling to let Willard see her fear.

"Who wants to be first?" he asked lasciviously, trailing the gun barrel between her breasts, down her stomach, and lower.

The three men looked at him in amazement and backed away, holding their hands out in front of them as if warding off an evil spirit. Clink was the only one who spoke. "You're as crazy as she is if you think we're gonna touch her." He was still clutching his wounded arm. "Hey dude," he called to Case. "Tell Willard how it is."

Frustrated with the knowledge that January's future depended on how convincing he could be in the next few minutes, Case forced a deliberate nonchalance into his tone. "It's a sad story. You see, J.J. used to be a real popular *fille de joie*."

"A whut?" Willard and Clink asked in unison.

Case appeared to consider a delicate way of putting it. "A *demimondaine*?" At their blank looks he tried, "A frail sister?" Comprehension still wasn't forthcoming. "A woman of easy virtue?"

"Oh!" they said with relief. "You mean a whore?"

"Yes, well, that's right. I made plenty off her until the damned sickness started eating away her brain. We got run out of Carthage because she attacked a customer. I guess I should've seen it coming, but I never thought she'd start turning on people and inadvertently kill a few of them." He shook his head as if the memory pained him and added, "Three young men, right in the prime of life, too."

He could see Clink and the others were suitably impressed by the horrible details, but decided to embellish the ridiculous story for Willard's benefit. "Go ahead and have your way with her. No charge. She'll be all right once she gets back into harness, so to speak. Be sure to stuff a kerchief in her mouth so she can't bite you, though. That's how she got it herself; some foreigner fresh off the boat got a little too frisky and bit her." Case frowned. "I sure would've killed him for that, but he died the very next day. You boys'll probably have to take a turn at holding her. Just watch out for those deadly teeth."

"Not me," Clink responded quickly.

"Now, don't get me wrong, there's still a lot of life in her and you might enjoy the few charms she has left," Case said encouragingly.

January shot him a look that would've felled a charging buffalo. "Damn you, Latimer. Now, see here. I ain't never been no filly . . ."

Case glared back and closed in for the kill. He wasn't worried about the others, and by the time he was through, old Willard wouldn't want anything to do with her either. "Don't get her riled. It makes her slobber."

Willard used the gun barrel to lift her chin for closer

scrutiny. "She's purty young to be used up already, ain't she?"

"She started young and she's older than she looks," Case fabricated.

"She's kinda scrawny, too."

"That she is. But before she caught the curse, she was as round and plump as a peach." Case shook his head sadly. "That's the way of it. The sickness starts inside, eats its way out. By the by, she's got some bad places on her, so be careful not to touch them."

Clink dropped her like a hot potato and she scrambled away from him on all fours. She'd caught on to Case's scheme and decided to help him out. She forced her eyes wide open in what she hoped was a demented look. She hissed and spat, then curved her fingers into clawlike weapons, threatening to scratch out the eyes of anyone who came near her.

Backing off, Willard took a long look at her, all carnal interest suddenly evaporating. "Tie 'er up, boys," he barked as he made for his horse. "We'll leave 'em for buzzard bait."

His men argued among themselves for brief moments. Mounting up, Clink called out, "You want her tied up, boss, you can hog-tie her your own self. I'm gettin' to the nearest sawbones before her pizen has a chance to spread." He turned to Case with a baleful look. "How long's it usually take, dude?" he beseeched.

"About forty-eight hours," Case told him solemnly. "She's been bathing real regular."

Lefty swooped down as he passed Case and plucked off his black hat. "I been fancyin' that hat and I don't reckon I can catch nothin' but a few nits by takin' it," he said, spurring his horse cruelly.

Willard climbed into the saddle and galloped off in pursuit of his cohorts. He threw a last, fearful glance over his shoulder and January obliged him by jumping up and charging after him for a few hundred yards, screaming like a banshee.

When the last of the bandits were out of sight, she returned to the scene of her tussle with Willard and retrieved her hat. Holding it in her hands, she marveled that the battered headgear was the only possession she had left. With that thought, she frantically patted her behind to assure herself that the silver dollars were still safe in their hidden pocket.

"January!" Case called. "Bring your frog-sticker over here and cut these ropes."

She looked at him, distracted from his dilemma by the far more pressing nature of her own. "You're such a big rat, Latimer, just go on ahead and gnaw yourself free."

Case laughed, relieved her experience with Willard and company hadn't daunted her spirit. "Come on, now, girl. Don't be peevish."

"Peevish? Is that what I am?" She stalked over to where he was tied. "Well, *dude,* being called a poxed-up strumpet puts me in a disagreeable temper. I have half a mind to let you rot here."

"What was I supposed to do? If I'd let on what a sweet, innocent little virgin you are, you sure as hell wouldn't be one now. I saved you from the fate worse than death, you know." He sighed dramatically. "Now, show some gratitude and get me out of these ropes. Being tied to a tree puts *me* in a disagreeable temper."

"Oh, yeah," she retorted. "The very thought of you being mad at me has me shakin' in my boots. And speaking of boots . . ." She paused, looking pointedly at his thin socks, and with a gloating look added, "Which of us ain't wearin' none?"

Case looked up with pious distaste, bristling at her cocky attitude. "It seems my personal dignity is just as much at stake here as I am. You're absolutely right. I shouldn't have told them that hideous fabrication. I should've told them you're just as pure as the day you were born. And right this very moment you'd be—"

"Hellfire, Case! Just shut the hell up." The fear, or anger, or whatever it was that had given January courage was seeping out of her and she felt suddenly weak and a little sick now that the immediate danger was past. She had faced down an outlaw band and come out of it alive, so why did she have the craziest urge to sit down and bawl? Instead, she went about the business of cutting Case loose.

"January? Are you all right?" He could have sworn her eyes were filled with unshed tears.

"No, I ain't!" she snapped, momentarily abandoning her task. "I've just been robbed of all my worldly goods. I'll never get to Oklahoma in time for the run now and I'm stranded with a fast-talking gambler."

Case straightened indignantly, as best his bonds would allow. "Which of the three distresses you most?"

"I haven't decided yet." She took off her hat and slapped him with it. "Hellfire! Ever since I tied in with you, I've had nothing but trouble. You're a dadblamed jinx, Latimer." She whacked him again for emphasis.

"A jinx?" he echoed. "Look who's calling who a jinx. Before I ran into you, all I had to worry about were the Buscus brothers. I didn't know how easy I had it. In the past twenty-four hours, I've had to save you three times, so don't go calling me a jinx," he ended huffily.

"Who're the Buscus brothers and why are you worried about them?" she wanted to know. Hadn't she been through enough? Now she had the added nuisance of a group called the Buscus brothers dogging after them.

Realizing his mistake in mentioning his pursuers, Case countered, "It isn't your concern. You've been nothing but bad news."

"I know," she yelled. "So I've been told most of my life."

"Well, J.J., are you going to satisfy my curiosity or not?"

She stared at him blankly. "About what?"

"About why you did what you did. I'm dying to know what's in those damned boots that you were willing to get us both killed for them. Your life savings? A map to buried treasure? The deed to the world?"

She shrugged. "Nothing."

"Did I hear correctly?"

"There ain't nothin' in my boots 'cept my feet. It was the principle of the thing." His scowling face wasn't a pretty sight. "Just because people are bigger, or stronger, or meaner than I am don't give them the right to scare me."

"I'll concede two out of those three," he mumbled crossly.

"They can only scare me if I let 'em. And I wasn't about to let 'em steal my boots."

She didn't know quite how to explain, but she was truly sorry to be such a nuisance. In reality she wanted nothing more than to fall down and bawl like a damned baby, but she wouldn't give Case the satisfaction of knowing just how shaken she felt. She sawed at the ropes with a vengeance.

"Are you crying, January? Tell me I'm crazy, but could it be you really were afraid? Just the tiniest bit?"

"If you think I wasn't scared, then you ain't as smart as I had you pegged. Only a fool wouldn't have been afraid," she said disdainfully. "But I wasn't going to show it." She'd been terrified by the certainty that she was dealing with evil in a pure form. Willard had looked mean enough to bite her himself.

"You did a good job of hiding it." Case chuckled wryly. He truly admired her spunk and her philosophy. "You didn't seem very scared to me. In fact, you were downright formidable. I know the man you bit will never be the same again."

He laughed aloud and the sound of it warmed her heart. She cut through the last knot and secreted the knife inside her coat, then sank down on the cold, damp ground before her legs deserted her completely and leaned against the tree.

"Well," she said softly, then smiled. "I was putting on."

"The hissing and spitting were absolutely inspired. You really should forget homesteading and consider a career on the stage."

"I might be forced to do just that. I'm not too sure how long it'll take to walk to Arkansas City." Looking into Case's blue eyes, she realized her surge of temporary courage had been the result of concern for his well-being. That idea alarmed her almost as much as the quivering that ribboned through her. She hoped that feeling wasn't reflected on the face she turned up to him, since she didn't have the artifice to hide it. "I was worried you might be dead," she admitted.

"Would you care if I was?"

"Yes," she said before she had time to think about it.

"Why?" Case's own voice had dropped to match the breathless timbre of hers.

She fought back an urge to fling herself into his arms. She'd never been petted and made over and she so wanted Case to pet and make over her now. Instead, she jumped up and dusted her palms together. "Because I ain't got time to be diggin' no graves." She didn't tell him it had wrenched her heart to see him lying unconscious, not even knowing if he were dead or alive. "And I felt sorta responsible."

Case cupped her face in his hands, turning it up to his own. "And well you should. Your stubbornness and temper could have gotten us both killed. I ought to wring your sweet little neck."

She leaned toward him, drawn by something she couldn't understand. The churning inside her made her doubt her ability to keep her feelings secret. An aching started deep within her and she longed to kiss him on the mouth, to hear him tell her that she was safe from all harm.

She'd only briefly known this man's lips on hers, but that moment had changed her life. Now she trembled with newly awakened passion, yearning for comfort and something else. For the first time, she questioned her father's wild warnings, suspecting they hadn't been entirely unselfish.

Could it be that he hadn't wanted her to experience the feelings that now threatened to overcome her because he'd been unwilling to lose a good worker? She pushed those thoughts aside, to better concentrate on what was happening. Case's thumbs gently stroked her cheeks. His fingers toyed with her hair. She shivered as though a cold wind had kicked up, but in reality, the evening was balmy, the light breeze unseasonably warm. All around her were the sounds of nature, the fragrance of verdant spring. Her eyes fluttered. It'd be so easy to lose herself among those sounds and smells. So, so easy.

"Could it be, little January, that you care what happens to me?" Case asked softly, his face drawing ever nearer her own.

His words snapped her back to reality and she stiffened, her eyes blinking open. Yes, it would be easy to lose herself to Case, but not at all possible. He wasn't the kind of man who could share her dreams, her visions for the future. And she wasn't the kind of woman who could become a gambler's doxy.

"No more than I care what happens to any helpless critter," she said sharply, wrenching from him and stalking away.

Case was startled by the sudden change in her behavior. For a few moments last night and again just now, she hadn't seemed like an innocent young girl at all. Her eyes had held a woman's promise; her body had strained with a woman's longing. He'd had a glimpse of the feminine softness beneath the hoydenish swagger. He knew how easy it would be for her fragile heart to be broken.

And what about his own? He'd clearly heard the warnings, but still he'd welcomed the stirring that made him want to take what she was unknowingly offering. He wanted to reclaim her lips, to feel her soft, young body beneath his again. He wanted to give to her until he heard her moan with fulfillment. He wanted to take from her until he finally found his own. He wanted . . . God, how he wanted her!

Such feelings were not only dangerous, they were foolish. He had places to go and cards to play. It would be a long time, if ever, before he was ready to settle down. And every time he looked into her eyes, he could hear the sounds of a picket-fence prison being nailed up around him.

January, on the other hand, was as much a part of the land as the flowers and trees and hills. She was like a wildflower, tough and delicate. Right now she was looking for a place to put down roots, and when she found it, she'd survive against all the odds fate cast her way. Those roots would go deep and they would tangle up a man, holding him.

"Who are you calling a helpless critter?" he responded in self-defense.

"Let's see here," she said matter-of-factly, crossing her arms over her chest and whirling to face him. "Do you have a weapon?"

"Well, no, but . . ."

She held up her knife with one hand and produced her slingshot with the other. "I do. Do you know what plants are edible, which ones are poison?"

"Maybe, a few . . ."

"I do. Do you have any boots?"

He glanced down at the thin socks, which were the only covering his tender feet now had. "No, but . . ."

She extended first one foot and then the other for his inspection. "I do. Now the big question. Do you have any ideas?"

"Not yet, but . . ."

She grinned triumphantly, her face lighting up in the gathering gloom. "Well, I do."

Chapter 6

Two days of enforced barefoot marching with January as self-appointed trail boss had begun to erode Case's normally winsome disposition. She had yapped at him every step of the way until he almost regretted having saved her ornery hide in the first place.

After their encounter with the robbers, she had stomped off down the road, determined to catch up with them. Her big idea was to find the brigands and make them give back her property. However, she wasn't too specific on exactly how that trick was to be accomplished. Given the run of luck Case had been having since he'd met her, he'd been sorely tempted to strike out in the opposite direction. Very tempted.

But as he had watched her stride resolutely away, arms swinging and head up, he'd realized he couldn't let her go alone. Convinced he had to be as crazy as she was, he'd limped after her.

"Just shut up, J.J." Case bathed his battered feet in the cool water of a stream, hoping it would have the same effect on his disposition.

"Don't tell me to shut up. You ain't my boss."

He smiled falsely, whisked off his hat, and clutched it to his chest in mock apology. "I do beg your pardon, ma'am. What I should have said was, please cease your endless chatter and let me die in peace."

She snorted. "You ain't gonna die."

He leveled a hard look at her. "Oh, yes, I am. If I have

to listen to your nagging for another ten miles, I'm going to drown myself right here and now."

"Ten miles!" she exclaimed. "That's a big windy for sure. It's been nearly two days since we was robbed and I'd ventured we ain't covered more'n five or six miles in all that time."

"Venture?" Case pretended shock. "Why, January Jones, I thought you were opposed to gambling. I'm appalled you'd even consider making such a wager."

"That was just one of them figures of speech you're so fond of, Latimer." She flopped down beside him and pressed her case. "You know as well as I do that we ain't traveled more'n a hop, skip, and a jump since we was bushwhacked. I thought we agreed to catch up to them outlaws and get our stuff back."

"That was your ridiculous idea, not mine."

"It don't matter whose idea it was, because those skunks are probably long gone by now. We've had to cold trail them because you sit yourself down every little whip stitch to rest."

He closed his eyes and tried to ignore her. The way she'd been harping at him you'd have thought he'd drawn a pistol and shot their damned horses. That it was through his own treachery that she was losing precious time.

It didn't help Case's mood much that he felt inadequate in her company, a feeling he'd never experienced around a woman before. He wasn't equipped to forage for himself in the woods like a damned ridge runner, finding supper under rocks and on bushes. His expertise ran in more sophisticated directions and he preferred the convenience of using legal tender to buy whatever he needed.

The fact that he didn't have a red cent now wasn't the real issue. If he were in a town, he could win some easily enough. His name and word alone were good enough to back his bets. But he could hardly get up a game in the middle of nowhere.

January's resourcefulness on the trail galled him and he resented having to depend on a woman. Especially an insufferable woman who pointed out his shortcomings at every turn. That, plus frustration and his raw, bruised feet, made him ill-tempered and quick to snap at her.

"All you've talked about is how we should hurry up and catch Willard's gang. What the hell are you going to do then? Pitch rocks? Have you forgotten they have guns—not only their own, but ours as well? I may be a gambler, but I don't like those odds. If you're planning to challenge them, do keep one thing in mind; your chances for survival are severely limited in a showdown of pebbles against lead."

"Are you done?"

"Yes." He rubbed his sore feet, thinking he'd like to be *done* with the whole damned mess, including her.

She folded her legs beneath her and spoke carefully as though explaining a difficult concept to a doltish child. "People who steal from others only do it on account of they're too lazy to work for what they want. Agree?"

"Usually," he said grudgingly.

"And they can't be too smart. If they was, they wouldn't go into the holdup business in the first place. Agree?"

"Perhaps."

"Being creatures of comfort, thieves are also lazy, so I figure Willard's gang is holed up in some town, spending your money and preying on other unsuspecting folks."

"That's a fair assessment, I suppose."

"And towns usually have a lawman, don't they?"

"Usually," he conceded.

She smiled brightly, concluding her backwoods logic lesson. "So, all you got to do is go to the sheriff and demand he put those no-goods in jail where they belong and give us our stuff back."

"And where, pray tell, will you be during this little interlude?"

"I'll be laying low in case Pa's circulated a wanted poster on me or something."

Case rolled his eyes. "And just how am I supposed to convince the law to take the word of a gambler?"

"Hellfire, Case, do I have to think of everything?"

"Well," he snapped, "you've been doing all of it so far."

"I can't go to no sheriff's office, seeing as how I stole old Brownie in the first place." January frowned thoughtfully, then snapped her fingers and smiled. "Why didn't I think of it before?"

Case groaned. "Why do I have the feeling I don't want to hear this?"

"No, this is foolproof. We'll just find them and take everything back our own selves. It probably wouldn't be a good idea to get the sheriff in on it, anyhow. Not under these circumstances, that is."

"Let me get this straight. The plan is, we just walk up to them and without a by-your-leave steal everything back, right out from under their noses."

"It ain't stealing when it belongs to us."

"And it isn't smart to get your brains blown out. Sometimes your sense of honor amazes me, Miss Jones." Case shook his head. "It's not stealing when you decide it isn't. And it wasn't lying when you led me to believe you were a boy. And it wouldn't have been murder if you'd killed me when I found out differently."

"That's right."

"And I suppose you think it's all my fault I lost control and kissed you. That I'm to blame for you kissing me back." Case hadn't meant to bring the subject up, but now that he had, he placed his fingers on her lips, silencing whatever protest she'd been about to make. "And you're determined to make me pay for forgetting myself when I sensed your own sweet response and the willingness of your wriggling little body beneath mine by getting me shot." Or by nagging him to death, whichever came first.

For once January was speechless. She knew she was guilty of the wriggling and willing part, as guilty of wantonness as any barroom tart. But she had no intention of getting anyone shot. Didn't he know she, too, was paying a high price for those heated moments on the creek bank?

Her conscience hadn't given her a minute's peace. "I don't know why you're bringing all that up now," she said evasively, averting her flushed face from him. "We've got more serious things to think about."

Case stroked her cheek. "Some people take their love-making very seriously." He didn't know why he was so drawn to her or how she managed to bring out the worst in him. She made him think of things he'd long forgotten. Things he didn't care to think about. He should tell her goodbye and forget her. He should let her out of his life for good. That's what he should do.

But Case generally chose the "should nots" over the "shoulds" and this time was no exception. He knew he was forever making a fool of himself where she was concerned. His verbal insults and sparring were only an attempt to overcome the yearning to take this child-woman into his arms and show her a thing or two. To turn her rantings into sighs of pleasure. To make her a woman in every sense of the word. *His* woman.

Dangerous thoughts, yet delightful. The kind he'd always avoided. He had to get away from her, but the idea of abandoning her went against all his deeply ingrained ideas of chivalry. Still, trying to protect her was utterly ridiculous when she could do a far better job of it herself.

As he watched, she unraveled a line from her pocket, tied a stick to one end, and impaled a fat caterpillar on the improvised hook at the other. Wordlessly, she cast it out in the stream. He'd never known a woman like her. Her stoic resourcefulness and fiery unpredictability fit into none of his preconceived categories of feminine behavior.

Separating was the best solution because he wasn't sure how much longer he could be trusted to keep his lusty thoughts to himself and his hands off her. All this noble resistance was enough to drive a man completely around the bend.

She might even be better off without him, he thought, trying to convince the nagging voice of his conscience. In his present condition, she could certainly make better time on her own.

"Feel free to go on whenever you like. I'm only slowing you down," he told her. "Besides, you don't need me for anything. You do most of the hunting and fishing." He gestured at her suddenly taut line, which gave every indication it might snap due to the size of her catch. She gathered it in efficiently, removed the fish, and tossed it aside. Pulling another caterpillar out of her coat pocket, she repeated the process.

Case's nose wrinkled in disgust. "Where did you get those ugly things?"

"I found 'em on a rotten log a ways back while you were resting your dogs. There's a lot of wooly worms around. It means a bad winter's coming. They're more black than brown; that's another sure sign. Fish love 'em, I guess because they can't crawl out of the water to get 'em theirselves."

Angry at himself for changing the subject, Case went on. "I wouldn't blame you for going on without me. I haven't contributed much to our survival so far." He hadn't meant to sound self-pitying. Since he had, he mentally gave himself a good swift kick.

"Hellfire, Case! I ain't complaining about that. I'm only worried about getting our horses back and making the run before it's all over. If we keep stopping all the time—"

"I know, I know," he said wearily. "I realize you still have your boots, but dammit to hell, don't your feet ever hurt? Don't you ever get tired?"

"Sure I do. I just don't whine about it, is all."

"Of course not," he scoffed. "Not the invincible January Jones who can kill two rabbits with a single bullet and catch fish with a goddamned sewing needle. Not the little spitfire who can whip a whole passel of outlaws single-handedly!"

She stared at him, so unnerved by his spiteful words that she lost the fish on her line. For a reason she couldn't name, he had cut her to the quick.

She swallowed the lump in her throat and willed the tears away. All she'd been trying to do was to show him she wasn't some helpless, clingy female. To show him she could take care of not only herself but him, too. Who would've ever thought men like crybaby women?

"I never said I killed two rabbits with one bullet. Them's your words, not mine." She *had* gloated at the time, but she'd only wanted him to admire her skill. Her voice was soft and shaky when she explained. "I got one with my slingshot. I've been hunting and fishing ever since I can remember—sometimes it was the only food we had."

The hurt look on January's face stung him and he wished he could call back the hateful words. "I'm sorry, J.J. I guess it's no excuse, but my sore feet are a constant reminder of how I gave up my boots without a fight. What makes it even harder to swallow is the fact that you were foolishly brave and I took the coward's way out." It was mean and small to let concern for his manly pride make him condemn her for doing what came naturally.

"You ain't a coward, Case. You just used your head. It shames me to admit it, but I'll confess my biggest weakness is I seldom think things through. I don't stop and ponder the upshot of what I do or say. I just get all het up and the next thing I know . . ." Her hands flew up, indicating an explosion. "Boom . . . I'm in trouble again. It's like a curse or somethin'."

His mustache twitched. Her pulled-down hat made her ears stick out and she looked so cute and innocent with her little upturned nose and wide doe eyes.

"You kept a cool head and I admire that," she told him. "My big mouth nearly got us both shot. If you hadn't thought up that story, we'd both be dead right now and it would've been all my fault."

It wasn't exactly an apology; she wouldn't go that far. But never having had any fences to mend before, she found contrition surprisingly easy. Making things right between her and Case felt good. She didn't want him to know she cared what he thought of her, so she avoided his eyes by fussing unnecessarily with her fishing line.

He hooked his finger beneath her chin, bringing her gaze to his, and once more she was struck by the knowledge that he was the handsomest man she'd ever seen. It didn't seem right for him to have such long eyelashes or such beautiful lips. It wasn't fair that his hair was sleek and soft when her own was a wayward tangle, or that his eyes were the color of a jay's wing while hers were more like a mud hen's. Hellfire, but he was far and away prettier than she.

They stared at each other for long moments and a strange throbbing began deep within her. She fell to hoping he'd kiss her again and wondered what "having your way with" a body involved. Whatever it was, she wouldn't holler help if it was Case doing the having.

Case was overwhelmed by the twisting sensations this girl stirred in him and he longed to tumble her to the ground and cover her upturned face with kisses. But at the same time he wanted to protect her, to save her from herself and from him. Because somehow he wasn't worthy of her. He was as confused as a hog on ice.

It required supreme effort to fold his arms and put distance between them, but forced hostility was the only way to deal with her and the libidinous thoughts she induced. "Yes, it would have been your fault," he said, "and since dying young isn't in my plans, do me a favor. When you feel another explosion coming on, kindly have it somewhere else."

This was a far cry from the kiss she'd been expecting. "Maybe I *will* go on without you. You're just slowing me down anyhow."

She could make better time alone, but she had to admit to herself that she didn't want to leave him. She told herself it was only because she liked having someone to talk to. She'd never really had anyone to fuss over before and she liked doing for Case, even if he didn't appreciate it.

She'd never felt so necessary and that was the best feeling of all.

"Just go on then." He waved his hand dismissively.

"Maybe I will. Maybe I'll just get along and leave you sittin' here like you ain't got a care in this whole world." Her voice rose in frustration. "You know what, Latimer? If you sit here long enough, life will just pass you by and so will I."

"That may be, but I intend to stay put until someone comes along and I can hitch a ride."

"I'll never make it to Arkansas City in time unless we get the horses back. And I can't do that without your help, so get off your butt and start cleaning these fish. After we eat, we walk. We should come to a town sooner or later." She turned her attention back to fishing.

Case grimaced at her dictatorial manner. It was so nice to be wanted. All his internal debate had been for naught, because he wasn't going to leave her. "I'll see that you get a new horse when we get to town." He drew his damp foot into his lap to inspect the stone bruises.

"You seem to forget that those snakes took all your money, too," she pointed out. "Besides, I've got further to go than just to the next saloon."

"So do I. But saloons are my office, so to speak, and if we're lucky, I'll soon be back in business." Gesturing at his feet, he added, "I don't know what I'm going to do about these. My socks have worn clean through."

She ran her fingers gently over swollen and bruised skin that had once been lily white and soft as a baby's. She gasped at the damage and was sorry she'd made light of his pain. Having gone barefoot most of her life, the soles of her feet were toughened by the rocky landscape. Not so Case's. "I know just what you need," she said softly.

"So do I. But how would that help my feet?" he asked in the teasing tone she found so maddening.

Come hell or high water, she wouldn't let him know she'd understood the implications of his question. "You need some brown paper soaked in apple cider vinegar to wrap up your feet. It's the best medicine I know to reduce swellin' and tenderness. Fact is, apple cider vinegar will cure just about anything that ails you."

"You're a veritable fount of backwoods lore, aren't you?"

January bristled up like a porcupine at what she interpreted as an insult. "Ain't no lore to it, just common sense."

"I was just thinking how you're full of vinegar, yourself. Too bad you're so set on Oklahoma. You'd be a nice diversion where I'm headed."

"Do tell." A thrill of curiosity rippled through her, but January pretended disinterest. In reality there was nothing about him that didn't thrill her, nothing she wasn't dying to know. However, Case wasn't very forthcoming with personal information. She'd like to know where he'd come from and what had led him to the life he lived, where he was bound and what he really thought of her. "You're headed to hell in a handcart, but I'm not going along for the ride," she added.

Case put a finger to his lips and cocked his head, listening. "Shhh."

"What?" she whispered.

"I hear horses coming. Several, I think."

"Hot damn!" She jumped to her feet and scrambled up the bank.

"Wait!" he commanded, hot on her heels and oblivious to the pain in his feet. "You never know what sort of riffraff you'll meet on these trails."

"If they have horses and are willing to give us a ride, I don't care much about their station in life. Maybe you should stay out of sight until we know for sure. Nobody'd harm a helpless little kid." She winked and ran up the hill, leaving him behind.

"Indeed!" Case watched her clamber up the bank. He had the feeling another explosion was in the offing. January had spunk, but he couldn't help thinking her impulsive nature would yet be her downfall, not to mention his own.

Topping the rise, she stood smack dab in the middle of the road, her arms rotating like a windmill to flag down the approaching wagon.

Suddenly the blast of a trumpet cut through the air and a team of matched bays appeared, pulling a big black rig. It was decorated with golden curlicues and ornate red letters announcing "Dr. Goodnews's Miracle Cure." Garish pictures depicted the assorted ailments the wonder drug would remedy.

January had seen traveling medicine men back in Possum Holler and had always thought the shows great fun. Usually the hawker was an earnest, fatherly-looking man with smiling features, dressed in a rusty black suit and top hat. First a pretty little gal with the voice of a lark and the face of an angel would sing to attract a crowd. Then the "doctor" would lecture about his wondrous elixir and collect money from believers.

It'd seemed exciting at the time and she'd wished she could be that sweet-voiced girl and travel in a grand wagon. But she'd been a child then, filled with romantic ideas about escaping her life. Now she knew the only hope for the future was in planting roots, of owning a place she'd never have to leave.

The wagon halted in a flurry of dust and January coughed. She was staring up at the stranger when Case joined her. The sun was a blinding ball of light behind the man and she had to squint her eyes nearly shut to see him. As she watched, he looped the reins around the whip bracket at his feet and stood up.

He wore a black frock coat and chimney-pipe hat. His poor posture and rounded shoulders belied his tall stature and gave him the appearance of a large crow crouched for flight. One look at his pockmarked face and January knew she and Case should have stayed down by the creek.

The mean-eyed stranger must have done in the owner of the wagon, for he sure wasn't like any of the cherub-faced hawkers she'd ever seen. The hair that hung to his shoulders was as dark as his handlebar mustache, with streaks of gray. He licked full lips and one eye peered suspiciously down the length of his nose. The other was covered by a black eyepatch.

January patted the rump of the horse nearest her, shielded her eyes from the bright sunshine, and commented conversationally, "These sure are some mighty fine-looking horses, mister."

The man's crafty face and formidable manner seemed less threatening when he smiled, revealing uncommonly white and perfect teeth. "You two aimin' to buy 'em or steal 'em?"

Case took offense and January laughed, hoping he'd catch on that the man was only joking. At least she hoped he was. "Neither. We was hoping you'd give us a ride to the nearest town," she explained. "I'm J.J. Jones and this here's Case Latimer."

"Pleased to make your acquaintance, friends," he said, doffing his dusty hat. "I'm Dr. Clarence Goodnews. You men got business in Branson?"

"Unfinished business, you might say," Case mumbled.

The "doctor" scratched his pointy, stubbled chin. "I reckon I could give you a ride, once I have a bite to eat and rest the horses."

"We've got fish, but no gear," she informed him. "We was robbed two days back and the low-down skunks took everything we had, even his boots."

Clarence chuckled and the warm sound imbued him with a measure of affability. He swung gracefully down from the wagon seat. "We're going to make a good team. I have all kinds of gear, but no fish. I don't mind sharing if you don't."

January was about to follow Clarence to the back of the wagon, but Case grabbed her arm. "I don't think we should trust him," he said in a low voice. "And I'm not so sure we should ride with him either. Goodnews, hell. He looks like bad news to me."

January had reconsidered her first impression and knew they had nothing to fear from Clarence. He seemed kind and generous. It wasn't his fault God had seen fit to give him a pirate face. "Hush, you'll hurt his feelings," she scolded. "Besides, we ain't got nothin' left to lose."

"Only our lives," Case lamented.

"Don't be so suspicious. We ain't had so many offers we can afford to be choosy." She shook off his protective arm.

"You two sound like kin." They were on Clarence's bad side and when he glanced in their direction, he had to turn his whole head toward them. "Are ya?"

"No," said January.

"Yes," said Case, simultaneously.

"Which is it, then?" Clarence handed her a frying pan and a coffeepot out of the back of the wagon.

"We might as well be," she grumped, thinking how Case had treated her like a pesky little sister for the past two days.

"We had the same ma," Case explained lamely, sticking with the story she'd concocted for the robbers. "But we don't claim each other."

Clarence shrugged and asked January, "Want some help frying up that fish, young man?"

She grinned slyly and passed the frying pan to Case. "Ask him. It's his turn to cook."

Chapter 7

After dinner Clarence shaded his face with his hat and stretched out for a nap, but not before finding a bottle of apple cider vinegar and brown paper for January.

"You don't have to do this," Case protested when she lifted his feet into her lap. He couldn't recall the last time anyone had touched him so gently. The intimacy of her ministrations gave him a strange feeling of being trapped.

"I know I don't, but I want to." She carefully rubbed his left foot, finding it warm and fevered. "The hot cider's going to sting these cuts and scrapes like the dickens, but it'll make the swellin' go down and that's what's important. Tomorrow you can wear the moccasins Clarence gave you and we can make better time."

Case watched her work and wished there was a way to tell her to leave him be without revealing how deeply her gentle touch affected him. Intent, she didn't notice the lock of hair that had fallen onto her forehead. He smoothed it back and she glanced up, her wide eyes sweet enough to melt a man's heart. She smiled almost coyly and ducked her head.

Case marveled at the contrasts she presented. She could look as fragile as a snowdrop, but she had an iron backbone any man would envy. She could be soft and womanly, as she was now, yet she could fight like a cornered wolverine. She was unschooled, yet she exhibited astonishing native intelligence. She was tough and tender, like a cast-iron violet.

Arguing was the last thing he wanted to do when January was in an intractable mood. But he was determined to fight the feelings she inspired and it was the only surefire way to break the spell building up between them. "That hurts, dammit."

"Didn't I tell you it would? Stop bein' a baby." She'd never really noticed a man's feet before, but Case's were wondrous beautiful and, like the rest of him, so different from her own. They were long and thin and white as virgin snow, having never before walked bare across anything rougher than carpet.

Under the pretext of cleaning his injuries, she stroked him until her throat felt like she'd swallowed a fuzzy peach. A commotion set-to inside her, proving she had the shameless heart of a strumpet. She was pretty far gone if merely washing a man's feet made her heart hammer and her head swim.

As far as Case could tell, the vinegar held no medicinal powers—the healing magic was in January's touch. It didn't require much imagination to picture her hands elsewhere on his body, stroking, caressing, creating a fever of their own. He felt an undeniable stirring and knew he had to stop her before he lost control completely.

"J.J., I don't . . ." he began, but his voice seemed to have rusted. He cleared his throat and tried once more. "You shouldn't be doing this."

"Doing what?" she asked innocently as she dipped the brown paper into the vinegar and wrapped his foot. She took up the other one, but he tried to draw it away.

"You shouldn't be touching me . . . um . . . my foot."

"Why shouldn't I?" He wouldn't have believed she was even aware of what was happening between them, but she stared him down, challenging him to confess her effect on him. He pulled his foot away, but she tugged it back into her lap.

"Because you're an unmarried woman and I'm . . . because it just isn't seemly, that's why." This time he jerked the appendage from her soft lap and tucked it under his leg, Indian fashion.

"Seemly? Is that what you're worried about?" Hers was the smile of Eve. "Hellfire, Case. Are you afraid I'll become so becrazed with lascivious thoughts from just lookin' at your seductive feet that I'll throw you down and have my way with you?"

From the shade of a nearby tree came the sound of Clarence's surprised snort of amusement.

Case was angry she'd let the medicine drummer find out her true identity and was infuriated by the embarrassment her teasing had caused him. "Since when do you know anything about lascivious thoughts, becrazed or otherwise?"

"Since I started riding with you, Latimer. What's the matter? Can't you take it when the funnin' is on the other foot?"

Exasperated, he didn't want to get into a discussion of malapropisms. "Actually, I rather enjoy finally seeing you where you belong, January Jones. Worshipping at your man's feet."

Clarence cackled, giving up any pretense of sleeping. He rolled over and watched their sparring unashamedly.

January yanked off her hat, the only weapon at hand, and clobbered Case with it until he was forced to grab her arms and subdue her. He pressed her back against his chest and held her tightly.

"You ain't my man and you never will be," she yelled, feeling the vibration of his heart between her shoulders. "No man of mine would ever expect me to sit at his danged feet."

Clarence cleared his throat loudly. "Did I hear correctly? Did you just call this gal January? January Jones?"

"That's right," Case said in a you-want-to-make-something-of-it tone of voice.

Clarence held up his hands. "Now, don't get your bowels in an uproar, young man, but I may just know her. I haven't run across too many redheaded Januarys in my travels. You related to the Joneses in Butler County?'' he asked her.

''I am.''

''Would your mammy be Daisy Jones?''

January's heart fluttered like a hummingbird's wings and she shook so that Case had to hold her tighter. He put his lips against her hair and she leaned into the solid reassurance of his chest.

''Yes, yes,'' she whispered. ''Do you know her? Is she alive? Where is she?''

Clarence shrugged. ''Slow down, gal. Last I knew she was in Springfield, but I heard she moved on.''

There was so much she wanted to know, January was hard pressed to think of the questions. Eventually she asked them all and learned that Clarence had found Daisy beside the road not far from Possum Holler on the day Jubal had driven her away. She was sick and out of her head, crying for her baby, and at first Clarence assumed she meant the child she was soon to deliver. But she called January's name over and over, and he soon realized she was grieving for a child she'd been forced to leave behind.

He took her all the way to Springfield and stayed until she was brought to bed with a baby girl. Touched by the woman's tragic plight, he kept in touch with her for a couple of years, periodically sending gifts of money ''for the baby.'' Whenever he passed through, he stopped to see her at the boardinghouse where she worked as a maid.

''Maybe I'll go see her,'' January said quietly.

Clarence sniffed. ''Can't. She ain't there no more. I was in Springfield—I guess it was the fall of '80—and I tried to talk Daisy into going on the road with me. Even offered to marry her and give the little girl my name. But she said she was still married to your pa and the road was no place to raise a child. She wanted me to find someone else but I never have.''

January saw the sadness in Clarence's face and knew he'd cared for her mother, that he still did. That thought made her happy because Daisy had received little love from Pa. "What happened?"

"The following spring, I stopped by to see her and the baby, but it was too late. She was gone. The lady at the boardinghouse said she just lit out one night. She left no forwarding address. I guess she didn't want to be found." He went around to the back of the wagon and returned with a small wooden box. Opening it, he took out a battered piece of paper which he held reverently, staring at it with his good eye.

He handed it to January. "She left me this letter. She was your mammy so you're welcome to read it if you want to."

January took it, gently unfolded it, then turned to Case with a pleading look.

Knowing how her illiteracy shamed her, Case took it and said softly, "Allow me. You're probably too upset to make heads or tails out of it." He held her with his left arm tucked firmly beneath her breasts and read the letter:

Dearest Clarence,

Oh, how I hate to tell you goodbye. My life is filled with goodbyes and I know not if I will ever see my beloved daughter January again. It is my hope that she finds the happiness which has eluded me these many years. Perhaps with time she will find it in her heart to forgive me. For that I pray.

I wish you and I could have met at a different time. As you know, I am tied to another and there is no future for us. You are a kind man. Thank you for coming along when I had forgotten such men existed. I have not done many right things in my life, but it is time for me to make my own way and stop depending on the charity of others. And you must forget me.

Please do not try to find me. It would only hurt us both. Take care of yourself and be happy. You will long be in my thoughts.

Daisy

Filled with emotion at the pain he glimpsed between each line, Case handed the letter back to Clarence and put his hand on January's shoulder. "Are you all right?"

"I'm fine," she lied softly. She often prayed her mother was alive and now that it seemed she was, it was too much to hope that she could ever find her. But if she could! The thought made her weak and she leaned against Case. Here she'd been thinking she was all alone in the world and it turned out she had not only a mother but a sister as well. A sister she'd never known. The thought filled her with excitement. "What about my sister?" she asked Clarence.

"I don't rightly know," he admitted sadly. "I took Daisy at her word and never tried to find her."

Knowing she had a mother and sister somewhere in the world gave January a sense of belonging. Even if she never saw them, it was enough just to know they existed. She refused to cry, but the pain of her suddenly realized loss left her weak and numb.

She trembled in Case's arms and he knew how shaken she really was. Given the lack of paternal affection in her life, the deprivation of her mother and sister was cruel, indeed.

She turned to Case, her face composed and grim. She wouldn't dwell on this new development. It made her too angry and sad. Angry at Pa for causing them so much grief and sad for her own loss. After she'd made the run and established a place for herself, she'd figure out a way to find her family. Once she had some money saved, she could hire a Pinkerton detective to find them if necessary. "We're just burning daylight standing here," she said. "We'd best be on our way."

Case helped her onto the wagon and kept a comforting arm around her as they bounced down the rutted road, axles groaning and bottles rattling. Exhausted from pent-up emotions, she soon fell asleep.

"What're we gonna do with her?" Clarence asked.

"She's my responsibility." Case eased January over until her head rested on his chest and noted it was the first time he'd ever seen her in repose. She didn't look fully dressed without a gun or knife in her hand, or a scowl on her face, but he was fascinated by her innocent beauty. He felt Clarence's eye gazing curiously in his direction. "I can take care of her."

"I can see that," Clarence said. "I figure you'd give her heaven if you could pry a corner loose. But what are your plans for her?"

"No one plans anything for January. She makes up her own mind and the devil take anyone who tries to change it. She's dead-set on getting in on the land run." If it were Case's decision to make, he'd send her somewhere safe, some clean, quiet place where she could have everything life had denied her. She needed time to be a carefree girl, to forget about survival and instead worry about dresses and beaux and other silly things. She needed learning and books to challenge her mind, a good man to teach her love and trust. She needed stability, but he had no idea where that could be found.

"It ain't no good her goin' to Oklahoma. You know what it's like out there?"

"I know." Case's thoughts had made him gloomy. "But her mind is made up. She's got it in her head to get some land of her own."

"It's sure enough a no-man's-land out there. Ain't nothing but renegade Injuns and outlaws." He shook his head sadly. "The girl's got grit."

Case sighed. "Yeah," he scoffed. "Grit and two bits will buy her a drink in any saloon from Galveston to Deadwood."

"True enough," Clarence agreed. "She'll be lucky to get as far as Arkansas City on her own."

"I'll see she makes it," he said vehemently. "I'll take care of her till she's settled somewhere."

"See that ya do. Children are a mighty big responsibility. Never had none myself, but my sister had two. Her and the brother-in-law was drowned in a flash flood near St. Louis a few weeks ago." Clarence took a twist of tobacco from his pocket and bit off a chunk. He offered it to Case, who declined.

"That's too bad. Did the children get out safely?" Case felt obliged to make polite conversation with the man even though his thoughts were still on January.

"Yep, and I'm grateful for that. Some good-hearted folks took 'em in and sent for me. Seein' as I'm their only livin' kin, I'm on my way up there to do my duty." He spat tobacco juice over the side of the wagon. "I'll be hanged if I know what I'm gonna do with them or their farm. I ain't no farmer and the road is no life for kids."

"I know what you mean. I'm a traveling man myself. As soon as I get January settled, I'm headed for Alaska," Case confided. He hadn't thought much about that since he'd met her and now felt strangely ill at ease with his intentions.

Clarence nodded in commiseration and the two fell silent for the rest of the trip into Branson.

They said goodbye to Clarence on the outskirts of town. As they piled off the wagon, January asked him to give Daisy a message if he should ever run across her.

"Tell her I'd be proud to see her someday. The past don't matter none to me. She's my mama and she always will be."

"I reckon she'd be mighty glad to hear it and I'll be sure to pass that on if I get the chance. God go with you." Clarence lifted the reins and whipped the horses into a trot, heading northeast for St. Louis.

January and Case walked the rest of the short distance into town in uneasy silence. She was thinking about her mother, her sister, and her future. He was thinking about his future as well. Getting to Alaska didn't seem so urgent now. He hadn't seen hide nor hair of the Buscus boys for several days and wondered if he might have heard the last of them.

January scuffed down the road. She had to get things settled about where she was headed and what she would do when she got there. Damn Case anyhow. Why'd he have to turn out to be a no-account gambler? And what was wrong with her that made him treat her like a case of the itch? Maybe if she had a dress and made herself up to look more like a lady. But it was no good wasting time on foolish thoughts like that when her whole future was at stake.

When she first heard Daisy was alive, she wanted nothing more than to go to her. She had faint memories of her mother's sweet lilac scent, of her soft, soothing voice. She wanted to be taken into a pair of comforting arms and told not to worry. But she couldn't go to her mother if she couldn't find her. And she couldn't stake a claim in Oklahoma if she wasn't old enough.

As much as she hated to do it, she'd just have to get some lonely man to do it for her. The money she had tucked away would be her dowry. She'd come too far to give it up because of a few little setbacks. Things would work out; she'd make them. Armed with a new determination and a somewhat brighter outlook, January smartened her steps.

But as they neared town in the rosy haze of twilight, her gaze locked with Case's and she had to keep reminding herself that she wasn't sweet on him. Sometimes hours went by without her thinking of the wonderfully disgraceful things they'd done that first night by the fire. Then some small incident—an accidental touch or something he said or did—sent them rushing back all over again.

"January?" he said loud enough to be heard over the tinny dance-hall music floating out of a saloon down the street.

"What?" She looked up and found him watching her intently.

"I need to find a game and . . ." His words died on his tongue, he was so caught up in her. Dammit to hell, he'd been on the trail too long when a mere slip of a girl could make him forget what he was about. "Get us a stake. Do you have anything I could gamble with?"

Cold awareness pinched off the melty feeling inside her.

He wanted something from her, that's why he was looking at her like she was a piece of peppermint. "I got my hat, but that's about it," she said in tight-lipped disapproval.

"Don't go getting righteous on me. We've got to get a stake somehow. You want a horse, don't you?"

"I don't want nothing that's won by wagerin'. I'd just as soon make my way without any ill-gotten gains, if you don't mind."

"Well, it's a good thing I don't share that holier-than-thou attitude or you'd be walking all the way to Oklahoma."

"Better that than—"

"I know, I know. Spare me the lecture. Do you want to get there on time or not?"

"Of course I do." She knew she had no business trying to change him and no right to be mad at him for being what he was. It was like being mad at the wind for blowing. Hellfire, he never should've been saddled with her in the first place, but she knew he felt responsible for her. She just wasn't sure why.

He wouldn't be happy unless he was free of her and he wouldn't be free of her until she made him mad enough to leave her behind. With that thought firmly in mind, she glanced knowingly at the saloon. "Now that you're home, so to speak, and don't need me no more, I reckon I'll just go the rest of the way by myself."

Case glared at her with disbelief. "You can't be serious."

"You've held me back long enough. We agreed this wasn't no ball and chain situation." The red tinge creeping up his neck told her he was riled now for sure.

"Well, if that don't beat all." Case slapped his thigh. "Maybe I'll mosey on along the rest of the way alone," he mimicked sarcastically. "Are you sure that's wise? Whatever will I do without you to protect me?" He straightened his collar, turned his back on her, and walked away. "I relieve you of your duty, Miss Good Deed."

"Where're you goin' now?" she asked with a sigh.

"I'm going to find a bath and a little diversion."

"You're the bathin'est man I ever seen."

"And how many have you seen?" he flung over his shoulder, then muttered something under his breath. It sounded like he said a little scrubbing sure wouldn't go amiss with her. Then he said she wasn't no Connie something or other.

Forgetting that her purpose was to make him mad enough to go on without her, she hurried to catch up. He didn't even look at her, just kept on walking. Head erect and arms swinging, he strode purposefully down the main street of the first town they'd seen since they met. Had it been only three days ago?

"You think you're so smart?" she flung at him. "You and your ten-dollar words. You don't know what it means either," she challenged, hoping he'd explain it to her.

"What?" he grumbled.

"That word," she said as patiently as she knew how. Hot damn, he made her madder than a hornet. "Connie sue-er," she said slowly, trying out the strange feel of it on her tongue.

Insulting her wasn't something he felt good about. It was unforgivable to berate her about her lack of knowledge where men were concerned, especially when that very innocence pleased him immensely.

"Forget it, January."

"Why, Case?" she hounded. "Is it a highfalutin cussword?"

"No, it isn't a cussword at all. Far be it from me to teach you any more of those." Though he tried not to, he grinned as the humor of the situation began to override his anger.

"If it ain't a dirty word, then why won't you tell me?" she persisted.

Case sighed. The girl was more determined than an egg-sucking dog. "A connoisseur is an expert, a person who understands the details or the techniques of an art and is competent to sit in judgment."

"Why'd you say I wasn't one, then?" she demanded.

"How many men have you known in your life, January? Me and your pa?" he asked with a raised eyebrow, his bad mood returning.

"Old Mr. Hibley down at the store and . . . hey, what difference does that make?"

"I was merely pointing out that you're no expert when it comes to men. You aren't qualified to judge one from another."

"Ain't much to judge," she scoffed. "And I'd hardly call men an 'art.' Most of 'em are lazy good-for-nothings who don't care about nothing, save themselves."

"You're such a hypocrite." He smiled. "A hypocrite is a person who takes on airs or qualities—"

"I know what a hypocrite is," January said authoritatively, wrinkling her nose with disdain. "That's in the Bible."

"I thought you couldn't read," Case pointed out thoughtlessly.

"Damn you!" she yelled. "Don't be mad at me 'cause I ain't as smart as you."

"I'm not mad at you," he said, gritting his teeth. "But if I ever find the men who stole our things, I think I'll give you to them. Hell, I'd have to *pay* them to take you even if I did manage to convince them you'd had a miraculous recovery. But it just might be worth it to be rid of you."

"Well," she drawled haughtily, "I'm glad you ain't *mad* at me."

"I thought you wanted to go on alone," he reminded her. "I'm not holding you back. And I didn't point a gun at you to make you stay with me in the first place."

"Maybe not, but if you set your mind to it, you could talk a horse out of his tail," she accused.

"Good God, woman! What do you want from me?" Case stomped away, not really wanting an answer. He knew what he wanted from her and that was scary enough. The sooner he got in a poker game, the sooner he could get her a horse and be rid of her. Contrary females! "You're the most hardheaded woman it's ever been my misfortune to meet."

"What put you in such a snit, anyhow? I'm the one ought to feel put upon."

He stopped, turned to her, and stuck his thumbs in the pockets of his vest. "For what?"

"For all the bad luck you've brought me."

"I've brought you bad luck?" His voice was as cold as the blue gaze that pierced her. "Since I met up with you, I've had nothing but trouble. It was bad enough losing Shadow, my boots, and my hat, not to mention my money and my gold watch—but I've had to put up with your bad temper and nagging as well. That's bad luck in its purest form."

Case glared at her as if she alone were to blame for all the bad things that had ever happened to him. He knew it was mean of him, but it was too late to call back the words he'd already spoken. Poor kid—for a moment there, he'd thought she was going to cry. Hadn't she been through enough? He was about to swallow his pride and apologize when she got that muley gleam in her eye.

"It ain't my fault we was robbed. And it ain't my fault you lost your prissy soap and was deprived of a sweet-smellin' bath every single day."

Case uttered a sound of frustration and took off again. She had to run to keep up. Glancing at him as they strode along, she couldn't help noticing how blue his eyes were—eyes that begged her to come closer one minute, then warned her to stay the hell away the next. She didn't know what to make of him. "Now that we're in town, you go your way, Latimer, and I'll go mine."

"Nothing would please me more, Miss Spitfire Jones!"

"Fine!" she yelled at his retreating back.

"Fine!" he yelled over his shoulder. Without another glance, he swaggered up to one of the houses that lined the street.

January flounced away with her nose in the air, hoping

she could get a horse cheap. She patted the money in her underwear and was comforted to know it was still there. "The day I met you wasn't exactly the high point of my life, either!" she muttered.

Her angry steps slowed as disappointment ate away her bravado. Damn him for letting her go so easily, for not caring. There was no telling the trouble he'd get into on his own. Convinced it was for his own good, she doubled back to follow him. Ducking behind a bush, she watched in dismay as Case leaned over a fence and tipped his hat to a blushing young woman who'd stepped onto her front porch.

January listened with disgust as the silver-tongued devil delivered his line of bull. Now she knew what he'd meant by a little "diversion." The woman hastily smoothed her hair and ran her palms nervously down her skirt. January knew just how she felt. She'd been on the receiving end of that smile herself. Her stomach knotted up at the sight of Case flirting so outrageously with another woman. Jealously. It was a feeling she didn't much cotton to.

When she could stand it no longer, she left her hiding place and stumbled down the street, convinced she was better off without him, but fearful her heart would break.

She decided her quivery stomach was a result of hunger, so she slipped a dollar from her pocket to buy herself a real meal. She asked directions to the nearest hotel but, when she'd found it, she hesitated in front of a sign she couldn't read, disliking the feeling of inadequacy civilization imposed on her. Hunger won out and she figured someone would let her know if she violated a written rule.

As soon as she had wolfed down her supper of fried ham and potatoes, she found the livery stable. Across the street, light spilled out of a noisy saloon, but there didn't seem to be anyone around. She went inside the barn to look over the horses and was shocked to see Shadow and Brownie munching hay in comfortable stalls.

"Brownie!" She flung her arms around him as if he were a long-lost loved one. "I never thought I'd hear myself say this, but I'm plumb glad to see you." He continued his mindless chomping, scarcely noticing her. She patted his rough neck. "I know you're as happy to see me as I am to find you, you contrary old . . ." She changed her mind about calling him a name and hugged him again. "How'd you come to be here?"

Brownie's head came up with another mouthful of hay. "It don't matter," she crooned. "The important thing is now that I've found you, I won't have to spend any of my money on another horse. Right, boy?" It was an extra bonus to find their saddles and gear tossed over the railing.

"What the hell you doin' there, kid?" A big black man in a leather apron filled the doorway, each of his arms as big as her waist. She swallowed and opened her mouth, but no sound came out.

He closed in on her and all January could manage was a tiny squeak before he lifted her by the scruff of her neck and seat of her pants and tossed her out into the street. "You got no bizness here, boy. Now, git."

January got.

Hellfire, now she'd have to go to Case. She hated the thought of asking for his help but loved the idea of having an excuse to do so. It wasn't as if she was running to him just because she'd met up with a little snag in her plans. Shadow was in there, too. That blacksmith was as big as a mountain, but Case would want to help retrieve their horses. He was mighty fond of that stallion.

If it meant getting his horse back, maybe he wouldn't be upset if she interrupted him in his pursuits. She hoped she wouldn't have too much trouble finding him. They didn't have a lot of time to spare.

Chapter 8

As it turned out, January ran into Case on the street and quickly apprised him of the situation. He followed her to the stable where he checked his belongings. There was now no sign of the big blacksmith who had earlier chased her away.

"Bring Shadow and Brownie down to the saloon. Then wait out front for me." He winced and pulled on his boots.

"This ain't exactly a good time for you to go drinking and socializing, Latimer," she said, checking Brownie's cinch. "We ought to git while we still can. If those fellers find out we took back our horses, they're liable to come after us."

"They won't have to find out, they'll know. They have something of mine and I want it back." His father's gold pocket watch contained a miniature of his mother and was all he had left of his old life. He'd be damned if he'd leave without it. Retrieving the derringer from his saddlebag, he tucked it into the strap on his arm and tugged his coat sleeve down over it. "This won't take long," he said over his shoulder as he strode purposefully out the door.

January grabbed the reins of both horses and took off after him. "Dammit, Case, we got most everything—our horses, our bedrolls, all our gear. What's so all-fired important that you'd risk getting shot over it?"

"I don't have time to discuss it." He had to do this, but there was no sense risking January's pretty little neck.

"On second thought, it might be a good idea if you didn't wait."

"Is that what you want? If you want to be shut of me, just say so right now and I'll be outta here so fast I won't even leave tracks."

"I'm only thinking of your safety."

"Hellfire, why do men always say that when they're really and truly thinking of themselves?"

"You wouldn't understand." She was the most unsentimental woman he'd ever encountered.

January glared at him. "How do you know? I swear, Latimer—"

"Yes," he agreed, "you do swear. A lot. You really should try to cut down on that, J.J. It gives a bad impression and isn't ladylike at all."

"That's good, 'cause I ain't no lady."

"I don't have time to argue with you now," he told her. They'd reached the saloon and he looped Shadow's reins around the post out front.

"Be careful," she pleaded.

He grinned, his eyes full of wicked amusement. "Are you worried about me?"

"Some," she admitted recklessly.

"Why, January," he drawled, his gaze sparring with hers as he took up her hand in both of his, "I didn't know you cared."

"I never said I did," she denied impatiently, watching his thumb as it gently stroked her knuckles. "But don't forget, you're outnumbered. Don't trust those bushwhackers with your back."

"Are you going to wait for me?" he asked in a husky tone.

"Yes, but not forever." She wished he'd asked for more of a commitment than that.

"No," he agreed, his thumb massaging her knuckles while his gaze warmed her face. "For someone with plans as grand as yours, that would be asking too much."

She gulped and her eyelids fluttered as he slowly brought

her fingers to his lips. Her heart hammered and her stomach churned when he brushed his mouth over each finger in turn.

Gently turning her hand over, he kissed the palm with a noisy smack, spoiling the sweetness of his gesture. "That ought to hold you until I get back," he teased with his red-hot demon grin.

She closed her fist as if to trap the caress for all eternity, then glared at him and rubbed her hand furiously on her pants leg.

"You're wasting time. If you ain't out here in thirty minutes, I'm leaving without you."

"Fair enough." He winked at her and stepped through the saloon's batwing doors.

She leaned against the hitching post and listened impatiently to the music and raucous laughter. After what was surely more than half an hour, she got down on all fours and sneaked a peek beneath the swinging doors. It was her first glimpse of such an establishment and her eyes widened with surprise. Wanting a better look, she swaggered through the doors with a bravado that belied her trembling knees.

For a business whose primary goal was to corrupt innocents and promote sin, she'd expected something more hellish-looking. Perhaps a dim room in whose gloomy corners iniquity and mayhem flourished unchecked. Instead she saw an intricately carved walnut bar behind which a diamond-dust mirror reflected the light of two dozen burners, suspended from the ceiling in cut-glass chandeliers. The glasses and bottles beneath the mirror sparkled like fallen stars, adding their own brilliance to the setting.

Enormous brass cuspidors were lined up between the men at the bar and, judging from the discordant pinging arising from them, they were being put to good use. The hardwood floor was covered with sawdust and its fresh piney scent mingled curiously with the aroma of cigars, whiskey, and crowded humanity.

Strains of "Pop Goes the Weasel" twanged from a fiddle accompanied by an overzealous piano player. Some of the patrons paired up with bargirls and a wild, foot-stomping dance ensued. In the midst of this cacophony a rumble of male voices, amplified by infusions of drink, called out orders and placed bets. Poker chips rattled at green cloth-covered tables in the back.

Deciding that was where she would most likely find Case, January inched her way toward the tables, trying to make herself as inconspicuous as possible. Despite the ample lighting, there was so much smoke she couldn't spot Case among the gamesters.

A young woman wearing an ill-fitting dress that threatened to give up the fight and release her thrusting bosom poked January in the ribs with her elbow. "What do you think you're doing in here, sonny? You looking for your pa or were you hoping to get a glimpse of a real woman?"

January's retort was lost in the boisterous greeting of a man who stumbled over to escort the brazen-faced blond to the dance floor. "C'mon, Rowdy Jane." The woman clung to the rough's arm, allowing him to whirl her around the floor with more enthusiasm than skill.

Now that she'd had a good look-see, January decided all the fancy trappings didn't change a thing. A saloon was still a place where a rattlesnake wouldn't take his mother.

Disgusted, she was about to leave when she spotted Case at a far table. Rowdy Jane was there now, hovering at his side like a loco honeybee on the make for nectar. Not only was Case gambling, he was playing cards with a couple of Willard's men!

It struck January with sudden clarity that she was viewing Case in his natural habitat. Maybe he wasn't much of a hand when it came to roughing it on the trail, but he looked happier than a hog in mud now. He seemed right at home behind the fans of cards in his hand, his polished looks and fancy clothes lending a high-toned touch to the tawdry surroundings.

She tore her gaze from him and glared at the half-naked woman hanging on him like a dirty icicle. Rowdy Jane had more heft on her, but January didn't think she'd be much good in a rush and tumble ruckus. Contemplating potential ways of dispatching the painted cat, January wasn't aware that trouble was brewing until it was almost too late.

Rowdy Jane was getting on his nerves and Case told her so. She shot back an insult as he was about to rake in his winnings, which included his father's watch. Willard chose that moment to mosey over from the bar and, being less drunk and less stupid than his companions, he recognized Case at once.

"Whoa, there, dude. Whatta ya thank yer doin'?"

"I'm reclaiming my property." Case slid the derringer into his hand and picked up the watch. Kicking back the chair, he rose and brandished the pistol. "Don't anyone try to follow me or I'll shoot."

As January watched Case back away from the table, she made a beeline for the door. She turned just in time to see the traitorous dress-straining floozy stick out her red-booted foot and trip him. Case sprawled on the floor, the derringer spinning out of reach.

Case had been mentally complimenting himself on how well he'd handled the situation when the next thing he knew, he was flat on his face, his mouth full of sawdust. He scrabbled for his gun, but Willard's men quickly regrouped, giving every indication they planned to tear him apart. As they closed in on him, he thought fleetingly of January and hoped she was safely on her way to Arkansas City.

Thinking frantically how best to help Case out of his predicament, January dropped to all fours and backed out the door, bumping into a gun-toting cowboy passed out on the sidewalk. His gunbelt held two revolvers and two more were stuffed into his pants, more weapons than an unconscious man could use. Not stopping to consider that any man so heavily armed was sure to have a sorry disposition, she decided to borrow some of the drunk's firepower.

She grabbed two of the pistols and mounted Brownie, urging the reluctant animal up onto the sidewalk and in through the swinging doors. She was leading Shadow. Inside, she clutched the reins in her teeth and cocked one of the pistols. She fired and the bullet struck the painting of a well-endowed nude right between her endowments.

The brawling ceased so suddenly that some of the scrappers stood with legs braced and fists drawn back, surprised looks on their faces. The musicians dove for cover and the girls fell to the floor.

"Latimer!" January yelled, counting on the advantage surprise would give her. "Catch." She tossed him the other gun, thinking too late that she should have checked it for ammunition. He caught it, but instead of making his escape, he just sat there with his mouth wide open. "Hellfire!" she yelled in the sudden quiet, "what'd you want me to do about the boys?"

"The boys?" Case scrambled to his feet.

"Yeah. You told me and the boys to wait outside," she improvised, motioning with Shadow's reins that Case should mount his horse. "Should I call 'em in so's we can finish off these scalawags?"

"Go ahead on," Willard shouted. "Call 'em on in, ya poxy bitch."

"Shut yer face, Willard, afore she comes over here and does us both in," Clink piped.

"Goddammit, Clink, there ain't nothin' wrong with her. Lookit. She ain't even a-frothin' at the mouth. It was a trick."

Willard made a move for his gun but Case had the drop on him. "Go ahead, Willard," he warned in a frighteningly calm voice. "Blink and you'll die in the dark."

January yowled like a rabid coyote. "These snakes are making me awful mad. We better git before I'm overcome and hurt somebody."

Case plucked his black hat from Lefty's head and clamped it on his own before swinging into the saddle. Knowing better than to show his back to bushwhackers, he pulled tightly on Shadow's reins and urged, "Back." The spirited animal danced expertly through the doors.

January watched in amazement as Case's mount did his bidding. Fat chance Brownie would be so willing. With more confidence than she felt, she yanked on the reins and gave the same low command. She was shocked when her usually stubborn horse stepped smartly backward as though they backed out of saloons every day. Evidently, riding with Shadow had been a favorable influence on the gelding. They'd scarcely made it to the street before the music started up in the saloon and the whoop-up resumed.

Inside, Rowdy Jane glared at Willard with scorn. "Those two just made a jackass out of you. Ain't you going after them?"

"Yeah, Willard," Clink put in. Not that he wanted any more dealings with that crazy gal, but because he couldn't believe his eyes and ears, he asked, "How come you to just up let 'em go like that?"

Willard smiled and flipped a silver dollar into Rowdy Jane's cleavage. "Because while y'all was riding hell-bent-for-leather for a doc, me and Lefty took a little detour and got into a fracas with a stagecoach." He and Lefty exchanged knowing glances. "Why chase after those two when the law'll do it fer us?"

Clink scratched his head. "I don't get it."

"We was riding those two horses when we held up the stage," Willard clued.

"So?"

"Lefty was wearing that black hat," he prompted.

"Yeah? I still don't get it."

Willard and Lefty shook their heads at Clink's failure to comprehend. "Go git drunk, Clink. Maybe that'll clear yer head."

Rowdy Jane laughed. "Come on upstairs, Willard. I ain't had a man like you in a coon's age."

Willard followed her and Clink turned to Lefty. "Why would the law be after 'em? Stages get held up all the time."

Lefty sighed. "You are one dumb hombre, Clink. Ain't you heard about the senator's nephew what got shot in the foot during that holdup?"

"Nope," Clink replied.

"You mean to tell me you ain't heard how the senator's chompin' to hang the two men responsible?"

Clink's blank look told him he hadn't kept up with current events and that meant he didn't know about the five thousand dollars they'd gotten away with, either. Lefty didn't bother to mention he and Willard had hidden the loot in a cave outside of town for the time being. No sense burdening the poor dolt with all the details.

Feeling generous, he did explain that the law was looking for a man in a black hat with a silver band, riding a black Morgan, and a smaller, younger man on a rawboned gelding.

"How come you and Willard shot the senator's nephew?" Clink asked when he finally got wise.

"That's the best part. The dang fool shot his own self trying to keep us from getting all that money." Lefty laughed, but stopped short when he realized how much he'd let slip.

"How much money did you get?" Suspicion registered in Clink's unperceptive eyes.

"Five dollars." Lefty hooted.

Not one to be taken in, Clink leveled his gun on Lefty and pulled back the hammer. "Since we're partners, I want my share."

Lefty was still laughing as he slid two silver dollars across the table. "Here, take my cut, Clink. You deserve it."

Whipping Shadow into a gallop, Case remembered the last time he'd ridden like fury out of town during the night. He certainly hoped such narrow escapes weren't becoming a habit.

January was proud of Brownie. She wouldn't have thought he had the inclination or the stamina to keep up.

He hadn't balked, not even once, and she thought it might be a matter of equine pride that a gelding keeping company with a fleet-footed stallion like Shadow put forth his best effort.

Case, the ungrateful louse, hadn't even thanked her. As they galloped toward Galena, she could tell he was madder than a wet hen, but she didn't know why. Hadn't she saved his pretty face from taking a beating and worse at the hands of Willard's gang? Hadn't she shown ingenuity and bravery in staging that dramatic rescue? Hadn't she proved once and for all that she loved him?

Hellfire! Love? What did she know about that? Since she'd never felt it before, how could she even be sure that's what it was? She had nothing to compare it to except the negative feelings of disgust Mose had inspired in her.

Yet it no longer seemed important that Case drank or gambled or did any of the things she wouldn't want her man to do. Did that mean she loved him in spite of his character flaws or did it mean she was becoming so corrupted that those sins didn't seem so bad anymore?

And if she was falling into wicked ways, whose fault was it?

She leaned forward on Brownie's neck, enjoying the night wind in her face. Her thoughts were meaningless, of course, because Case Latimer would never belong to any woman. He'd made it clear that permanence of any kind wasn't in his future and after getting a load of the kind of place where he preferred to spend his time, she knew she'd be lost if she threw in with him.

Maybe it wasn't love at all, just harloty feelings Case alone could inspire. Maybe it wasn't logical, but January decided that if she was destined to be a fallen woman on the run from God-knew-what, it was high time she just got it over with and found out for sure.

If only she could get Case into a creek again soon . . . if she was destined for ruination, he'd be the best damned guide she could have.

It started to rain and the horses grew weary, stumbling

on the rocky trail. It seemed to January that they were riding in aimless circles and she said as much to Case. "What in tarnation are we doin'?"

"I don't know about you, but I don't like riding around in the rain," he snapped. "I'm looking for some kind of shelter. Keep your eyes open for a rocky overhang, or better yet, a cave."

A cave? January's heart froze at the thought of spending the night in such a dark and scarifying place. She immediately began looking for a rock formation that would protect them from the weather. Spotting a likely looking pile of boulders off to her left, she called above the mounting wind. "How about over there?"

Case looked where she pointed. "There is a God! It's a cave and a big one from the looks of it. There'll be room for us and the horses."

Big or little, it made January no never mind, she wasn't about to sleep in a place like that. As Brownie followed Shadow's lead, she tried to think up a reasonable excuse why she should spend the night out in the open.

Dismounting, Case gathered wood and went inside to build a small fire. January fussed with her horse, delaying the inevitable moment when she'd have to confess her fear to Case. Panic swamped her. When he stepped out to collect brush to cover the opening, his impatient words made her jump in alarm. "Come on, this is as far as we go tonight."

"I'll just bed down out here," she said stubbornly, eyeing the dark hole in the wall.

"What did I do to deserve this?" Case implored the stormy heavens as the rain pelted down in earnest. "Don't give me any more trouble, January. Just get inside."

"I need some privacy. I'll be in later." She didn't want him to see how nervous she was.

"It's a big cave; you'll have plenty of privacy in there," he argued. "It's raining, for God's sake, and you're soaked."

"A little water never hurt a body." She was reluctant to admit her fear of close, dark places.

"Don't be ridiculous. We have to get out of sight. This cave is an ideal hiding place."

"I can't go in there."

Her voice sounded small and scared and so utterly unlike the January he knew that he pulled her to him, his gaze searching hers. Her eyes were wide and frightened, her face pale. She was shaking. "What's wrong, January? What is it?"

"I can't. There might be spiders and snakes in there."

"Since when have such insignificant creatures ever deterred you?" he teased. He sensed there was more to her reticent behavior than a fear of unseen insects and reptiles, but he didn't know what it was.

"I didn't say I was deterred," she argued. "I said I wasn't going in no hole in the ground."

"And I say you are." He walked the horses to the cave's entrance and slapped their rumps. Hooves clattering on the hard-packed earth, they trotted inside. He turned to her, and taking her hand in his, led her to the entrance, where she balked.

"Don't you dare slap my butt, Latimer, and expect me to trot in there like some high-bred filly." She'd meant the words to sound heated, but they came out feeble and, much to her disgrace, she heard a tremble in her voice. Humiliating tears pooled in her eyes, threatening to overflow at the least provocation. She plopped down on the wet ground and breathed deeply, fighting for control.

Feeling foolish, Case sat down beside her in the mud and waited, water cascading off his hat brim. She glared up at him and, though she was obviously trying for defiance, her look was one of heart-stirring dejection. He put his arm around her and looked away, trying to ignore the rain dripping down his collar.

"I've built us a nice little fire in there, if it's the darkness that frightens you."

January sniffed. "Don't be nice to me, Case Latimer."

He frowned. Remembering her abnormal fear of men in general, he removed his arm. "You needn't be afraid of me," he said softly, trying to keep the hurt from his voice. "You know by now that you can trust me. I wouldn't harm you for anything."

"Oh-h-h!" January burst into tears and flung her arms around his neck.

Good God, he didn't know what to do. If she'd hit him or screamed at him or cussed him out, he would have had a clue. But tears? That was new, uncharted behavioral territory. They'd been through a lot together, but this was the first time she'd shown womanly weakness.

Should he wrap her in his arms and comfort her or would she mistake the gesture for something else? If he touched her right now, it was entirely possible he'd end up wanting much, much more. He'd been doing that a lot lately.

If he sat stiffly while her tears and the rain soaked his last clean shirt, she'd think him an uncaring bastard. He was damned if he did, but sometimes a man had to do things that went against his better judgment.

As he gathered her into his arms, something tightened in his chest. A wistful longing for life as it had once been, uncomplicated by feelings of tenderness and concern for another person. He suspected prisoners felt the same sense of entrapment as their shackles were clamped inescapably into place.

But he forgot all about such things when January scooted closer, brushing her small, firm breasts against his pounding heart. Whatever she was afraid of, it must be terrifying for her to allow such intimacy.

"January," he pleaded, "please tell me why you're crying. Maybe I can help."

"I'm afra-a-aid," she sobbed brokenly. "Afra-a-aid to go in the-e-ere."

"I'll take care of you," he promised. A tingling sensation rippled through him when his lips tenderly touched her forehead. "We're getting drenched out here. I'm going to carry you inside now, but I promise nothing will hurt you as long as I'm with you."

She burrowed her face into his neck as he slipped an arm under her legs and stood easily. He shifted his slight burden and ducked to enter the cave, kicking the gathered brush into place with his foot. Once inside, he was able to stand erect and stopped near the warmth of the fire.

He found her mouth and brushed it tenderly with his lips. January knew it was meant as some kind of reassurance, but she feared she'd surely melt from the heat.

"Are you all right?" he asked, his concern evident.

Unable to speak coherently, she nodded.

He smiled and she felt it on her lips. Her heart swelled. Surely the dizzy commotion storming within her was what a woman in love was supposed to feel.

"Are you still frightened?"

"Not when you're with me," she admitted shamelessly.

"We should get out of these wet clothes," he suggested softly as he removed her hat.

"I reckon we should." He loosened his hold, allowing her to slide down the length of him. "We might catch cold or come down with a fever."

"What do you do for a fever?" he asked playfully. "Drink some of that precious apple cider vinegar Clarence gave you?" He didn't tell her he'd already succumbed to a fever that only her sweet body could cure. He stepped away from her, not wanting to frighten her with his evident state of arousal.

"I'd find a stream and pick peppermint, put it in a jar, pour cold water over it, and drink it." January thought how peculiar it was that she already felt so much better, free and exhilarated. Who would have thought giving into a fit of bawling could be so curative?

Deep in thought, she loosened two buttons on her shirt before Case tossed her a blanket and resolutely presented his back.

In the shadows cast by the flickering fire, she shucked off her wet clothes and draped them over boulders to dry.

She wrapped herself in the blanket, tucking it under her arms so she could boil coffee and warm a can of beans over the fire.

While she bustled around, Case unsaddled the horses. He was also wearing a blanket and seemed surprisingly nervous as he sat down on the opposite side of the fire.

"Coffee? Beans?" she asked pleasantly, but what she really longed to know was why he'd put the fire between them as though it were some sort of boundary line he was loathe to cross.

"Thanks," he mumbled. Balancing the tin plate on his lap and holding on to the blanket for dear life, he ate pretty fast for a man with only one hand to spare. He sipped the hot coffee and stared into the flames.

"Are you going to hold all that there bawlin' against me?" she asked tentatively, hoping to scale the wall of resistance he'd built between them.

"Of course not," he drawled. "But I was worried about you. Crying isn't something you do often."

"No, it isn't. I haven't cried since the day my mama left home." Her glance bounced around the cave and the walls seemed to close in on her. "Talk to me, Case," she pleaded, her fears returning. "Tell me about the place where you grew up."

He recognized that look on her face; it was the same one she'd been wearing just before she'd burst into those awful tears. "What's wrong?"

She glanced around and breathed deeply. "Hellfire, just talk to me," she demanded.

He crossed the distance, sat down beside her, and held her. "I was raised on a tobacco plantation in Louisiana," he began, digging deeply into his memories for something pleasant to take her mind off whatever terrors plagued her. With the telling of one particularly happy event, others surfaced and he was surprised he could still conjure up those blissful, long-forgotten days.

"On my sixth birthday, my mother surprised me with a big party. I remember all my friends were driven over for the day. There was a huge fancy cake with lots of sweet frosting and an apple pie all my own. It seemed I opened presents for hours, but the most memorable part of the day was the snowball fight."

He smiled wistfully and January could almost picture the scene he described so vividly. "What with everything else that was goin' on, why does the snowball fight stand out in your memory?"

He grinned. "I guess because my birthday is in July."

She regarded him doubtfully. "I know y'all were rich, but just how did your ma manage that?"

"When the winters were cold enough, our servants cut ice from the river and packed it in sawdust deep underground to preserve it. We used it for cooling drinks and making ice cream in the summer. That year, mother had instructed the servants to also store enough snowballs for a good fight."

January relaxed against him, understanding him a little better now that she'd had a peek at his past. She begged him to tell her more about the home he called River Ridge, about his strong, doting father and beautiful Creole mother. He related tales of his many childhood adventures, all conducted under the watchful eyes of devoted servants.

"I wish I'd known you then. What happened to the plantation?"

"I was born during the war and surprisingly enough, River Ridge survived nearly untouched. Unlike many southerners who were ruined by the war, never to recover, my father made a fortune during Reconstruction."

"You mean he was one of them scalawags who turned against his own?"

"Not at all. His dream was to see the South restored to her former glory. He had foresight, my father, and recognized an opportunity to fulfill his dream and profit at the same time. He had large holdings of what many considered to be worthless land. But Dixie was rebuilding and badly needed his timber, so he began a lumbering operation."

"Why'd you leave all that?"

"I didn't leave it; it was gone. Father lost everything in the crash of '79. I was sixteen at the time, away at school and into self-indulgence, totally unaware of what was happening until it was too late. I was summoned home for his funeral."

"What happened to him?"

"He couldn't face his failure and declined into self-pity. He blew his brains out with a pearl-handled dueling pistol." Case was surprised at how easily he'd related his family history. Never before had he told anyone the story and he wondered why he was telling it now. He leaned back against the wall of the cave and January laid her head on his shoulder, resting her hand on his chest.

"How awful it must have been for you. And for your poor mama."

"I left school to help her, but neither of us had any sense when it came to farming the small piece of property we'd managed to hang on to. We mortgaged it to make it through the first year, then lost it when the crops failed."

"Is that when you took up gambling?" she asked.

Case smiled. "Not until later. Mother and I moved to Baton Rouge, where I found work in a shoe factory. I didn't make much money, barely enough to keep food on the table and pay the rent on the little house we lived in. Mother had never been very strong. She was an aristocrat and unaccustomed to work and privation. One wet winter she got sick. I don't know if it was the pneumonia that killed her or the loss of Father."

"You were left all alone," she said softly. "Why do you suppose life is so unfair?"

"I don't know. Fate can be cruel. It has a way of taking those we love best."

January wondered how it would feel to be counted among those Case loved. She knew he'd be leaving her someday and it seemed he knew it, too.

Just thinking of losing him made her stomach hurt and her heart ache. She must love him for sure. "Does it have to be that way, do you reckon?" she whispered.

"I don't know, January. I decided a long time ago that owning things and caring for people is a painful business I'm not cut out for. Losing them is an unbearable hurt that never quite goes away."

Beneath her palm, the hammering of his heart marked his statement as a myth he'd adopted to ease his pain. Surely, the right woman could dispel the wrongheaded notion that caring for others was too risky. "Where did you go from there?"

"I worked my way down the Mississippi and eventually became a deckhand on a riverboat. I found I had an aptitude for cards and some of the old-time gamblers took me under their wing and taught me the tricks of the trade."

"What tricks?"

"I realize I'm a fascinating subject, but I've grown weary with all this talk of myself. I'd rather hear about you. How did you learn all your survival techniques?"

January laughed self-consciously. "Weren't no technique to it. It was learn to hunt or go hungry. I soon figured out that critters are just naturally suspicious and I'd have to sneak up on them or do without supper. Pa never worried too much about food when he was drinking and that was most of the time, especially after he run Mama off."

January snuggled close and Case absently rubbed her bare back, delighting in the silken feel of her skin. "I cried myself to sleep that night and swore I'd never do it again. It was the last time I ever cried. Until tonight."

"What happened tonight?"

She hesitated, then related the whole story. "The day Mama left, I tried to run after her." She could still see her mother standing in the dusty yard, begging Pa not to send her away. Tears streaming, Mama had pleaded, "Don't do it, Jubal. I swear I've never even looked at another man." But Jubal Jones had ignored the tears and waved the Winchester wildly. "That's a lie. You jest married me 'cause you had to, 'cause you was ketched-up. I was a fool to ever think you keered. I was handy, that's all."

"Jubal, you know you were the only man who ever touched me," Daisy had sobbed, cradling her large belly.

"I listened to you then, but I ain't listenin' no more. You was used to better than I could give you. You had edjication and too many big ideas. Well, I'm tired of hearin' how I should git my own place. I reckon you didn't know how hard times could git when you married up with a dirt poor sharecropper."

"Why do you say these things? I don't care about money. We'd be happy if you'd let us." At the time, January had been too young to understand what her parents were arguing about, or how Pa could resist the pleading look on Daisy's pretty face.

But he had. Daisy had started to leave then, trying to take January with her. Instead, Pa had jerked her out of her mother's comforting embrace and flung her aside. "Leave the gal be and git out. You ain't takin' her, not with your corruptin' ways. Now git, or I'll kill the both of you."

January closed her eyes, trying to shut out the painful memories.

"You mean she left you?" Case asked.

"I reckon she had to. Pa wasn't offerin' her any choice in the matter. I tried to follow her, but he caught me and dragged me back. Twice. I wouldn't give up, so he locked me in the root cellar and told me I couldn't come out until I promised not to run off. I can still remember how dark it was, how the walls seemed to close in around me. How I couldn't get enough air to breathe and how it stank of rotten potatoes and decay. But, stubborn as I was, I screamed for hours for him to let me go with Mama.

"Then I got scared and begged him to let me out. I promised not to run away again, but he didn't come. More than likely, he was passed out somewhere and never even knew I'd repented."

"Dear God," Case exclaimed, shuddering at the brutality she'd endured. "How long were you down there?"

"I don't rightly know. A couple of days. I never went in that cellar again. I couldn't even look at it without remembering how scared I'd been."

Thinking of the love and privilege of his own childhood, Case was outraged. "How could he have done such a thing?"

"Drinking is a sickness, only it eats a body up slower than most. A circuit rider who came to the holler to preach said the body was God's temple and we shouldn't abuse it with the devil's brew. He said the Lord was vengeful and he'd smite us down. I reckon he knew what he was talking about."

Case frowned. "Between your father and that holy roller, it's no wonder you hold men in such contempt."

"I got some dire warnings about men from Pa, but it was Mose who made a believer out of me."

"Mose?" he asked.

January told him all about Mose and gave him a brief accounting of the Cleek family in general. She included the story of poor Yarnell and his tales of the bog-stalker and of the mistreated little Almafae.

"No wonder you ran away. To think I tried to talk you into going home," Case ranted. "Your pa should be thrashed and I won't even say what I'd do to Mose Cleek, if I could get my hands on that bastard."

"I like to think he's still hanging in that tree. I can just picture Toad taking little bites out of him until he's completely et up. Did I mention that Toad's the best hogdog in the holler?" she asked, her eyes wide and matter-of-fact.

Case laughed and kissed the tip of her nose. "Yes, you did. I'm surprised to learn you have a vengeful streak."

"I can be ruthless when I have to be," she allowed, basking in the warm circle of his arms.

"Do you still want to go to the Territory?"

"I don't have anywhere else to go. I won't go back to Pa and Mose."

"Of course not," he agreed emphatically. "I wouldn't let you."

"I don't know where my mama is, so I can't go to her. I know I'm not old enough to participate in the run, but I've been thinking maybe I can find me a good man who wants to stay in the same place forever and get him to marry me."

"You're not serious." Case sat up and took her by the shoulders. "How could you even think of doing such a coldhearted thing? Tell me that was a joke."

"Hellfire, Latimer," she hollered, shrugging off his hands, "I know I ain't much to look at and all, but I'm a hard worker and loyal. I'm capable of doing what needs to be done if I set my mind to it."

It was obvious that he wasn't the good man to which she'd referred and that knowledge rankled. It also galled him to think she'd give herself to just any man on the basis of his property rights. Case was hard-pressed to understand his anger, especially since he was unwilling to be the type of man she sought. "I pity the poor sodbuster who's fool enough to take you on," he said, rising to his feet.

"Any man would be lucky to get his hands on me," she shouted.

"Is that so? I had my hands all over you the very first night we met and Lady Luck hasn't exactly been smiling on me lately."

"It's just like you to bring that up. If I live to be a hundred, I'll never forgive you for the liberties you took with my body in that damned creek. It was downright degrading."

"I was trying to save you from drowning. What's so degrading about that?" he yelled, looming over her.

January jumped to her feet. "You know what I mean. I was frightened by the things you did to me."

"I don't believe that for one moment," he bellowed. "As I recall, you were enjoying the kissing as much as I was. You responded with more passion than a virgin ought to feel."

January's cheeks heated up. It was true. Too true. "You're a damned liar, Latimer. If I was so passionate, why'd I threaten you with my knife?"

"Because you were afraid of the desire I brought out in you."

"Go to hell, you slimy snake."

"Where do you think I've been the past few days, lady?" He hated talking to her like that, but he couldn't afford to let the tender feelings overwhelm him. He didn't want to succumb to his yearning.

He marched to the rock where his damp clothing still lay and dropped the blanket. Modesty be damned. Propriety be damned. January Jones be damned, too.

"Where do you think you're going?" she asked the back of his neck, careful to keep her eyes above his waist.

"I haven't decided yet. Anywhere. As long as it's far away from you and your caterwauling." He picked up his pants and had one leg in them before he realized she'd failed to come back with a hot reply.

"Please," she said softly. "I'm asking you to stay."

"You don't want that," he said reasonably, keeping his back to her, suddenly as breathless as if he'd run a long way.

"Oh, yes," she said, lifting her chin.

"You'll feel differently in the morning." He felt honor-bound to warn her. It was the least he could do.

"I want you so much. It feels right tonight, so how can it be wrong?"

He dropped his pants and scooped up the blanket to hold in front of him as he turned toward her. "I'll stay," he qualified. "But I can't promise you forever."

"I know."

"Do you realize what will happen if I stay?"

"Not exactly."

He went to her. He'd known it would happen sooner or later and he was resigned to his fate. Hell, he reveled in it. He spread his blanket on the ground and pulled her down beside him.

"I don't know much about these things," she admitted skittishly. "I don't know what to do."

"That's okay," he said softly, grinning. "I do." His hands cupped her cheek, guiding her mouth to his. He placed her arms around his neck where she curled her hands into his hair. "I've got enough ideas for both of us," he said cockily.

"That's good," she sighed, happy he was smarter than she about one thing at least.

Chapter 9

"Don't hate me for this, January." Case's whispered words took her heart hostage before he slanted his mouth over hers in another bone-melting kiss. It had taken only a few moments for her to get over the shock of having a naked man lying beside her, his hot flesh branding hers with a fiery, unmistakable message. She was doomed. The heat from his body was more intense than that radiated by the smoldering fire.

"Case Latimer," she breathed against his lips, "you must be the best kisser in the world."

He chuckled and nibbled her bottom lip before drawing back to gaze into her eyes. "I was just thinking the same thing about you," he confided. His fingers played with the edge of the blanket still tucked tightly under her arms. "Are you sure you haven't done this before?"

Her eyes widened in indignation until she realized he was teasing her. "I haven't, but you can't say the same." His mouth had explored hers with practiced ease, his tongue performing a languid dance. Once she'd gotten used to the strange sensation, she'd found she rather liked his boldness.

"Would you want to sail with a captain who'd never been to sea?" He'd been unsuccessful at loosening the blanket. It was wrapped around her at least twice. How was he going to remove it gracefully?

He nuzzled her neck and whispered into her ear, "We should have a tintype made of you, frame it in gilt, and have it engraved: 'January Jones, World's Fastest Learner.' ''

She struggled in his arms, but it was a token protest. Secretly, she was happy to please him. His lips nipped her earlobe, then slipped downward. She arched her neck to give him better access to her sensitive skin.

Before she could stop them, her fingers launched an unplanned exploration of his back, tracing the ridges of rippling muscles. He was warm and hard and she ached with a wanting she didn't understand. Anything that made her feel so good couldn't be all bad, and with the heart of a truly passionate woman, she gave herself up completely to the feelings, willing her mind to stay out of it.

When his searching mouth found hers and turned her insides into a sweet, shivering jelly, it was easy to ignore her father's drummed-in warnings. Knowing instinctively that she had to remove the final barrier between them, she lifted her body into his and tugged at the blanket.

Skin burnished skin at last. Her heart hammered wildly against his and Case groaned, sucking her upper lip into the warm moistness of his mouth. He trailed tiny, hot kisses like liquid fire from one shoulder to the other, his sweeping mustache adding to the exciting sensations. Holding her tightly, he nestled his face in her hair.

''Are you sure?'' His breath beat against her ear.

''Certain sure,'' she murmured, not caring about tomorrow. ''Hurry up and kiss me again.''

He felt compelled to warn her about what she was getting into, but there wasn't time before his lips fell over hers. All his good intentions and better judgment melted like snow on a warm day as he lay across her, chest to chest, heart to heart. Resting most of his weight on his forearms, he dipped his tongue against hers, slipping away only to explore, to entice.

January imitated his actions with abandon. She was cautious at first, but as her pleasure grew, so did her confidence. Brazenly, she slid her hands across his shoulders, down his ribs, over his hips, to the tops of his thighs. Not knowing where the impulse came from, she stroked his naked backside and massaged the base of his spine.

He moaned and his breathing became as labored as a hard-run horse's. His tongue dove deeper, delving, teasing, then withdrew to slide down over her chin, her neck, and the hollow of her throat. When he swiped enticingly near her breast, she felt her nipples harden and strain for his touch.

"May I have a little taste?" he asked huskily, his tongue drawing damp circles around the erect bud.

"Is that the way it's done?" She was breathless and a little shocked.

She felt his grin. "Sometimes, but only if you'd like."

"I'd like." She was going to hell anyway. Why should she miss anything?

Lovingly, Case's mouth closed over the hard, expectant nipple and he sucked gently. A coil tightened within her and she feared she would shatter into a million pieces. Would she expire from the sheer forbidden pleasure of it all? While he wooed her with his lips, his hands slid down her hips and she gasped when he touched her intimately.

"Don't be afraid. I won't hurt you," he whispered.

Shaken that she craved his touch with such intensity, she wriggled beneath his gently exploring fingers, the coil of need twisting within her with a ferocious life of its own.

Case wasn't sure how much longer he could last. With growing desire, he watched January, her eyes closed, her head tossing from side to side as he brought her ever closer to fulfillment. It was important to him that her introduction to lovemaking be gratifying. In a way, it was a first for him, too, since he'd never been with a virgin before. Her innocence made the experience brand-new and he was filled not only with tenderness he'd thought himself incapable of, but also with an overwhelming sense of responsibility.

Needing to be touched and sensing her readiness, Case guided her hand to him, dying a small death when her fingers closed tremulously around the hard shaft.

Her eyes widened in surprise and she gasped at the shocking size and heat of him. Suddenly afraid and uncertain as to what would happen next, her body stiffened involuntarily.

Immediately, he rolled away from her and threw an arm over his eyes. "I'm sorry," he said, his breathing ragged. "I should've waited and given you more time to get used to the feel of me." She deserved more than to be taken on the cold, hard ground. Her first time should be in a feather bed with white sheets and lacy pillows. He'd wanted to make the experience memorable and he'd failed.

The delightful sensations were cut off suddenly and she felt bereft. Feeling the loss of his warmth, she turned over and flung herself across his chest. Peering under his arm, she asked hesitantly, "Is that it? Is that all there is to it?" If it was, carnal knowledge between humans wasn't anything like what she'd witnessed between farm animals. She felt empty and unfulfilled. This wasn't even worth going to hell for. "Is it over?"

"No," Case spluttered, laughing. He pulled her onto his chest, hugging her as though he'd never let her go. "It isn't nearly over yet. Not by a damned sight."

"Stop laughing at me," she warned.

He stopped and gazed at her instead. My little spitfire, he thought, what are you trying to do to me? They lay for long moments, staring into each other's eyes. Without movement and without speech they communicated on a very basic level.

"I was laughing at me." He shook his head. "I always thought I knew so much about . . ." He paused. Dammit to hell, Latimer, this is hardly the time to bring up past conquests. He began again. "I misunderstood when you tensed up. I was afraid you were repulsed."

"Does repulsed mean I didn't like it?" she asked.

"It means disgusted."

"Then I wasn't. It just surprised me. I didn't expect it . . . I mean you to . . ." Her words trailed away.

"What?" He grinned, rubbing her round bottom.

"Well," she began, suddenly embarrassed by the topic of conversation. "I . . . um . . . it felt . . . um . . . different than it looked." She burrowed her scorching cheeks against his neck and knew she was making a complete fool of herself. She felt the laughter rumbling in his chest before she heard it. "You're not the gentleman I first thought you were."

"I'm a gambler," Case said softly, cupping her face in his hands and rubbing her perky nose with his. "Make no mistake about who or what I am, my little wildcat. I'm no gentleman and I'm no farmer."

"I don't care," she said honestly. What he was or wasn't didn't seem to matter much at this point. "And I'm no Rowdy Jane!"

"Good. I can't tell you how delighted I am to hear that." Jane's practiced moves wouldn't be nearly as delightful as January's tentative ones.

"I only meant that you'll have to show me how it's done."

"That will be a pleasure in more ways than one," he whispered. His marauding mouth sent spasms of desire rippling through her every nerve. Emotion stormed her senses and passion claimed her body.

He rolled over, tucking her beneath him. He lowered his head and watched her eyes flutter shut, her lips part in anticipation. He brushed his lips against one temple then the other before sampling the delicate arch of her brows. He tasted her, dallying over the silky softness of her face. Her lips beckoned enticingly, but he nipped along the line of her jaw and the hollow of her cheek, denying himself and making the pleasure last.

His thumb stroked her bottom lip as he whispered feathery kisses over her breasts and abdomen. January shivered at the surprising pleasure his lips gave her. He retraced the path to her lips and sipped at the corners of her mouth, making her yearn for more. With a moan, she slipped her fingers into his hair and pulled his mouth down. Wrapping her arms around him possessively, she thrilled as a tremor convulsed his body and delighted in the newfound power she had over him.

Case wasn't oblivious to the enormity of the moment, to his aching need. He'd never felt like this before and it was both thrilling and terrifying. He marveled at her beauty, her softness and her strength. He slid his palm down the curve of her hip to her thigh and found her soft and yielding.

"Don't be frightened, love," he whispered in her ear. "It will hurt, but only this first time."

The first time? Did he think they would be doing this again? But she had no time to dwell on such matters for his hands and his lips were everywhere, discovering, guiding, teaching. They did delicious things to her and left her weak with longing, wanting more.

She writhed beneath him, unsure of exactly what she wanted from him. But as his hot, throbbing flesh burrowed between her thighs, trying to gain entrance into previously unchartered territory, she was positive *that* wasn't it.

"Don't," she said, resisting, trying to push him away.

"Relax, love," he pleaded huskily, retreating. Then his mouth smothered hers harshly and his tongue plunged in and out, demonstrating what was about to happen. His hand fanned over her stomach in a burning caress, then up and down her thigh, caressing her until her skin began to heat and her blood began to hum.

January was past thought. His knowing strokes were kindling a fire and something hot and fierce was trying to erupt deep within her. It began anew, that nameless hunger that made her hips search for the root of heated flesh she'd earlier tried so hard to avoid.

This time he entered her quickly, pressing heavily against her maiden skin and thrusting past all barriers, to nestle deeply within her warmth.

"Hellfire," she gasped. Pa had been right to warn her; it hurt like the very dickens. That awful, excruciating pain and that terrible tearing sensation were surely to be her penance, no more than she deserved.

"I'm sorry," Case said softly, but control was beyond him now. Knowledge of her body had taken over and all he could feel was her tightness and the hot velvet pulsing around him. "Please, January, don't ask me to stop now."

She lay still and quiet beneath him. Everyone paid for their sins. Why should she be any exception? Pain was her punishment for wanting him in the first place. Seeking comfort, she rubbed her temple against his lips, eager for the touch of them on her own. Then his mouth smothered hers, his tongue and hips thrusting rhythmically as his knowing fingers plied her body and quickened her senses all over again.

Within moments, the hurting stopped, replaced by a pleasure of such thrilling proportions that she thought it was the end of the world. Her body bucked and clamored beneath his, pulling him deeper inside her until he touched her very soul. She moaned, demanding a release she couldn't understand.

"January, January." Her name escaped him as spasms of heat pulsated through every part of his body and he fought for control, fully intending that she share the experience. He wanted to teach her the joy of lovemaking, so he diligently set his mind to other things. He went through the multiplication tables twice before he deemed her sufficiently aroused.

She lost sanity. She was aware only of his manhood slipping in and out of her with exquisite slowness, of his tongue invading the soft inner sweetness of her mouth, of his hands capturing her breasts, eliciting gasps of pleasure from her. He fondled the pointed tip between his thumb and finger, gently rolling and squeezing until she no longer knew where her ardor came from.

Case vowed that by the time morning arrived, she'd know all the wonders she could give a man and the many pleasures a man's body could bestow upon hers. Right behind that came the thought that it would be damned hard to let her go once this night was over. Banishing it from his mind, he kissed her again.

She moaned in abandon, thrusting herself against him. Once again he was overwhelmed by the realization that she was like no other woman in the world. She was all feeling, all fire, and she burned only for him, because of him. As he rocked in the cradle of her hips, ripples of bittersweet yearning washed over him.

Delving deeper, harder, he spun her breathlessly into a sweet mindlessness. She writhed against him until the tension uncoiled; the burning heat finally exploded. Ribbons of sparks spiraled from the core of her being in one colossal burst of overpoweringly sensual pleasure. She dissolved in a fireball and cried out his name in ecstasy.

Case captured her scream in his trembling mouth just as his own pulsating climax sent him into oblivion.

She floated, hovering where the loss of her innocence no longer mattered, where fear and warnings could no longer reach her. The nameless hunger was at last satisfied. Only now it had a name. And it was Case.

He kissed her tenderly, thoroughly content. Afraid of hurting her, he rolled half his weight to the cool damp floor of the cave, but kept his arms wrapped around her, holding her possessively against him. A need to protect and take care of her grew in his heart, a need so fierce that he was frightened by its intensity.

He braced himself on an elbow, gazing at her, and rubbed a thumb over the skin just below her breast. It was a different smile he wore now, almost tender yet somehow tense, and she hardly knew what to make of it.

"I'm sorry I hurt you, January."

She shrugged and kept her gaze firmly riveted on his thumb as it strummed her sensitive skin. She wanted to tell him that the pleasure far outweighed the pain, but she couldn't find the words. She longed to throw her arms around him and tell him how much she loved him, tell him she'd shrivel up and die if he ever left her. But she didn't dare speak.

He'd been honest when he'd told her not to expect forever. She would have to be equally honest and let him go.

Her heart missed him already and he hadn't even left. Was all-encompassing loneliness to be yet another bridge to cross on her road to perdition?

"Don't look at me like that."

Case blinked in the dim light of the fire. "Like what?"

"Like I was some kind of floozy."

"I said I was sorry for hurting you and I tried to stop when you asked me. I really did, but it was too late." Why did she always want to fight when he needed closeness? Had their experience meant so little to her that she'd already forgotten how special it had been? He snatched his arms away and sat up, propping his elbows on his knees. "And I wasn't looking at you like you were a floozy. Nothing could have been further from my thoughts."

January sat up, yanked the blanket right out from under him, and held it over her breasts, shielding her nakedness from his scrutiny. "Hellfire, I don't know what you're so mad about. You weren't the one in the throes of pain."

"I'm not mad about anything," he ground out. Hadn't he apologized for hurting her? "You were in the throes of something a few minutes ago, but it sure as hell wasn't pain."

"I begged you to stop," she defended, knowing it was a lie.

He rested his forehead in his palms. "I don't want to fight with you, January. Not now. One minute we're as close as a man and woman can be, closer than I've ever been to anyone, and the next, we're arguing again." Case sighed and turned to face her.

"I ain't in the mood for talking." She lay down, showing him her back, taking pains to cover herself from his prying eyes.

Good God, she had the ability to confuse him until he didn't know up from down. Then it finally dawned on him that she wasn't mad. She, like himself, was merely confused with all these new and unfamiliar emotions.

"Seems to me you're carrying on about one thing when

it's something else that's got you riled up.'' Quick as a wink, he lifted a corner of the blanket and crawled in behind her. Before she could splutter a protest, he rolled her to her back, threw his arm about her waist, and pinned her leg with his. She was his prisoner.

''I told you to leave me be,'' she said peevishly, trying to wriggle away, careful lest she succeed. It was sinful enough that she'd actively participated in fornication with him and enjoyed it as much as she had, without having to talk about it.

''Well,'' he drawled, ''I don't want to, January.'' Case's breathy words tickled her ear. ''You asked me to show you how it's done and I obliged.'' He gave her a randy smile. ''But there's more, so much more.''

''Jesus,'' she gasped as she felt him growing against her hip.

''Jesus won't help you now,'' he whispered, running a finger down the line of her jaw.

And why should he? she wondered. She couldn't even help herself. She must be bad clean through, for she was much too thrilled by the prospect of doing it all over again.

She sighed in ecstasy and gave herself up to Case's magic.

''January.'' He said it like a caress, then whispered sweet, meaningless words in her ear that made her tremble. Like a lover's litany, he breathed her name over and over until everything about her turned pliable and wanting, and she reached out for him.

His breathing grew easy and he knew this shared closeness was as near to perfect as he'd ever find with a woman. January Jones, the little hellion, captivated him and he marveled at the passionate strength and courage she put into everything she did, especially lovemaking.

They lay tightly wrapped in each other's arms, her forehead nestled beneath his jaw, his hand rubbing her shoulders in lazy, satisfied circles. Their chests rose and fell in the sublime cadence of lovers.

She was just about the most perfect woman he could

ever hope to meet and he was puzzled by the emotions she stirred in him. He only hoped he'd have his fill of her before the time came for him to head for Alaska. They still had a few days before then, he consoled himself as he drifted off to sleep.

Chapter 10

By morning, the thought of his impending departure had lost some of its luster and loomed up like an outhouse in the fog. Sometime during their sleep, he'd wrapped her body against his own, spoon fashion. Case moved his hand from her hip, possessively cupping her breast.

When his mustache tickled the back of her neck, January's eyes opened. The way his hand moved over her body told her he was wide awake. He sure picked a fine time to become an early riser, she thought with trepidation. A chilling wave of reality washed over her as she recalled her wanton abandon of the night before. She squeezed her eyelids shut. How was she ever going to face him in the cold, hard light of day?

She decided the best thing to do was just to get up and get dressed in a hurry and try to act as though nothing had happened. But when she would've rolled out of the tangled blankets, his arm tightened around her and hauled her back.

"I've never slept the night through with a woman before," he admitted. "And I must say I enjoyed it. You were wonderful."

When his warm lips pressed a provocative kiss on her shoulder, the rhythm of January's heart picked up and she scurried out of his clutches. Their lovemaking last night had been spontaneous and out of control. They'd both been swept away by the feelings of closeness they'd shared. But if she allowed it to happen again, it would be premeditated and unforgivable. No need to compound already staggering transgressions.

Hiding behind the horses as much as possible, she yanked on her dry clothes. "We're burning daylight, Latimer, and I ain't got that much to waste on such trivial pursuits."

"Aw, January," he purred, "don't get all tensed up on me. We've got plenty of time." He patted the place beside him. "Come on back to bed. We'll sleep late."

"No." He sure was in a good mood, she thought, tugging on her boots. She almost put them on the wrong feet when he stood, bare-assed as the day he was born, to stretch and growl. The sight of him caused the blood to cascade to her face and her ears seemed in grave danger of igniting from the heat. She tossed him his things. "Put your clothes on."

"Say please," he instructed.

She glared at him and Case hopped around on one leg while he slipped the other into his pants. "Does my nudity offend you?" he asked with a half smile. He stretched again and rubbed the furry surface of his chest.

"Yes." She busied herself saddling the horses and packing their gear.

"It certainly didn't bother you last night," he pointed out mischievously.

"I think it's best if we forget last night ever happened." Her tone was as self-righteous as a temperance leader's.

He considered that for a moment and cocked his head to one side. "Just how the hell do we do that?"

"We just do, that's all. We'll pretend it never happened. And it ain't never gonna happen again." She spotted something and bent down, peering behind the rocks. Now, *why* would a leather pouch be wedged into that crevice? And *who* had put it there?

"I don't think I can stretch my imagination that far," he groused.

"See if you can bend it enough to accommodate this . . ." She paused, crawling behind a boulder. By reaching far into the groove and using considerable effort, she managed to latch on to a leather strap.

"What?" he asked curiously, standing impatiently behind her.

"This." She hauled the pouch out of its hiding place and triumphantly slapped it down on the ledge in front of her. Case stepped around her, examined the fine workmanship of the leather, then unfastened the thongs of what was obviously an expensive item.

"Hot damn!" he exclaimed, looking inside. "Hot damn!"

"Just a bunch of old letters," January scoffed, standing on tiptoe to see over his shoulder. "Hellfire, it's money!"

"And lots of it." Case spread it in his hands like a fan and threw it up in the air. As it drifted down around them, he lifted her in his arms and whirled her around. When he stopped, they stood toe to toe and he kept his arms locked around her waist. "Enough to buy you a damned farm. Now you don't have to go to Indian Territory at all. Isn't that wonderful?"

"Wonderful?" Pushing against his chest with her palms, she twisted out of his grasp and backed away from him. She stooped to pick up the scattered currency. "It ain't my money, Case, and it ain't yours. We can't spend a cent of it."

"And why not?"

"It's not ours. It just wouldn't be right."

"Don't be an idiot." Dropping on one knee to help, he rationalized, "Don't you see, somebody probably stole this money and hid it in the rocks, planning to come back for it later. Since we have no way of knowing who it belongs to, what harm could there be in putting it to good use?"

He had a point. If they knew who the rightful owner was, there would be no question of what should be done. But since they didn't . . . She straightened and tried to count the bills as she tucked them back into the fancy pouch, appalled that she would even consider the idea.

Filled with self-disgust, she shook her head as she ran her fingers over the smooth leather. There was a tiny split in the lining and she pulled out a small printed card and handed it to Case.

"'Wesley Tyrone,'" he read aloud. "'Washington, D.C.' Sounds like some tenderfoot came all the way to Missouri only to get robbed."

"Now we know whose it is, we have to give it back." January took the card and jammed it deep into the saddlebags she'd already tossed over Brownie's rump. She led the horse outside.

Case grabbed Shadow's reins and followed. "How?"

"We know who and where it belongs. We'll leave it with the sheriff in the next town we come to," she said with finality, hoisting herself into the saddle.

Filled with disbelief, Case stared at her. "Are you crazy? Finding this money is a sign that my luck is finally changing for the better." His tone grew loud and angry. "Why not just take it and buy the land you're so all-fired determined to have?"

"Because I have enough sins chalked up against me without adding theft to the lot."

Mr. Tyrone was lucky such an honorable person as herself had found his money, she decided. Now that she knew where his fortune was, she'd see that he got it back somehow despite Case's objections. She sat up proud and straight and urged Brownie to take to the trail. But the contrary critter looked toward Shadow as if waiting for his leader to give the word. "Are you gonna mount up so this fool horse of mine knows it's time to go?"

After that querulous comment, she ignored him and he didn't like being ignored. She was the first woman he'd ever made love to without paying for the privilege. Now she wanted to pretend it hadn't happened, as if nothing had changed. Exactly what had changed he didn't know, but something had.

When January cooled off, she'd surely realize that turning so much money over to the authorities was a bad move. If not, he'd have to figure out a way to bring her around.

Sweet talking wouldn't work. They'd have spent the better part of the morning in that cave if that had any effect on her. He mounted Shadow and took off down the trail at a fast clip.

No sooner had Case's bottom slapped leather than Brownie, trying to keep up with the Morgan, stretched into an unsteady, bone-wrenching lope. January jiggled and bounced with every hoofbeat and felt a raw tenderness in her nether regions. It hurt, but she considered it just another divine punishment.

For a man who hadn't wanted to get started this morning, Case seemed to be in a right smart hurry, January observed. Brownie hadn't been blessed with the same smooth gait as Shadow and January was damned uncomfortable. Let Case ride as if he couldn't reach their destination and get rid of her fast enough. She wasn't about to let him set her pace. She tried to rein Brownie in, but the contrary beast ignored her.

"You goldurned lop-eared old nag," she scolded, but the horse wasn't listening. He was too busy trying to stay abreast of Shadow.

They rode without talking until the sun was high and Case insisted they stop for a quick meal. He silenced January's arguments by reminding her he'd been rushed away this morning without breakfast.

She would've ridden off and left him right then and there, but Brownie wasn't about to move a muscle unless Shadow moved one first. They sat down to eat, the air bristling around them.

Avoiding physical and eye contact, they spoke in short, angry sentences.

"Coffee?" January offered to pour.

"Please." Case held out his cup.

"More?" he asked, helping himself to the last of the vittles.

It was a good thing she didn't want any. "No, thanks."

"Welcome," he mumbled, his mouth full.

"Ready to go?" She packed up. He'd cooked while she'd watered the horses.

"Nope." He reclined against a handy tree as though he had plenty of time and stretched his long legs out in front of him, crossing them at the ankles. With the tip of a brown forefinger, he pulled down his hat brim.

"You're not taking a nap!" she exclaimed.

"Five minutes to rest and let my food digest," he said as if that were the end of the matter.

Much later, they'd gone a good ways down the road and she'd managed to work herself into a huff by the time she glanced at him. "Those five minutes turned into twenty," she said grumpily, unable to hold her tongue any longer.

It was plain Case didn't give a tinker's damn that she was annoyed. He didn't answer, didn't even look her way. She swore not to speak to him again until hell froze over.

As twilight descended, Case found a pretty little stream and set up their camp. She resented him making all the decisions just because her cockeyed horse didn't have any initiative. Brownie had never seemed more worthless.

She might be forced to travel with Case for the time being, but not forever. To hell with him. Brownie, too. The next town they passed through, she'd swap the old nag for an animal that didn't require the leadership of another horse.

"I'll see if I can scare up some game for supper," she said, sliding the Winchester from its sheath.

"No need," Case drawled, building a fire. "We have plenty of supplies." Someone had left them a nice little legacy. He'd be damned if he'd sit around while she went out like some kind of female Daniel Boone to hunt for him. He tossed thick chunks of salt pork into a sizzling pan and dumped a can of beans over it.

"No need to waste supplies when there's plenty of critters to eat," she pointed out sensibly.

"We can restock tomorrow. There's another town not

too far from here.'' Grabbing the coffeepot, he took off toward the stream.

''And just what will we use for money?'' If she parted with any of her hard-earned silver, it'd be for something worthwhile. Like a new horse to get her away from this insufferable man.

He paused and gestured with the pan. ''You sound like a damned wife, always harping about money. Or the lack of it. We've got what I won in the poker game, although I'll admit it's not much. But there's over five thousand dollars in that pouch.''

''We ain't spending any of Wesley Tyrone's money.'' January shot him with a withering glance and crossed her arms over her chest. ''It wouldn't be right.''

He said something she couldn't make out, slapped his thigh in frustration, then wheeled around and stomped down to the creek.

After they finished another silent meal, she stacked the dirty utensils and carried them to the edge of the water. When she'd cleaned them, she piled everything on a rock.

From the corner of her eye, she could see Case was still pouting near the fire. She sneaked into the trees and stripped down to her underwear. Removing the silver dollars from their secret pocket, she stashed them in her jacket for safekeeping, then hid everything in a pile of brush.

She scrubbed, using only water and her hands. It was no real hardship to do without Case's fancy soap. She'd only tried it that one time and a body could hardly miss something they hadn't had a chance to get used to.

That wasn't strictly true. She'd just had a fair sample of Case's lovemaking and she was sure going to miss that. God brand her for a hussy, but she would.

She splashed the cold water over her face, trying to forget those less than pleasant thoughts. The water was chilly, but not as cold as it had been when he'd saved her from drowning.

She smiled, recalling how frightened she'd been that

night. He'd merely touched her breast and she'd fought and scratched as if he'd been trying to kill her.

Despite the cool air, her cheeks heated up just thinking about him and the exciting things he'd done to and for her. She ducked her head under the water, trying to clear it of such shameful thoughts. He would be leaving her soon and she'd be on her own again. She would miss him something fierce.

Case had watched her slip out of her clothes. Then, clad only in her chemise and drawers, she had hidden them in a brushpile. If she thought the tall grass at water's edge secluded the scene of her toilette, she was mistaken. He groaned, remembering how soft and yielding she'd been in his arms last night. He'd thought her beautiful then, but she'd been absolutely breathtaking this morning when she'd turned stubborn and sassy.

If he weren't such an honorable man, he'd walk down there, scoop her up in his arms, strip off that flimsy see-through underwear, and make love to her right in the stream. He'd never tried anything so adventurous and was still wondering if such an act might be possible when he watched her tippy-toe into the shallows, picking up her feet like a cat in wet grass.

Suddenly he remembered she couldn't swim. It was dangerous for her to be down there alone. What if she stepped in over her head? It had happened before.

Without making a sound, he sneaked to the edge of the creek and hid behind some bushes. He had to keep watch, to make sure she didn't drown. Didn't he? Of course he did. She might need him.

He debated his choices. She'd never believe it if he stumbled upon her "accidentally" while pretending to take a bath himself. But staying put and watching her in the moonlight wouldn't be so easy, either. He felt a familiar aching longing and could almost taste her sweetness, could almost feel her warm flesh beneath his.

A person shouldn't have to go through life without knowing how to swim, he rationalized. It was an important bit of survival knowledge and he owed her that much. He skinned off his clothes in a fevered rush. He'd just wade in there and give her a swimming lesson. Even January couldn't condemn him for wanting to help her.

One minute she was alone and the next she was scooped up in Case's arms, her hands clasped instinctively around his neck. "What do you think you're doin'?" she shrieked.

"Teaching you to swim." He waded out until the water covered him. One look at him and she'd know he was a liar. "Are you afraid?"

"Not of the water, I ain't." She tightened her grip on him.

"Surely not of me?" he teased.

January refused to be taken in by him. Allowing him to make love to her last night had been a big mistake. She'd listened to her heart and her body when she should have paid more attention to her head and her pa. Fornication was wrong; she'd been duly warned, and she knew better. She'd not make that same mistake again. She wouldn't. But surely something as innocent as a swimming lesson couldn't be sinful.

"You can trust me, January. Do you?"

"Yes," she breathed, though she knew she shouldn't.

He waded further out. "Take your arms from my neck."

With great reluctance she did so. She obeyed each of his softly voiced instructions until she was lying on her back, on top of the rippling water. One of his strong hands supported her shoulders and the other, her hips.

"What do I do now?"

"You float, but first you have to relax. Just lie back and look up at the stars. Come on," he coaxed. "Don't be so nervy. That's it, let your hands lie on the water." His words trailed away and his fascinated gaze traveled from her bobbing hands to the water pooling around the ripe fullness of her breasts. Her nipples jutted enticingly at the clinging wet chemise and he cut his eyes away. Traitorously, they slid down to the soft indentation of her navel, then lower to the dark mound of auburn hair floating tantalizingly just below the surface.

His hands ached to caress her, to find the throbbing bud hidden there and bring her to ecstasy. The need was so painfully acute that he stared out over the water and said, "I'm going to take my hands away now and you'll be—"

"Sinking?" she asked impishly, to lighten the tension. She recognized that devilish gleam in his eyes.

Once he removed his hands, she promptly sank below the surface, but he caught her in his arms, clasping her to his chest. She coughed and spluttered and he pounded her back and carried her out of the water. He was disgusted with himself. He'd been so caught up with his lusty thoughts that he'd nearly let her drown.

Gently, he laid her on the grassy bank and knelt at her side, concern evident in his features. "Are you all right?"

Her eyes met his. "I'm fine." She was fascinated by the movement of his lips and his dark mustache. A strange paralysis set upon her and she couldn't move as those hell-hot eyes of his touched her everywhere.

Her breasts strained for his touch and when it came, her heart skipped into double-time. Her hips shifted beneath him and she was nearly giddy with relief and wanting when his hands cupped her bottom. She was his for the taking and she wished he'd get on with it.

"I love it," he said. "I love the taste of you." His teeth and tongue ravished her earlobe. "I like touching you and it feels so good when you touch me." One hand slid inside her drawers to knead her heated flesh. The other guided her to his manhood. "In fact, I like it so much, I may not go to Alaska until next year."

His words chilled her. Next year? This year? *When* was immaterial. The fact that he was planning to leave was the issue. January stiffened and rolled away from him, her expression hard. "Alaska? So that's where you're headed? Why didn't you tell me before?"

"Because at first I didn't think it was any of your business." Case tried to take one of her clenched hands in his, but she jerked it away. "Later, there were too many distractions. You've turned out to be the biggest distraction of all."

She couldn't think of anything vile enough to say, her misery was so acute. How was it possible her own body had betrayed her in such a way? Or had Case done the betraying by not telling her of his intentions? He didn't belong to her. He never would. The thought made her sick, but how much worse would it hurt if he were truly gone?

"For God's sake, what have I done now?"

"Nothin', Mr. Latimer, nothin' at all." Shakily, she got to her feet, snatched up her clothes, and marched back to camp.

He followed. "You'll have to explain, because I'm damned if I know what's got your feathers all ruffled."

She wheeled on him, her hands on her hips. "Just because I was curious about . . . about what goes on between men and women and . . ."

"Don't stop now."

"I only let you show me . . ."

"Let? *You* let *me?*"

"Just because we . . . well . . . Hellfire, what happened don't give you the right to think I'd want to do . . . um . . . that again. I'm not your personal property to take when you feel like it and throw out like a broken boot when the spirit strikes you."

"Say no more!" Case grabbed up his pants and pulled them on with jerky movements. He thrust his arms into his shirt and jammed his feet into his boots. "I've never forced myself on a woman before and I'm not about to start now."

Tight-lipped, she watched him saddle Shadow. She had to bite her tongue to keep from asking where he was off to. The sudden overwhelming urge to tell him she was sorry and confess her innermost feelings bore down on her like an anvil on her chest. She longed to beg him to stay but fought the urge. It was better this way. Her innocence was lost but she still had her pride.

She wrapped up in her blanket and sat down, waiting. Brownie snorted, shifting restlessly. She had half a mind to tell Case that since he was leaving with her heart, he might as well take her horse, too.

He swung onto Shadow and stopped beside her. "Despite what you're thinking, I'm not deserting you. I intend to see that you make your destination safely."

January stuck up her chin. "I can take care of myself."

"Probably better than I can, but allow me my illusions." He sighed, pushing up his hat brim. "We need a rest from each other's company and I'm going into town. I'm in a real hardship of need for a drink and some friendly companionship. I need to play some cards and relax."

"Fine." January stared into the campfire, feeling his gaze on her but refusing to meet it. After what had happened the last time he'd sat in on a game, she didn't think she could relax until he got back safely.

All she had to do was ask him to stay and he would. But her icy silence told him he could wait until doomsday and she'd never give an inch. Muttering a frustrated "Dammit to hell," he lit out.

Resolutely, she put on her clothes and lay down in her blankets near the fire's warmth. Sleep was a long time coming.

Befuddled with dreams of Case, January was confused when she was awakened by four strangers riding into camp. When she saw it wasn't Willard and his gang, she felt relieved but pulled on her hat and felt for the Winchester just the same. One of the men spoke and her finger curled around the trigger.

"Don't shoot, feller. We're jest lookin' for someone. A man what calls hisself Case Latimer. You seen 'im?"

"Since I was sleeping," January scoffed, "how was I supposed to see anyone?"

"I reckon as you're the only one here, right?"

The fire had burned down, the embers didn't cast enough

light to make out their faces, and one of them seemed to take great pains to stay in the shadows. "Right now. My brother's in town, but he'll be back soon," she lied.

The same man spoke for them all. "You seen anybody else?"

"Not since we left Branson." Who were these men and why were they looking for Case? Had he gotten into some kind of trouble when he'd gone to town tonight? "How come you're looking for this here Lattimore feller anyway?"

"Latimer," the stranger corrected. "It's personal. He's gonna be a pappy and we aim to take him back to Hot Springs with us."

January's heart sank. "A pappy, huh?"

"That's right," he agreed vehemently. "We plan to see he does right by our poor sister. Else he'll pay fer what he done to the Buscus family."

So these were the Buscus brothers Case hadn't wanted to tell her about. Now that she knew why they were looking for him, she could understand why he hadn't. It appeared her first impression of that devil Case had been right on target. He truly was a no-account, low-life, good-fer-nuthin'. With shame, she recalled the intimacies they'd shared, intimacies he'd obviously also shared with Miss Buscus.

January hoped Case got his just desserts, but she wasn't about to let these farmboys get their hands on him before she did. "Good for you," she said, pretending to encourage the stranger. "You know, we did meet up with one feller. Said his name was Smith. He wore a black hat with a silver band and was a real dandified sort. He was ridin' a black Morgan."

"That's him." The man nodded eagerly. "Which way was he headed?"

"North. He talked to my brother and mentioned something about Alaska." That should discourage them. They didn't look like they had the gumption to chase a man clear out of the country.

The rider in the shadows threw back his head and yowled like a pain-crazed coyote. The spokesman whispered frantically to his companions before exclaiming, "God a-mighty! We'll get that slippery varmint if we have to follow him clear to kingdom come. When'd you say you saw him?"

"Nigh on to two, maybe three days ago."

January waited until the horsemen had galloped off in the wrong direction before she made a move. Quickly, she packed up and doused the coals.

"One more time," she grumped, swinging into the saddle. "I'll help him just this once and then he's on his own."

She nudged her horse in the flanks. "Hellfire, don't fail me now, Brownie." He must have sensed her desperation for he actually raced down the moonlit trail.

Chapter 11

"Hellfire," January mumbled under her breath. "How do they stand it?"

Swearing this would be the very last time she ventured into a helldorado in this life, she tugged her hat down over her ears and marched into Big Betty's Barrelhouse. Her nose wrinkled at the unfragrant medley of odors that assailed it—stale cigar smoke, sour malt beer, and overworked spittoons.

This was the second time circumstances had forced her into such a place since Case Latimer had shot into her life like a wayward bullet. Walking into this one didn't feel as strange as it should and that worried her. She had enough bad marks against her without turning into a barroom fixture.

"What do you think you're doin' in here, kid?" asked a deep voice behind her. "This ain't no Sunday school."

January turned and looked up at the owner of the voice. A raven-haired doxy, tall as any man, glared down, her hands splayed over wide hips. Her homely features were rawboned and angular and there was the slight suggestion of dark hair above her lip. Despite the painted face, frizzed-up hair, and spangled dress, January wondered if the saloon "gal" might not be a man having everyone on.

"I asked you a question, kid."

January thought fast. "Just looking to find my brother is all."

"Well, tend to your bizness and get out. This is my

place and I don't need the likes of you comin' in here and reminding these bardogs they got wives and kids waitin' home. Who's your brother?''

January glanced around and her heart drummed against her ribs when she spotted Case. ''He's right over there. I'll get him.''

''Just be quick about it,'' Big Betty threw over her shoulder as she pushed through the crowded room to the bar, looking for all the world like a steamboat huffing through deadwood.

Case, relaxed and jovial, leaned over the table and raked in his winnings. For a moment, January stood behind him, reluctant to spoil his good mood. She studied the way his dark hair curled over his collar and the play of muscles straining against the fabric of his jacket. The sound of his laughter set little fires in her stomach.

''Hey, kid, you skeedaddle on out of here. Go on back to your ma.'' The dealer who'd spoken stopped passing round cards and scowled at her. January wondered if all saloon patrons just naturally had a grudge against kids. ''You hear me now? Go on, git.''

Dammit to hell. Case had a sneaking suspicion whom he'd see when he glanced over his shoulder. He reared back in his chair and their gazes clashed. He knew it! January had a way of turning up when her company was least welcome. Thinking he'd be better off with a millstone around his neck, he turned back to his cronies, masking his displeasure that she'd followed him.

''I ain't goin' nowhere till I fetch my brother,'' she said stubbornly. Crossing her arms, she planted her feet in a stance that the most obstinate mule would envy.

The dealer persisted. ''Big Betty don't feel too kindly disposed toward sprouts like you. One was in here a while back and got himself into a game that damned near broke the bank. He started a riot that busted up the joint something fierce.''

January looked around at the squalid surroundings. ''Tearing this place down would be an improvement.''

Case sighed and jumped into the conversation before her mouth got them both in trouble. "The kid's my responsibility." His look was so hot it nearly singed her eyebrows and a frown marred his handsome face. "What are you doing here, J.J.?" he demanded.

"I . . ." She started to answer, then reconsidered. What did he have to be so mad at her about? Like a softheaded fool who couldn't learn to stay away from the stove no matter how many times she got burned, she'd thought to save him again. She was tempted to find those Buscus brothers and hand him over herself.

Then she remembered what they had in mind for Case. It would serve him right if he had to get hitched up, but it wasn't going to be to no faceless Buscus sister. She glanced meaningfully at the others around the table, then back at him. "I need to talk to you. Private-like."

"I'm busy."

"You have to come," she muttered through clenched teeth, unwilling to divulge this newest problem in front of the others. If the Buscuses showed up later asking questions, she didn't want any sore losers to set them on their trail. Rolling her eyes toward the door, she nodded imperiously. "It's important."

Inwardly, Case was pleased she'd come to her senses and missed him enough to come after him, but his poker face displayed nothing. Although he was tempted to grab her and plant a big kiss on her mouth, he restrained himself. Her disguise would invite serious speculation regarding his manhood. He fanned his cards, showing her no apparent interest. "Not now, J.J."

"You're making a big mistake."

"I'll go when I'm good and ready."

He was acting like a damned fool and it took all of January's formidable willpower not to walk right back out those swinging doors and leave him to his fate. Then she remembered exactly what was at stake. It'd be a crying shame if he wound up on the wrong end of those Buscus boys' shotguns.

"If you don't come with me right now, you're liable to find yourself in dire straits again," she warned in a sing-song tone. She wanted to throw "holy matrimony" in for a clincher, but didn't dare.

"He can't leave," a loser put in crossly, pointing out the large pile of money in front of Case. "That wouldn't be fair. He's a-winnin'."

"I'll be along. Later," Case said firmly. January needed to learn right off who was the boss. He couldn't allow her to follow him, then start ordering him around like a Yankee sergeant. He'd lose a few hands to pacify the other players and make her sweat. Then he'd go.

"It's more important than you know." She drew her finger across her throat in a cutting gesture but Case wasn't looking. Suddenly inspired, she piped up, "Ma says I'm to fetch you. That I shouldn't leave here without you."

The men at the table guffawed. Case gave her a dirty look. "I don't take orders from anyone," he gritted. "Especially women."

"Have it your way," she relented. "But you ought to know the baby's on the way."

Case looked up, startled. "What baby?"

"Why, little baby Buscus," she said pointedly.

"What?" he exclaimed, instantly on his feet. How could she know about that? Since he hadn't told her, she must have encountered those hounddog farmers after he left camp. It had been so long since they'd intruded in his life, he'd been convinced they were no longer a threat. Dammit to hell!

"You remember," she said impatiently, rocking the cradle she'd made of her arms. "Baby Buscus?"

Hurrying, Case nearly forgot to rake the money into his hat. Disgruntled protests rose around the table from players who would now have no chance to even the score.

"Sorry, men, but a matter of utmost importance requires my attention." Thinking his apology lacked sincerity, he shoved a pile of money across the table. "Drinks for the house on me," he said magnanimously. Grabbing

January's arm, he steered her outside. "Where are the horses?" he said, looking around.

She jerked her arm away, loath to let him touch her after what she'd learned about him from the Buscus brothers. "Over there, you damned polecat." Not waiting for a response, she stalked to the dark alley between Big Betty's and a dry goods store.

"What's gotten into you now?" he asked in exasperation, confused by the sudden intensity of her anger.

"I ain't talkin' to you," she spat out, the words falling like hard pebbles in a blackened pool.

"Well, you're going to talk to me, like or not. What's all this about a baby?" The best course of action was to find out exactly what she knew before he confessed too much, too soon. Dumping the money into his saddlebags, he plopped his hat on his head and bent to scoop up Shadow's reins.

"Damn you for getting some farmers' sister ketched-up." Furious at him, at herself, and at the whole damned Buscus family, she drew back her arm, doubled her fist, and walloped him a good one right in the middle of the back.

Caught off guard, Case's chin jammed into the saddle and he rounded on her. "What the hell's got into you?"

She told herself her outrage had nothing to do with the fact that he'd nearly seduced her in the stream, then run out on her when she was in a fever of need. And it had nothing to do with the fact that his past misdeeds were catching up with him, or that he'd soon be a not-so-proud papa. Or that now any hope she might have had for a future with him was dashed.

"You ought to be horsewhipped, you . . . you despoiler of women! You corruptin' satchel-crazy tomcat!" She searched her vocabulary for other suitably demeaning epithets and latched on to the most appropriate one of all. One that carried a special brand of scorn. "You . . . man!"

"I hope that made you feel better."

"No, it didn't!" she yelled and suddenly her fists were pounding his chest.

"What's gotten into you?" He grabbed her shoulders, pulling her against him to restrain the assault. She kicked him in the shins and squirmed out of his grasp. Free, she backed away, her fists thrust up in front of her like a pugilist's.

"Nothin's got into me but you," she screeched. "Just leave me the hell alone from now on."

"What's this all about?" He took a tentative step toward her, suspecting her behavior was prompted by feminine jealousy.

"Don't come near me," she warned. "Don't you dare touch me."

"I'm not going to hurt you. I'd never hurt you." He held out his arms, hoping she'd regain her senses. This was more then just a jealous snit. Her suspicion and doubt reminded him of the first night they'd met and how she'd fought like a demented bobcat when he'd discovered her true identity.

"Not anymore you won't," she declared, her eyes flashing. "Even though you do drink and gamble and frequent parlor houses, I thought that down deep you had a good heart. But you don't have a heart at all or you wouldn't have done what you did. A good man wouldn't steal a woman's virtue and fill her with his seed, then leave her to face the consequences all alone." It occurred to her that she could very well be in the same trouble this very moment and a cold dread creeped through her.

Case stopped dead-still and his hands dropped to his sides. Anger threaded his words. "I can't figure you out. If that's how you feel, why bother to warn me at all?"

How could she tell him she'd warned him because she loved him? "I told you, I don't think things through. I'm like a half-cocked pistol. When something happens, I just shoot off without seeing it clear-like. Seems like I always end up making a passel of bad mistakes." The only thing that kept her from mounting Brownie and riding away from him forever was the overwhelming need to hear him deny the Buscuses' allegations. "I have to be crazy. If I weren't, I wouldn't be keeping company with the likes of you in the first danged place."

"Are you ready to listen?" He didn't know why but suddenly it was crucial for her to understand there had been nothing between Ardetta Buscus and himself. To his surprise he found himself doing something he'd never done before—explaining his actions.

Soon he'd told her everything. "And if she really is in that delicate condition, I swear to you, it isn't my child. Do you believe me?"

He'd spoken with such conviction, imploring her with his eyes and his words to trust him, that January could do little else. How could she *not* believe him when she needed so desperately to trust him? She couldn't bear the thought of him being with any other woman, much less forced into marrying one.

"I believe you," she replied when she could manage to force out the words.

"That means a lot to me, January." The feeling came to him as a surprise but admitting it was a regular shock.

He said her name so softly and longingly that she ached for things she had no right to want. Gone was the cold wedge that had threatened to tear her heart asunder, but her pride still held sway over her emotions. "I probably shouldn't listen to a thing you say. Your sweet talk is what makes you so good at seducing innocent young virgins into your bed."

They faced each other silently, his eyes sparkling blue fire. She wished she could call back her rash retort, but the words hung in the air like early frost. When at last he spoke, his words were made all the more startling by the quiet, wistful way in which they were delivered.

"I didn't hold a gun on you. I never forced you into the intimacies we shared. You wanted it to happen as much as I did."

"Stop it," she cried, clamping her hands over her ears. "Don't say that."

Case gently pulled her hands away, holding them in his. "What we did went against my principles, too," he admitted. "But making love with you . . ." He paused, confused by the feelings she'd dredged up. He'd never thought of sex in such tender terms, but when he'd lain with January, it had been more than the casual, businesslike encounters he was used to. What they'd shared had been so special he couldn't bear the thought that it might not have meant as much to her.

"Making love with you," he repeated softly, enjoying the foreign feel of the words on his tongue, "was the most memorable moment of my life. The sweetest, most precious thing that ever happened to me. And I won't allow you to make less of it."

His gentle hold on her arms and his heartfelt revelation were almost her undoing. She wanted to throw herself against him and admit how important their lovemaking had been to her, too. A beautiful memory. A treasure to be locked away in her heart forever and taken out like a faded rose when he was long gone, to be savored and relived whenever she needed to feel cherished.

But admitting such sentimentality would threaten her hard-won independence and demolish her already battered pride. For as sure as geese went barefoot, the day would come when he'd leave her. Maybe not tonight, or tomorrow, or even the next day, but eventually they'd reach a crossroads and she knew they could never take the same path.

"I didn't know what I was doing," she defended, refusing to admit her part in the deed. "You should've known that and you never should've taken advantage of me. You're nothing but a selfish, no-account gambler, a wastrel, a . . . a vagabond, a—"

"Don't forget despoiler of innocents," he prompted with a grin.

"It's bad enough it happened at all, but it's downright humiliating to make light of it."

"I'm sorry," he said sincerely. "That was not my intention. However, I won't deny myself the pleasure of remembering how it was between us. Why can't you admit that you wanted me as badly as I wanted you? Or is it the idea that a mere gambler, a low-down hellraising jack of aces, could kiss you and wake your own passions that's so repugnant?"

There was nothing repugnant about how she'd felt with Case. That was the problem. She had enjoyed it, all of it, and that made her a wanton, shameless woman. He surely read the truth in her traitorous eyes, for his own turned soft as he stared at her lips. She knew he was going to kiss her and, God help her, she wanted him to. The melting had already started. Yearning and waiting for his touch, she scrunched her eyes tight, unable to watch his mouth descend slowly to her own. She waited breathlessly for his lips to cover hers and touch off the fires smoldering within her.

He pulled her body against his own and an eternity passed while she anticipated the joyous mindlessness that his wonderful, coaxing mouth could bring on. When it didn't come, she blinked up at him. He smiled.

"If you want a kiss, January, you'll have to take it," he challenged softly. "Never let it be said that Case Latimer forced you to kiss him."

She wanted to jerk her hands from his chest, but instead her willful fingers curled around the lapels of his jacket. She was tempted to take that kiss, to prove to him that she was a full-grown woman, not the mewling cub he treated her like most of the time. She longed for the warmth of his mouth on hers, opened wide, his tongue dancing suggestively, intimately with her own. But she could only stare at those lips while her wild imagination ran amok.

"What makes you think I'd want to kiss you?" she whispered.

He flashed his devil grin. "I don't know. Maybe the

way your head is thrown back, ready and waiting. Or the way you're all over me like a cheap suit of clothes. But mostly it's the way you're hanging on that convinced me." He glanced pointedly at her hands and she snatched them away as if his lapels had suddenly caught fire. "Your eyes are begging me to take the initiative, so you'll be absolved of guilt. That way all the sin you engage in won't be your fault, will it?"

She gaped at him, her chest contracting painfully. How could he be so uncouth and unchivalrous as to point out such things?

"Aren't you going to defend yourself?" He waited for her to spit back one of her barbed insults.

She stuck her nose in the air. "If it does your manhood good to believe such balderdash, why should I try to change your hard head?"

"Don't be afraid of feeling, January," he coaxed, aching with need for her. He lowered his head and his lips brushed her ear. "Give in to your desires. Take a kiss if that's what you want."

There was nothing she'd rather do. She was tortured by the knowledge that if she turned her face just a smidgen, their lips would meet. "I don't have any desires," she denied.

"Oh yes, you do." His warm breath fanned her cheek. "Someday you'll admit it."

"Don't hold your breath. Good, God-fearing women don't give in to bodily cravings."

He didn't know whether to contradict her or not. He had no experience with such women. "Then we'll never kiss again." He sighed. "I won't take anything that's not freely given."

She breathed deeply. Her stubborn pride was strong, but her flesh was weak. Lacking the willpower it would take to push him away, she rubbed her forehead against his jaw in an unconsciously sensuous gesture. She caressed him until her insides became a liquid fire that rushed downward to throb in her secret places.

Forgetting his ultimatum, Case encircled her in his arms. One hand cupped her bottom and pulled her ever closer to the hard length of him. His knee slid between her legs and she gasped when his thigh rubbed that throbbing place.

"Say it, January." His voice was thick with mounting desire. "Tell me you want to belong to me. Tell me . . ." He stopped when a drunk, a railroad man by the looks of him, stumbled into the alley.

The man stared at them curiously, then shook his head in apparent disgust. "Men like you two make me sick!" he told them. "Ain't there enough wimmin in this world to go around? Don't you know what you're doing goes against the laws of God?" He waved his arms dismissively and stumbled on down the alley.

The man's loathing look made Case laugh, but he wasn't about to ease the poor fellow's mind by pointing out his mistake. The interruption was just what he needed to remind himself that this was neither the time nor the place for what had been about to happen.

Not only that, but he wasn't the man for January. He'd never be willing to put down roots and sweat behind a plow. There were too many places to go, too many sights to see. He had no intention of tying himself down with a good woman, so what was the point of tangling the knots even more?

"I shouldn't have done that. I'm sorry. I don't know what came over me." He didn't want to hurt her and he had no wish to inflict further pain on himself. "I had no right."

She noticed the change in Case and her willing confession of just how much she wanted to do all those things died on her tongue. As if she was a fish too small and insignificant to keep, he'd decided to throw her back. The pain of rejection did nothing to quiet the tawdry palpitations of her flesh. She gulped back tears and her voice grew unsteady. "Forget it. We'd better get along. There's no telling when the Buscus gang will wise up and be on your tail again.'' She scrambled out of reach and swung into the saddle.

Case didn't understand how he'd allowed himself to get caught up in such a farcical situation. He'd always been a man in command of his destiny, a man renowned for steely nerves and boundless wit. A man of his talents shouldn't have to be on the run from a bunch of slow-headed farmers. He never should've allowed a little spitfire with a penchant for attracting trouble to get the upper hand.

''Compared to the perils of your companionship,'' he grumbled as they galloped out of town, ''the Buscus brothers would be a welcome relief.''

Chapter 12

They traveled all night and it was nearly noon when they finally reached Joplin, a thriving lead and zinc mining town. January was appalled at the sight of so many saloons, but Case laughingly explained that the large population of miners needed them more than they needed mercantiles and churches. She smiled and an unspoken truce was forged between them.

Riding through town, they passed a big white house with a sign nailed to its picket fence. Case dismounted and tied Shadow's reins to the hitching post, then held up his arms to help January dismount.

"What's in there?" she asked suspiciously, waving away his offer of assistance. She slid off Brownie's back and eyed the place. There were flowers in the yard and a fat yellow cat dozed on the porch, but for all she knew the establishment might be some fancy gambling hall or sporting palace.

"It's the nicest-looking boardinghouse in town. The sign says the rooms are the best accommodations in Joplin and boasts meals beyond compare." When she frowned, he quickly added, "It's reasonably priced."

"You stay here if you want. I'll camp outside of town," she said stubbornly as he entered the yard. "No need to waste good money."

He held the gate open for her. "Come on, it's my treat. It's time we had a proper bath. A place like this will have plenty of clean towels and hot water and fancy soaps to choose from.''

She stood her ground. ''I've never had plenty of hot water,'' she said petulantly. Hellfire, she'd never had plenty of anything and it'd be just one less delight she'd have to learn to do without later. ''But I wouldn't say no to a bar of homemade lye soap to take with me.''

''I want to sleep in a bed instead of under trees and rocks. I'm accustomed to more comforts in life.''

''Well, I ain't.''

''Please.'' He folded his hands in mock supplication and she had to squeeze back the grin she felt coming.

''Nope.'' Her balkiness arose more from fear of the unknown than from thriftiness.

''I'm a city slicker,'' he reminded her, kneeling at her feet and bowing his head melodramatically. ''I've been denied too much lately and I can't take it anymore. Please say we can rent rooms and live like real people for just one night.''

Two little boys peeped around a large tree in the yard next door, then ran giggling into the house. January laughed, tugging at Case's hands, but he stayed where he was until she said, ''Oh, all right. We'll stay, but you'd better get up before the owner sees you acting like this. He'll think you're crazy and won't let you in such a fine place. Then I'll be sleeping under them clean sheets all alone.''

She reddened, suddenly aware of how provocative her words had sounded. The last thing she'd wanted to bring up was their potential sleeping arrangements.

Case sensed her discomfort and, for once, knew better than to tease her about the slip. ''Come on, let's see if they have any rooms available,'' he said, emphasizing the plural.

January sank down in the luxurious suds. She wouldn't be surprised if heaven turned out to be a brass tub filled with hot, lilac-scented water.

"Thank you, Mrs. Randall." The grandmotherly proprietress brought up a kettle of fresh water to rinse January's hair. Modestly, January crossed her arms over her breasts. "It smells so good under all these bubbles, I kind of hate to rinse them off."

"Just call me Ocie." The woman handed her a towel. "That may be, but you'd better climb on out of there. Your man will be back soon and you don't want him to see you all shriveled up and waterlogged." She held the kettle high. "Bend over and close your peepers."

"You don't have to do that, Ocie. I can manage. And just so's you'll know, Case Latimer ain't my man." He'd never belong to any woman as long as he had his wits about him.

"Funny. He acted like he was. He paid me extra to assist your bath and help you get dressed. So bend over and let me earn it."

Knowing all about doing honest work for honest pay, January didn't argue. She'd have a few choice words for Mr. Latimer when she saw him for thinking she couldn't even bathe and dress herself.

"Where's my clothes?" she asked, still clutching the towel in front of her.

"Right there on the bed."

Her eyes widened at the resplendent garments spread out for her inspection. "Those ain't mine. I've never seen 'em before."

"Mr. Latimer sent them up. Said to tell you they're a birthday present."

A birthday present? "What day is it?"

"Why, the thirteenth."

It was her birthday! And Case had remembered. She'd never had a proper gift before. And she'd never had such clothes. Why, they were fit for a fine lady. She eyed them longingly. The delicate fabric and wispy lace didn't look like it'd hold up on the trail very long. "Where am I supposed to wear such a getup?"

"Mr. Latimer is planning to take you out to dinner tonight to celebrate your special day." Ocie smoothed a hand over the frothy underpinnings and waited expectantly.

Her special day? January felt the sting of tears at his thoughtfulness. She'd never celebrated her birthday. It had always come and gone without notice.

"Well, what are you waiting for, dearie?" Ocie held up an elegant pair of lawn drawers, trimmed with row upon row of delicate lace and ribbons. "Not bad for ready-mades," she dismissed. "Of course, a lady lavishes more attention on her handmade things."

"Of course," January agreed absently, though she didn't have the slightest idea what Ocie was talking about.

"It appears he thought of everything from the skin out."

Accepting unmentionables from a man was just the next step down on her descent to perdition, but January was nonetheless touched by Case's misguided generosity. Slipping the garment on, she delighted in the way the soft fabric gently caressed her skin. She donned a matching camisole, thinking it was a shame to hide such beautiful things under a dress.

Suddenly remembering the money sewn into her old drawers, she looked around frantically. "Where's the clothes I had on?"

"In the corner to be washed later."

She heaved a relieved sigh. "If it's all the same to you, Ocie, I'd as soon wash my own drawers."

"Whatever you say." Ocie stepped forward with a piece of stiff white cotton. "Ready to put on your stays?"

January had seen corsets in the mail-order book, but she'd never quite understood their purpose. "I ain't wearin' that," she said resolutely.

"Every lady above the age of fifteen wears a corset. It's highly essential to fashion and beneficial to the female figure."

"I don't see how it can be beneficial to truss yourself up in a contraption like that."

"It rearranges the torso and pushes up the bosom." Placing her hands beneath her own ample breasts, Ocie lifted them to demonstrate. ''It'll make your waist several inches smaller.'' She made as if to fasten it around her large girth, but the Little Pet was designed for young ladies and not stout matrons.

''But how in tarnation does a body breathe?'' January couldn't believe women would willingly subject themselves to such suffering.

Ocie laughed. ''That part takes practice. More than one lady has swooned because her stays were too tight. Want me to lace it up for you?''

''No.'' She gasped in alarm. ''I don't care much for any fashion that says I have to gird up my waist and squash my ribs.''

''Really, Miss Jones.'' Ocie smiled indulgently. ''Don't you care what you look like? My mother always quoted the *Ladies Hand Book:* 'The female who is utterly regardless of her appearance may be safely pronounced deficient in some of the more important qualities which the term ''good character'' invariably implies.' ''

''What's that mean in regular talk?''

''It means you wouldn't want to disappoint Mr. Latimer after he went to so much effort procuring these pretty clothes for you, would you?''

He *had* gone to a lot of trouble on her account and she wondered with embarrassment if he'd selected the clothing himself, though it didn't seem right to wear something next to her bare skin that he'd seen and maybe even touched. She chided herself for her inappropriate sensibilities. Hadn't he seen and touched things more personal than a few scraps of cloth?

''All right,'' she said hesitantly. ''Bind me up. But if it gets to hurting too bad, I'm taking my knife and cutting myself out of it.''

She clutched the bedpost while Ocie yanked and squeezed and laced her into the corset. The older woman explained that the best results were obtained by adjusting the corset while it was damp for a snugger fit. When January was fashionably encased, Ocie stepped back to admire her tiny waist, then picked up a large horsehair pad that looked like a flattened pillow.

"What's that for?" Resigned to her fate, January was no longer amazed by the odd articles Ocie produced. She didn't have the breath to waste on gasps of surprise.

"It's a bustle, dearie."

"What's it for?"

Ocie shook her head and clucked her tongue. "It's worn under your petticoats to effect a fashionable fullness in the rear."

"That's the craziest thing yet!" she exclaimed. "First I squeeze into a corset to make my waist small, then you tell me to wear that thing to make my hind end stick out! It doesn't make a lick of sense to me."

"Fashion rarely does, my dear," Ocie consoled as she secured the bustle in place. "Now slip into these petticoats." She held out a pile of rustling silk taffeta.

"All of them?" January asked in wonder.

"All of them."

Once the underpinnings were in place, Ocie began fussing with January's hair. "I don't know what I'm going to do with this mop. Who performed this desecration?" she asked as her fingers sifted through the short curls.

January wasn't sure about the desecration part, but she was more than willing to take full blame. "I did," she mumbled.

"Whatever for? You didn't have lice, did you?"

"No!" January was indignant. "It was part of my disguise." Since the older woman seemed interested, she gave her an abbreviated version of her flight from Possum Holler, her encounter with Case Latimer, and her subsequent arrival in Joplin.

As she talked, Ocie began trimming and snipping her hair with a pair of sewing scissors. She cut and combed, brushed and primped until she was satisfied with her efforts. Handing January a hand mirror, she asked, "Well, what do you think?"

January stared at the beguiling face peering out at her.

Was that winsome, pretty girl really she? Ocie had arranged her hair in curls on her forehead, sweeping up the sides and creating a fascinating cascade of curls from crown to nape where she'd pinned a cluster of myrtle-green silk roses that matched the dress on the bed. Wispy ringlets dangled saucily over her ears.

"I don't look like myself."

"The style's a bit dated, but what with it being so short, it was the best I could do. Your hair's such a glorious color, no one will even notice how it's arranged," Ocie assured her.

January stared into the gilt mirror for long moments, feeling proud and vain and not even caring that she did. Was this what Case saw when he looked at her? Had he seen past the swaggering, dirty-faced tomboy she'd been and recognized what amounted, God forgive her vanity, to beauty?

Numbly, she allowed herself to be fastened into the silk gown. The neckline was scooped off her shoulders, baring an immodest expanse of bosom. Ocie assured her it was the latest fashion. The polanaise skirt was drawn back with more of the silk roses and draped dramatically from the bustle in back. The fairy gown produced an alluring rustle when she walked awkwardly around the room, sweeping the full skirt from side to side.

"What's wrong, dearie?" Ocie asked when she saw January's frustration. "You look beautiful."

"Just because a cat has kittens in the oven don't make them biscuits. Maybe I look like a lady, but I ain't one. I feel foolish in this fancy getup. I don't even know how to get around in it."

"Maybe we have time for a quick lesson on poise. Put on your shoes and let's get started."

In the tiny, high-heeled kid slippers, January felt more uncomfortable then ever, but after several minutes of Ocie's diligent coaching, she began to think she might be able to face Case after all. When she was deemed ready at last, she gave her teacher an exuberant hug. "Thank you. Don't ever let anyone tell you you can't make a silk purse out of a sow's ear."

"You were no sow's ear, my dear, just a diamond in the rough." Ocie's eyes misted and she covered her emotion by steering January through the door. "Mr. Latimer said he'd be ready and if I were you, I wouldn't keep a man like that waiting too long."

January walked carefully down the stairs in the unfamiliar shoes and paused on the landing. Case, standing in the foyer, looked up as she descended. When his gaze fastened on her, his brooding blue eyes seemed lighter and brighter. Doffing a new black Stetson, he smiled lazily.

"Good evening, Miss Jones," he drawled.

"Good evening to you, Mr. Latimer." Her heart picked up speed, reminding her a little of Brownie's loping gait, and she waited for Case to make fun of her for trying to be something she wasn't.

Case had known the right clothes and a judicious combing would enhance January's naturally good looks, but he hadn't expected such breathtaking results. The dewy-skinned charmer who smiled back at him so shyly was undoubtedly the loveliest woman he'd ever seen.

"You look quite beautiful, Miss Jones, and I'm proud to be your escort tonight." He pulled back his black jacket and reached into his gold brocade waistcoat for his watch. Checking the time, he asked, "Shall we go?"

With one shaky hand trailing the banister, she went down the rest of the stairs slowly, afraid her new slippers would tangle in the voluminous petticoats and trip her up. She carried her paisley shawl and beaded bag with studied casualness, just as Ocie had instructed. "Have you been waiting long?" she asked when she joined him. It sounded like something a coy lady in a myrtle-green silk dress would say to her handsome beau.

Case couldn't get over her appearance and had to concentrate on not letting his reaction show. It might hurt her pride if she thought he was too surprised. The vivid green dress emphasized her flawless complexion and enhanced her elegant bone structure. If he hadn't known better, he'd have sworn there was a high-born aristocrat on some limb of her family tree.

"Yes, I have, but it was worth every minute and more."

"Thank you," she said softly. "For the clothes. You didn't need to buy me anything for my birthday. It was enough that you remembered it." Feeling shy, she smoothed her hands over the folds of her skirt. "I've never had a present as grand as all this." She laughed. "In fact, I've never had a present at all."

"There's a first time for everything, January," he said, thinking that if he showered her with presents from now until doomsday, he could never give her anything as precious as the gift she'd given him in that cave. He took her hands in his.

"I feel like a Christmas goose," she said, laughing nervously.

"You sure don't look like one." The admiration and approval in his voice made her discomfort seem insignificant.

He kissed her cheek and commented on her flattering coiffure. He hadn't thought anyone could tame the wayward mass of curls into anything so elegant. "You're a vision," he said sincerely before opening the door and proudly escorting her to the finest restaurant in town.

Being with Case in such a fancy place made January feel as though she were, for tonight anyway, a grand lady. He'd pulled her chair out and seated her as she'd noticed another man in the dining room do for his wife. She didn't think it would hurt if, just for a little while during dinner, she pretended that's what she was. Case's wife. She was willing to forget he drank whiskey and gambled and womanized, and that surprised her. She hadn't thought there was a man alive who could make her want to forgive his vices.

Although the food was of the highest quality, she scarcely tasted it. She was so worried about embarrassing both of them that she watched Case's every move, duplicating them precisely. When the soup was served, she waited until he selected a silver spoon from the sparkling array of flatware beside his plate. Striving for inconspicuousness, she copied the way he held the utensil and the way he sipped delicately from the side of the bowl. He left a minute portion unconsumed and so did she.

The main course, a thick beefsteak served with buttered potatoes and rich gravy, presented its own problems. She couldn't quite get the hang of holding her meat with her fork, cutting it with her knife, then laying the knife aside and switching the fork from left hand to right. It seemed a powerful lot of trouble to go to when it would so much easier to simply eat it off the point of her knife.

He sensed her dilemma and pointedly ignored the way she mimicked his every move. When he lifted his napkin to his lips, she lifted hers. When he took a sip of water, she sipped. She didn't cut her steak until he cut his, then matched her rate of chewing to his. After a while, he felt he was caught up in some kind of theatrical comedy act, her concentration was so acute. He was tempted to jump onto the table and do a jig, just to see if she would follow suit.

He dared not laugh or draw attention to her exaggerated miming for fear of humiliating her. That was something he'd never do. He enjoyed feeling in charge and having her look to him for guidance for a change. She was as unfamiliar with snowy white tablecloths and dessert spoons as he was with slingshots and fishing hooks.

It pleased him that she was a much faster learner than he.

After dinner they took a stroll, pausing briefly in front of a general store to admire a colorful poster advertising a traveling circus due in town the next day. Case was indulgent at her wonder and interest in the wild animals and performers depicted on the handbill. Tucking her hand securely in his, he guided her across the street to avoid a raucous saloon.

It was late and as they left the busy section of town, the only light came from a big silver-dollar moon.

They reached the boardinghouse and January felt a little tingle on her back where Case pressed his hand against her spine to assist her up the porch stop. Although she didn't need the help, she allowed it, for even such an innocent touch from him thrilled her.

It had been a perfect evening and she hated to see it end. Proudly, she felt she'd given a good accounting of herself in the fancy restaurant. Even though she'd been raised in an environment devoid of the finer things in life, she didn't think any of the other patrons had guessed she was an illiterate backwoods tomboy. Memories of her mother had come to her aid tonight and she knew it was because Daisy had been gentle-raised and had tried to instill some of her good breeding in her daughter that she'd fared so well. Once learned, never forgotten?

"It's a lovely night," Case said. "Would you care to sit outside a spell?" He couldn't bear going into different rooms, separate beds. This would be the first time since he'd met her that there would be anything more substantial than an argument between them.

"Sounds nice," she said, thinking her voice was a bit too dreamy to suit her.

They sat in the porch swing and she fussed with her skirt. Her old dress from home and her britches had never been such a botheration. "There ain't very many stars tonight," she commented inanely.

"No, there aren't," he agreed. "The sky looks as though some housewife might have had an apron full and decided to shake them loose. They look so near, just barely out of reach." That's how he felt about her. Though only a few inches, the distance between them was too great.

Now that they were sitting down, he had no legitimate reason to touch her and he wished they'd kept walking. He folded his hands in his lap and nudged the swing into action with his foot.

"That's a nice thought. It's like a poem." She watched

him cross his black-booted ankle over his knee and was vitally aware that each glide of the swing caused his knee to brush her skirt. She was entranced by the rippling play of muscle in his lean, tightly sheathed leg and had to fold her hands in her lap to keep them from straying where they shouldn't.

They'd made love and Case's hands had been all over her. Now she was filled with a shameful desire to acquaint herself more fully with the feel of him. With every push of his foot, the yearning grew stronger to feel, firsthand, the intimate shift of that muscle.

"We had a good time tonight, didn't we?" he asked, draping his wrist casually over the back of the swing. "We should do this more often. Do you realized there hasn't been so much as one harsh word between us this whole evening?"

"Yes." His hand dangled so near her shoulder that it made her breath come too quickly. Her heart flopped like a fish on dry land and she dared not look at him for fear he'd guess what was happening inside her. "I just remembered something else."

"What's that?"

His voice drew her gaze like a magnet. She turned to him with a smile. "Do you realize that since we met, this is the first town we've been to that you haven't made a beeline to the nearest saloon? You even took pains to cross the street so we wouldn't pass near one."

Case grinned back at her, allowing his hand to touch her shoulder, and was immediately filled with a sense of being where he belonged. Right behind that came the sudden, intense need to get up in the morning and head for Alaska before any more silly notions overtook him. "Maybe we should have gone inside that saloon. Just for old times' sake."

The hand resting on her shoulder made her pulses beat crazily and the blood rush to her head. "That's one bad habit I'd rather not get started, if you don't mind."

"But I do mind. We'd have a lot of fun," he protested.

It sounded so good to him he didn't see how she could possibly refuse. "I could teach you to gamble. We could go everywhere, January. I could show you things you've never dreamed of. We'd make a great team."

It sounded like heaven. Almost. The mere thought of being the other half of any team Case was on was so inviting that she actually considered it. But only briefly. She didn't doubt they'd have fun doing those things together, but it wasn't the life she wanted or needed. "No. I want to settle down, not go from pillar to post with a man as shiftless as Pa. You may have more spit and polish than he does, and you're more successful," she said, aware of how brutal her honesty sounded. "But you're rootless and that don't suit me."

Her words cut him like a razor, but Case shrugged nonchalantly to cover his hurt. How dare she compare him to that despicable father of hers. Donning his best poker face, he drawled, "If you won't go to Alaska with me, how about at least taking in that circus tomorrow?"

She nearly refused. They didn't have time to waste on a circus. Then she remembered the poster with its pictures of elephants and tigers and high-wire artists in scandalous costumes. What was one more day? They were fairly close to her destination and the run was over a week away. What was the harm in spending one more day? One more day of having a good time with Case. She'd have the rest of her life to get used to being without him.

"It'd be a pure dee shame to miss such a spectacle, Mr. Latimer. I'd be proud to go with you."

Chapter 13

The circus didn't quite live up to the thrilling promise of the poster, but even the halfhearted performance of the elderly elephant and toothless tiger couldn't lessen January's enjoyment of the day. She took in the sights with childlike fascination. Case, amused and indulgent, plied her with lemonade and popcorn and spun-sugar candy treats.

Once inside the tent, she insisted on taking a front row seat. She leaned forward expectantly, elbows on her knees, chin in her hands, spellbound by the tired-eyed, second-rate trapeze artists and equilibrists in their shabby, oft-mended spangles. Though Case was unimpressed, the mediocre spectacle drew astounded "ooohs" and "ahs" from January and he was happy because she was happy.

She wore another of the new outfits he'd given her, a soft gray flannel skirt with black braid trim and a white embroidered shirtwaist. The green silk dress had imbued her with an aura of coquettish sophistication, but this prim ensemble with its wide-brimmed straw hat and shiny boots lent all the allure of a schoolgirl playing hooky.

January Jones was an intriguing puzzle, a study in contrasts Case found increasingly bewildering. Her moods were as changeable as quicksilver, her temper awesome. She lived with a fierce and breathless passion that threw him on his beam end and made him fear for the future.

She knew her mind and spoke it. She was bold and absurd, audacious and irrational. She was moralistic, irreverent, self-righteous, and eminently corruptible. She was fractious as a hessian, high-handed, hardheaded, and dear. She was full of flaws which with time would evolve into full-blown personality defects.

She was a beautiful woman who would love long and love hard and demand to be loved back in kind. In a very short time their lives had become inextricably entangled and he knew it would be painful to say goodbye when the time came. And it would come. They could no more reconcile to a mutually satisfying life than a donkey could sprout wings and fly. The two of them were as different as night and day, as at odds as chalk and cheese. He stood for all she disapproved of and she stood for everything he feared.

Case astonished himself by admitting he'd come to care for the happiness and well-being of the child-woman who'd tumbled headlong into his life and changed it forever. Never again could he view the world from quite the same jaded perspective. Never again would he be capable of complete self-interest. Never again could he see a dogwood blossom or eat a fish without thinking of her.

He knew such thoughts were dangerous and banished them from his mind, concentrating all his attention on January and her delight in the broken-down circus.

As they strolled out of the big tent following the last performance of the day, a burly, sharp-eyed man stepped in front of them, blocking their exit. Case took January's elbow and tried to shoulder his way past, but the man drew his gun and made it infinitely clear that he wasn't about to let them go. Because they were momentarily shocked at being accosted in public, it was a few seconds before they realized the significance of the silver star pinned on the man's vest.

"You aren't going anywhere, mister." The lawman's voice was as cold and hard as a December icicle. "You're under arrest, so just come with me quiet-like and nobody will get hurt."

"I beg your pardon." Case yanked his arm out of the

man's grasp, affronted by what was clearly a case of mistaken identity.

"I said, you're under arrest." The man patted him down for concealed weapons while January looked on in horrified fascination. "Come peaceably and you won't get hurt."

"What are the charges?" Case finally asked.

"Is that your black Morgan down at the livery stable?" the flinty-eyed lawman asked.

"It is."

"How long have you had him?"

"About four years. Since when did it become illegal to own a Morgan horse in Missouri?"

"It ain't against the law to own Morgans. But it is to rob stages while you're riding on one."

"Stage? I've held up no stage. Where'd you get such a preposterous idea?"

"Your horse and saddle matches the description given by the driver and passengers, and so do you. It might go easier on you, however, if you tell me where your accomplice got off to."

"What accomplice?" Case still couldn't believe what was happening.

"Don't play dumb with me. The other feller's chestnut is in the stable alongside yours. Where's that little weevil now?"

"I don't know what you're talking about," he maintained, when in reality he was beginning to have a very good idea.

Willard and Lefty must have staged the robbery while in possession of Shadow and Brownie. He and Lefty were both tall and they both had dark hair and mustaches. In her shabby boy's clothing, January and Willard shared superficial similarities. Fortunately, as she was now dressed, no one would ever mistake her for the bandy-legged holdup artist.

January's eyes widened when the sheriff clamped a pair

of handcuffs around Case's wrists. "Sheriff, there must be some mistake," she said.

"Young lady, the only mistake is the one your beau here made when he held up the stage and robbed Wesley Tyrone."

"Wesley Tyrone!" she gasped. "Why, we—"

"Never heard of him," Case finished for her. He trod her foot heavily, indicating with a wrathful look that this was one time she'd better obey him. If she shot off her big mouth, they'd both wind up in the hoosegow.

"Watch where you're steppin', Latimer," she squawked, belatedly reading the warning on his face. She knew him well enough to understand that if she valued her hide, she wouldn't say so much as boo. As much as it pained her, she bit back the words trembling on her tongue. They were in his element now and she'd have to defer to his judgment for a change.

"That's right," she said, batting her lashes at the sheriff in a surprisingly practiced manner. "We never heard of him."

"Save your story for the judge. Lucky for you, Mr. Tyrone was only injured or you'd hang for sure."

Case groaned with the unwelcome knowledge that Willard and Lefty had not only robbed the stage but had also stashed the cache of money in the cave. No wonder the thieves hadn't followed them after January's daring rescue in the saloon. They'd known the law would catch up to them sooner or later. Who would have thought those boneheads could be so clever?

Case studied the sheriff's grim face. Had he already discovered the leather pouch hidden in the bottom of the wardrobe back in his room? If not, the arrest was based on circumstantial evidence that would never hold up in court. But if he had, the presence of that money in his room was enough to see him convicted.

January's thought tumbled. She'd known Wesley Tyrone's money was nothing but trouble. Hadn't she tried to persuade Case to hand it over to the authorities? He'd just laughed at her suggestion, claiming they shouldn't look a gift horse in the mouth, or some such sheepdip. The satisfaction she felt in being right was short-lived.

It didn't take long for her to put the pieces together and figure out Willard's and Lefty's roles in the robbery. Those human skunks were to blame and Case was innocent of everything but poor judgment. But would the sheriff believe him? They couldn't afford any more delays and she was reluctant to ride on and leave him sitting in jail, even if he did have it coming for being so shifty about the money. If only she could talk to him and find out what he thought she ought to do.

"Sheriff, this man's been with me for the past week and I swear he didn't rob no stage." She had to say *something*. Playing dumb as a mop just didn't set well with her.

"That's fine, young lady. You may just get a chance to do your swearing in court."

January and Case exchanged frantic looks as the hard-faced lawman hauled him off to the brand-new, escape-proof brick jailhouse.

After two long hours, Sheriff Ruggles still didn't believe Case, but at least he was listening with some degree of interest. Case went over the story again and again, explaining how Willard's gang had held up him and his traveling companion, stealing everything including their horses. He told how they'd retrieved their property and faced down the men in a Branson saloon.

Throughout the telling, he took pains not to name his companion. At least if he didn't get out of this, January would. When his story failed to convince the sheriff, he related his theory about when the stage had been robbed and by whom.

An honest lawman, Ruggles finally relented and agreed to telegraph Branson in an attempt to verify his story. Case didn't think Rowdy Jane and her barroom cronies would be much help and they weren't worth spit as character witnesses. But he was counting on there having been at least one man with integrity in the saloon that night who would want to see justice done by corroborating the truth.

Meanwhile, Case had no choice but to cool his heels in jail, as panic-inspiring a situation as he'd ever been in. All that day and the next, January moaned about wasted time until the sheriff, obviously as exhausted as Case was by her stomping around, suggested she go have some supper. Case heaved a sigh of relief. Being locked up for a crime he didn't commit was bad enough, but being a captive audience for January's histrionics was cruel punishment, indeed.

January sat in the hotel dining room, her supper growing cold as she stewed and fretted over Case's untimely incarceration. Having right on his side, he seemed confident that it was only a matter of time until he was free, that those toughs in the Branson saloon would be only too happy to vouch for him. Suffering from no such delusions, she was in a high state of aggravated nervosity.

What if the sheriff searched Case's room and found the stolen loot? She had no experience with the justice system, but she understood the phrase "caught red-handed." Not even Case could fast-talk himself out of jail if such incriminating evidence were brought to bear against him.

She had begun to pick at her food when four men entered the dining room and clumped down noisily at a nearby table. She sputtered in her water goblet, her shock was so acute. The newcomers were none other than the Buscus brothers themselves. After much chair-scraping and napkin-tucking, they proceeded to order and promptly consume staggering quantities of food.

Eavesdropping shamelessly, she learned that the men were not at all happy about having been sent on a wild-goose chase by "some dang-fool kid who must have been in cahoots with Latimer."

"I don't like bein' hornscriggled and when I catch up to those two," the eldest of the group vowed, "I'm gonna make that little goslin' holler calf-rope."

"A good hide-tannin' will make him sorry he crossed us, Byrell," another concurred.

"Hell, Carvel, why waste our time thrashin' him?" the third asked. "Let's just drown him for the sorry, rump-sprung pup he is."

The younger of the two couldn't seem to agree on which manner of death would be the most fun to mete out. "Now you're talkin', Jory. Why don't we tar and feather 'em while we're at it?"

"I'm for bashin' 'em about the head with a two-by-four, myself." Jory's eyes glinted with anticipation.

"Nah, too much work," the one called Carvel demurred. "Let's just stomp 'em a good 'un."

Gooseflesh rashed out on January's arms as she listened to three of the brothers debate, with mounting ardor, all cogitable methods of painfully and vilely dispatching her and Case. The fourth diner remained curiously silent during the discussion of their impending dismemberment and ate with his hat pulled down throughout the meal.

"I got an idee Latimer's in this town somewheres," Byrell speculated, "and I aim to find him or die trying. I'm sick of all this gallivantin' around. We got crops to put in and can't afford to squander springtime on a no-account tinhorn like him."

"Yeah, maybe," Jory drawled. "But ain't chasin' Latimer a hell of a lot more fun than plowin'?"

His question was met with general agreement and laughter all around.

Terrified the men would recognize her, January paid for her meal and dashed from the restaurant. After hurrying to Mrs. Randall's boardinghouse, she took the stairs two at a time to Case's room. She tossed his belongings haphazardly into saddlebags, with none of the care he usually lavished on his clothing.

She knew Case didn't have Tyrone's money packet on him or the sheriff would have found it. That meant it had to be here somewhere. Standing in the middle of the small room she chewed a thumbnail and tried to figure out where he had hidden it.

Asking herself where she would have stashed the money if she were Case, she concentrated for a few moments, then with sudden inspiration went to the wardrobe where she triumphantly retrieved the pouch from under some soiled towels.

Lordy, she was even beginning to think like a gambler. What iniquity would she cleave to next?

In her own room, she had to make a painful decision regarding the lovely clothes Case had given her. She couldn't take them all and, with regret, left the fancy green dress and taffeta petticoats behind, taking only the two plainer outfits. There wouldn't be much call for silk dresses and kid slippers where she was going. The corset she tossed aside with delight; if she never saw another one of those torture devices, it would be too soon.

When everything was packed, she sneaked out of the house. She was sorry to leave without saying goodbye to Ocie, but it was for the best. Her new friend would not approve of what she was about to do. January would miss the older woman and her many kindnesses, and though it wasn't likely, she hoped she would get a chance to see her again someday. Ocie had told her that if things didn't work out and she needed someplace to go, she would always be welcome. What Ocie didn't know was that January had a way of *making* things work out the way she wanted them to.

She reached the mercantile store just as the clerk was locking up and persuaded him to reopen for a last-minute sale. She chose two outfits of boy's clothes with little regard to style or fashion and paid for her purchases with two of her precious silver dollars. She couldn't wear dresses on the trail and had to have something practical that was clean and well-fitting.

Surprisingly, she had enjoyed her brief respite as a lady but it was time once again to don her disguise. The livery was deserted so she changed in an empty stall. She enjoyed the freedom the pants gave her as she saddled the horses and led them outside. Sticking to alleys, she was soon out of town.

Being in jail, Case was a sitting duck for those Buscus brothers and it wouldn't be long before they discovered him. Knowing she couldn't just stand by and let them haul him off into holy matrimony with their sister, January made another rash decision.

She rode to the outskirts of town, to a mine company supply shack they'd passed on the way into Joplin. There she waited until the night watchman sauntered into the woods to answer the call of nature, then scuttled inside and snatched up a bundle of dynamite. Recklessly stuffing the explosives inside her coat, she mounted Brownie and galloped back to town, trailing Shadow behind.

Case paced the confining cell, each turn punctuated by a fist smacking into a palm. He was beginning to fear the sheriff would discover Tyrone's money in his room before word came from Branson that would release him.

Even more vexing than worrying about rotting in jail was the fact that January had not been back since she'd left for supper several hours ago. As hot-tempered and harebrained as she could be, there was no end to the mischief she might be getting into. Case was beset with a sense of foreboding.

He was also concerned for her safety. She was alone among strangers in the biggest town she'd ever seen. She was more than self-reliant in the woods, her survival skills as honed as her knife blade, but she had no experience with the kinds of predators that prowled rough-and-tumble mining towns. He raked his hands through his hair and willed her to burst through the jailhouse door.

Case hadn't been able to eat much of the supper the sheriff's wife had sent over and the rangy deputy removed the tray. No sooner had the cell door clanged shut than Sheriff Ruggles stormed in and began yanking rifles out of the cabinet. "There's a big ruckus under way down at the Rusty Plug. The miners are really tearin' the bone out."

"Ah, shit, not again." The deputy checked his ammunition. "We should've closed that hellhole after the last one. What started it this time?"

"I don't know. Best I could make out, some goddamned peach-faced kid waded in and set the Marvel Mine boys against the Little Wonder boys."

"Not that it'd take much to get those gangs to go at it hammer and tongs, but what happened?" The deputy loaded a shotgun with buckshot and shouldered the weapon.

A muscle twitched in Sheriff Ruggles's jaw. "The way I heard it, the kid told one of the Marvels that one of the Wonders called him a sorghum-lappin', ellum-peelin' hog-ranger and that there was so many Marvel miners in hell their feet were stickin' out the winders. That's when the fight started."

"Aw, shit. Those boys don't fight. They just kill and drag out."

The two men ran out, leaving Case to worry about what he'd just heard. He had a cold, sinking feeling about the identity of the peach-faced kid who'd started a free-for-all in the roughest saloon in town. It sounded like January's style. The only question was, why had she done it? What was she up to? She'd never go into a joint like that without a good reason. And what was she doing dressed in boy's clothes again?

Didn't they have enough trouble without her jumping into more with both feet? His pacing grew more frenetic and he strained to peer out the small, barred window. It faced the alley and he couldn't see a thing, but he could hear the sounds of mayhem and destruction rolling down from the Rusty Plug.

"Pssst, Case!" January stepped out of the shadows into the moonlight. "Case, are you in there?"

"January!" Relief that she was alive and unharmed was evident in his tone. That relief was immediately replaced by anger of thunderous proportions. "What the hell is going on? Did you start a riot in a saloon?"

She shrugged dismissively. "I had to. I couldn't do anything with the sheriff and deputy breathing down my neck."

"Just what the hell *are* you doing here?" Case wasn't sure he wanted to know.

"I don't have time to explain." She withdrew a bundle from inside her coat and set it under the window.

"What do you have there?" He scowled through the bars, trying to see what she was up to. "Answer me!"

"Dynamite."

"Dynamite! Where in the hell did you get dynamite?" He'd thought nothing she could do or say would surprise him, but he'd been wrong.

"I stole it from the Little Wonder Mining Company."

Case clutched the window bars, barely maintaining white-knuckled control. "That's just swell. What other crimes have you committed since the last time I saw you?"

Thinking of the bloodbath in the saloon, she smiled sheepishly. "You don't really want to know."

"You're right, I don't. What exactly are you planning to do with that dynamite?"

"I'm gonna bust you out of there," she announced triumphantly.

"Oh no, you aren't. I haven't broken any laws and I won't start with jailbreaking. What's your damned hurry, anyway? The sheriff will hear from Branson in a day or two."

"We ain't got a day or two." She fumbled in her pocket for the matches she'd stashed there.

Case slapped the bars in frustration and anger. The run! She was forever worried about not getting to Arkansas City in time for that cursed land run. "Dammit to hell, January. If it means that much to you, just go on without me. I'll catch up when I get out of here."

"No, you won't."

"What's that supposed to mean?"

"It means, guess who had supper in the hotel dining room tonight?"

"You, I hope."

"Yeah, me and the ever-lovin' Buscus brothers. They're here in Joplin and you don't even want to hear what they've got planned for you when they catch you." She produced the matches with a flourish. "To say nothing of my own disembowelment."

Case thought hard for a moment. So they'd finally caught up with him. Should he risk a showdown or allow January to carry out her preposterous plan? The decision came quickly. "Forget it. I'm innocent of any crime so far and I'll stay here and face the music. An honest man has nothing to fear from the law."

January laughed. "When's the last time you heard of a gambler being held up as a shining example of respectability? Besides, it ain't the law you need to worry about, Latimer. It's those fellers what feel obliged to make their sister a wife and a good widow in one fell swoop. Noble gentleman that you are, I guess you're willing to make an honest woman of Ardetta Buscus and die with a clean slate."

"I'm not afraid of those farmboys."

"Those heavily armed farmboys," she clarified.

"It doesn't matter. I'm not running from them because I'm afraid of what they'll do. I just don't want to have to kill any of the damned fools in self-defense."

"Maybe you should be afraid of them. All this chasing around the country has turned 'em mean. Think about it, Latimer. My way may put you crosswise with the law, but at least you'll be a few steps ahead of your future in-laws."

While he was deciding between the two evils, January took the matter into her own hot little hands. She plucked a match from the box, drew it along the brick wall, and held it aloft. "Take cover, Latimer, all hell's fixin' to break loose."

He was about to protest when she touched the flaring

matchstick to the fuse, clamped her hand on top of her hat, and dashed down the alley.

"January! You get back here this minute. January! January?"

All was silent and he waited impatiently for her reply. Then he became aware of the hissing sound of a short fuse being rapidly consumed by flame. He dove beneath the iron cot not a moment too soon.

The world exploded in red, earsplitting violence that shook the foundation and vibrated deep in his chest. His ears hurt and he feared permanent deafness would result. Falling bricks and crumbled mortar crashed around him and the air was thick with charred splinters, bits of paper, and singed feathers from the mattress ticking.

His eyes smarted from the swirling smoke as he huddled under what was left of the cot, his arms thrown over his head. Coughing as dust and smoke filled his nose, he flinched when the slop jar clanged disgustingly near his head.

"Did I kill you, Latimer?" January called tentatively into the devastation. The explosion had been much worse than she'd expected. She'd only wanted to blow a little hole in the side of the building, not lay waste to the whole damned place.

When Case didn't answer, her worst fears were confirmed. "Latimer!" she screamed desperately. "Please say I didn't kill you."

"Not quite, but you did your damnedest," he called back in a shaken voice. He thwacked his head with the flat of his hand in an attempt to restore his hearing. "Dammit to hell, you've rendered me deaf."

January was relieved he was alive enough to snap at her. "Is that all? Get a move on. Everybody and his pet coon will be here in a minute." She clambered over the debris and ran inside to toss Wesley Tyrone's money bag on the sheriff's brick-littered desk. She passed a wobbly Case on the way out and danged if he didn't look stunned. Hellfire, she hoped none of the bricks had gollywhomped him.

She paused long enough to pat out a few insignificant fires smoldering in the folds of his coat. Then, clutching his arm, she propelled him over the tumbled pile of bricks to the horses. Climbing on Brownie, she urged Case to hurry.

He couldn't believe his own eyes. The whole side of the building was gone. The iron bars of his cell stood intact, but just about everything else had been blown into oblivion. It was a miracle he was alive and in possession of all his bodily parts. "Jesus, woman, you nearly blew me to hell. How much dynamite did you use?"

"I didn't count the sticks," she said in exasperation. "Come on, let's ride." She waited for Shadow to take the lead so Brownie would follow.

"Sticks!" he bellowed. "You mean you used more than one?"

"Hellfire, I ain't no miner. How was I supposed to know how big of a boom it'd make?" She could tell by the murderous look on his face that her reasonable question didn't sound so reasonable to him.

"She didn't count the sticks," he called heavenward. "My God, were you trying to kill me or just maim me for life?"

She pulled herself up smartly in the saddle, insulted by his apparent lack of gratitude. "As a matter of fact, I was trying to keep the Buscus brothers from doing the job."

Case heaved himself onto Shadow and urged the Morgan into a gallop. Under cover of darkness, they rode abreast out of town. "This is the last straw," he yelled above the clatter of the horses' hooves. "Don't you ever save me again. Do you hear me, you hotheaded little incendiary? Don't help me, rescue me, offer me succor, or do me a favor. Do you understand, you nihilistic dynamitard! Don't you *dare* ever save me again!"

January suffered his raving in smug silence, the insults she didn't fully understand rolling off her like water off a duck's back. How the man could carry on when he got wound up! He put on a regular show and if nothing else, she was sure learning a spate of new words.

Let Case holler and cuss and call her names. When he cooled off and his ears stopped ringing, he'd realize just what she'd risked for him and thank his lucky stars for the day they'd met. It was comforting to know she was right and would eventually receive the credit she was due.

But best of all, she thought as they left Joplin's escape-proof jail far behind them, was the satisfaction of having once again saved the bacon.

Chapter 14

"Hellfire, Case, do you really think we should chance stopping here? What if that sheriff is still on our trail?"

Case glared black murder at her and continued to smooth out his bedroll—some distance from her own, she noticed.

"So don't answer me." Peevishly, she flopped down on her own blanket and tucked her legs beneath her, reaching out to the warmth of the campfire he'd built. She hadn't thought she'd ever be willing to spend another night in a hole in the ground, but finding the abandoned mine shaft that afternoon had been a stroke of luck. "I reckon we've crossed into Kansas now, so more than likely the posse has turned back. Is that how you figure it?"

Case didn't trust himself to address her in a civilized tone. He was still angry and shaken from having nearly been blown to kingdom come three nights ago and knew that totally ignoring her was all that kept him from wringing her neck. He didn't like losing control and if he got started again, he was liable to do and say things he'd regret.

"What're you so miffy about anyhow?" January couldn't believe he was still vexed about that little dynamite disaster. "You ain't said a word for hours."

He continued to glower at her, his fine black brows drawn down like a blackbird's broken wing, his lips set in a grim line that issued a clear, though silent, warning.

Maybe she shouldn't push. Maybe she'd caused enough commotion for a while. He was all horns and rattles now, but then, such a close call with his Maker was bound to make a man touchy. He'd get over it. A conniption fit of such proportions couldn't last forever.

Immediately after the jailbreak, he'd given her what-for for several miles. According to him, she was nothing but an aspiring arsonist. She wasn't sure just what being an arsonist entailed, but the way he said it, she knew it wasn't somebody you'd invite home for Sunday dinner and she resented the comparison. She strained toward the fire, watching him out of the corner of her eye, and wished he'd lambast her again. Cursing and meanness she understood; she knew how to fight back in kind. But icy silence was something else.

She'd make him speak to her if it was the last thing she ever did. "Reckon this rain will last long?" she asked conversationally.

He set the coffee to boiling. "Probably." The way his luck was going, it could very well turn into a full-blown typhoon. Sitting out yet another storm with the woman who'd nearly killed him seemed the perfect finale for the melodramatic events of the other evening.

His one clipped-off spoken word was a triumph, but January was never one to leave well enough alone. She considered her next move. She didn't cotton to staying in the shaft, but at least it was dry. The walls weren't closing in on her as they had in the cave and there was plenty of fresh breathing air and light from the fire.

It occurred to her that maybe telling Case about being locked in that long-ago root cellar had banished the ghosts of her fears. She'd never say so because it was such a silly thing to admit, but maybe it was easier to face something dreadful when you were with someone you loved.

They'd shared much more than memories that night and the mere recollection of their lovemaking made her flush hotly. Her pulses skittered and heat swelled up inside her.

Besides helping Case shake off his black mood, a little friendly conversation might take her mind off voluptuary matters. It would also calm her nerves and assuage her hurt feelings. She didn't like being treated as if she was no more significant than a pesky gnat. "No doubt we've lost the Buscus brothers, too."

His response, a brief, sharp glance, was not encouraging. "I figure we're in the clear and it's a straight shot on into Arkansas City," she added.

No answer.

Damn him. "Hey, Latimer?" she sang. When she was sure she had his attention, she prodded, "What do *you* think?"

He shrugged, examined his silver pocket flask, then added a healthy dollop of whiskey to his coffee. Holding the cup with both hands, he stared into the fire like a charmed snake.

If things were different and it wasn't such a snibbling night, she wouldn't put up with the surly company he offered. But it was a gullywasher out there and nobody was going anyplace until it let up.

She tried again. "So far, this has been an uncommon damp and stormy springtime, hasn't it?"

He snorted and his long face informed her he was still as grumpy as a woodpecker with a headache. She made up her mind. Either she'd force Mr. Uppity to talk to her or she'd bust a gut trying.

"You aiming to git drunk?" There was nothing so effective as a simple question to get the conversational ball rolling.

"That, by God, does it!" A muscle twitched in his jaw and Case lost control. "I promised myself I wouldn't talk to you until I could do so with some degree of rationality, but you never quit, do you?"

She met his glance without flinching. "Not while there's a breath left in me, I don't." She poured herself a cup of coffee.

"You're the most unyielding, pertinacious, unregenerate, rock-ribbed female ever born of woman."

When she'd wanted him to talk to her, she'd had English in mind. She didn't understand much of what he'd said, but "rock-ribbed" was an insult if she'd ever heard one. "Now, Case." She struck a coquettish pose, peering at him from beneath quivering lashes. "Such flattery's sure to turn a gal's head."

Eschewing the empty cup for the flask, he saluted her and proposed a toast. "To the slings and arrows of outrageous fortune. Or misfortune, as the case may be." He took a long, steady drink.

"What is it about liquor that makes men spout nonsense?"

"Don't try to weasel out of an argument by changing the subject."

"I wouldn't dream of it. I'll leave all the weaselin' to be done in this outfit to the one best qualified."

"Meaning?" he demanded.

"Meaning it's a pretty currish critter that don't appreciate being sprung from a trap. I think it's called bitin' the hand that feeds you."

He growled like a cornered wolf, then jumped up and stalked a few yards down the tunnel. He marched back and loomed over her. After taking another fortifying sip, he drew a deep breath. "You should be more careful with that viper's tongue of yours," he warned. "The painful poison goes right to the heart of its victim. Someday it might just get turned back on you."

"That's right. Blame me, so's you'll feel better."

He ignored her tart rejoinder. "No, I blame myself for being taken in by a sad-looking ragamuffin I found sprawled in the mud. Since then, that same rash, wrongheaded child has given me nothing but hard times, headaches, and . . ." He'd almost said heartbreak, but stopped himself in time.

Child? January bristled at the slur on her womanhood. Had he forgotten all that had transpired between them in that other hidey-hole? "I never asked you for nothin', especially help. Your own befuddled sense of duty is responsible for durn near every tight spot we've been in, so don't go heaping the dadblamed guilt on me."

He sighed and his smile was forced and tired-looking. "You're right, of course."

She eyed him suspiciously. "I am?"

"Yes. You *didn't* ask for my help. I assumed because you were a young—pardon the expression—helpless female that it was needed. I apologize for being wrong."

January sensed she'd won something but she felt no elation at the victory. "Well," she mumbled, edgy and tense. "Just so you understand how it was. If you hadn't killed that snake and spooked poor ole Brownie right out from under me, I'd be in Arkansas City by now." Alone. She choked on her coffee and didn't know if it was the brew or the thought that was so bitter. Holding out her cup, she demanded, "Give me some whiskey. It's time I found out what I've been missing."

He ignored her, drinking greedily. Why did he even bother to argue or explain things to her? She was an uncomplicated person living in an uncomplicated black and white world. A world where events and people either helped her attain her goal or hindered her and were judged accordingly. A world where a plot of hard-packed prairie was a golden fleece worth fighting for, an end that justified all manner of means.

She was making a mistake, throwing her life away on a dream that didn't exist, that wouldn't be good enough for her even if it did. But she was so uncompromising, no amount of reason could change her mind. How could he convince her to join him and hitch her buggy to a star when she was bound and determined to hitch it to a sodbuster's plow?

"Come on, give me a taste." She nudged his arm with her cup.

"Cut it out."

"I've lived with whiskey all my life and I've never even tasted it. I think it's high time we were properly introduced." January knew she was courting trouble, goading Case beyond reasonable limits, but she felt reckless. Besides, she needed something to take her mind off wanting him to kiss her.

"What's the matter with you?"

"I don't rightly know. I haven't felt like myself since I met you. What a black day that was. If you hadn't seduced me and assured me of a place in the devil's band—"

His words were low and mocking. "Never has anyone been so willing to be ruined as you were." Out of spite, he poured most of the liquor into her cup.

She was shocked that he'd called her bluff, then reminded herself that he was, after all, a gambler who took chances for a living. "I was innocent. I didn't know—"

"Don't give me that. You knew very well what you were doing. You're just too cowardly to admit your own feelings."

"I ain't a coward!"

"No, you're the most fearless woman I've ever met. You'd square off with a grizzly armed with a hatpin, jump into a roaring river to save your hat. You'd marry a stranger in cold blood, someone you care nothing about, just to get what you want. But there's a big difference between fearlessness and courage."

She stared at him, taking in what he'd said. "Is that a fact?"

"It is. A fearless person doesn't acknowledge danger, won't admit limitations or weaknesses. A fearless person denies the obvious and never accepts the possibility of defeat."

The way he put it, being fearless meant being stupid. She didn't like the implication. "So?"

"A courageous person understands danger, knows it intimately, and fears it. He lives with it and it becomes a part of him. He knows what's at stake, knows that in a confrontation with that which he fears he just may lose. But because he has admitted his terror, he can never really be defeated."

Her eyes narrowed as she worried his words in her mind. It was a compelling notion that admitting your fears could make you brave. Her mind, acute and restive, had never been challenged by ideas. It had always been too busy with survival.

He went on. "You're a passionate woman who rejects that passion. But you can't make it go away by denying that it exists."

She didn't like talking about things like passion. It wasn't seemly. "And you can't make something real just by saying it's so."

He sighed and stared into the fire. "Apparently not. I guess we've reached an impasse."

She didn't know what an impasse was, but his air of resignation told her the discussion was over. She'd gotten him to talk to her, so why didn't she feel any satisfaction? She didn't like how quiet and thoughtful he'd become.

She could handle his anger—she'd grown up dealing daily with a father whose bad moods, or the severity of them, depended on the amount of whiskey he consumed. She learned early how to badger him into noticing her, and though getting Pa's attention usually meant being cuffed around, a hard biscuit was better than no biscuit at all. So she learned to duck when the blows came, to sass from a distance, and to have the last word.

What she couldn't handle was tenderness. It was something she'd always longed for without really knowing what it meant, like a bird hatched in a cage longs for freedom. But like that bird, when finally faced with her heart's desire, she was frozen by uncertainty, her wings untried and weak. She reacted in a time-tested fashion.

"All this talk about fearlessness and courage is well and good, but I've got some ideas on the subject myself."

Case looked up, his eyes widening.

"Hell's bells, don't look so surprised. I've got a mind and it does get ideas sometimes. I think the world is divided up into two sides."

"That landowners and everybody else?"

She gave him a look that told him she didn't appreciate his sarcasm. "No. The doers and the watchers. The doers take what they want, so long as they don't hurt nobody doing it,'' she qualified. ''And the watchers sit back and let 'em. Nobody gives nobody nothing in this life.''

''That's a mighty callous opinion coming from one so young.''

''Calloused or not, it's true. I figure that's where we're different.''

''It's an interesting theory, one deserving of further debate. But I'm too tired to do it justice tonight. Just be quiet for once in your life, January, and let me rest.''

''Ain't that just like a man! Get a woman riled up, then beg out of the tussle.''

''Don't goad me. I'm fighting mad already and I've had just about enough from you.''

''I'm fit to be tied my own self.'' She saw a spark of emotion in his eyes and knew she was close to prodding him into action. She couldn't bear to see him sit around like a schoolmaster spouting scholarly ideas. It wasn't becoming.

Without thinking, she jumped to her feet and thrust her fists out before her in a boxer's stance, bouncing her weight from one foot to the other. ''Where I come from, that there would be took as a challenge to go to Fist Holler. You want to fight, let's get after it.''

''Don't be silly. I refuse to spar with a female.'' He pursed his lips sternly, trying not to grin at her antics.

She playfully punched him on the arm. ''Come on, you old spoilsport, you said you were *fighting mad.* So get your dukes up.''

''Absolutely not.''

A chuckle escaped under the guise of a cough, but she'd caught that teasing twinkle in his eyes—he was laughing on the inside. ''Aw, come on, Latimer,'' she teased, faking jabs to his stomach. ''I thought you were a sportin' man.''

''Cut it out.'' How did she do it? One minute, she had him so furious he wanted to throttle her. The next, she made him want to laugh out loud. And the next . . . well, she just made him want.

''What's the matter? Afraid I might lick you?''

"Maybe I'm afraid you won't." Case's tone held a suggestive challenge.

January's cheeks flamed when she realized her innocent question had a suggestive double meaning. Judging by the lusty gleam in his eyes, her playful attempt to improve his mood had set his mind on those same voluptuary matters she'd been trying to forget.

Case laughed at her acute embarrassment and drew her to his chest, holding her in a relaxed embrace. He held her lightly while giving every indication he wouldn't be averse to further dalliance. Clearly, the choice was hers but at the moment, it was one she couldn't bring herself to make. Endeavoring to resist his roguish charm and lowering lips, she backed away. "That ain't fightin' fair and you know it."

Still wearing that rakehell grin, he shrugged. "I never claimed to be a fighter."

"Just like that? No fisticuffs? I win?"

"You win."

"Are you still upset with me?"

He nodded.

"Well, hellfire, didn't we settle that? All I done was break you out of jail. How ungrateful can a body get?"

"For starters, I am now a wanted man. Thanks to you."

She began to tell him he'd always be wanted, at least by her, but the declaration died in her throat.

"We're talking wanted posters, January. My picture is probably on its way to every sheriff between here and New Orleans."

"That wasn't my doin'."

"Wasn't it?"

When she failed to answer, he continued. "If you hadn't interfered, I'd have been cleared of those trumped-up charges by now." He took up his flask for another swig, building up steam. "But no. All you could think about was yourself and that damned land run."

"I was thinking about you," she insisted. "If the Buscus boys had run across you laid up in jail, you'd be a married man by now."

"I told you before, I'm not afraid of those boys. I can outwit them and outshoot them anytime."

"I never said you couldn't."

"I left Hot Springs because I chose to. I didn't want to kill those boys then and I still don't. Thinking back, though, maybe I should've winged one of them as a warning of what would happen if they persisted."

"You know what they say about hindsight. And about violence begetting violence."

He laughed. "You're a fine one to talk about violence. You're the one who just blew up a brand-new jail. Now, that's what I call violence." He swigged on his drink.

"You're just sore because you didn't think of usin' dynamite your own self."

"Only an idiot would have done what you did."

"I did it for you and all you've done is holler at me. For all I care, you can go back to Hot Springs, or to Alaska, or straight to hell, you damned ingrate."

"Ingrate! My ears and reputation will never be the same. Not only that, but you nearly blew my head off. As well as your own." That was the crux of the problem, he realized. His fearful concern for her. "What I'd like to know is, why did you have to use so much?"

"I told you. I'd never seen that stuff before. I only had three or four little ole sticks. How was I supposed to know it was enough to send us to glory?"

"Even if the sheriff uncovers the truth about the stage robbery, he's not going to take too kindly to having his jail demolished. By breaking me out and leaving that money, you gave him all the evidence he needs to prove me guilty."

"That money had to be returned to its rightful owner." Maybe she'd done everything all wrong, but she'd only been trying to help. The devil take him. "I was stupid enough to think you'd be glad I'd saved your miserable hide."

"There you go again." Since he'd met her, his manly

pride had taken a profound beating. "Maybe I could've handled it myself. Did you once stop to think about that? I'm a full-grown man and it might surprise you to know that I've been taking care of myself for a long time now."

"You could've fooled me." He made her so mad she could spit fire and she wasn't even warmed up. "If your brains weren't all in your britches, you wouldn't be in this mess anyhow."

His look of astonishment was genuine and her fists relaxed at her sides. She'd gone too far lashing out at him that way and with such an untoward remark! She hung her head and tried a tentative apology. "I'm sorry, Case. I didn't mean it."

That was a first. As far as he knew, she'd never apologized before and he realized how much it must have cost her. Trying to make light of the tense situation, he gave her a teasing grin and snapped his fingers as though she'd just imparted information he'd long been seeking. "So that's where my brains are. I was beginning to wonder myself."

Her smile started slowly, then spread upward and outward until she was laughing out loud. Then Case was laughing, too, and they fell into each other's arms. They laughed at themselves and at each other. They laughed at the twisted sense of humor fate had displayed in bringing such disparate souls together. They laughed at the storm, the night, and the world.

At long last they sank down beside the fire, still touching, intensely aware of that other heat building between them. After long moments, Case released the tension. "So much laughing and scrapping makes a man thirsty." He gestured at January's brimming cup. "Are you going to drink that or throw it in my face?"

"I'm gonna drink it." She snatched it up hurriedly to keep it from him.

Case watched in openmouthed surprise as her shaky hands turned the tin cup to her lips and she gulped its contents. "Hey, take it easy with that stuff."

His warning came too late. Now she knew why whiskey

was referred to as firewater. It burned all the way down. The explosion that resulted when it assaulted her stomach resembled the one back in Joplin, though she didn't let on. Her eyes smarting with tears, she wiped her mouth with her sleeve as she'd seen Pa do many times.

Case leaned toward her. "You all right?"

"Why wouldn't I be? And what do you care?" She took another sip, a smallcr one this time.

"I do care. And I'm sorry. I never thought I'd see the day Hard Case Latimer would have to caution January Jones about spirits." He sighed melodramatically. "Is there no end to the wickedness and corruption I've dragged you into? Being in my company has reduced you to dynamiting jails and allowing demon drink to pass your innocent lips. I should be horsewhipped."

"You should take to the stage." Stifling a ready grin, she excused her actions. "It's purely for medicinal purposes. I'm colder than a spinster in December."

Case laughed as he took the cup and diluted the spirits with coffee. "It'll go down easier this way."

January took a tentative sip and found it surprisingly good. Generously, she made an offer. "Want some?"

After a moment of nervous silence, he leaned forward and sipped from her cup. They stared deeply into each other's eyes. His gaze left hers only long enough to set the cup aside. He turned back to her and held her hands in his. "You might be cold, but the possibility of your ever being a spinster is nonexistent."

She hoped he wouldn't notice her trembling. "Because of . . . because we've known each other?" At his puzzled frown, she explained, "In the biblical sense."

"Not just that." His eyes gleamed with a message that warmed her blood and made her heart thrum. "Because you're a beautiful woman," he said softly. "Even when you're dressed like a man." Wrapping her in his arms, he kissed the top of her head.

She nestled her cheek against his chest, overjoyed that

his heart was racing as erratically as her own. "I wouldn't think a rock-ribbed woman could be beautiful."

Squeezing her, he laughed delightedly. "I didn't mean that literally and you know it. But you have to admit that you can be pretty stubborn at times."

Placing her hands on his chest, she leaned back, peering up at him. "But why were you so mad at me? About the jail, I mean?"

Cupping her face in his hands and leaning into her until their noses touched, he confessed his concern. "You could have been hurt." He kissed the tip of her nose, her temple. "I couldn't bear to see you hurt on my behalf. I wouldn't want to be responsible for ever giving you pain."

His frankness made her snatch up the cup and gulp the fiery contents. In the process she splashed some over the edge.

"Be careful, you're spilling it. That's all I have left and, considering the circumstances, it promises to be a long night."

"You men are all alike, never thinkin' past your pleasures."

"Maybe I won't have to worry about them so much now that you're finally thinking about them for me."

She grinned. "Go to hell, Latimer."

He grinned. "Come with me?"

It was a request, a challenge, a provocative invitation. Oklahoma seemed far away. The sheriff and the Buscus brothers faded in and out of her mind like smoke on a blowy day. All she could see, hear, smell, touch, or taste was Case and the wondrous loving his twinkly blue eyes promised. He'd said he would never force her but his power over her was undeniable as she searched for his lips beneath the silky mustache.

"Don't be tender, else we might end up in another brawl."

He groaned, his lips brushing her neck. "I can't think of anyone I'd rather wrestle. Can you?"

"No." With his lips so near, she couldn't think of anything else at all. She knew it was shameful the way her mouth yearned for his and her body clamored for his touch. She knew her overwhelming need made her no better than the floozy she'd accused him of making her. She knew she should stop. Lordy, how she knew. But she ignored the warning voices within her. One whispered, *Don't do it, this man can never be yours*. Another, prompted by her traitorous desires, demanded she take full advantage of the moment, conscience be damned.

The devilish suggestions were much more tempting, so she grabbed Case by the hair and guided his lips back to where they belonged—on her own. The air around them grew close and heated. His tongue danced, dueling with hers as he massaged her back. She plastered herself against him, yearning for more warmth, more contact, more . . .

He gasped when her frantic hands burrowed beneath his shirt and tangled in the mat of hair on his chest, then moaned his pleasure. Her leg twined with his and she writhed sinuously over him. Her eyes were open, filled with the deep and glorious passion he'd always known was there. "January . . ."

"Shut up, Latimer. You talk too much." She covered his face with kisses, her tongue flicking erotically over his skin. When he tried to hug her to him, she clasped his wrists in her hands and forced them back until they were pressed down on the blanket. Feeling the fire rage up, she was frantic to feel his bare skin against her own.

"January," he moaned.

He assisted her out of her clothing and she longed to indulge herself likewise, but he couldn't wait for her shaking hands to do the job. Soon they were naked on the blanket beside the fire.

She shuddered as he moved over her, his lips, eyes, and hands teasing her to unheard-of heights. His eyes smoldered with need for her and she decided that, if loving Case meant going to hell, maybe heaven wasn't meant for her.

Chapter 15

After their exhausting lovemaking, Case pulled his lips away from hers and nestled them against the pounding pulse in her neck. "I don't want you to go to the Territory," he admitted softly. "I can't bear to think of you married to a dirt farmer."

She couldn't bear the thought of being married to anyone except him, but since he wasn't asking, a dirt farmer was her only hope. "I don't like depending on men, never have. But I don't have much choice. A woman alone don't stand a chance in this world." She leaned back and their gazes met and held.

Case smiled, his look consuming. "That may be true of most women, but it hardly applies to you."

"I don't have any learning. I can't teach school or work in a shop. I can't sew fanciwork and I can only cook enough to keep from eating it raw. All I know is farming. But I'm good at that. I know land and animals and I'll make a good farmer's wife."

"I've never met anyone like you."

"No, I don't reckon you have," she agreed softly. "Us unregenerate, pertinacious females are as scarce as hen's teeth."

Her quick mind was a constant source of delight to him. "I've never met anyone as beautiful as you, January. You're pretty on the inside where it counts most. Out of your headstrong impulsiveness comes loyalty and strength. Those are traits becoming in a woman. I admire you."

She couldn't believe her ears. Had he just paid her a compliment? "You do? Really?"

He nodded and a quirky grin forced the end of his mustache to stretch toward his dimple. "You're very rare, very special. Why not come with me? Alaska is as wild and untamed as you are. We could oversee the making of history together."

Heart racing and pulses pounding, she actually considered it, briefly, before coming to her senses. She was being propositioned again, but it wasn't the one she wanted to hear. Even if she were foolish enough to call his bluff, what would happen to her when he grew tired of overseeing history being made? What then?

After all, she was an illiterate girl from the hills and he was a refined gentleman from a good family. If he ever decided to give up gambling and settle down, it wouldn't be on no hardscrabble farm. It would be somewhere bright and clean and perfect. And she could never fit into a life lived in such a place.

"I may be impulsive and wild, but I ain't crazy. What kind of life would I have traipsing after a gambler, spending my nights in saloons, my days in cheap hotel rooms? Living in tall cotton when the cards were right, in the gutter when they weren't? No, I can't go with you," she murmured sadly. She turned her back to him, needing to put some distance between them.

"Sure you can. There's nothing holding you here." He rolled her over to face him.

"Just because we've . . . *known* each other ain't no call for you to go thinkin' I'd want to be a gambler's doxy. I'd just as soon enter the frail sisterhood. Which is what I'd have to do when you got tired of me."

At first he was hurt by her vehement protests and by the fact that she had so little faith in him. But she'd formulated objections, so she'd obviously been thinking about it. Was she weakening? "But we'd be together," he coaxed. "Would that be so bad?"

"That ain't it." She sat up and wrapped herself in the

other blanket. "You just don't understand and that's what makes it all so hopeless. I need a place to call home because I've never had one. I want land of my own that nobody can't never take away from me. A place where I can put down roots and raise a family.

"I want to be one of them gum-suckin' old ladies that sit in the shade at family get-togethers and bore her kinfolk with tales of the old days. I want to be a mama, a grandmaw, and a great-grandmaw and see the fruit of my labors grow and multiply and fill up the world. I come from nothin', Case, but I want to leave somethin' behind. Can you understand that at all?"

Her words touched him and he found himself thinking about being the gum-sucking old man in the rocker beside her. He shook his head. It was a pleasant enough picture, but it wasn't how he had his life planned. He wanted freedom. Freedom to come and go as the spirit moved him. Freedom from the chains of love and family. "I just don't see why you're so set to get to the run when you can't even participate."

"But you could," she said brightly, suddenly filled with inspiration. "Why don't we get hitched? It's the answer to everything."

He clenched his jaw and felt a muscle quiver there. He opened his mouth, but nothing came out.

January hastened to explain. "You're over twenty-one. If we're married, you can make the run for me."

He was appalled. Not by the idea of marrying January. If he was going to get married, she was as good a choice as anyone else. But the thought of willingly undertaking the role of a sodbuster was ridiculous and he told her so.

"You've got some romantic delusions about a homesteader's life, but you don't know anything about it."

"And you do?" She drew herself up haughtily.

"As a matter of fact, I spent some time on the plains of Kansas once. Not as a matter of choice, but I was hurt in a saloon brawl and a very nice farmer took me home with him to recuperate. You can't imagine the poverty."

"Oh, can't I? Just how luxurious do you think my life was back in Possum Holler? I think I'm on closer terms with poverty than you."

"Perhaps so, but the prairie is a far cry from the Ozarks. The brown horizon goes on forever and the summer heat is as relentless as the freezing wind in winter. There's no lumber available so homes are dug out of the sides of claybanks. I can't see myself living in a windowless hovel that drips mud when it rains and spiders and insects when it doesn't."

He looked at her. "Do you know what squaw wood is?"

She gave her head a quick shake.

"Squaw wood is another name for dried cowchips. Can you imagine keeping warm during frigid winters by a fire fueled with cowchips?"

"I've done and heard of worse."

"Well, I haven't. I have plans for my life and they don't include taking time out to break my back busting virgin sod with a flimsy plow. Any crops you manage to coax from the unforgiving ground probably won't survive the droughts. That is if the locusts and prairie fires don't get them first. No, January. The life of a homesteader is not for me."

The painful depiction he presented was a mocking insult. It sounded worse than what she'd left behind in the holler. Maybe the cabin was so small you couldn't cuss a cat without getting hair in your mouth, but it was above ground and watertight. The wild woods and streams teemed with life, so unless a body was too lazy to hunt and fish, he never had to go hungry.

Her life had never been easy and she knew she could adapt to the hardships of the prairie, but she would miss the Ozarks. She'd never thought about being poor and doing without when there was so much beauty free for the seeing. A turtle taking the sun on a riverbank was a simple springtime pleasure. She found joy in the fleeting wonder of the bloodroot flower whose single, starkly white bloom lasts but a day. The dogwood tree offered its riches twice; once in May, when its blossoms turned the woods white, and again in fall when it was heavy with bright red berrylike fruit.

How she'd miss the old eight hooters, the great horned owls whose evening call of eight notes echoed around the cabin in an eerie lullaby. The melody of the woods was rich and varied; besides the songbirds, the slap of a beaver's tail on water, the distinctive "gobble-up" of the wild turkey, even the sleep-piercing bobcat's cry were all part of the wild symphony.

She hoped there would be whippoorwills in Oklahoma. She'd grown up listening to that chunky little bird who was said to be a predictor of the future and a grantor of wishes made on the first call heard in the spring. It was accepted in the Ozarks that the listener who shouted at the bird upon hearing the first call of evening could predict the length of his own life by counting the number of times the bird continued to call.

Accordingly, January expected to live at least two hundred and twenty-two years.

Without such beauty, she would, indeed, be poor. Without Case, she would be very lonely. She didn't much miss Pa. He'd never taken up room in her heart and had squelched any overtures of warmth she'd ever tried to make. She felt only the smallest twinge of sadness that she would probably never see him again and that was prompted more by pity than love.

She did long for her mother and unknown sister, but she knew it was unrealistic to ever hope to be reunited with them. Knowing she would lose Case set up an uncharacteristic flow of self-pity and she was tempted to roll into a ball and give way to the tears and misery welling up inside her. Then one look at his face sparked her anger and changed her mind. He'd been looking through her as if she weren't there at all.

"I know you're too fine a gentleman for such a life. Forgive me for insulting you with my proposal of marriage. I was just trying to come up with a sensible solution. After all, married to me, no matter how distasteful that might be, you wouldn't have to go back to Hot Springs and Ardetta Buscus. I can see you prefer to take your chances with her trigger-happy brothers than be stuck with me."

"January, that's not it. I'm a rambler. I can't see myself locked up in marriage."

"Locked up? You make it sound like some kind of jail sentence."

"Isn't it? Maybe the bars are made of pickets instead of iron, but it's a prison just the same."

"A picket-fence prison? Is that what you think?"

"I always have."

"Well, go to hell, then. I never intended to lay claim to you—only to the land, which is all I ever wanted anyhow. I never thought to try and hold you. Once I was settled, you'd have been free to go on your merry way. I figure the Land Bureau wouldn't kick a poor abandoned wife off her claim if she met all the requirements."

So she thought he was the kind of heartless bastard who could go off and leave a woman on her own in that godforsaken land. He'd always prided himself on being a man of principle and honor. A lot of good those worthy attributes did in a confrontation with January Jones.

"No," he said firmly, angry that after all they'd been through together, she didn't know him better. "The idea's not only ludicrous, it's unthinkable. I'm not going to Oklahoma and neither are you."

"The hell you say! I'll go anywhere I please. You're not my boss!" Stung by the humiliation of his adamant rejection, she took refuge in anger. "I spent the first part of my life with a low-down, hard-drinkin', card-crazy skunk. I sure ain't thrilled about tying myself to another one. I was just thinking to help you, that's all."

"Don't trouble yourself." He congratulated himself on the touch of cold indignation in his tone. Amid the red dust of his fury, he felt the unwelcome stirrings of physical craving and knew he had to get away from her. What he needed were spirits to numb the pain of needing her and knowing he couldn't give her what she wanted so desperately.

"Hard-drinking, card-crazy skunk, huh? Never let it be said that Case Latimer ever disappointed a woman." He yanked on his clothes, then stalked over to his saddle and hefted it and his gear to his shoulder. Snatching a flaming stick from the fire, he took off toward the back entrance where they'd left the horses.

January clamped her teeth down on her lower lip and stifled the urge to run after him, to beg him not to leave without her. "Are you running out on me?" she called defiantly, her hands on her hips.

Case stopped dead-still and lowered his head for a moment, but when he turned to face her, there was an element of sadness in his eyes. "No," he said quietly. "I'm fresh out of whiskey and all out of patience. I find your company requires an abundance of both. I'll be back after I've had some time to think." He walked on.

"Latimer? Aren't you forgetting something?"

He stopped again, certain that if he turned around and saw her holding her arms out to him, he'd forget all about the whiskey, the soddies, the cowchips, everything. "What?" he asked with a satisfied smile on his face.

"Your gosh-damned boots!" She tossed them down the passage and they landed with a splash in a puddle.

He muttered curses under his breath, jammed his feet into them, and strode away, squishing with every step.

Satisfied that she'd had the last word, she shrugged as if it made absolutely no difference to her if he never came back. His torch was barely out of sight when the keening wind wailed through the passage, sending shivers up and down her spine.

"Damn you, Case Latimer." Her curse echoed in the empty chamber. January collapsed to her knees on her bedroll. At first she wept silently into her hands, then she began to whimper softly, until her sobs became agonized moans of despair.

She wept for herself. She loved him, yet she would lose him and the thought was enough to tear her heart out. She cried for Case, because he didn't love her back and wasn't farsighted enough to see that he needed her in his own way just as much as she needed him.

She soon grew tired of weeping, for she'd learned long ago that tears solved nothing and self-pity was a waste of time. Did she want Case enough to fight for him? Yes, God help her, she did.

Did she want him enough to accept him on his terms? No. She'd have to make him come around to her way of thinking. Men were so easily influenced by their "passions," as he called it, that there were sure to be ways to get around minor differences such as they shared. January was proud of the fact that if she was anything, she was resourceful. In the past when she'd been faced with a problem, she'd blundered into it and hope for the best.

"Why should this disaster be any different?" The words, spoken in the cryptlike closeness of the shaft, rattled her more than the ghostly wailing of the wind.

From a tiny thought, a plan began to take form. She dug into her pack. There had been only one period of time during their short acquaintance when they hadn't been fighting tooth and toenail. When they'd been in Joplin and she'd worn the pretty dresses Case had given her, he'd treated her with caring and respect.

Those too-few and too-short hours had been sweet, filled with fun and laughter. They'd discovered they truly liked each other despite their differences and they'd been happy for a little while. She'd wash up and put on a dress and her best ladylike behavior. When Case returned, they'd talk quietly and laugh about their silly quarrel. Her plan included making the most of whatever time they had left together and maybe, just maybe, he'd come to his senses and change his mind about being a farmer.

But what if it didn't work? She wouldn't be any worse

off than she was right now. No, she'd make it work. She had to show Case that there was more between them than fussing and kissing, that they had a future together and, like it or not, there was nothing he could do about it. Maybe she wasn't a genteel Southern lady like his mother had been, but she would be a good wife.

She'd love him and bear his children and do for him for the rest of his life, if only he'd give her a chance. She'd be as faithful as an old hound, as hardworking as a mule. Why, a man would be lucky to have her!

Amazed that she no longer found the close walls of the gloomy mine menacing, she washed with water from her canteen and dressed in the plainest of the three outfits Case had given her for her birthday. It was a blue-sprigged calico with a ruffled collar, a demure, wifely dress, exactly what she should be wearing when she next encountered him.

She worried that it was *too* right. That her intentions would be so obvious, he'd think she was foolish for hitting him over the head with them. Then she admonished herself. A gal could never look too sweet and innocent. She fluffed her curls with her fingers, wrapped the paisley shawl more tightly around her, and settled down to await his return. She hoped he wouldn't come back so drunk he'd ruin her scheme.

These were high stakes and she was a novice when it came to gambling, but she loved him. Her niggling conscience insisted that her heart and her pride were too much to risk, and warned that she was being a little sneaky. She had to try, she thought as her eyelids grew heavy. If she didn't, she'd never forgive herself.

The storm finally blew itself out and she fell asleep listening to the constant drip of water from the ceiling.

A little while later, she was startled awake by the sound of someone stumbling down the shaft. Instinct told her it wasn't Case. The fire had long since burned down and she hurriedly kicked up dirt to cover it. Plucking out a stick, she blew on it until it flamed feebly and gave her enough light to quickly gather her belongings and retreat into the recesses of the mine. She hoped whoever was coming didn't know about the rear entrance where Brownie was tied.

By the time she reached her horse, January realized the tunnel carried and amplified noises. She heard angry voices which she recognized as belonging to the Buscus brothers.

Hellfire, not again! She was good and weary of the brothers' unwelcome persistence. She didn't like it, but it seemed that warning Case was becoming a way of life for her. She'd have to find him fast and be quiet about it. If she could hear them, it stood to reason they might hear her and become suspicious enough to investigate. Stealthily, she saddled Brownie in the dark and led him out the tunnel and down the muddy, rocky trail before she dared climb onto his back.

She couldn't find any tracks—the storm had taken care of them—but she had an idea where Case might be. They'd passed a sprawling mining camp and she suspected he had doubled back to patronize the tavern there.

Once she'd located the camp, she stopped to change into her boy's clothes. A lone female in such a place might give all those miners wicked thoughts and that could prove disastrous. But in the rearranged clothing, the first thing she pulled out was the horsehair bustle she'd absentmindedly included when she'd packed. Maybe it wasn't so frivolous after all.

Hoisting up her skirt, she tucked the pad beneath her breasts and fastened it upside down around her waist. Positioned as it was over her stomach, it simulated an advanced state of pregnancy. In such a state, she was certain to be safe from even the most evil-minded miner.

It wasn't difficult to find the saloon. It was the only place in camp where lanterns still glowed and a few saddled horses dozed outside the entrance. It was a jerry-built false-fronted building constructed of unpainted pine and its doors were propped open with empty rum kegs. Mustering her determination, January picked her way into the rough establishment with all the obvious distress any self-respecting mother-to-be should exhibit.

She paused inside the door, taking it all in. She was gawking, but she'd never seen anything quite so sordid, even in her undesirably vast experience with dens of iniquity. Evidently intent upon keeping peace, the bald bartender hulked behind the rough-hewn bar, a pistol stashed in a glass within easy reach. A small number of customers, miners from the rough look of them, drank, gambled, and consorted with fast women. Much to her dismay, there was no sign of Case.

"You lost, sugar?" asked an aging, kohl-eyed slattern who strolled up beside her.

"I . . . I . . ." January didn't quite know how to begin. Case wasn't here. Did that mean he'd skipped out on her? Had she passed him in the night without knowing it? Was he on his way back to the mine or had he already been ambushed by the Buscus brothers? Would she ever see him again? Much to her surprise and embarrassment, her eyes filled and tears spilled down her cheeks.

"Now, now, don't cry." The woman's arms embraced January's shoulders comfortingly. "Come over here and tell Goldie all about it, sugar. What's your name?"

"January Jones."

"Don't you cry now, Mrs. Jones." A scruffy-looking but polite miner hastily vacated his chair for her. "We'll help you find that husband of yourn."

January was touched by the kindness with which she was being treated and felt a twinge of guilt that she had deceived such nice folks. Her tears had begun sincerely enough, but they now seemed a mockery. However, she recognized sympathy when she saw it and knew she could use all she could get.

She sobbed anew, as if all the tears of a lifetime had been stored up behind a suddenly weakened dam. She'd done more crying, real and otherwise, since she'd met Case than in her whole previous life. But then, she observed wryly, she'd had more to cry about.

"I ain't married," she blubbered. At least she could set some of their misconceptions straight and create a more pathetic picture in the process.

"Just go ahead, sugar. Cry it all out." Goldie motioned for the bartender to join them.

"I never cry." Her voice came out all quivery and she snuffled. "Not usually, anyhow. I just don't know what's got into me lately."

The bartender, setting a bottle and a glass in front of her, stared meaningfully at January's protrusion. "We already know *what* got into you. The question is *who?*"

"That ain't no way to be talkin' to a lady, Burt. She's upset enough." Goldie frowned at him and his handlebar mustache drooped.

"I didn't mean no disrespect, miss, I surely didn't," he said sincerely. "Now, you just tell me which one of these low-livin' debauchin' miners is to blame for your delicate condition and Burt will mop up the floor with him."

Cheeks burning with embarrassment, January lowered her gaze. "It ain't a miner I'm looking for, but a gamblin' man." She sighed forlornly. "But I can see for myself he ain't here. Would there be another saloon nearby?"

Goldie and Burt exchanged I-knew-it glances, then his eyes narrowed and his lips were pinched when he spoke. "Would he, by any chance, be a tall, clean-lookin' feller in a black hat?"

"Yes, yes," she said eagerly, sitting forward in her chair. "He was here? How long ago did he leave?"

"That rascal was here all right." Burt slapped the table. "He still is, but he's in the back room with Gert."

"Who's Gert?" January asked innocently. No one answered and, judging from the sheepish looks on their faces, it became apparent that Gert was a woman of questionable virtue. "Never mind. I don't reckon I need to know."

"If it's any comfort to ya, he was real drunk when he took her up on the offer," Burt said apologetically.

"Thank you. That does make me feel a whole sight better." Wondering how she was going to induce Goldie and Burt to drag Case out of wherever he was, she sighed dramatically. "I shouldn't have come here. I've made my bed. I'll just have to lie in it now."

Burt muttered a curse. "What kind of man would do something like this to a nice young gal like you? The dirty, rotten, no-good."

Clasping her hands over her heart, January fluttered her lashes at the big man. "No man ever sinks so low that some dog or woman won't take up with him."

Goldie patted her hand with sisterly affection. "Ain't that the truth. Now, don't you fret. Burt and Goldie are gonna help you."

"Help her do what, Goldie?" the bartender asked, clearly puzzled by what his role was supposed to be.

"We're gonna solve her little problem," she replied as if he were dense for having to ask.

"And just how we gonna do that?"

Goldie smiled, revealing a big gold tooth. "Why, we're gonna stage us a little weddin' right here."

January sucked in a deep breath and would have protested, but no sound came out. A wedding? In a dirt-floor saloon? Conducted by a beefy bartender and a soiled dove? She suppressed the laughter that bubbled up inside her. Why not? Stranger things had happened.

Burt leaned across the table. "You want me to git the shotgun?"

"No, you find Preacher and sober him up. See if he's got any of them weddin' certif'cates left." Goldie stood up, issuing further instructions, not only to Burt, but also to the miner who'd given up his chair and a sulky-faced bargirl.

January knew she should stop them, that what they were proposing was ridiculous. But things were snowballing so fast, she had no idea how to slow them down. She was flabbergasted.

"Shucks, Goldie," Burt protested. "Bringin' Preacher to his senses is gonna take some doin'. He passed out hours ago."

''Just pour some cold water in his face, then wave a bottle under his nose. It works every time.'' Burt was already on his way when Goldie remembered something and called out, ''But don't let him have no whiskey until the knots have been firmly tied. Etta Ruth!'' The sullen girl looked up at the sound of Goldie's booming voice. ''See if you can find some flowers and a Bible.''

''There ain't no flowers around here. And even if there was some, they'd all be squashed in the storm,'' Etta Ruth whined.

''Then go rip some off those god-awful dresses of yours. Scat!''

The girl shot Goldie and January a dark look and ambled off, muttering about knocked-up farmgirls and crazy, sentimental whores.

January finally found her voice. ''Really, Goldie, I can't let you do this.''

''Hogwash. I want to. It won't be no trouble. Nothin' nice or fun ever happens around here. I'm just sorry there won't be much fanciness, it being such short notice and all.'' When Goldie saw the forlorn look on January's face, she asked, ''What's the matter, kid? Don't you want to marry your baby's pappy?''

She wasn't sure how to answer. She did want to marry Case, but there was no baby. At least none that she knew of. Then she had an alarming thought. There very well *could* be a baby. ''Well, yes, but—''

''Then that settles it,'' Goldie boomed as she enclosed January in a big bear hug. ''Honey, you're gettin' hitched.''

Chapter 16

When Case had reached the Lucky Strike saloon, he'd tried hard to forget January and the constant yearning he felt for her. In fact, he'd tried so hard to numb his mind to that maddening attraction, he'd inadvertently anesthetized his body as well.

He simply had to get all thoughts of January out of his head. Lately, he'd been thinking in terms of love and that wasn't good. He knew what he felt wasn't love because he didn't want it to be and he certainly wasn't ready for the kind of commitment love would require. Not by a long shot.

So when a sloe-eyed erring angel approached him with detailed carnal suggestions, he jumped at the chance to prove to himself once and for all that it wasn't Miss Jones he needed—that any woman would do. They'd adjourned to her small, shabby room, but filled as he was with mixed emotions and rotgut, he'd been unable to do anything more than fall into a deep slumber.

Not only did January torment him during his waking hours, she also haunted his dreams. A dream so vivid, it would have been frightening had it not been so absurd and amusing.

Having spent the major portion of his adult life in saloons, Case didn't find it particularly odd that their dream wedding should take place in one. The scene was blurry at best, the voices distant and echoing like someone calling from the bottom of a well. The wedding party was composed of those he'd last been in contact with—which was typical of dreams. The bald bartender made a passable best man, but the soiled dove acting as January's maid of honor was carrying illusion to a ridiculous extreme.

Having imbibed heavily himself, Case was quick to notice—even in his sleep—that the participants were incapacitated by varying stages of drunkenness. From the tipsy floozies and wobbly miners right down to the belching, but sincere parson.

Case viewed the nocturnal spectacle objectively, as though he were standing at some distant point watching the proceedings unfold in a tunnel. His body was weightless, a common condition in dreams, and he had to be supported on one side by the best man and on the other by January.

A very lovely, very symbolically pregnant January!

That's when he knew for sure he was dreaming.

January was relieved and surprised that Case was taking everything so well. So far, he hadn't humiliated her by voicing any protests or denouncing the institution of wedded bliss as she'd expected him to do. In fact, he seemed rather pleased with the whole idea, if the goofy grin on his face was any indication.

But, truth to tell, he was only semiconscious and not quite as coherent as she would have wished. Taking advantage of him wasn't exactly fair, but she couldn't allow guilt and self-recriminations to stop her now.

He obviously had no idea a shotgun wedding was taking place—his own. Boy, was he in for a surprise come morning! She could only hope the debilitating effects of the hangover he was sure to suffer would sufficiently deter him from killing her and all those involved. Wobbling momentarily on the cutting edge of indecision, she argued with her conscience.

If she and Case were united in holy wedlock, he couldn't be expected to commit bigamy with Ardetta. Therefore, the Buscus brothers would be forced to give up the ghost. That was good. Since she harbored no ill-conceived plan of holding Case to their vows, he'd be a free man again. That was good, too. And she'd have a chance in the run. That was the best part of all.

By marrying him, she was actually doing him yet another favor. After Joplin, he'd warned her against doing him any more favors, but this was one he was sure to thank her for someday. And he would, too, just as soon as he realized he needed her as much as she needed him.

"Dearly be-e-e-loved," Preacher slurred. "We are gathered he-e-e-re to join this couple in holy matri— marti— wedlock. If anybody objects to this here union, let him so say, or forever hold his pe-e-e-ace." The long pause that followed was interrupted by a noisome belch.

Case laughed aloud at the comic overtones, but stopped short when the dream January jabbed him, very realistically, in the ribs. "No wife of mine is going to manhandle me," he pronounced with male aplomb. Then, reconsidering, he leered and added, "On second thought, go right ahead—manhandle me all you want."

"If you don't want to take me as your lawful wedded wife, then this is your last chance to speak up, Case." Her voice floated out from afar.

"Why, shore he does, dontcha?" Burt applied painful pressure on his arm.

Case nodded vigorously and his head swam. "I don't suppose I could lie down for a few moments first." He glanced at the large man at his side. "No, I suppose not."

"Come on, Preacher, at the rate you're going, these two'll be parents before they ever git hitched," Burt urged, fearing the groom might pass out before the "I do's." Not only that, but Latimer was a heavy sonuvagun.

"Snap it up, will ya?" Goldie urged. "Before one of 'em changes their mind."

Preacher belched again. "I need a drink."

"Me, too," Case agreed, but was too dizzy to worry about it overmuch.

"Plenty of time for drinkin' later. Drinks are on the

house, once these two are ball-and-chained.'' Goldie held up a bottle and waved it enticingly.

Preacher began again with renewed fervor and Case smiled benignly in deference to the solemn occasion. Even if it was just a dream, it deserved a certain amount of decorum. Then came another interruption from unexpected quarters. Gert, wearing a threadbare wrapper and little else, sniffed loudly.

''Wha'sa matter, Gertie?'' Preacher seemed to forget he was in the middle of a ceremony and placed a consoling arm around his favorite whore. He thrust his dingy handkerchief into her hands.

She dried her tears and blew her nose before deeming herself ready to speak. ''It's a cryin' shame, but a woman's only noticed three times in her life—when she's hatched, matched, or dispatched.'' Blowing her nose again, she added, ''I feel sorry for the gal. He might be a cocky-lookin' rooster, but he shore weren't nothin' to crow about. Git my meanin', Preach? He never even tried before he conked out.''

January giggled. That news alone made the world a brighter place and she was as tickled as a baby with a feather that Case had resisted Gert's dubious charms.

Raising his voice above the snickering inspired by Gert's remark, Preacher concurred. ''That's the way of his kind, Gertie. All show and no go.''

''I resent that remark, sirs,'' Case objected to the two men holding the Bibles, but neither of them paid him any mind. Soon he was seeing two of everyone and it was difficult to remember just what it was he'd taken such offense to. The world tilted beneath his feet and he knew his condition was grave, and that was putting it mildly.

''Still, can't help feelin' sorry for the bride, ya know?'' Gert rolled her eyes meaningfully.

Case rallied long enough to defend himself. ''She's damned lucky to get me,'' he said smugly. Hoping the bobbing images would merge into one solid mass, he scrunched one eye shut and peered down his nose at the painted cat. "Many have tried and failed."

"Lucky?" January frothed up. "I'm doing you a favor, you damned self-happy fool. Though why I bother to save your ass—"

"Cusses like a mule-skinner. That's my little spitfire," he announced triumphantly. Since one eye closed hadn't worked, he tried narrowing both eyes until the two Januarys blended and came into sharper focus. He had enough trouble with one of her; dealing with two of her was a staggering thought, indeed.

He lovingly caressed her protruding girth and was about to point out just exactly who was doing whom the biggest favor, but his feeble constitution took a turn for the worse. A wave of nausea washed over him like a swell on an angry sea. He clamped his lips together and concentrated on the impossible task of merely standing erect for the duration.

Dammit to hell, how long did dreams last, anyhow?

"Enough!" Goldie threw up her hands in an impatient gesture. "If ever'body's ready, and even if they ain't, let's at least git these two in bed before they split the blanket."

January glared at Case, no longer feeling any compunction about taking advantage of him in his inebriated state. Preacher droned on and on and she fairly gloated at her bridegroom's apparently delicate condition. Let this be a lesson to him. If nothing else, it ought to teach him the evils of abusing demon rum.

However, the sweet taste of victory soon turned as bitter as gall on her tongue, because when Preacher asked for Case's "I do," he didn't. As all eyes turned expectantly to the couple, the mocking silence became even more pregnant than January had made herself appear.

Case didn't feel so good. He knew everyone was waiting impatiently for him to vow his everlasting devotion, but he also knew that if he opened his mouth, he would disgrace himself. He was sicker than a foundered horse and totally absorbed with calculating the distance to the nearest door or window.

January implored him with her gaze to say something. Anything. Even a no would be preferable to that pinched look his green-tinted face had assumed. How dare he just stand there with his Adam's apple bobbing up and down.

Case had another problem. Not only was he sicker than a dog on a gutwagon, but where there had been double vision before, there was only encroaching black vertigo now. He blinked rapidly, but to no avail. He'd been struck blind. This was no dream. It was a nightmare.

January bit her lip and closed her eyes, silently begging for divine assistance. What had she ever done to warrant this public disgrace? Was he suddenly so underwhelmed to find himself on the threshold of marriage that he'd lost his voice? Or had he chosen to give her her comeuppance by humiliating her at the last possible moment?

He'd succeeded, but she wasn't about to let everyone know. She laughed derisively and shrugged as if it were all a big joke. "Looks like the groom needs a little prodding. You got a shotgun in this place, Goldie?"

As sick and blind as he was, Case became aware of the nervous giggles and self-conscious throat-clearings and admired his bride's indomitable spirit. He mustered his remaining strength and opened his mouth to tell them all how proud he was to say "I do."

At least that was the plan. The only sound he emitted was one very loud, very drawn-out, relief-inducing *hic-c-cup* before blessed oblivion snatched him away.

Construing the sound as an affirmative reply, the wedding party cheered and Preacher quickly pronounced them man and wife. After the well-wishing and congratulatory back-slapping were over, Goldie announced that drinks were on the house.

Someone grabbed up a devil's music box and fiddled away, singing "Skip to My Lou." It was of little importance that men outnumbered the women; they merely danced with each other. One swung around, holding up imaginary skirts, while the other stomped and clapped in time with the music. The festive occasion demanded they whoop and cheer one another at the top of their lungs.

The sight made January laugh so hard, she had to dab tears from her eyes. Someone patted her shoulder. Turning, she watched in uneasy silence as Burt hefted Case by the boots while a burly miner held his shoulders. Her new husband was even worse off than she'd suspected.

Burt eyed her sympathetically. ''It's your honeymoon, gal. Where do you want the groom?''

''I don't suppose he's in any condition to ride a horse?'' she asked doubtfully.

Unsuccessfully hiding a grin, Preacher pursed his lips as if he were mulling it over, then scratched his chin stubble. ''I reckon he could if we was to tie him on.''

Goldie intervened. ''Put 'em in my room fer the night, boys.''

''Oh no,'' January said. ''We couldn't put you out of your own room. You've done too much already.''

''Nonsense,'' Gert put in. ''Ain't nothin' we like better'n a weddin' unless it's a party. This 'un's liable to go on all night anyways. Too bad we can't say the same for him.''

Amid the ribald laughter following that remark, January ducked her head and followed as Case was hauled to one of the back rooms. With sad looks and head shakes, the men offered to put him to bed. Nervously, she paced the short hall while she waited.

Common sense told her that Case would be madder than a hornet when he woke up in the morning a married man. But he wouldn't have gone through with it if he hadn't been willing, would he? Of course not.

There had been moments when his eyes had sparkled with the same gleam they got when he made love to her. And that smile. Whiskey hadn't been behind that grin. There had been real tenderness in it. Wasn't that proof enough that he cared? Maybe just a little?

By the time Burt and the miner left them alone in the

room, January had herself convinced. Once she explained how the evening's events had transpired, Case would understand. It was his own fault he'd been so drunk that she'd been forced, as usual, to take charge. Surely he would see the reason behind her hasty actions and all would be forgiven.

Case knew she wasn't just another scheming female, out to take advantage of him. Hellfire, if he couldn't trust her, he couldn't trust anyone.

Lovingly, January smoothed back his hair and kissed his forehead. Burt sure had a strange sense of humor. He'd made Case look as though he'd been laid out for burial rather than a marriage bed. His hands were folded on his chest and all his sheet-shrouded form needed was a white lily to complete the morbid, but amusing, picture. Totally incongruous to his deathlike stillness was his snuffling, sibilant snoring, which was loud enough to rival the celebration in the saloon.

"Maybe he didn't actually say 'I do.' Maybe he only sucked wind down his pipes at an unlikely moment," she argued aloud. But hiccup notwithstanding, they were still married. She had the paper to prove it. She stripped off her clothes and crawled into bed beside him. If he awakened during the night, she wanted to be ready.

"Case's wife." She sighed dreamily, scooting closer to his warmth. "Mrs. Case Latimer." Daringly, she rolled her head onto his shoulder, allowing her lips the luxury of kissing his bare flesh. He was out cold for now, but he had to wake up sometime and when he did, she planned to consummate their vows. It was only natural to do so. She wouldn't worry about tomorrow. Things always had a way of working themselves out.

It was still dark when Case awoke to the not-too-distant sounds of revelry. His head throbbed painfully and he was still woofy from all his imbibing. To top it all off, he was slightly befuddled from the disconcerting dream he'd had.

That had been some fantasy, he thought with a pained smile.

He stretched and rolled to his back. When he felt the soft female form beside him, he remembered where he was and was thoroughly disgusted with himself. Not only had he run out on January, which was inexcusable, but his head pained him something fierce. What in the devil was he doing in bed with a trollop when the only woman he'd ever really cared about was all alone in a damp, deserted mine shaft?

He should be ashamed of himself. He was suddenly struck with an overwhelming urge to see January, to apologize for leaving her alone when he knew how she hated the darkness. He sat up quickly, deciding to slip out of the strumpet's bed and hurry back where he belonged.

"Don't go, Case." January had awakened the moment he stirred, at the first delicious touch of his warm skin feathering against her own.

"January?" he gasped, surprised. In a single fluid motion, he knelt over her on the sagging mattress, his face level with hers. He'd trade Shadow for a candle, he thought as his gaze traveled the sheet-clad length of her, lingering briefly on her breasts. "Is it really you?" he asked stupidly.

She nodded, smiling. He leaned over her in all his glory and she wished for more moonlight than the stingy amount penetrating the dirty window.

She watched, mesmerized, as his rakish grin tilted his mustache. His hot gaze slid over her, then returned to capture hers. His hands slipped around her neck, securing her head at the nape, and his thumb caressed the delicate line of her jaw. She couldn't speak and didn't dare breathe for fear of breaking the magic of this endearing moment.

Slowly, inevitably, his face came closer to hers until she thought she'd go mad if he didn't kiss her quick. He stopped just a hairbreadth away and she wanted to scream with frustration.

Case rubbed gentle fingers over her lips. She felt real

enough, but then, that other dream had seemed awfully real, too. Maybe he'd simply conjured her up. Maybe this, too, was only an illusion, albeit a warm and excitingly realistic one. Her lovely face could very well turn into a pillow when he kissed her. He blinked several times, but she didn't disappear. She lay there, a smile on her too-kissable lips, a hungry gleam in her beautiful brown eyes.

"Tell me it's really you," he implored huskily. "Tell me you aren't merely a figment of my overactive imagination."

January heaved a sigh of relief. "I ain't no dream woman," she assured him softly. Taking his hand, she pressed it against her thudding heart. "I'm only a woman."

Finally his lips touched hers—gently at first, nipping, teasing, and playful, but then increasing in pressure until she opened her mouth to him. His tongue swept inside, hinting at the pleasurable delights of things to come.

"Ah, January," he breathed hotly against her cheek, then his lips explored her face and ears as she clamped her arms around his waist. "God, I want you."

"For how long?"

"I can never get enough. All I have to do is look at you and I ache."

"Even when I look like a scrawny, half-growed boy?" She grinned triumphantly. As a reward she drew tiny circles on the small of his bare back.

"Especially when you're wearing those infernal britches." His words came out in quick, panting breaths as his lips covered her face in brief kisses, sliding down her throat to the soft swell of her breasts.

She put her hands on his chest, pushing slightly to peer up at him. "But I've caught you frowning at me with your eyes aimed right at the seat of my pants. I always figured you didn't like it because I didn't dress like a lady."

"God, do you have any idea how you look in those britches of yours? Or what the sight does to me?"

Shaking her head, she urged, "Tell me."

He had to have another kiss first. "It was almost more than I could stand, riding behind you and watching your cute little bottom bouncing up and down in that saddle. Many's the time the mere sight left me breathless and hard. I was willing to die to touch you. Most of the time it was all I could do not to drag you off old Brownie and into the nearest clump of bushes, where I could ravish you until you cried for mercy." With one hand, he stroked her side, caressing her hip through the sheet.

January framed his face with her hands and looked deeply into his eyes. Her voice sounded rusty when she spoke. "I know this ain't no clump of bushes we're in. And since I ain't cryin' for mercy, do you think you could just get on with the ravishin' part?"

Reverently, he pulled the sheet away. The breath caught in her throat as he admired her. The gambler's mask was gone and his wondering expression made him look young and downright vulnerable. His skin was flushed with desire and his lids were heavy above passionate eyes.

He bent his head and bestowed gentle, heated kisses across her chest and stomach, laving her warm skin. A moan escaped her when he took a rosy bud between his lips, gently nudging it to a throbbing peak, and again when he practiced the divine torture on her other breast.

No longer inhibited by thoughts of sinful, out-of-wedlock coupling and fears of eternal damnation, January reveled in the knowledge that she could touch him all she wanted to because Case was now her husband. She could finally do what she'd longed to do before they were married. By catching him off guard, she was able to roll him to his back and push against his chest, pinning him to the bed. She straddled him on her hands and knees.

"What's going on?" he asked, surprised.

"Would it be improper for a lady to ravish a gentleman?" she asked tentatively, suddenly embarrassed by her aggression.

Recognizing the passionate twinkle in her eyes, the stubborn slant of her chin, and the blush on her cheeks, he knew she was waiting for his approval. Case relaxed against the pillow, propped his hands behind his head, and pretended to mull it over.

"Well?" she demanded. "Would it?"

"In some social circles such wantonness might be considered improper behavior, even downright indecent. But this must be your lucky day, because *I'm* not a gentleman." With one hand he stroked her collarbone, then his fingertips traced her breasts, trailing down her rib cage where he lingered to tease her navel.

January giggled and squirmed over him. If only she had some idea what to do next. "You're pretty lucky your own self."

"How's that?"

"It's certain sure I ain't no lady."

His fingers locked in her hair, imprisoning her face, forcing her to stare into smoky blue eyes. "A lady is a woman of gentle manners. It's also a courteous form of address. You," he insisted, "are definitely a *lady* and anyone who dares to say differently will answer to me."

A tiny whimper of love and desire rose from her throat and she took his hands in hers and pressed them back on the bed. She bent her head and kissed him. A long, deep, bone-melting assault that left her all atremble. She snatched her lips away to blaze a fiery path across his cheek to his earlobe which she tasted with her teeth and tongue.

Case groaned. Grasping her hips, he tugged her body until it rested atop his. She shivered at the delightful full-length contact of his flesh, then tingled as his roaming hands explored her back from top to bottom. When she could bear no more, she caught his hands in hers.

"It's my turn, remember?" she whispered breathily. Without waiting to see if he agreed, she dipped her tongue inside his mouth for some delightful explorations of her own.

He squeezed her hands, his only anchor in the dizzying whirlpool January had pulled him into. She'd been shy and slightly backward during their previous lovemaking. Just when he'd thought he had her all figured out, knew everything there was to know about her, she now proved him wrong. She never failed to surprise him.

Wiggling her hands from his grip, she stretched out beside him, propping herself on an elbow, feeling free and happy, liquid and lazy at the newfound power that wifehood had given her. She rubbed one hand over his chest and tickled his ribs as she caressed his hip with the other. Her gaze followed each and every movement as her hands glided over his straining flesh.

She didn't even hesitate as her curious fingers found their way into the nest of curly hair between his legs. Stroking his swollen manhood, she leaned over him, treating her lips to an exploration across his chest and down his ribs. Growing bolder with each passing moment, she even flicked his belly button with her tongue.

Case's breathing became more and more difficult. He couldn't take much more of the delectable agony. Pulling her face up to his, he kissed her long and mindlessly.

He rolled over, tucking her beneath him. "Why did you do that?" she mumbled into his mouth. "I wanted to send you to paradise."

He grinned and tugged her bottom lip into his mouth. "I know, but I decided I didn't want to go without you." A soft breath escaped him then and he tightened strong arms around her as his hungry lips feasted on hers.

Arms and legs all atangle, she returned kiss for kiss with a hot, relentless passion that grew wilder still in her efforts to excite him, to convey her love for him. It was gratifying the way he trembled at her touch, the way he seemed to enjoy touching her. Still, she felt at a disadvantage when it came to pleasing a man.

She worried that, because she was green and unschooled in amorous advances, she would fail to excite him to the same degree he aroused her.

She could only hope that instinct and Case himself would guide her. When he nuzzled her neck, she nibbled his shoulder and found the taste delightful. When his lips found her breast and fastened greedily upon the bounty, she stopped worrying and gave herself up to sheer bliss.

His hot mouth moved down her stomach and his educated fingers fondled the secrets between her legs, soon discovering all her tender, most responsive places. The gentle massage intensified until the blood boiled in her veins and threatened to explode within her. She gasped with surprise when his warm mouth followed the path his hands had blazed. Her fingers plowed into his hair, but he slid farther down her body, his lips and tongue sending spasms of sensation and urgency through her.

This was something she hadn't even guessed at. "Please, Case." She clutched at his shoulders, writhing in the ecstasy he was urging from her. But it wasn't enough. She needed to feel him inside her. "Please, come up here."

Sensing her urgency, he breathed against her navel, stopping to kiss and nibble with agonizing slowness along the way. He gazed at her, fondly rubbing her nose with his.

"I thought you'd never get here." She smiled, cupping his devilishly handsome face in her hands.

He raised himself on his elbows so that their lower bodies touched intimately. She looked adorable and captivating as she lay beneath him, breathing hard and fast, her hair love-mussed, her lips swollen from his kisses. He winked at her. "Tell me what you want, January. Name it and it's yours."

She parted her legs, sensuously rubbing her toes up and down his calves. "You," she said breathlessly. "I want you."

"Not nearly as much as I want you."

Case's lips were soft as they covered her own, then grew more demanding when she felt him thrust rock-hard against her. She returned his kiss, wrapping him tightly with her arms and legs, and wriggled beneath him. Using hands and mouth, he tantalized her with amazing restraint, building her passion to a fever pitch until she was spinning out of control.

"Case." His name was a sigh from her lips, her arching body an invitation he could no longer resist. He'd never experienced anything so moving as when she reached for him, guiding him home. At long last, he was inside her. January Jones was a force to be reckoned with. Even as he filled her body with his, she filled his heart with an unnameable emotion so profound it was unbelievable, so moving it destroyed all rational thought.

Clasping him with her legs, January brought him even more deeply inside, chipping away at his dwindling control. The blood roared in his ears and he realized they were almost there, to the point of no return. Every move she made further inflamed his blazing passion. When she churned her hips in wild response to his burning thrusts, he urged her on, coaxing her with his fingers and mouth. He swallowed up her cry of pleasure as she crested the peak, and he shuddered against her, sharing that blissful oneness he could find only with her.

They'd found it. Paradise.

The sharp edge of pleasure receded slightly, leaving January lazy and languid. Warm devotion filled her heart as Case collapsed atop her, his breathing fast and ragged. She was smugly content as he rolled to his side and settled her into the crook of his arm. He kissed her hair, rubbing his cheek against it.

As she relaxed in his strong arms, her last conscious thought was that she'd been right to marry him. Everything would work out just fine. It had to.

January woke at dawn, long before Case. She took advantage of the time to study his features, committing them to memory. He was a beautiful sight first thing the morning and a silly smile curved her lips. He belonged to her now and there would be many such mornings as this one. She gazed lovingly at his profile. Just watching him sleep made her pulses skitter.

Unable to face her just yet, and unwilling to ask how she'd ended up in bed with him, Case had quickly closed his eyes, feigning sleep when she stirred in his arms. After their amorous night, he'd awakened earlier than usual. Something—he couldn't quite put his finger on it—had been bothering him.

Now he remembered. It was all this newborn emotion she'd managed to dredge up in him. What did it all mean? Could it be that she was in love with him and, sensing that, he'd imagined stronger feelings between them?

He pictured her in his mind's eye—the glow that lit up her face, the possessive glint in her eyes when she thought he wasn't looking. It all added up. Instinct said she loved him, though his heart cried out against it. She couldn't love him, she just couldn't. Because if she did, it would be so much harder to give her up.

He'd never meant to hurt her, but if he accepted her love without returning it, she would inevitably be hurt. He could never conform to her expectations. Her way of life would never suit him.

Last night she'd given herself completely. The passionate, exciting way she'd made love to him, eager to please and be pleased, free of previous inhibitions, proved only one thing. She was in love with him.

Dammit to hell! That unwelcome revelation, coupled with a morning-after hangover, might just make life intolerable.

"Case, are you asleep?" she whispered softly.

He frowned and January wished he'd wake up and kiss her, chase away the doubts that morning had brought. "Case?" she asked a bit louder. "Case?"

"Hmmm?" He kept his eyes closed, not wanting to see the look of pain he suspected would be on her face.

"Did I wake you?" she asked cheerfully, leaning over him.

He withdrew his arm and sat up quickly, which turned out to be a painful experience. "There's no need to shout, January," he snapped. "I'm awake."

The realization that he didn't seem especially glad to find her in his bed made her lash out defensively. "I wasn't shouting. *This,*" she shrieked in his face, "is shouting." She scrambled from the bed, yanked the sheet from it, and covered herself as a sudden surge of modesty swamped her. So much for self-confidence.

"Keep your voice down," he muttered. "My head is killing me." He found his pants and slipped them on, then bent to look under the bed for his shirt. "What the hell are you doing here anyway?"

He'd asked that question as if she had no rights at all. So he'd been too drunk to remember last night. Why should she remind him he was a married man, that she had ample right to be in his bed or anywhere else she wanted to be?

What made her think he'd wanted her in the first place? No doubt he'd have enjoyed Gert just as much. Didn't all women have the same equipment? January tensed. He didn't deserve her.

Stuffing the dress she'd worn for their wedding into her saddlebag and recalling what Case had said about the way she looked in pants, she defiantly skimmed them up her hips with a show of womanly pride.

"I asked you a question, young woman. What are you doing here?"

"Well, you see, I was on my way to the Oklahoma Land Run," she sassed, "when all of a sudden—"

"You know very well what I'm asking."

"Do I?"

"Why are you here in this room, in my bed?"

It riled her to think he had no recollection of anything that had passed between them last night, not even their wedding ceremony. Well, far be it from her to inform him of the recent nuptials. She'd just stop at the first damned courthouse she came to and have the damned thing annulled.

"As much as it pains me to admit it," she said, her tone oozing sarcasm, "even sleeping in a bed with the likes of you was preferable to spending the night in some gosh-damned haunted mine shaft with them Buscus boys.''

"Is that your only excuse?'' He pressed his fingertips to his throbbing temples, perversely disappointed that she appeared so totally unscathed by his rejection. Especially after the most glorious night of lovemaking he'd ever known. Why was she behaving as though it meant nothing to her? "January Jones to the rescue, huh? It must be tiresome, indeed, always having to save my ass.''

She yanked on her boots and tucked in her shirt. "Not that it's worth saving, but yes, that's exactly why I'm here. And the only reason I hung around was because you were so damned drunk you passed out before I could warn you.'' She shrugged and glared at him. "Satisfied?''

"Are you saying you didn't come here to . . .'' He broke off, staring meaningfully at the bed.

"Me? Never in a million years,'' she lied. "I got sleepy and since there was no where else to lay my weary bones, I ended up in bed with you. Just because I let you have your way with me, don't flatter yourself by thinking it meant anything special, 'cause it didn't.''

"I guess that explains everything,'' he grumbled. He had it coming, anything she cared to dish out and more, for jumping to the wrong conclusion after a simple, uncomplicated night of passion. After all, it wasn't the first time they'd made love and it wasn't as though she was unresponsive, either. If not for that crazy dream about weddings and such, he wouldn't have mistakenly fancied that she had fallen in love with him.

She'd simply come galloping to the rescue again and fallen asleep beside him. The lovemaking hadn't meant a thing. After all, two bare-assed people in the same bed were duty bound to make love. A little ring of sadness tightened around his heart as he pulled on his boots.

"Have you seen my shirt?''

January plucked it from the bedpost and tossed it over his head as she stalked past him. Her hand on the doorknob, she hesitated, throwing him a sad look over her shoulder. "I'll go saddle up the horses while you finish dressing. We're burnin' daylight."

Case stared at the door she slammed between them, then sighed and pulled on his shirt. He didn't blame her for being mad and he vowed that somehow he'd make it up to her. He sighed, knowing there was only one way to do that.

Outside, January set herself to saddling the horses, relieved that it was much too early for the witnesses of last night's debacle to be up and around. She was practically choking on tears, but she refused to shed them over a no-account gambling drunkard like Case Latimer. Not now. Not ever.

They rode hard and exhaustingly, stopping only when darkness made it dangerous for the horses to proceed. They ate in silence and slept on opposite sides of the campfire, barely managing to coexist in an atmosphere of estrangement.

Late one day, they stopped to water the horses in a stream. January nearly jumped out of her skin when Case took her hand and pulled her down beside him on a log.

"I figure we'll make Arkansas City by midday tomorrow," he said.

"So?"

"It's going to be a wild place, crowded with so many people." It was impossible to look at her without starting a fire in his body, so he carefully kept his gaze on the soothing, rippling water.

"So?" She stared at his profile, wondering what he was getting at. He knew she wasn't old enough to make the run. He'd also told her, in no uncertain terms, that he wouldn't be making the run for her. Unless she could get an annulment soon, she couldn't even look for a husband among the other hopefuls. What a mess she'd made of things.

"What are your plans?" He hoped she'd given up the crazy notion of finding a homesteader to marry. How could she even consider exchanging the use of her body for a damned farm? All she'd get out of that bad bargain would be a passel of starving kids and a lot of backbreaking work that would make her old before her time.

"I've told you before," she said. "I aim to have my own land and I don't care what I have to do to get it."

This is it, Case decided. The moment of truth. After mulling it over long and hard, he couldn't think of a single way to help her that didn't set his teeth on edge. "Since you're so stubborn about it and determined to go through with this thing . . ." He paused, momentarily balking at what he was about to propose. Still, he had to help her; he owed her that much. "And since you can't make the run yourself, I guess I'll just have to marry you and do it for you," he offered magnanimously.

January glared at him. When she opened her mouth to give him what-for, he held up a warning hand. "But don't go getting any wrong ideas about me sticking around for the duration. Once I've got you settled, I'll be heading for Alaska."

"Now, don't that just beat all?" January slapped her thigh. "Just when I'm beginning to think you're nothing but a stupid, lop-eared jackass, I'll be damned if you don't prove me right."

His stare was icy. "I was only trying to ease your mind about your somewhat questionable future. This is one time you'll be forced to allow me to save *your* butt, Miss Jones. Because, no matter how independent you like to think you are, this is something you can't do for yourself. You may as well admit it. This time you need my help."

"Maybe I don't want your help," she fired back.

Angry and careless, Case and January were too engrossed in their heated argument to hear the riders stealthily approaching their camp. At the ominous sound of rifles being cocked at their backs, their eyes met and locked in surprise.

They froze when a laughing voice observed, "I think

you're both shit out of luck and need all the help you can get. Reach for the sky!"

Both Case and January cursed at the familiar voice of Byrell Buscus. Hellfire! January's alarm was tempered by disgust at herself for being so caught up with Case that she'd let the fools sneak up on them.

Case was more philosophical. The relentless Buscus brothers seemed to have an almost supernatural way of showing up when a man least expected them.

Chapter 17

"Keep your dirty hands off me!" January lashed out with fists and feet at the Buscus brother who was trying valiantly to hold her.

"Dammit, Carvel, tie her up, too," Byrell Buscus instructed his younger brother. "Leastways until we decide what to do with her."

"Leave her alone. She's no threat to you." Trussed up the way he was, Case wasn't in much of a position to be making demands. He'd been shoved into an abandoned cabin by the two younger brothers, while a fourth, as yet unidentified, member of the gang stayed outside to tend the horses.

"Neither is a razorback with a snoot full of bees," the youngest deadpanned.

"Shut up, Jory! I've gotta cogitate on this." Byrell pushed his hat back on his head and rubbed his mouth with his hand. After a few moments of hard thinking, he tugged a red bandana from his hip pocket and mopped up the sweat that had accumulated on his forehead as a result of such strenuous activity.

"What's to think about?" said Carvel. "We been chasing this rascal for weeks so we could make him marry Ardetta. Well, we caught him. Looks to me like a weddin' is the answer."

January was bound hand and foot, then pushed down on the dirty, leaf-strewn plank floor beside Case with an order to keep her mouth shut. Orders from men never had set well with her. "He can't marry yours nor nobody else's sister."

Byrell spun around, a wrathful look on his face. "Is that so, little missy? And just why cain't he?"

"Because he's already married to me, that's why."

At that very moment, the loose-hinged door swung open and the fourth rider stood in the doorway, silhouetted by the late afternoon sun. "He's *what!*"

"I said, he's married to me."

Staring at January, Case was about to question her wild tale when a loud, keening wail erupted from the person in the doorway. The fourth brother snatched off his hat in a furious gesture and long, tangled blond curls tumbled down around his shoulders. Except that it was suddenly clear to January that *he* was really a *she*.

January had no idea who the woman was, but Case did. "Ardetta!"

"That's right, Latimer, it's me." Ardetta's pale blue eyes flashed venomous hatred. "I've been herding these shiftless plow-benders ever since we left Hot Springs. I knew I couldn't trust them to bring you back to me, so I made sure they didn't give up the chase. Do you have any idea what I've endured to find you?"

"Some," he said mildly, still shocked to see her. No wonder the brothers had hounded him so relentlessly. Ardetta had been riding roughshod over them the whole time. He recalled some lines from Congreve's play: *Heaven has no rage like love to hatred turned, Nor hell a fury like a woman scorned.* He'd never quite understood what all that meant, until now.

"Some! Is that all you've got to say?" Ardetta pulled a Colt revolver from the waistband of her baggy pants and aimed it at Case's heart. "I ought to kill you, Latimer."

"Ardetta!" All three brothers rallied around her, but she waved them off with the pistol. "Oh, shut up, all of you, before I kill you, too."

"Now, Ardetta honey, you don't mean that," Byrell

cajoled. "Killin's a sin, especially when it's your own kin."

"Try me, big brother."

"Careful," Carvel warned. "Don't upset her none. She's so riled, she might just have to kill somebody to improve her mood."

Jory snickered.

Ardetta rounded on January, whose fierce scowl gave the impression it was lucky for them she was totally immobilized. "I don't believe he'd marry a skinny little bitch like you."

"So you're Ardetta Buscus." January raked her up and down with a hard look and wondered how Case had ever been suckered in by such as her. Some might consider the short, plumply round girl pretty and no doubt men would be attracted by her wide hips and pouter-pigeon bosom. Her skin was as pale as milk, but her nose was red and peeling and large splotchy freckles had erupted across her sun-ravaged face.

She had china-doll eyes and full lips that were probably more appealing when they weren't cracked and chapped. The hand holding the gun was shaking visibly and January wasn't sure if it was the woman's anger or disappointment that made it tremble.

"Did you think his taste ran to lardy little bitches like you?" January asked conversationally.

Ardetta squealed in outrage and squeezed off a shot. A chunk of wood flew out of the log wall a few inches from January's head, but she didn't even flinch. She wasn't about to give the crazy woman the satisfaction of knowing she was scared out of her mind.

The brothers made a move to take the gun from their sister, but Ardetta warned, "Stay out of this." To Case she screeched, "Are you really married to her, Latimer?"

With his eyes, Case questioned January silently. Was it possible or was this just another of her impetuous schemes? Her eyes narrowed as she nodded almost imperceptibly. Maybe that dream hadn't been a dream after all, he decided. But it had to be. No wedding could have taken place in that saloon, conducted by a half-drunk preacher turned miner and attended by barroom habitués.

Was it possible that he was married? To January? Case had a flash of sudden, shocking insight. Their lovemaking had been so good that last morning in the mining camp. January had given herself to him in a totally different and breathtaking manner. With all her worry about brimstone and damnation, she never would have been so uninhibited unless she'd had the sanction of legal license. Case glanced at her again and the smug look on her face spoke volumes. God, it was true!

"It appears so." His emotions were in turmoil, but his face betrayed nothing.

"I don't believe it!" Ardetta stamped her foot and waved the gun. The brothers all ducked.

"Just take a look in my saddlebag," January instructed archly. "The certificate's in there, all legal and proper."

Jory was dispatched to locate the document. When he returned, he handed it to his sister. As she read it, her face became even redder and more dangerous-looking than before.

"It's true then." She sounded like a person who'd just run out of choices and knew it. "Looks like there's only one thing to do now."

Byrell tried to take her arm. "Come on, little sister. There's nothing to be done now. It's all over so we might as well go on home."

Ardetta jerked away. "It's not over by a damned sight."

"Hell, girl, the man's hitched. He can't very well marry you, too. It ain't legal."

Her eyes were blue ice and a scary smile played around her lips. "The way I figure it, a grieving widower needs someone to step in and comfort him in his hour of need. Right, Latimer?"

It took a few moments for the meaning of her words to sink into the men's heads, but January understood at once. She was going to die. She'd been married only a few days, had had only one chance to love Case as a wife should. She'd never see Oklahoma and she'd never sit in that rocking chair. There wouldn't be any "good old days" to relate to her descendants because there wouldn't be any descendants.

She recalled what Case had told her about how facing up to a fear could make a body strong. Well, she was looking death right in its evil eye and she was still as scared as hell. This wasn't how she'd planned to spend her last hour on earth. The worst thing was, she hadn't gotten around to telling Case how much she loved him.

She stared at Ardetta, trying to determine if she was the kind of woman who could kill someone in cold blood. She heard the hammer cock and the bullet drop into the chamber. It appeared she was.

Behind the shaking woman, her brothers were exchanging frantic hand signals and, before Ardetta knew what hit her, they'd wrestled her to the floor. The gun fired in the scuffle, the loud report reverberating in the broken-down cabin. Seconds passed and neither Case nor January knew who, if anyone, in the pile had been shot. At last the men all got to their feet, pulled a snarling Ardetta to hers, and disarmed her.

"Now, you just get your ass over there, sis," Byrell directed. "And don't give me no more trouble. "You're lucky you didn't hurt somebody or miscarry that baby."

"What baby?" she scoffed. "There's no baby, you idiot. Never has been."

Byrell, Carvel, and Jory stared at her, dumbfounded. Case and January exchanged puzzled looks.

"You're all fools," Ardetta sneered derisively. "All men are fools." She tossed the marriage license aside.

January didn't care much for Ardetta, but she had to agree—men *were* fools. That was a pure dee fact. But women were right behind them in the stupid race, she decided as she watched the license drift down beside her.

"But you said . . ." Byrell began.

"I know what I said. What I don't know is why y'all

believed me. You men were so all-fired worried about my honor. I guess the joke's on you because honor never was at stake here."

"Well, what the hell was, then?" Carvel demanded.

"My pride, brothers. My feminine vanity. I threw myself at Latimer and practically begged him to have his way with me. He turned me aside. He was the one with honor, not me."

The brothers, whose collective intelligence wasn't equal to their righteous indignation, looked to one another for guidance. "What'll we do, Byrell?" Carvel asked.

"I don't know," Byrell snapped. "Let me think on it."

"In that case, I reckon I'll get me some grub," Jory cracked. "We're liable to be here all night."

"Shut up!" all the other Buscus family members shouted in chorus.

Ardetta turned to Case. "I still don't understand why you did it. Why'd you go and marry a scrawny little wretch like her when you could have had me? Wasn't I good enough for you?"

Before he could answer, Byrell snapped to action. "You hush, Ardetta. None of that matters anymore. We'll deal with you when we get back to Hot Springs."

"I'm not going back to Hot Springs," she corrected. "I'm sick to death of that farm and the way you boys and Ma and Pa boss me around. I'm nothing but an unpaid servant. I wash and cook and tend and clean from sunup to sundown. Ma's not as sick as she lets on. Did you know that? She can't do nothing about Pa's philandering, so she takes her bad temper out on me. Did you really think that stick she's always carrying was just for walking?" At that, Ardetta yanked up the back of her shirt and displayed the ugly scars of accumulative beatings on her back.

Her brothers stared in disbelief as she went on. "And Pa? He's such a hypocrite. He never lets me go anywhere. I can't go to dances or parties or anywhere I might have a little fun. I never would have met Latimer if I hadn't sneaked out of prayer meeting and gone to that medicine show.

"The reason Pa's so afraid some old man'll get his hands on me is because he's had his all over half the hurdy girls in town."

"That's a lie!" Byrell looked appalled by his sister's shocking denouncement of their parents.

"Don't you just wish? You boys just turn a blind eye and deaf ear to the goings-on in that house. Well, I'm tired of the whole bunch of you. I want to be free and I want the kind of life Latimer can give me, not the early grave I'll get if I stay in Hot Springs. I've even been learning card games."

She ignored her brothers whose mouths were gaping open and directed her words to Case. "I'd make you a good partner, Latimer. I don't care that you're married, I'll take you anyhow. Just deny her"—a toss of her curls indicated January—"and we can leave together. Right now. We'll ride out of here and never look back. What do you say, Latimer?" she asked desperately. "You're a gambling man. Are you willing to take a chance on me?"

Case was moved by Ardetta's story. He'd had no idea of the kind of life the poor girl had endured. He understood her bitterness. She hated her brutal life so much, she was willing to do anything to escape it. Just as January had.

But unlike January, who'd had the spirit to go it alone, who had enough confidence in her own abilities to take such a risk, Ardetta needed someone else. What she didn't understand was that she would never be free as long as she depended on others. It was unjust that women didn't have the same options as men, but there was nothing he could do about the way of the world. And there was nothing he could say to Ardetta. Though she stirred his sympathy, he had no desire to form an illicit relationship with her.

January waited for Case to hotly reject Ardetta's suggestion. When he didn't, her heart began to break. He was considering the woman's offer, damn him. He was actually trying to decide whether to walk out and leave with the little bitch. Or maybe he was debating the merits of shooting her, his wife, first so he could keep his precious freedom intact!

She looked hard at Case's profile, then quickly away as tears blurred her vision. He didn't love her. He never had. All they'd shared—all the adventure, the joy, the tenderness—meant nothing to him. *She* meant nothing to him. Her gaze fell on the marriage license. She couldn't read it, but she knew her numbers and her eyes focused on the date of the ceremony. The eighteenth. They'd been married on April eighteenth, eighteen hundred and eighty-nine.

"What's today's date?" she demanded of anyone.

"Let me think," Jory spoke up. "I believe it's the twenty-second."

"The twenty-second?" A cold wind of desolation swept through her as she realized she'd missed the land run. At exactly twelve o'clock noon today, hopeful settlers had lined up in Arkansas City and at the other starting points and had made the run into Indian Territory.

It was late evening now and all the claims had been staked. All the men were busy getting down to the business of scratching out a living. Those who needed wives had found them by now. Even if they hadn't, she was still married with no hope of getting an annulment before they did. Life had cheated her out of her last chance. It was almost too much to comprehend. The run was over and she'd missed it.

Her goal had slipped through her fingers while she was dallying with Case Latimer. She couldn't go back to Possum Holler and, without a destination, she felt bereft. For the past few weeks she'd managed to keep going because of the promise the future held.

Now she had nothing. No Case, no land, no hope.

Case saw the expression on January's face and knew what she was thinking. Because of him she'd missed out on the one thing she wanted more than anything else. The golden fleece had been snatched away from her. He was elated and miserable and sad all at once. A young woman's dreams shouldn't be shattered so carelessly.

"January?" He spoke her name tentatively, but she didn't answer him. She just stared straight ahead as though nothing else mattered. As though nothing would ever matter again.

January glanced at Ardetta and the girl's expression surprised her. She didn't look mad anymore. She didn't look hurt. She looked about as numb as January felt. Her heart went out to the woman who only a few minutes ago had tried to kill her.

January knew what it meant to be disappointed by life, to be willing to do almost anything to escape the domination of others, to be desperate enough to offer yourself to a man you didn't love just to get what you wanted. Hadn't she almost done the same thing? She'd wanted land and a home so badly she would have given up the man she did love to get them.

Ardetta didn't love Case. There'd been no mention of that. Her offer had been strictly business. So January approached the problem in a businesslike way. "What will you do now, Ardetta?"

The blonde's eyes sparked at the question. "What do you care?"

"Where will you go?" she prodded gently.

"I don't know."

"Would money help?"

Ardetta laughed mirthlessly. "Doesn't it always?"

"I have some. I'll give it to you if you and your brothers will let us go. It ain't much, less than two hundred dollars, but it's all I got. You're welcome to it."

Ardetta regarded her suspiciously. "Why?"

January glanced from brother to brother and back to Ardetta. "Because I think you need it more than me. Let us go and I'll see that Case throws in whatever he has, too. For your trouble."

"Now, wait just a damned minute." There was over eight hundred dollars in his saddlebag and Case didn't feel generous. And he wasn't about to let January be altruistic at his expense. This little scene convinced him once and for all that he would never understand women. The two cats had been ready to go at each other tooth and claw a few minutes ago and now January was acting as if she had final say over the disposition of his property.

"Ardetta, check Case's saddlebags and help yourself," January insisted.

Ardetta thought over the offer. She had no idea why the girl was willing to help her, but she seemed sincere. It had been a long time since anyone had shown her any generosity. She looked first at the girl, then eyed Case. She knew. The girl loved him!

She smiled conspiratorily. "He's your husband. Why don't I untie you and you can fleece him for me."

Once Case's poker winnings had been transferred to Ardetta's bags and she'd sent her disbelieving brothers packing, she paused to speak to January and Case outside the cabin.

"No hard feelings, I hope." Ardetta adjusted her hat to a rakish angle.

"None to speak of," Case allowed grumpily. While he'd decided there was no point mourning for his eight hundred dollars, he still resented the way January had taken control of the situation.

"What will you do?" January was glad that at least one person had a chance to make her dreams come true.

"I'm not sure. Right now, it's more than enough that I'm getting away from my family. With the money, I can make a new life for myself. I may even open up my own gambling parlor." She smiled at Case. "Maybe if you and the missus are planning to stay in the trade, we'll run across one another again someday."

"Maybe."

Ardetta turned to January and the two women exchanged an impulsive hug. "Take care of old Hard Case. He needs a good woman like you."

"I will. Good luck, Ardetta. Take care of yourself."

They watched her ride off, wondering what life had in store for her. "I have a feeling Ardetta Buscus has what it takes to be a successful businesswoman," January commented.

"Yeah," Case agreed with ill humor. "My money."

"Oh, don't be such an old grumpus. There's always more where that came from, remember?"

"Why'd you do it, January?"

"Do what?"

"Well, lots of things. But for starters, why'd you help her? She nearly killed you."

January was silent for so long, Case thought she hadn't heard him.

She *had* heard the question; she just didn't know how to answer it. She couldn't bring herself to tell him she knew now that he didn't love her and never would. She'd glimpsed his trapped expression when he'd realized their marriage was legitimate.

She didn't know the words to explain, but since she'd already lost everything, she wanted to help the other woman realize her plans. "I just wanted to see something good come out of all this."

He shook his head. The good thing was that maybe now she'd give up her foolish quest and listen to reason. "The world is in desperate need of another fallen woman and gambling den."

"I wanted to see someone end up happy."

He gave her a hard look. "And you're not?"

"Hell no, I'm not. I narrowly escaped bein' shot. I missed the run, and I'm married to . . ." She'd been about to say *to a man who doesn't love me,* but she couldn't. It hurt too much.

"To whom? A worthless, tinhorn gambler with clean hands and no plow? Is that why you gave Ardetta our money? Out of spite?"

"Spite for what?"

Case hadn't planned to argue. He'd gotten used to the

idea of being married and, when Ardetta had called January "the missus," he'd smiled with pleasure at all the word connoted. How did January make him so mad so fast? "For me being drunk enough to marry you. Why the hell didn't you tell me we were married when I woke up in bed with you that morning?"

"Why the hell didn't you ask?"

"You weren't exactly acting like a blushing bride."

"Oooh!" She yanked off her hat and slapped him on the chest. "A body would have thought your life was ruined because we'd finally done what we done in a bed instead of on the cold, hard ground like a couple of animals. The whole thing was a big mistake. I didn't plan to marry you. It just happened. I was forced into it just as much as you were. And when I realized what I'd done, I kept it from you, thinking I could get it annulled."

So she hadn't wanted to marry him. The knowledge hurt him more than any other loss he'd ever suffered. "Is that what you're planning to do?"

"It is. If it weren't for you and those dang-fool Buscuses, I'd be homesteading in the Territory by now."

"Hitched to some farmer and destined for an early grave."

"At least I would've died happy!" she shouted.

"And you'd be buried on your own land!" he shouted back.

"That's right. Land is the only thing that matters."

"You are a cold woman, January Jones. Your single-minded purpose in life is to get your name on a deed."

Feeling rejected and furious that he'd lost the upper hand, he spun away from her and stalked over to where the horses were tethered. "You're totally devoid of tender emotion, you heartless wench."

Heartless? He was accusing her of being heartless? She'd had a heart once upon a time. Then he'd come along and stolen it. He'd tromped all over it and left it torn and bleeding somewhere on the trail. If she was heartless, it was all his doing!

"That's right. I'm heartless, penniless, *and* homeless and it's all your fault. Every bit of it. I rue the day I met you."

He heard her voice crack and went to her, but she wouldn't allow him to touch her, comfort her. She blamed him for the loss of a dream that had never been possible. "You don't want to be married to me," she sobbed.

"Yes, I do." He'd say anything if only she'd stop crying.

"You don't love me. You never cared about me. I've been nothing but a millstone around your neck, a tribulation and a trial. I tried to do right. I tried to help you and show you that I could be good for you. But nothin' I do ever makes you happy. The only thing that'll please you is to see the last of me. Well, I'll do that for you. I'll leave and you can get on to Alaska."

He tried to contradict her, but she was beyond listening, beyond reason. He grabbed her by the shoulders and shook her. "January, what do you want from me?"

She yanked away from his rough handling and wiped her eyes with the backs of her hands. Drawing herself up, she snapped, "All I ever wanted from you or anyone else was a home, some happiness."

"And I can't give you that?"

"Can't and won't."

"Then I guess this is it."

She sniffed inelegantly. This was that crossroads she'd been so worried about. "I reckon it is. There's no place for us to go to from here. Not together anyhow."

"What will you do?"

"Don't worry about me. Like you, I've been taking care of myself for a long time." She marched over to Brownie, swearing under her breath that if the horse gave her a dot of trouble about leaving without Shadow, she'd shoot the cussed critter right between the eyes.

But the horse obeyed her commands as though he understood her need to get away cleanly and with some small measure of dignity. She sat in the saddle for a moment, the reins in her hands, trying to decide which way to go.

Oklahoma was hopeless. To be honest, she'd known that long before today. She wasn't a person who could be happy in the flatlands. She wanted the Ozarks. She'd always feel at home in the hills. She clucked to Brownie and turned east down the road, back the way they'd come.

She'd return to Joplin and take Ocie Randall up on her offer to live with her. She didn't know how she'd support herself, but it was a destination and she felt better having a purpose. Now that she had a goal, she didn't feel so naked and vulnerable.

As she passed Case, she half expected him to grab her off the horse and kiss some sense into her. But he didn't. He just stood rooted to the spot like an ancient, implacable tree, his eyes hard-edged, his mouth grim.

This would be her last glimpse of him and she didn't want to remember him without that lopsided smile. "Hey, Latimer!"

"Yes?" he asked, hoping she'd changed her mind.

"Watch your back. I won't be around to save your butt anymore." Riding off, she left him standing in front of the abandoned cabin. A cabin that was evidence of someone else's broken dreams.

Chapter 18

Case watched January ride away and willed his feet not to run after her, his mouth not to call her back. This was it. She was leaving and she was taking trouble and complications with her. Without her, his world would stop tilting at such a reckless angle. His life could get back to normal. In a few months he'd be in Alaska preparing to embark on a whole new adventure. He was free of the maddening female and he was glad.

She disappeared around a bend in the road and his throat tightened. If he was so damned glad, why did he feel like such a sonuvabitch? As if an emotional life sentence had just been pronounced against him? He was bleak in his soul, as though he'd just seen the sun go down, never to rise again.

He'd been a loner most of his adult life. He'd never associated being alone with the feeling called loneliness, because he'd never cared about people enough to want them in his life. Until now. Without January he didn't feel completely alive. It was as though he'd lost a part of himself. The knowledge that she had become so important made him furious, with her and with himself. God, he hadn't thought he would miss her so much!

Her jerked off his new hat and threw it on the ground. ''Dammit to hell! What has she done to me?'' The woman drove him crazy, twisted him up in knots. He was better off without her.

He mounted Shadow and headed the stallion in the opposite direction, determined to get as far away from January Jones as was humanly possible.

His thoughts were jumbled as he rode along. Warring internal voices cross-examined his motives. *Where is she headed?* one voice asked.

What do you care? answered another.

It isn't right to let a woman ride the trail all alone.

She said she could take care of herself.

How can you just abandon her after all you've been through together? challenged the first.

Who's abandoning whom here?

She doesn't need you or any other man.

Case urged Shadow into a gallop.

He'd traveled several miles when his conscience got the best of him. He couldn't just let her ride off like that. It was too dangerous. The way she attracted trouble, there was no telling what might happen and he didn't want to be responsible for loosing her upon an unsuspecting world. It would take a better man than he was to get through that hard head of hers, but at least he could make sure she got to wherever she was headed safely.

Feeling trapped by his own feelings, he could almost hear that picket fence being nailed up around him. "Dammit to hell!" Fully aware he was making a big mistake, Case yanked on the reins and wheeled Shadow around in an abrupt turn. "Some people just don't know when they're well off," he muttered between clenched teeth as he galloped down the trail after her.

He followed January all the way back to Joplin, careful not to divulge his presence and equally careful to stay out of cussing and shooting range. Being followed and nursemaided wouldn't set well with Miss Independence.

When they reached town and he saw she was headed for Mrs. Randall's boardinghouse, he breathed a sigh of relief. He'd had a lot of time to think and he'd come to a decision. Since land seemed to be the only thing she wanted out of life, he'd see that she had some. Never let it be said that Case Latimer didn't provide for his wife.

He rode to Carthage and did something he'd never done before and couldn't believe he was doing now. He used Shadow as collateral for a stake. That done, he managed to get himself in a poker game with some very serious players. The high-stakes game lasted for four days and he didn't quit until he'd parlayed his initial winnings into enough money to carry out his four-step plan.

Step one had succeeded beyond his wildest dreams. He left Carthage with nearly twenty thousand dollars, more than enough to do what had to be done. Step two would be a bit trickier. He was reluctant to show his face in Joplin since Sheriff Ruggles was probably harboring some hard feelings regarding his jail. But being a gambler, by heart and by choice, Case took the chance.

He made discreet inquiries around town and, finding his face on none of the posted wanted bills, he walked, bold as brass, into the sheriff's office one early May morning.

"Hello, Sheriff Ruggles. Remember me?"

The lawman's boots were propped on the desk, his chair tipped back against the wall in a misleading posture of indolence. He drew and leveled a gun on Case so fast, Case didn't even see the movement. "I sure do, Latimer. What the hell are you doing in my town?"

"I was just passing through and thought I'd stop by and see if there was a bounty on my head."

"You lookin' to collect it?"

"No. I'm looking to clear my good name of false charges."

The chair rocked down with a bang, but the gun never wavered. "You should've hung around a little longer. I got a telegram the day after your . . . er . . . hasty departure."

"From the sheriff in Branson?"

"That's right. He was just notifying me that he'd arrested the men who held up the stage and robbed Mr. Tyrone."

"That's nice. Was Mr. Tyrone happy to get his money back?"

"He sure was. Come to find out, he'd shot himself in the foot. Isn't that funny?"

"Very. I guess that clears me then, huh?"

"Of the robbery charges. I checked around and unfortunately you're not wanted anywhere. At the moment. However, there's still the little matter of that." He motioned with his gun to the back of the jail where raw timber had been nailed over the blown-out walls.

"Since I didn't have any dynamite on me when you locked me up, you must realize I couldn't have done it."

"I do. And believe me, that's all that's keeping me from blowing the same kind of hole clear through you."

"I'm real sorry you were troubled by that . . . um . . . little inconvenience."

"Lucky for you, I haven't had to arrest anyone lately. I wouldn't be in such a good mood if I'd had to put lawbreakers up in my spare room at home."

Case surveyed the damage and shook his head. "That is a mighty big hole you've got there."

"It's a nine-hundred-dollar hole, to be exact."

"Would you stop pointing that gun at my head if I paid for the damages?"

"I might." Ruggles made no move to lower the weapon.

Case tossed a bag of money on the desk. "There's three thousand dollars in there."

The sheriff's eyes grew cold. "I said it was a nine-hundred-dollar hole. You trying to bribe a law enforcement official?"

Case feigned horror. "I wouldn't dream of it. I'd just like to make a sizable contribution to the Widows and Orphans Fund. Joplin does have such a fund, doesn't it, sheriff?"

"It does." Looking sorry he wouldn't get to use it, Ruggles returned the gun to his holster.

"I knew it." Case stuck out his hand and the lawman shook it—reluctantly. "It's been a pleasure doing business with you, sir."

"Sorry I can't say the same. You know, Latimer, it

might be a good idea if you don't spend too much time around here."

"My sentiments exactly."

Outside, Case breathed a sigh of relief. He hadn't expected to pull it off that easily. Lady Luck had smiled on him once more, as she had ever since he'd parted company with January. He'd try not to think about that.

Now that he was square with the law, he could start on step three. This one would require some travel, but it was sure to be simpler than step four—getting January to agree.

January was out behind the boardinghouse hanging laundry on the line, but her mind wasn't on her work. It was still on that damned deserter, Case, though it had been over two weeks since the day they'd parted. She was trying with all her earnest heart to get on with her new life in Joplin, but somehow she felt as though she weren't really living at all. There was an emptiness now, a longing she'd never known before.

A stiff breeze popped the wet sheets, which flapped and snapped like the sails on a schooner. They tangled around her, impeding her progress, and fanned her anger at Case into a full-fledged hissy fit. She was mad at him and at herself. But it was the hapless laundry that took the brunt.

"Hellfire," she muttered as she shook out a sheet and tossed it over the line. Before she could take a wooden clothes peg from her mouth and force it over the bucking muslin, the wind flipped it over her head. Struggling out of the sheet's clammy grasp, she lost her balance and went down in the dirt, dragging the clean laundry with her.

That's when she realized she was no longer alone.

A pair of shiny boots was moving toward her between the rows of sheets. She knew those feet, but she hadn't expected to ever see them again. She held her breath as a slim brown hand gathered back one of the sheets and exposed a familiar smiling face.

"Hello, January."

She was so shocked by Case's sudden, unexpected appearance she couldn't speak. Her teeth clamped down on the remaining pegs and she stared at him in wonder and astonishment. She'd prayed for this day, imagined it a million times, but when two weeks had gone by without a word from him, she'd given up hope. She wanted to hug him and kiss him, but she couldn't even say hello. Hellfire, she couldn't even get to her feet.

"Nice blowy day for laundry." He leaned casually against a clothesline pole, his arms folded across his chest.

He was really here. She hadn't conjured him up out of her unspeakable loneliness. She was both glad and mad. Where had he been all this time? And what had he been doing? The way he was acting, a body would think they'd just spoken at breakfast. How dare he stand there grinning, cool as a cucumber.

Didn't he realize she'd died a hundred deaths since she'd ridden away from that cabin? That foolish girl was long gone. In her place was a woman, made old and wise by nights of crying herself to sleep.

Gradually the shock of his nearness wore off. "Watr ya dun her?" she mumbled around the pegs.

His mustache twitched and he reached out slowly and extracted the pegs, one by one. His blue eyes, twinkling at full power, never left hers as he dropped the pegs into her apron pocket. Pulling her to her feet, he asked, "What did you say?"

She looked abashed. He *would* come on laundry day when her hands were red and wrinkled, her face chapped. Her hair looked like a rook's nest and she was barefoot, for God's sake! What would he think of her? "I asked you what you're doin' here."

"I came to see you, of course." A sheet flapped in his face and he lazily brushed it aside.

"Now that you've seen me, what're you hanging around for?"

"If I didn't know better, I'd say you weren't happy to see *me*, Mrs. Latimer."

"Mrs. Latimer!"

"That is your name, isn't it?" He regarded her with mock reproach. "You haven't gone and gotten that annulment yet, have you?"

She busied herself shaking out a sheet so he wouldn't see the flush on her face. "I haven't had time."

She was even prettier than he remembered, but she looked different. She wore a pale blue dress and a big white apron. Red curls whipped around her face and she impatiently shoved them away. Her eyes were still defiant, but now they held a knowing sadness as well, a look of vulnerability. Was he responsible for putting it there?

"I guess you've been pretty busy."

"I have. Is that all? Did you just come to see if we was still hitched?"

"That's one reason. How have you been keeping?"

"Just fine. Don't I look fine?"

"You look better than fine."

She blushed and hefted the laundry basket. "I thought you'd be on your way to Alaska by now."

He shrugged. "I had some business to attend to."

They stared at each other for several long minutes, neither knowing what else to say. She was afraid to open her mouth lest she make a fool of herself by begging him to kiss her. He was trying to adjust to the faster rate his heartbeat had assumed the moment he saw her.

The silence drew attention to itself and January wiped her damp hands on her apron. "I can't stand around here jawin' all day. I got chores to do."

"Oh yes, you can. I've already spoken to Mrs. Randall and she told me to tell you she was giving you the rest of the day off. Come on, January." He took her hand. "We need to talk."

She lost all resistance the moment he touched her. She couldn't think or talk or breathe, her mind was so busy drinking in the sheer wonder of him. He'd come back. She didn't know why, but right now it was enough that he had. She didn't know what he wanted of her, but she was prepared to do anything, say anything, to keep him here.

He led her to a bench under an elm tree and sat down beside her. "How have you been getting along?"

"Fair. I've been workin' for Ocie for my keep. She's been mighty good, takin' me in and all."

"Are you happy?"

A wistful look stole over her delicate features. "Happy enough, I reckon. I got plenty to eat and a nice room. But I don't much cotton to town livin'. I'd rather be back in the hills."

He smiled and drew a folded piece of paper from his breast pocket. He handed it to her. "I'm glad to hear that."

She took the legal-looking paper and turned it over in her hands. "What's this?"

"It's a deed."

"A deed to what?"

"A farm."

Her eyes narrowed suspiciously. "What farm would that be?"

"Do you remember stopping at a little place near Gainesville while we were traveling together? Where I talked the lady of the house out of supper for us?"

"I remember you *saying* you talked her out of it."

He laughed at her haughty look. "I went back to see the Widow Green. Don't look so put out. When I was there the first time, she told me she wanted to sell out so she could go to her folks' in Springfield."

"So?"

"So I bought it."

"*You* bought a farm?" She couldn't believe it. Case had groused all the time about being tied down in one place. All that talk about picket-fence prisons had made it perfectly clear he had no intention of settling down. So what was the catch?

"Don't look so surprised. Stranger things have happened, you know."

"Yeah, I heard tell of a two-headed calf once, but I didn't believe that, either."

"You're holding the deed in your hand. How much more proof do you need?"

She couldn't read the paper, but it did look official. There were notary seals and everything. "Okay. So you bought yourself a farm. Why ain't you on it, workin'?"

"First of all, I didn't buy myself a farm. I bought it for *you.* Second of all, I have no intention of working it. I'll leave that to the owner." He smiled. "She's far more qualified than I."

"You bought me a . . . ?"

"A farm. Your name's on the deed, legal and binding. It looks like you're in business, Mrs. Latimer."

She still didn't understand. What did it all mean? He said he wasn't going to work the place. Was he planning to live there? With her? "How'd you manage to buy a farm? Last I saw you, you couldn't have bought a pound of coffee."

He resisted the urge to remind her his temporary indigence had been all her fault. "I was in a card game and got lucky. When it was over, I realized I had more than enough to get to Alaska, so I decided to make sure you had some security."

Alaska! He was still going to Alaska? "You shouldn't have troubled yourself, Mr. Latimer. I can take care of myself."

Now, what had he said wrong? "I know that, *Mrs.* Latimer. You've told me often enough. But knowing how you feel about having a place of your own, I couldn't leave without seeing you settled. Maybe you don't want to be married to me, but I'm still the head of this family and I'll provide for my wife if I want to."

She remembered that place. It was a real pretty little farm. A body could do a lot with land like that. Still, it had been bought with wagered money. That was sure to taint it. But *she* hadn't wagered the money. It was like a gift and God wouldn't look ill upon someone accepting a gift, would he? "All right."

"I don't care how stubborn you act, that farm is yours and there isn't a thing you can do to change it."

Her thoughts were racing. If memory served, there was a barn and a chicken house and a smokehouse. Yes, a place like that could make a good living for the right person. "All right."

"And you're going to live there even if I have to tie you to your horse and drag you there myself."

There were cleared fields and a little orchard and a good, sunny garden spot. "Dammit, Latimer, all right!"

He looked up sharply. "What did you say?"

"I said all right. Ten minutes ago." A farm of her own! It was too much to take in. And it wasn't some broken-down soddy on the prairie, either. It was a snug, well-tended house on good, rich bottomland. The best part of all, it was situated in the hills she loved. It was a dream come real.

Part of the dream hadn't come true. Case wasn't staying. It wouldn't be the same without him, but maybe she could still change his mind. After all, he wasn't in Alaska yet.

"You mean you'll go?"

She jumped up, grabbed his hands, and spun him around in excited circles. "You just try to stop me, Case Latimer!"

He'd vowed not to let it happen, but in all the excitement he forgot himself and kissed her full on the mouth. Her warm lips parted and he was drawn into her, all his good intentions swept in a tide of desire . . .

They spent several days preparing for the journey to the hundred-and-twenty-acre farm. The widow sold Case some animals, tools and equipment, and some of the household goods, but he insisted on taking January on numerous shopping expeditions to purchase supplementary supplies. She argued it was a shameful waste of good money to buy geegaws like rugs and pictures and mantel clocks, but Case argued it was his money to waste.

She was till unsure of his intentions. He'd made it clear he was leaving for Alaska after he got her settled, but the optimism of youth was on her side and she was confident he'd choose to stay with her. If wishing could make it so, then it would be.

They were getting along better now, as though having a shared purpose diffused some of the tension that usually boilcd between them. As they shopped for things to fill the wagon Case had bought, January pretended they were no different from any other newly married couple preparing to embark on the voyage of life together.

There'd been no more kisses after the one under the elm and she accepted the disappointing fact that Case harbored no husbandly interest toward her. She'd thought she was lonely without him, but it was nothing compared to the empty longing that kept her company through the long nights when he was just a breath away.

Case's original plan was to keep a healthy distance between them since no possible good could come of further exploring the physical side of their relationship. But because they were married, Ocie naturally assumed they'd be sharing a room and put his things in with hers. January had been too embarrassed to tell her otherwise, so the first night he slept on the floor.

The second night she offered to share the bed, saying it wasn't right for him to camp out on the hard floor when he was paying for everything. Since the old mattress sloped down to the middle, she had to huddle on the far side and hang on to the edge to keep from being rolled up against him. Half the night she worried he'd try something and the other half she was perturbed that he hadn't.

The furrowed bed offered a special challenge to Case and it was through force of will alone that he managed to observe the invisible barrier between them. It was a trial, but throughout the long night he kept his hands, and other parts, to himself.

The third night he climbed into bed as he had before, prepared for sleepless hours of denial, and was surprised when January rolled to his side and snuggled up against his back.

He was shocked when her hand began caressing his bare chest.

He was delighted when his could do likewise.

Instead of the neck-to-toe flannel nightgown she'd worn before, January had gone to bed dressed only in what God gave her. He groaned and pulled her warm, naked body to his, knowing as he did that he was stepping in a deep pool. But he didn't care. Hell, it wouldn't be the first time he'd been in over his head. As his lips found hers, he asked her if she knew what she was doing. She answered in a provocative voice, "I should. I had a good teacher."

"It's even more beautiful than I remembered," January said softly when the house came into sight.

"It's no mansion," he teased. "Just four rooms and a lean-to."

"Yeah." Her smile widened and her face glowed. "But it's *my* four rooms and lean-to."

They moved in. January took delight in arranging the furniture and filling the cupboards. Maybe it wasn't a mansion compared to what Case was used to, but it was a castle to her. The house was well-built and had a tight roof. It would be warm in winter and in the summer the well-placed windows would conduct cooling breezes throughout the rooms.

There was an enormous black woodstove in the kitchen. It had a double oven and a water reservoir that January kept filled from the pump near the back door.

There were two bedrooms. She chose the back one because of the view and was disappointed and a little hurt when Case said, "That's fine. I'll take the one in front." After the intimacies they'd known in Joplin, she had expected them to share a single room, but it seemed he had other ideas. She wouldn't humiliate herself by asking him what the problem was, so she assumed she hadn't pleased him. Maybe her boldness had been out of line. It was possible men didn't like aggressive women.

The reason for the sleeping arrangements became obvious a few days later. It seemed Case still had an aversion to remaining in one place. He'd meant it when he'd said he was only staying long enough to see her settled.

As the days went by, it became harder and harder for January to accept the fact that Case would soon be gone from her life forever. Each day that he stayed made the inevitable parting more difficult, so she tried to reassure him that she was capable of handling the farm alone. That way he'd go and she could grieve, then get on with her life. To that end, she began dropping the phrase, "when you're gone," into discussions of future events. At first it killed her to say it, but with time, it became a self-defensive habit.

Case hadn't exactly expected tears and hysterics when January finally acknowledged that he wasn't staying with her on the farm, but a little judicious cursing might have been in order. Anything would've been easier to swallow than her stoic silence.

There wasn't much time to worry about emotional matters. Life on the farm was too demanding. While he couldn't understand or share her delight in rural life, he was nonetheless fascinated by her passion for the mundane. She was content to sit on the porch in the evenings, to turn in early and exhausted, and to rise before dawn to start the same dull routine all over again.

A hard taskmaster, January kept Case busy despite his distaste for menial work. He balked at learning to milk the cow, but she insisted and before long he could handle the job alone. He protested when she hitched Brownie to the plow and told him to put in a late corn crop, but she got her field. However, the day she tried to send him out to the pigpen with a bucket of smelly slop, he drew the line. There were some things a man shouldn't have to do.

"Why don't I chop some wood instead?" he suggested.

"We've got plenty of wood for the time being."

"But you'll need enough to see you through the winter. I'd best do it while I'm still here."

Why'd he have to keep reminding her? The time for cutting and stacking winter wood was fall. In words as brisk as that season, she said. "I know. You're gonna be in Alaska come fall."

He tried to interpret the hard look she gave him. "I thought that was understood. I'll have to leave here pretty soon. It'll take a while to get to Seattle by train and book passage north. It gets cold fast up there, you know."

"No, I don't know much at all about that place. Why is that frozen tundra so damned important to you?"

"It's the adventure of it all. The excitement of going somewhere new where the taming influence of civilization hasn't quite reached. Why can't you understand, January?"

"I understand." She bit back her tears. He'd never planned to stay; deep down she'd known it all along. "Seems like we've had this conversation before."

"I believe we have." Case was reluctant to leave her. That's why he'd hung around longer than he should have. But he couldn't wait much longer. There weren't many boats out of Seattle after the first of August.

She regarded him with hurt in her eyes. "So you really are goin'?"

"I always said I was. I never said any different." Why was she making this so hard? Why did he feel like such a bastard every time he did something *he* wanted to do for a change?

She was tempted to fling the contents of the slop bucket in his face. But he'd expect that. It was what the old January would have done. She drew herself up. "Just go on, then. Why don't you leave today? Right now? You won't be happy until you go up there and freeze your damned tail off and die. Enjoy your freedom, or whatever it is you call it. Get a craw full of adventure. But don't you ever come back here expecting me to welcome you with a kiss and a roll in the hay."

She flounced away. Even with a slop bucket so heavy she had to carry it with both hands, she maintained the cool bearing of an indignant queen. She needn't worry. If he left, there'd be no coming back. Would a man willingly lock himself up in jail and throw away the key? Damn, but she made him mad.

She was too proud to ask him to stay, he knew. Never in the most heated moments of their lovemaking had she once told him she loved him. Not that he'd told her, either, but he'd been waiting for her to go first. No doubt she'd offered herself to him in Joplin out of gratitude for the farm. That's all she'd ever wanted from him; she'd made that clear enough. Now she had it. She didn't need him anymore, so he might as well just go. God, but she infuriated him!

He stalked over to the woodpile and pulled the ax out of a length of stove wood. Hoisting it over his shoulder, he strode off toward the woods, determined to take his anger and resentment and hurt—yes, dammit to hell, hurt—out on some hapless trees.

Coming here hadn't been a good idea. The past few days had only complicated things. Hell, he should have mailed the goddamned deed! He chose a likely candidate for his wrath, a tall hickory with lots of dead limbs. With grim determination he began to work out his frustration. Each time the ax blade struck home, it seemed to chant along with his muttered oaths: damn, damn, damn.

The tree fell with a resounding crash and Case contemplated going for Brownie and the drag chain, then decided against it. He wasn't ready to face January and her recriminating looks just yet. He'd chop the tree into manageable lengths and bring the wagon back for it later.

He tried to clear his mind and concentrate on the release to be found in hard, physical labor, but he couldn't. He kept thinking of the way she'd looked when he'd loved her, of the way she'd felt wrapped around him. He was going to miss that. Damn!

There'd be other women in Alaska, he told himself reasonably. Wherever men gathered to work, a contingent of easy ladies was usually on hand to assist them in their play. But it wouldn't be the same. Even the brief time he'd loved January had spoiled him. He'd never again be satisfied to simply pay and be done with it. Loving her had made him want to be loved back.

He soon had all the limbs hacked off the fallen tree and began chopping the trunk. He placed his left foot on it to steady the wobble and brought the ax down with exceptional force. It was a moment before he realized what he'd done and even longer before the pain began.

He blanched white when he saw the ax imbedded in the foot of his boot. He thought he would pass out when he tried to pull it free, but he worked at it until he was able to toss the bloody tool aside. The hideous pain came then and he felt the warm, sticky blood flowing inside his boot. He sank down on the tree trunk, frantically thinking what to do.

The most important thing was to remain conscious. If he didn't, he might very well bleed to death right here. He set his jaw and struggled until he pulled the boot off. Stripping the bandana from around his neck, he used a stick to fashion a tourniquet. He didn't know if he'd struck bone, but he knew one thing; he'd never make it back to the house.

January was washing potatoes under the pump when Case's ax fell silent. Knowing he'd return soon, she gathered up the vegetables and hurried inside to start supper.

The corn bread was done and he still hadn't come in. She went to the back door and stepped out to the porch. Shading her eyes against the last rays of the sun, she watched the woods uneasily for a sign of him. Something was wrong. Very wrong. She bounded off the steps and ran to the barn for Shadow. If Case was hurt, he'd need her.

It didn't take her long to find him slumped, ashen-faced, against the tree he'd felled. "Case!" She ran to his side and sized up the situation immediately. There was so much blood and he was barely conscious. Trying not to weep, she tore off her apron and used it to bind up his wound. Don't pass out on me, she prayed. She'd never get him on the horse if he did.

January would never know how she managed to get him on Shadow. Nor did she remember much of the short ride to the house. Somehow she got him into bed and cleaned and wrapped the injury as best she could. The cut was deep and his big toe was nearly severed. If he lost it, he'd be crippled for life. The situation was beyond her limited medical knowledge.

He'd passed out and couldn't hear her but January assured him she would be back soon. She raced Shadow the twelve long miles into town and fairly dragged the doctor away from his supper. After relating the problem, she raced home, getting there far ahead of the tired old man and his worn-out buggy.

Chapter 19

January saw the doctor to the door, then returned to Case's bedroom. She stood at the foot of the iron bed, gazing down at him. He was resting quietly, his chest rising and falling in a gentle motion, but he was still pale. So very pale. His pallor made his long lashes and silky mustache seem darker than ever.

Just looking at him made her heart twist, he was that handsome. His aristocratic nose and high cheekbones lent him dignity in repose, but she knew that hidden beneath his closed lids were lively blue eyes that concealed the very devil in their depths. She stroked back the heavy lock of hair that had fallen onto his forehead. She was so hungry to touch him, she indulged herself in a little innocent petting. Sitting down on the bed beside him, she caressed his face gently.

She was sorry he'd been hurt, but one good thing would come of his injury. He wouldn't be going anywhere until his foot was healed and that could take weeks. She'd have him a little longer. She'd been given another chance to show him how much she loved him.

Maybe by the time his convalescence was over, he'd realize he belonged with her and not in some Alaskan boom town. Temporarily forgetting her many pressing chores, she sat for a long time and watched him sleep.

"Don't stop," he murmured. "That felt good." He opened his eyes and gave her a weak grin. "Doctor's orders, I trust?"

She smiled back at him. "No, just another old folk remedy. I'm glad to see it worked. You look plenty bright-eyed now."

"Do it some more," he said with mock fatigue as he sought to pull her down beside him. "I feel a relapse coming on."

"Is that what you call it? Let go of me, you randy faker, and I'll fix you some supper."

"I don't want any supper. I want you."

"Sorry, but I ain't on the menu." That was just like a man. He'd done his utmost best to chop his fool foot off, nearly bleeding to death in the bargain, and here he was thinking about his pleasures. She wiggled away from him and escaped to the door.

"I hope you're not going to be one of those nasty, difficult patients while you're laid up. I got enough to worry about running this farm without you giving me grief."

"Who, me?" His look was pure innocence.

She retraced her steps and sat in the chair at his bedside. "I think maybe we should get a few things straight before we go any further." Prolonged, enforced togetherness could prove very tempting to both of them and she'd do well to establish some rules.

"Like what?"

"The doc said you'll have to stay in bed for a couple of weeks. After that, you'll have to keep off that foot awhile longer. I know you're a gambler, but unless you want to take your chances with gangrene, you'd better do as he says."

"Surprisingly enough, it doesn't hurt all that much now. Was it very bad?"

She shuddered at the memory of the hacked flesh. "Bad enough. You ain't feelin' poorly now because of the medicine Doc gave you. When it wears off, that foot's goin' to be throbbing something dreadful and you're goin' to be in a world of hurt."

He grimaced. "Thanks for the prognosis, nurse. There's

nothing like a little cheerful optimism to hasten a patient's speedy recovery."

"I'm just telling you how it's gonna be. There's no way you can leave until you're well, so we'll have to live in this house together until then. That's liable to cause some . . . uh . . . beguilin' situations to arise."

"With any luck at all," he agreed.

"I just want to make it clear that living here don't grant you no husbandly privleges. I'll take care of you as long as you don't take advantage of the arrangement."

"You didn't seem to mind me taking advantage of the arrangement in Joplin. What are you worried about, January? That I might make love to you again? Would that be so terrible?"

It wouldn't be terrible at all and that was the main problem. "We both know you'll be leaving as soon as you're fit to travel. I ain't no gambler like you and I can't risk being abandoned 'that way.' I don't want to raise a child alone."

Case bristled. Abandoned? She'd been acting as if she couldn't wait for him to get on down the road so she could have her precious farm all to herself. All he'd heard was "when you leave, this" and "when you leave, that." She'd made it obvious from the very start that all she wanted from him was a pair of strong hands to help her get established. She'd never acted as though she wanted him. How dare she accuse him of abandoning her.

"Isn't that a little like locking the barn door after the horse is stolen? You could very well be 'that way' right now."

"I ain't, so don't worry about it." She sounded more certain than she felt. At least she didn't think she was pregnant. "You just get well. You got a boat to catch, remember?"

"I remember," he said tightly. He turned his back to her, wincing when pain sliced through his injured foot.

As the days passed and boredom set in, Case's mood quickly deteriorated from disgruntled to downright crotchety. It provoked him that the only times January paid the least bit of attention to him was when she brought in his meal trays and changed his dressing. Even those transactions she handled with cool, efficient detachment.

One morning she brought in a pitcher of warm water, along with a washbowl and some clean rags. "I think you're overdue for a bath." Brusquely, she placed the bowl on the mattress beside him and wrung out the rag. "I'll wash down as far as possible and up as far as possible."

"But what about possible? Who's going to wash it?"

Her eyes narrowed. He was doing it again. She flung the washrag in the bowl and water splashed over him. "Give your own damned self a bath. You've got a hurt foot, but you ain't paralyzed from the neck down."

No, he wasn't. Just the thought of her soft hands sponging his body all over caused aches to prove that statement. It might start out as a bath, but it could end up a whole different way. If he played his cards right, that is. "I don't think I'm able."

She eyed him, knowing he was naked under the thin blanket. She imagined she could see the muscles and the curly hair and the warm skin. If she perked her ear, she could hear his body calling her name. "Oh, yes, you are. That's why you're going to take care of your own damned bath."

"What kind of nurse are you, anyway?" he asked petulantly, disappointment and frustration underlining every word.

"A busy one." A needy one who yearned for him and all he could give her. A lonely one who laid awake in her room at night, contemplating ravishment like a shameless Jezebel. A cautious one who knew better than to start something both of them were only too eager to finish. She stared at him archly and, holding the bar of soap high over the bowl, she opened her hand slowly and let it drop with a splat before she flounced out of the room.

That afternoon, January was weeding the garden when

a wagon pulled into the yard. A middle-aged couple climbed down and hailed her. "Howdy!"

She howdied them back.

The woman stepped forward and shook her hand. "I'm Sarah Wilcox and this here's my husband, Henry. You can call me Aunt Sarah. Near about everyone does. We're your closest neighbors. We live about six miles over." She waggled her hand in an easterly direction. "Sorry it's taken us so long to come by. It's been a busy season and this is the first chance we had. We was on our way into town and decided to stop and meet you."

January liked the tall, sandy-haired woman immediately. Her face was tanned from the sun and little white lines radiated from the corners of her eyes. She had a loud, engaging voice and a friendly smile. She looked like a woman with plenty to be happy about.

Her husband was a few inches shorter than Sarah, thin and work-tough. January shook his hand and noticed that, although it was big and rough, it was also gentle. He was quiet, as if resigned to letting his spirited wife do all the talking.

"Pleased to meet you. I'm January Jones . . . uh . . . Latimer."

Aunt Sarah grinned. "Well, girl, which is it?"

"It's Latimer. I just got married."

"Now, ain't that nice? Newlyweds. Trot that there husband of yours out here so we can say howdy."

"My husband's in bed. He had an accident chopping wood and hurt his foot."

Aunt Sarah glanced at Henry, her concern evident. "Well, fry me brown! You mean you're running this big place all by yourself, a little scrap like you?"

"I'm stronger than I look," January assured her. "I'm used to hard work."

"Henry, go chop this poor girl some firewood."

Henry made a move for the woodpile, but January stopped him. "Please, don't. I can't ask you to chop wood when you've got your own chores to do."

Aunt Sarah hugged January's shoulders. "Honey, you don't have to ask. What are neighbors for? I'll pass the word that your man's laid up and folks'll be around to help out. There's a passel of nice people in these parts and they're always ready to help in times of need."

"That's very kind." She watched Henry amble over to the woodpile and slowly and methodically fall to work. "Won't you come in and have some coffee?" January invited, overwhelmed by her new neighbors' generosity.

"That'd be a pure pleasure. I can tell you all about everything."

That proved to be no exaggeration. Aunt Sarah was a wealth of information. Not only about the community and all its inhabitants, of whose lives she knew and was willing to share the most intimate details, but also about gardening, cooking, quilting, canning, and children. She and Henry had been married twenty-seven years and had seven children ranging in age from twenty-five down to thirteen, and six grandchildren, the favorite being little Jesse, her brag baby, and a regular angel to hear her tell it.

Not only was he the most beautiful child ever born, but he was good and smart and sweet, to boot. "Why, Jesse, he wasn't even born the reg'lar way," Aunt Sarah rhapsodized. "God jest greased his little fanny and slid him down on a rainbow."

She'd lived around Gainesville since before there was a town and had a firm grip on the community's pulse. "Anytime you need help with something, you jest holler 'Aunt Sarah' and I'll come a-runnin'."

January confessed her lack of training in housewifely skills and the older woman promptly reassured her with "When I got married, I was so green you could scrape it off'n me with a stick. Learnin' comes with livin', honey. There jest ain't no way around it."

It was comforting to know such a paragon was close by and January made up her mind to cultivate Aunt Sarah's natural friendliness and willingness to help in the days ahead.

Her guest had no compunction about entering a strange man's bedroom and stuck her head in to introduce herself to Case. He was napping so she backed out quietly. "My, ain't he a pretty 'un?" she gushed. "It's a good thing you married him before he got here. There's an ungodly amount of squirmy single girls in these parts."

When it was time for the Wilcoxes to leave, January walked them out to the wagon, certain she'd just made a lifelong friend.

"You think your man will be up to comin' to the box supper at the schoolhouse next Saturday night?"

"I don't know." January wasn't sure *she* was up to such a social occasion. She didn't know a thing about box suppers and was too proud to admit her ignorance of such matters. "The doctor's due by tomorrow. If he says it's all right, I reckon we could come."

"You see you do. It'll give you a chance to meet folks and let them look you over. You jest be sure you keep that pretty man of yourn on a short rein, if you know what I mean." Aunt Sarah's booming laughter rang out as the wagon lurched down the road.

The next day the doctor pronounced Case fit enough for short outings, so long as he used a crutch and kept his weight off his foot. When asked if he could attend the box supper, the old man scratched his whiskery chin and said, "I reckon that'd be all right. Just don't you go dancin' no jigs or cuttin' no rustys, young man." Case assured him he wouldn't. He didn't feel strong enough for dancing and hadn't the slightest idea what cutting a rusty entailed.

After seeing the doctor off, January returned to the kitchen where Case was seated, his injured foot propped on a low stool.

"What in tarnation is a box supper, exactly?" she asked him.

"You mean you've never been to one?"

"If I had, I wouldn't be askin'."

Case had had only infrequent experience with such events himself, but he endeavored to explain. "As I recall, the ladies all bring a supper for two in a decorated box and then they're auctioned off."

"The ladies?"

"No, the suppers. The man who bids highest on the box wins the companionship of the lady who prepared it for as long as it takes to eat the meal."

"Hmmm." She nodded as she thought it over. "What's the purpose of such as that?"

"The money goes to a good cause. Since this one's at the school, it will probably go for school equipment or books. It's also a good way for young people to court. A boy who buys a girl's covered box has an excuse to sit alone with her and make pie-eyes at her all evening."

She wrinkled her nose in distaste. "Folks really do that?"

"On a regular basis."

She had a sudden thought. "What if a feller gets the wrong box, not the one his gal made but some pruney old spinster's?"

"Since it's all supposed to be anonymous, that's the best part of the fun. The suspense brings out a man's sporting blood."

"Sounds like foolishness to me. Whyn't folks just give the money to the school and be done with it?"

Case sighed. January, having lived a self-reliant and solitary life, didn't understand the need people had for entertainment and social fellowship. "People need one another, not just in times of trouble, but during good times, too. You'd better get used to the idea if you plan to live in a community like this."

"I ain't never been around very many folks all at the same time," she admitted nervously.

"This isn't the holler where it's every man for himself and the devil take the hindmost. Rural folks enjoy their little get-togethers and if you don't take part, you'll be marked as standoffish and you'll never fit in."

He was right, of course. She'd learned that from talking with Aunt Sarah. "All right. But since I don't know nothin' about decoratin' fancy boxes, you'll have to help me."

Saturday evening was balmy and fair, a perfect ending to a perfect early June day. January assisted Case into the wagon and took the reins. Her box, a sad-looking little affair wrapped in yellow gingham and tied with a crumpled blue ribbon, was stashed carefully in the back. Case had given her directions regarding its construction but had insisted she do all the work herself.

She'd made an attempt to make it more attractive by tying a bunch of wild roses on it, but they'd already begun to wilt and only added to the box's dejected appearance. Actually, the box's facade was misleadingly promising. Any man tempted to bid on it would soon discover its appeal was mostly on the outside, since it contained overcooked fried chicken, slices of stillborn bread spread with salty butter, and unpalatably hard molasses cookies.

When they reached the school, it was already surrounded by buggies and wagons and horses. Older men stood in tight little knots discussing crops and school board business and children ran wild, delighting in the infrequent companionship of their peers. A large cluster of young men and boys lined the path hoping for a glimpse of their sweethearts' offerings.

"January!"

She looked around to find the owner of the voice and saw Aunt Sarah making her way toward her, a herd of small children tagging alongside her.

"You childurn git along now and let Grandmaw be. I'll see y'all later." She stooped down from her considerable height and bestowed a loud, smacking kiss on each of them. "Now, scat!" They ran off and Sarah laughed. "Lordy, they flat wear me out, but I love 'em all. How're you young people tonight?" She thrust out her hand to Case and introduced herself before January had a chance to do the honors. "I'm proud to see you could make it, Case. Mind you take it easy on that foot."

"Yes, ma'am." It seemed to him that agreement was the best approach when dealing with Aunt Sarah.

"That's a right pretty little box you brung, honey."

January couldn't help but notice Aunt Sarah's unconscious emphasis on the word "little." As they went inside, she realized with a sinking feeling that her contribution looked downright puny next to the other flamboyantly decorated masterpieces.

Aunt Sarah plopped her tribute down on the table. It was wrapped in pink calico, decorated with cutout paper hearts, and tied with a big white bow. It emanated a mouth-watering aroma of chicken and dumplings and apple pie and was attracting a lot of attention. January was glad Case knew the identity of her box. She wouldn't have to suffer undue embarrassment by sharing her unappetizing supper with a stranger.

After considerable socializing, the auctioneer got down to business. The man's job was not only to hold up items for sale and accept bids, but to provide amusement for those present. He poked fun at the bidders and fielded their inevitable insults. January suspected there were unspoken rules governing who could say what, but it was all done in the spirit of fun and everyone seemed to be having a fine time.

Although the auctioneer encouraged the bidding as high as possible, most of the boxes sold for between fifteen and twenty-five cents. That is until he held Aunt Sarah's creation aloft.

"Now, what do I hear for this heavenly concoction?"

A young man in the back bid twenty-five cents, which the auctioneer scorned. "Lee Roy, I wouldn't even let you sniff under the lid for no measly quarter. Who's ready to put their money where their mouth is?"

An elderly gentleman recklessly upped the bid to thirty-five cents. "You boys ain't serious?" the auctioneer asked. "Why, this here box has got thirty-five cents' worth of pretty on it. Who'll give me a real bid?"

January was startled when Case spoke up. "Two dollars!"

All eyes turned to them. "Two dollars, our new neighbor says. Anybody gonna tussle him over it?" When no more bids were forthcoming, the auctioneer gallantly carried the box forward and, in consideration of Case's injury, placed it reverently in his hands.

The bidding went on until it was time for January's box to be sold. The heat of the room had shriveled the pathetic-looking roses and their odor was no longer pleasant, either. She wanted to die from embarrassment when the opening bid was five cents. "Now, come on, fellers," the auctioneer goaded. "Looks can be deceivin', you know. Do I hear ten cents?"

A small boy waved a dime in the air and won. There were no more bids. Red-faced, January glared at Case, mad enough to butt stumps. How dare he put her in such a humiliating position. He knew which box was hers. Why hadn't he bid two dollars on it? Why had he left her to suffer such shame in front of her new neighbors?

Case was immediately sorry he hadn't bid on January's box, but he'd seen Aunt Sarah carry the pink one in and knew, without being told, that the woman was a skilled cook. Why, she even smelled like cinnamon! Besides, he never had been able to resist homemade apple pie and he was betting that box held one. Weeks of eating the results of January's earnest but clumsy culinary efforts had softened his resistance even more and the savory smell coming out of Aunt Sarah's supper box affected him like a drug. He'd catch holy hell when they got home, but it would be worth it.

It was soon time for partners to pair up. January felt a tug on her skirt and looked down into the small, smudgy face staring up at her so hopefully. In all good conscience, she wasn't sure she could inflict her cooking on an innocent child. "Hello."

"Hello."

"Ain't you one of Aunt Sarah's grandchildren?"

"I'm Tilly's boy, Jesse Clayton. Grandmaw sure was right."

"About what?"

"She give me that dime and said if I bought this box, I wouldn't be sorry 'cause it belonged to the purtiest gal in the county."

January smiled. He was a beautiful child. His fine-pored skin was the color of sun-warmed honey, his curly corn-silk hair making an unusual contrast. He had wide green, intelligent eyes, fringed with gold-tipped lashes. And he sure had a fine line of bull for one so young. "How old are you, Jesse Clayton?"

"I'm near a'most five."

"I reckon in ten years the papas around here'll be locking up their daughters when they see you comin'."

"Yes'm." He smiled engagingly and his green eyes sparkled with mischief. "That's what ever'body says."

Even though the food was cold and untasty, Jesse bragged on it like it was manna from heaven, making January wonder how much Aunt Sarah had paid him for his trouble. And she'd always heard children were basically honest. She listened to Jesse's lively chatter, but she couldn't keep her mind on the conversation for wondering how Case was enjoying his meal. She hoped the damned fool choked on that pie.

She drove home in stony silence. Any attempts Case made to josh her out of her sullen mood failed. "January, why are you being so hardheaded?"

She glared back at him in the growing darkness. "I ain't hardheaded, but bein' made a laughin'stock of just naturally puts me a little crossways with the world."

"You weren't a laughingstock."

"Was too. I saw the sly-eyed glances those gals were givin' me. That is, when they could spare me a look. Most of the time they was so busy ogling you they didn't know if it was windy or wet."

"They were not."

"Were too. I'll wager that right now there's two dozen

arguments going on about what that handsome Latimer man sees in his scrawny little wife. They're sure to know it ain't my cookin' since you didn't even bid on my box."

He took the reins from her and whoaed the horse. Turning to her, he said, "First of all, you aren't scrawny. There was some looking going on tonight, but most of it was those young bucks getting an eyeful of you. Second of all, what those simple-headed little girls don't know yet is that when a man chooses a woman, her cooking ability is not his highest priority."

"It ain't?" He was so near, his warm breath made his mustache tickle her lips.

"No, it isn't. I'm sorry I was seduced by Aunt Sarah's apple pie, which was delicious by the way, and I'm sorry if you were embarrassed. But I'm not sorry I married you."

"You ain't? I mean, you aren't?"

"No, I'm not." He took her into his arms and kissed her until she was breathless. She'd waited a long time for that and it was shameless the way her very blood sang out for him. She kissed him back.

After long moments, he set her away from him and took up the reins, urging the horse toward home. "Next time you have any doubts," he told her as he tried to regain some of his lost composure, "just ask me and I'll do my best to set your mind at ease."

Her fingertips brushed her swollen lips and she couldn't speak until the tingling died down. She tried to hide her pleased smile by pretending to admire the countryside. "I'll have to remember that."

Case's foot was slow to mend, but January kept him busy just the same. Through Aunt Sarah, she contacted the schoolteacher and arranged to borrow books and a slate. School was out for the summer and Miss Peel was only too happy to oblige her. Once January obtained the necessary equipment, she approached Case about teaching her to read and write.

He readily agreed. Not only would the lessons make him feel useful and give him something to do, but it would be an opportunity to repay her for all the farming lore she had forced down his throat. He now knew more than he'd ever wanted to know about how to treat hens with ruptured egg bags, how to force tonic down a cow, and how to plant by the signs.

As it turned out, January was a much more willing pupil than Case and soon mastered the alphabet and simple words. To facilitate learning, he wrote out the names of objects around the house on small pieces of paper and she delighted in identifying them. He'd even tried fooling her by mislabeling items, which she corrected eagerly. Before long, there were labels everywhere. She rapidly advanced to reading short sentences.

When she came in for her lesson one evening, she was amazed to see a label pinned to Case's shirt. It took her a long time to decipher it, since he'd give her no clues, but finally she triumphantly pronounced, "love-starved husband."

With a sly grin, she removed the paper and scratched through his elegant handwriting. In small, labored letters, she printed, "wishful dreamer." Their throbbing awareness was ignored in the laugh they shared before getting down to work, but both of them wondered how much longer they could maintain the hands-off policy she'd insisted on.

One warm evening, Case listened to January read from a primer but couldn't concentrate on the words. He was fascinated by the way the lamplight plucked the red out of her hair and cast dark shadows through the fringe of her lashes.

Her hair had grown out and was now nearly down to her shoulders, rich and curly and resistant to control. Case longed to see those silky tresses tossing on a pillow as he coaxed her willing body to fulfillment. He ached to tangle it in his hands as he pulled her lips to his for a taste of her sweetness.

It was incredible the way she'd blossomed. She was no longer thin and her ripening bosom strained the bodice of the dresses he'd bought in Joplin. She was calmer now, more at peace with herself, and he knew the gratification of farmwork had fulfilled inner needs he could only guess at. At times he resented not having been the one to make her so happy. But then, he'd made it possible for her to have the farm, hadn't he? Maybe he could claim a little of the credit.

He watched her acquire what she called "house plunder" with the voraciousness of a born housewife and was amazed at the joy she found in the simple, daily pleasures of her new life. He surprised even himself by sharing some of that joy.

Like the day the goslings hatched. She ran into the house holding a honking ball of yellow fuzz in both hands, as excited as if she'd personally been in charge of all creation and had given orders directly to God himself.

But sometimes she carried the pride of ownership too far. At her behest, Case limped out to the garden when the first green tomatoes appeared in order to properly admire that wonder. She was disappointed that he wasn't as enthralled as she was by all things green and growing.

Once, he caught her sitting on a limb in the apple tree, industriously inspecting the tiny nubbins that would eventually turn into fruit, but would probably never live a second life as an edible dessert. Another time she was down on her hands and knees totally absorbed in the slow progress of a tiny insect.

"What are you doing down there?" he called.

Completely serious, she answered, "Making sure my ladybug gets home all right."

She was in a towering rage the morning she went out to feed the chickens and discovered two of her best layers missing. A few bloodstained feathers was all that was left to tell the tale, but she knew immediately that a fox had been responsible and she started plotting its demise.

Normally an early riser who claimed a decent woman

was only in bed between the hours of seven p.m. and four a.m. unless she was in labor or dead, January took to getting up long before cockcrow, hoping to catch the villain red-handed. After several such mornings of being roused from a sound sleep as she stomped around the house loading the Winchester and muttering about thieving red devils, Case asked her why she didn't just sell her bed and buy lamps with the money.

Despite her efforts, the fox continued his marauding and her frustration grew. One misty morning they were having breakfast and she happened to glance out the window to see the culprit slinking around the hen yard. Without pausing to grab the gun, she raced to the door, threw it open, and ran down the steps barefoot, screaming like a loco Apache.

The "fox" turned out to be a hungry rogue wolf and not nearly as wily as his distant cousin the fox. Case wasn't surprised. Any predator stupid enough to steal from January was bound to use poor judgment when selecting an escape route. The wolf cut across the yard, a squawking hen still clutched in his mouth, and ran smack dab into the path of vengeance.

Outraged by such audacity, January grabbed up a broom, the only weapon at hand, and chased the wolf until he dropped the hen. The old broody shook her feathers and staggered back into the yard, without a backward glance for the foolish, heroic girl who'd just rescued her from the very jaws of death.

Case yelled at January about her recklessness. "That wolf could have turned on you before I had a chance to load the gun. How could you take such a risk? It was only a chicken, for God's sake!"

She yelled right back, still shaking from her experience. "Yes, but it was *my* chicken!"

Afterward she developed amazing restraint. She grew, right before his eyes, from brash girl to competent young woman. She managed the farm with skill, thriving on the sameness of the daily routine, the peace and quiet of early summer evenings, the hard work. When he pointed out that gambling was more profitable and a lot less work, she told him wryly that no man had ever drowned in his own sweat.

Case was reluctant to admit it, but he shared some of January's feelings. As the season progressed and he was able to do more and more, it was satisfying to know his efforts were helping to coax a living from the fertile land. He wondered what it would be like to work shoulder to shoulder with January for the rest of his life. To watch the seasons come and go and never venture beyond the boundaries of his own property. To grow old with the love of a good woman to keep him warm.

Then he thought about Alaska and its wild and provocative promise. There'd been talk of more and more gold being discovered and he had a feeling that the biggest strikes were yet to be made. Not that he wanted to mine, but those who did would be only too eager to part with their hard-won treasure for the sake of a little diversion. An honest gambler stood to make a lot of money, enough to last a lifetime of careful living.

Was that what he wanted? He no longer knew. Since he'd met January, things seemed to be out of focus, as if he was looking at life through a smoky glass. He had strong feelings for her, there was no denying that, but were they strong enough to last forever?

Forever was a mighty long time. He'd had plenty of money to start them out with and they hadn't had to do without a thing. But the money would run out eventually and the novelty of farming would wear off. Then what? Could the wonder of newly hatched goslings and green tomatoes see them through the grind of a harsh life?

On the other hand, he was a man who was used to comforts and amenities, and though the farm didn't offer an abundance of those, it surely had more than a rough frontier.

He'd vowed never to be tied down, to maintain his freedom at all costs, but hadn't freedom proved to be as imprisoning as iron bars? Hadn't it kept his feelings locked up since he'd lost his parents and all he knew? His dreams of adventure in Alaska didn't seem real anymore. Had they ever been? Or had he merely used those dreams to avoid taking responsibility for a love he might have already lost? And for what? Stubborn pride?

The longer Case knew January, the more he realized how much they had in common. She had a lively mind, keen as a briar, and it wouldn't be long before she progressed from reading primers to reading Dickens. He'd like to be around when literature opened up the world for her and he made a mental note to buy her some books of her own the next time the peddler came through.

On the man's last visit, Case had noticed her eyeing an applewood dulcimer and had bought it to surprise her. She'd taken to the instrument immediately, claiming her mother had played one for her long ago.

In the evening when the work was done and the air was soft with the whirr of insects, she'd sit in her rocker on the porch and gently coax lilting melodies and haunting ballads from its three strings, using only her fingers and a turkey quill pick. She sang in a clear, unfaltering contralto. Sometimes Case's arms rashed out with gooseflesh while listening to the tragic love songs that weren't meant to be only heard by the ears, but felt by the heart, as well.

Were they destined for tragedy also? Life would, indeed, be empty without her. He'd miss her enthusiasm, her zest for living. The world would seem empty without the sparkling laughter that erupted from her when things went her way and the muttered curses when they didn't. He couldn't forget the passionate lovemaking they'd shared and his skin grew warm and fevered every time he thought about her urgent responses.

No doubt about it, he was a better man for having known her. She'd helped him grow strong, both physically and emotionally. She'd taught him respect for the land and had given him a sense of belonging. By making him care for someone besides himself, she'd freed him from a painful past that had made him afraid to risk his heart.

It was a heart that no longer belonged to him. A red-haired girl now owned it lock, stock, and barrel.

Only she didn't seem to care. They'd grown close, but she'd made sure that closeness was a fraternal one. It killed him to be near enough to kiss her and know he'd have to settle for a good-night peck on the cheek before she retired to her own room. After the thrilling kiss they'd shared on the way home from the box supper, he'd hoped she would come to him, but she had kept herself even more aloof.

They didn't fight much anymore. It was as though they'd come to accept each other's flaws and shortcomings and made allowances thereof. But he missed the verbal donnybrooks that had once been so much a part of their relationship. They'd sparked a fire that had almost always culminated in fierce lovemaking.

Sometimes he could actually see her biting her tongue or counting slowly to ten in order to avoid a row. That kind of self-control disturbed him deeply. It wasn't natural. Not for January.

He feared she'd pinched back any budding feelings she might have had for him. Or maybe there hadn't been any to begin with. He'd introduced her to the pleasures men and women could offer each other, but maybe she was just a hot-blooded woman who would have responded to any half-tender man. Who would fulfill her when he was gone? The thought burned him and he brooded about the confusing state of their relationship.

Forcing all such thoughts from his mind, he watched her finger move across the pages with growing confidence. He'd reached a decision. Maybe he'd rushed her. Maybe he hadn't wooed her properly. Hell, he hadn't wooed her at all. He'd yelled at her, cursed her, blamed her for every bad thing that had ever happened to him.

She didn't encourage him or seem eager for his touch, but perhaps in time he could convince her of his love.

Love. There. He'd thought it and it hadn't hurt a bit.

He hadn't been struck down and the world hadn't come to an end. Dammit to hell, Alaska could just make history without him. For a man totally set in his ways, it hadn't been as painful as he'd thought to admit he loved January.

The big question was, how was he going to convince her?

Chapter 20

Case had vowed to win the affection of his wife if it took him the rest of his life, but judging from his progress of the past two weeks, forever wouldn't be long enough.

He'd tried everything he could think of and finally decided it was impossible to woo a woman who wouldn't allow herself to be courted. January was apparently immune to his charm, unappreciative of his chivalry, entirely too logical, and totally unsentimental. Work was her raison d'être and to her anything else was a frivolous waste of time.

Since none of his gallant gestures worked on his uncharmable wife, Case finally came to a sad conclusion. She didn't have a romantic bone in her body. If he rushed to open a door for her, she hung back, forcing him to go first or slam it in frustration. The days were growing longer and hotter and last Sunday he'd tried to entice her by suggesting they pack a meal and have a picnic down by the shady stream.

"Come on, January," he cajoled. "All the chores are done." When she hadn't refused immediately, he'd grown positively inspired with the idea. "We'll spread a sheet on the ground and laze around all day. We'll drink a little sunshine, get drunk on Mother Nature, and tell each other our innermost secrets. What do you think?"

She'd stared at him in consternation, as though he'd just invited her to accompany him to the moon. "I think you're daft, Latimer," she'd scoffed. "I ain't about to go to all the trouble of totin' a lot of junk down there, just to have to tote it all back again. I don't see no sense in sittin' on the ground, sharin' our food with ants, when we got a perfectly good table to eat from and chairs to sit on."

"I just thought it might be fun," he said lamely. He consoled himself that at least she'd considered it, momentarily anyway, right before cold-bloodedly shooting him in his hope-filled heart. God, she could be a hard woman.

January saw the hurt look on Case's face. Hellfire, she hadn't thought it was that important to him. Maybe she shouldn't reject the idea out of hand. No, it was too silly. "But don't let me spoil your fun. Go ahead, go if you want to," she said with a sweet smile. "But mind you don't get grass stains on my white sheets."

Flattery was his next ploy. Each day he made it a point to shower her with compliments about her beauty. But she always managed to turn or twist his words around and make them sound like criticism. When personal comments didn't work, he was reduced to dreaming up lies about her cooking.

"The green beans are delicious, so fresh and crisp," he remarked while gnawing on the half-cooked vegetable.

She smiled archly, letting him know she saw through the ruse. "They do go down a mite easier when I don't burn 'em, don't they?"

Just last night he'd pulled out her chair at the supper table, but she'd scorned that gesture as well, informing him in no uncertain terms that he should sit in his own chair across the table.

"I'm not trying to steal your seat, January," he said in exasperation as he motioned for her to take it. "I was only holding out your chair to help seat you. Just a harmless effort at courtesy."

She eyed him. He sure was acting strange lately. She recalled his holding out her chair in the restaurant in Joplin. She'd been so nervous she'd appreciated it then, but things were different now. "I don't need any help."

"Sit down, dammit," he commanded in a sudden fit of pique.

She sat, but not until she had a firm grip on the chair herself. He sighed noisily. She acted as though he had something malicious on his mind, like yanking the seat away at the last moment.

After two weeks of one disappointment after another, Case was desperate. He was down to trying to remember how he'd gotten himself invited into her bedroll the first time they'd made love.

Invited! Maybe that was the key that would unleash her passions once more. During the time he'd spent with her, he'd learned a few things about the hardheaded female he'd married. When January wanted something, she went after it with single-minded purpose and fought for it with everything she had. But no one could make her do *anything* she didn't want to do.

Yet, even fearing eternal damnation and divine retribution, she'd been the one to initiate things the first time. When she'd begged him to stay with her, she'd practically asked him to make love to her. Out on the trail, she'd proposed marriage and had seemed genuinely hurt by his condemnation of her way of life.

Maybe her intentions had been innocent when she'd stuck that bustle in the front of her dress and inadvertently caused a bunch of crusty miners and sentimental whores to whip up a wedding. But the fact remained—she could have stopped the charade anytime she'd wanted. So in truth, she'd chosen to marry him, in spite of his inebriated state. Why? Because she'd *wanted* to.

Although the unorthodox ceremony had seemed like a dream at the time, he clearly remembered the way she'd made love to him later. He hadn't imagined the bouncing marriage bed, or the intensity and profundity of the feelings that had passed between them. The next morning, he'd guessed she was in love with him. It could have been mere wishful thinking on his part, but if it wasn't love, it was damned close to it.

If she wanted him once, it stood to reason she'd want him again. As he saw it, all he had to do was make her admit desire and realize what she was missing.

He loved his wife and he wanted to stay married to her, but he wanted theirs to be a real marriage. He wanted January to bear his children and share his life. Forever.

That was the answer, then, he decided in triumph. She was keeping him at arm's length because of her fear of pregnancy. But if she *was* pregnant, even the hardheaded January would be forced to admit that she needed him.

He wasn't sure he could pull it off, but he had to try. If he waited for her to make any overtures on her own, they'd be that gum-sucking old couple she'd talked about—but without the added benefit of descendants. Subtlety and gentle nudges were lost on her, leaving him only one alternative. He'd have to push and shove, but he'd have to make her think their lovemaking, and whatever resulted, was her own idea.

January was disappointed when Henry and Aunt Sarah dropped by a few days later with the mail. Case's box of soap arrived, but there was no letter for her. As soon as she'd mastered the necessary skills, she had written her father and, despite the circumstances surrounding her departure from Possum Holler, she had hoped to hear from him. Although Jubal could neither read nor write, she knew Mr. Hibley at the general store often performed such services for his customers.

Maybe Case had been right. Maybe she didn't owe Jubal Jones an explanation or a place to live should he take her up on her offer, but he was all the family she had. He was rife with failings, but he was still her pa. She wasn't sorry she'd left him, but she wished they hadn't parted in anger.

His silence could mean only one thing—he didn't care.

By the time the older couple had left for home, January longed for a nap. It seemed she couldn't get enough sleep of late, but sleeping in the daytime went against her principles. No doubt all the hard work she'd been doing lately was responsible for her fatigue. There'd been so much to do around the place that she had to go at it from sunup to sundown just to keep up.

Case had worked right alongside her, harder than she'd ever dreamed he would. In the beginning, he'd griped and grumbled, but more than once she'd caught him staring out over the neatly cultivated fields with a smug grin on his handsome face.

The first time it happened, she'd questioned him. "What are you thinking? That you'll be glad when you can leave all this backbreaking work and sweat behind?"

He'd shaken his head. "I think I'm beginning to see what you mean about owning and working the land, about putting down roots. I suddenly feel good. Tired, but good." He'd laughed as though at himself. "I never thought physical labor could fill a man's chest with such pride."

Not only that, she'd noted with admiration, but it had also filled his chest and arms out. He sometimes worked without a shirt and she'd seen muscles bulging where they'd never bulged before. The sun had turned his skin warm and golden and enticing. Many were the days she'd had to turn away from him before her traitorous body could fling itself on her tan, work-toughened husband.

Although he invaded her senses, she resisted the lure of his blatantly beckoning sexuality. As one summer day faded into the next, she rose each morning wondering if this would be their last one together. When it wasn't, she was relieved to have him for a few more hours and angry that now she'd have to worry about tomorrow.

Granted, he hadn't mentioned Alaska for weeks, but that didn't mean he'd changed his mind about going. He'd made no plans she knew of and he was running out of time. Maybe he expected her to beg him to stay or give him a big send-off. If so, he'd still be waiting when hell froze over and the devil started passing out ice water.

There was nothing to keep him here. Certainly not her. She wasn't one of those women who was lost without a man. She'd never latch onto his coattails, bawling and begging. No doubt his peculiar behavior was a result of the resentment he felt toward her for detaining him.

Refusing to get caught up in the churning turmoil thinking about the future always caused her, January wandered to the window. Where had Case gotten off to? Today was Sunday, a day of rest, but she was so tense, rest was out of the question.

It was all his fault. Lately, he'd taken to fawning over her like a lovesick calf, reminding her of the way Aunt Sarah's boy, Billy Ray, acted whenever he was around Essie Peterson. If she didn't know better, she'd swear Case was trying to court her or something. But that was ridiculous. Men didn't court their wives. The courting should have come before the vows.

But with all their chasing around the countryside, they'd never had the time. Was he trying to make up for it now or was he simply getting an itch that he needed help scratching?

The first possibility made her knees wobbly and her head swirl with giddy thoughts, but she couldn't let herself get carried away. That would be asking for a broken heart. More than likely Case had a bad bout of the horn colic which a trip to the nearest saloon and fancy woman would cure right up. Her stomach lurched at the thought of him lying in another woman's arms and she forced herself not to dwell on it.

She'd set the rules and she'd damned well abide by them, even if it killed her. She wasn't about to fall into his bed and wind up with child. That would be a disaster. If he left, she'd have to raise the babe alone and if he stayed, she'd always wonder if he'd stuck around for her or for his flesh and blood. Things would be so much easier if only he'd leave her be.

But no, not him. He went around smiling and winking all the damned time like he hadn't a care in the world. He was always doing things for her, things she was perfectly capable of doing for herself. He was treating her like a helpless female and that riled her. He hadn't considered her helpless when they'd ridden together. How could he, when she was saving his butt every time he turned around? So why had he suddenly decided she was too weak and frail to lift a ham out of the oven?

He was acting mighty peculiar. Did he honestly believe she was too backward to know what a doorknob was for, too clumsy to climb down from a wagon, or too awkward to sit her fanny in her own chair without his thoughtful assistance?

He'd tried to tempt her with an invitation to picnic down by the creek and had made it all sound so romantic that turning him down had been painful, indeed. With each passing day, it grew harder and harder to refuse him when what she wanted most in the world was to say yes, yes, yes, to his every command.

There had been one outing she couldn't refuse and that was little Jesse's baptism. Ozarkers looked to the church to help identify and combat the devil's works. Their religion was sincere and fundamental, providing them with not only nourishment of the spirit but recreation for the body as well. It also gave the community an opportunity to gather in social fellowship.

But that morning January overslept, an unheard-of occurrence, and was late getting breakfast because something she'd eaten the day before hadn't agreed with her. She was so sick, she thought she might have to send Case to church without her, but as soon as her stomach had purged itself of its contents, she felt hale and hearty once more.

Case had looked forward to the outing himself and insisted they get an early start. He paced, as impatient as the horses hitched to the wagon, until she finally appeared. When she failed to load up quick enough to suit him, he placed his hands on her fanny and gave her a boost.

That didn't do her disposition much good and she was as cranky as all get out. But the meaner she got, the harder he tried. Even Aunt Sarah noticed his behavior and felt obliged to give January a bit of sage advice.

"Case is the most lovin' and thoughtful husband I ever did see," she told January. "I been watchin' and I notice these things. It ain't my bizness, but I feel I jest gotta speak up, honey. I don't know what's wrong betwixt ya, but somethin' sure is. Don't you love him no more?"

January hung her head. "I love him so much it hurts."

"Good." Aunt Sarah patted her hand. "But I gotta tell ya, I don't think your man knows that and he's hurtin' on account of it. He don't never take his eyes off ya and I saw the pain in 'em today when you scorned him."

"I wasn't scornin' him. He knows I can climb off a wagon without his help. He was just bein' nice for show." Turning her guilty gaze, January gestured at Billy and Essie. "I ain't like her. She's fragile and pretty and coddled. I been takin' care of myself ever since I can remember."

"You're the greenest gal I ever heard tell of." Aunt Sarah laughed. "Essie and Billy are in love. She ain't as fragile as she looks and both of 'em knows it. But it's a fittin' and proper way a man has to put his hands on his woman and her to do likewise in public. He's courtin' and flirtin' and struttin' his stuff. It's also a man's way of tellin' others that this is his woman."

"Oh." If that was true, she wondered, then why was Case doing it?

"I think your man is reachin' out for ya and you better take ahold of him, honey. You say you love him, but I've seen ya treat him like ya don't. There's sadness in his eyes. Ya gotta nurture a man. They need it even more than women. He's hungry and hunger makes a man do things he might regret. You understand?"

All too well. January nodded, unable to confide in Aunt Sarah as she would have liked.

"I'll just say one more thing, 'cause I can see ya don't like discussin' it. The wedding night"—Aunt Sarah's cheeks pinkened, but she steadfastly continued—"ain't always as easy on a new bride as the lovin' what comes later. If that's what's troublin' ya, you can rest assured. It gets better and better. If ya ever want to talk, I'll be glad to listen or answer a few questions."

For a woman so wise in the ways of men and women, Aunt Sarah was certainly wrong this time. Sex with Case was too enjoyable. January loved her husband. Unfortunately, the older woman had mistaken Case's unsatisfied lust for a love he couldn't give.

Still, January couldn't understand his strange behavior. If only she knew what he was up to. What ulterior motives had prompted him to discuss the farm with her, going so far as to admit being a farmer wasn't as bad as he'd thought it would be? Why would he pretend to enjoy the life he'd ridiculed?

Peeking around the curtain after they'd returned home, January saw Case come out of the barn and stride across the yard to the chopping block. Since his accident, she'd hated the sight of an ax in his hand. She held her breath when he bent to pull the ax from the block and left her vigil at the window to join him.

The squeak of the door announced her arrival, but Case didn't look up until he'd finished chopping the kindling. "Do you need wood for the stove?" he asked, stretching.

"No, I'm just on my way to the barn."

Case nodded. She seemed a little jumpy. Was that a good sign? His gaze riveted on her slim hips as she sashayed across the yard.

At the entrance she stopped to glance at him over her shoulder and called out softly, "Take care with that ax, now."

By the time the woodbox was filled, he was hot and thirsty. He hoped something would happen between them soon, because he was fast running out of patience and ideas.

"Case," January said breathlessly at his back, "I need you."

The dipper fell from his hand, clattering against the water bucket. Grinning, he spun around to face her, his eyes sparkling mischievously. "You do? Right here and now? In front of God and everybody?"

"Don't be silly. I need your help in the barn," she explained quickly.

"I knew it was too good to be true. In the barn, huh?"

She stifled a grin and took a step backward. "Jezebel's in trouble."

"Hey, you've got the wrong guy," he teased, holding his hands up in a gesture of innocence. "I swear I never touched her. I'd lay odds it was Sampson. I've always thought there was something sheepish about that ram."

As worried as she was, she couldn't help smiling. He could always cheer her. "Jezebel's lambing. Or trying to, but something's wrong."

"I'm afraid I don't know much about delivering baby sheep." Draping her shoulders with his arm, he let his hand absently massage the tenseness in her nape as they walked.

"Lambs," she corrected automatically, allowing his comforting arm to stay where it was, even though it caused their hips to bump with each step.

"Now, ain't that a pure dee shame?" he asked, borrowing one of her frequent sayings. Without so much as a break in their stride, he cupped her chin in his free hand and brushed her lips with his thumb.

"What?" The caress was so quick, January wondered if she'd imagined it. He'd been awfully flirty lately.

"Wouldn't you know that the very first time my wife actually admits she needs me, I'm powerless to help. Impotent." He grinned down at her.

"Why do I get the feeling that's supposed to be funny?" January chanced a glance at his glittering blue eyes. "What's 'impotent' mean?"

Case chuckled and couldn't resist squeezing her against him. "It means . . . um . . . lacking in strength or vigor." When she still didn't get it, he tried again. "Unable to copulate."

"That's a big windy for sure," she said without thinking. She lowered her gaze when she felt a telltale warmth spreading from her heart to her cheeks.

"Was that a compliment, Mrs. Latimer? Well, it just so happens I admire your . . . *strength* and *vigor,* too."

January twisted away from him. It was plumb dangerous the way he made her want to throw him down and make love to him right then and there. She scurried inside the dim barn, unable to conceal the pleasure his words had given her.

They knelt on the straw beside the laboring animal and Case ran a gentle hand over the ewe's heaving girth. Jezebel made a sad sound, like a plea for help, and tried to rally. With a valiant effort, she struggled to lift her head, then stared up at Case with pain-filled eyes. He could have sworn the animal was begging him to do something, making him feel even more helpless and inept.

"Poor little mother," January cooed in a singsongy tone, scratching the wooly curls between the animal's ears. Jezebel closed her eyes and seemed to relax. "That's right, little mother, rest while you can."

"I realize I'm not an expert," Case said, "but isn't the old girl's timing all wrong? Don't ewes usually lamb in the spring?"

"Yes. Sampson must have jumped the fence or something. That happens sometimes."

"I can certainly sympathize with the poor guy. I know just how he feels," he said softly.

"If you're so bad off, go on to the saloon in town," she snapped. Case was no better than Sampson. Any female would do in a pinch.

"Saloon! Do you honestly believe I can be satisfied with a strumpet . . ." Case paused and stiffened, wiping all traces of emotion from his face. He refused to wear his heart on his sleeve just to be coldly rejected. Turning back to the ewe, he changed the subject. "I haven't the vaguest idea how to help her."

"The lamb can't come out butt first. We have to turn it so he has a better chance."

"And just how do *we* do that?" he asked, still miffed.

"Just put your hands in, find the front feet and head . . ."

Jezebel stirred and January bent to soothe her.

"We put our hands in?" Case asked incredulously, not sure he had the stomach for it.

"Not we, you. I've already tried, but the little dickens is stuck or something. I couldn't budge him. You're stronger than I am. You can do it."

Case's mouth went dry. "I refuse to put my hands in there."

"Don't be ridiculous," she scolded. "It's only blood and water. Hellfire, Case, it'll wash off."

Jezebel went into another spasm and January was distracted.

"What happens if I refuse?" he asked, already knowing he wouldn't.

"I told you, I need help." When she looked up at his pale features, she couldn't pass up this chance to get back at him. "I never asked you to do nothin' you didn't want to do. But I'm asking you now."

Case sighed. "What do I do?"

January gave him detailed instructions while trying to calm Jezebel's noisy protests. Case pushed and shoved. It seemed to take forever before he finally felt the lamb's nose.

"Okay, it's turned," he declared triumphantly. "What now? Do I pull it out by the head or the feet?"

"Don't ever pull one out by the feet because you might pull its little hooves off."

Case wrinkled his nose with disgust. "Did I hear correctly? Its feet might come off? In my hands?"

"Not unless you pull 'em off," she said, her tone implying he had asked a very stupid question. "Besides, if you pull the feet, more than likely the head will get stuck."

Thinking males had the easy part in the reproduction scheme, Case considered January's words, managing to conjure up a horrible vision. "Isn't it a little risky to pull it out by the head then?"

She nodded. "I don't want to do that unless we have to. To get it out that way, we'd have to use a rope. If it isn't done exactly right . . ." She made a slicing gesture across her throat.

"Oh, wonderful," he muttered.

"Here, let me show you. Just pull it out by the fore-legs."

Case knew something wasn't right when the lifeless creature emerged from its thankful mother. Frowning, he said, "I'm sorry, January. I must have done something wrong. It isn't breathing."

"No!" she cried, leaping to her feet.

He placed the lamb on the straw. "It's dead. There's nothing we can do about that."

She pushed past him and scooped the animal into her arms before he could stop her. She raced out of the barn, toward the creek. Case, thinking she might be hysterical, followed, trying to calm her.

"January, wait. Listen to me," he called.

She ignored him. When she reached the shady, spring-fed stream, she splashed right in and dunked the animal. Case was shocked by her irrational behavior and thrashed in after her. "What are you doing?" he yelled.

She finally allowed him to help her back to shore with her pathetic burden. She beamed up at him. "It worked!" she exclaimed proudly.

"What?"

"Looky." She held out the lamb and he could see its sides heaving rapidly. It emitted a weak *ba-a-a*.

"Well, I'll be damned."

January rubbed the lamb with her apron and stood it on its wobbly legs in the grass where it proceeded to bleat for its mother. "The cold water shocked life into him."

"Well, you damned near shocked the life right out of me. I thought you were . . ." He couldn't go on. He longed to shake her until her teeth rattled. Instead, he sank to his knees and glared up at her.

"I'm glad we saved him," she said. "He's going to make a fine ram."

Case eyed the pitiful creature doubtfully. It was no bigger than a good-sized cat, all skin and bones, with a head much too big for its underdeveloped body. "Him?"

"Of course, him."

"Maybe you're not as good a judge of animals as I thought," he said with a laugh.

She glanced up from the lamb and caught his tender expression. "I confess I do better when it comes to judging husbands." Her wink was as bold as any he'd ever given her. Working shoulder to shoulder with Case, January had almost been overcome, not only by his sheer physical beauty, but by the goodness of his spirit. Gambler or no, he was a decent man with a loving and generous nature. Just the thought of living without him bore down on her soul like a crushing fist and she turned her eyes away.

Cuddling the lamb, she was suddenly filled with longing for a child of her own. A child sired by Case. Perversely, she realized such thoughts were in complete opposition to those she'd clung to stubbornly only a few days ago. But where was it written, she wondered, that a woman couldn't have a change of heart when she felt like it? If she did get with child, she'd never use it to tie Case down, so where was the harm? Then, if he did leave, she would have a small part of him to love forever.

The more she thought about it, the more it made perfect sense to her. A child would love her in spite of her poor education and backward ways. Maybe Case would never be truly satisfied with having her for a wife, but a baby wouldn't hold Possum Holler against her. She hadn't known much love during those brutal years with Jubal, but she could learn how to give it as well as accept it. She could prove herself by loving a child.

A fleeting image of that child—tall and strong and beautiful—filled her with a powerful new determination. No matter how much she'd tried to tell herself otherwise, she wanted Case, even if it was only for a little while. As she knelt by the stream, mentally talking herself into the audacious plan, she felt the heat rising like a wellspring within her. Inexperienced as she was, she recognized the primitive yearning. It was that passion Case had spoken of, but it was much more. It was love, as well.

In an effort to keep her decision secret, January drew herself up and defended Jezebel's offspring. ''You really have to know your sheep to be willing to start off with one such as him.''

She had to wonder if she could carry out the seduction she'd just plotted. Would Case be vulnerable to her fledgling wiles? His hungry look as he watched her answered that question.

''You know something, Latimer?'' she asked with a grin. ''For such an educated man, sometimes it amazes me how dumb you can be.''

Case wasn't sure what had happened, but something sure as hell had perked January up. Her face was a mirror of her emotions and, unless his guess was wrong, she was excited about more than just her new lamb. ''Sometimes I amaze myself.''

Chapter 21

"What do you think you're doing?" January squealed when Case stripped off his soggy boots and reached to unfasten the buttons on his shirt.

"I'm going to take a bath." Hands on hips, he challenged, "You got anything to say about that?" He wasn't sure even an extended dip in the frigid water would cool his ardor.

"Nope." Grinning like an idiot and happy that things were going to be much easier than she'd dared to hope, January picked up the bawling lamb and backed away. "I'll just take him back to Jezebel."

"You do that," Case said agreeably as he shrugged out of his messy shirt. Wadding it up, he flung it aside.

From several yards away she offered, "Want me to bring you some soap and a towel?"

"That would be nice." Pretending the utmost nonchalance, Case unbuttoned his trousers and waited for January's reaction. She stared boldly, daringly. He shucked them off and they landed atop his soiled shirt. He made no move to enter the water. He figured he could stare her down. He did. She wheeled around and struggled up the bank.

After depositing the lamb with its mother, January raced into the house. She snatched up one of Case's clean shirts, a towel, and a cake of the spicy-smelling soap he liked. Though she considered it a shameless extravagance, this was no time to be thrifty.

It was also no time to be bashful. Things were so ripe between them, the air fairly hummed with excitement. It would be foolish and coy to pretend she didn't want him when the ache was like a fever inside her. If Case wanted her even half as much as she wanted him, her bold plan of seduction would not only be successful, it would be downright fruitful.

There was no holding back now, but January worried about how to tell him of her changed feelings. She'd learned early in life to disconnect from her emotions. That way she could concentrate on the important things, like staying alive. An empty stomach could be a powerful distraction and she hadn't been able to afford to waste much time looking inward.

Unfortunately, Case liked to talk things over. What he called "philosophizing" and "intellectualizing." He didn't just *have* ideas, he discovered them, picking over them like he was sorting for diamonds in a pan of gravel. He turned ideas this way and that, inside and out, trying them on for size in his mind. Hellfire! Case could think a notion plumb to death!

No, it was better not to try and tell him. As poor a hand as she was with words, she'd be a wrinkled old crone before they got around to the good part. Better to show him. Words couldn't hold a candle to action, she always said. With any luck, during the showing, he'd come to realize they belonged together.

At least that's how she had it figured. She'd just traipse right on down to the water hole and make him hers, if not forever, then for as long as she could hold him. With that thought clutched firmly in the jaws of her mind, January marched resolutely down the steps.

"Hey, Latimer. Catch." She tossed him the bar of soap and, gasping at the sudden chill, held her breath and splashed toward him.

Case was so surprised to see January flailing around in her underwear, he almost forgot to catch the missile she hurled at him. Treading water, he called to her, "What a pleasant surprise. Are you planning to swim out here and wash my back?"

"Don't be silly," she demurred. "You know I can't swim." Silently, she implored him not to make her voice her intentions. "This water's like ice. How can you stand it?"

Recalling another day, another stream, he said, "Don't you remember? A bracing dip is good for the constitution." He didn't know what had come over her, but he didn't care. It was enough that she had come back of her own volition. Like a sleek otter, he glided smoothly toward her. "It isn't so bad, once you get used to it. Come all the way in. You'll see."

Case stood, holding out his hands as the water lapped at his navel. "Hold my hands. I'll take you out a ways."

January placed her hands in his and he slowly backed away, pulling her from her feet. As she skimmed across the water, her nipples hardened beneath her thin shift. "Don't take me out too far," she entreated.

He smiled with regret at the tremble in her voice. "Don't you trust me at all? Do you think I couldn't save you from drowning?"

"Maybe I think you might have trouble saving yourself from me," she sassed.

"Then we'll go back to the bank," he said with a grin, remembering how exciting that other rescue, and its aftermath, had been.

They stood in the waist-deep water and held hands beneath the surface. Late afternoon sun dappled through the trees and all around them busy summer insects filled the still, heavy air with the sounds of their industry. Case's gaze locked with January's for a timeless moment. Gradually, she lost awareness of a world that seemed to shrink away as though there was no room in it for anything except the two of them.

Slowly she withdrew her hands from his and splashed to the bank where she retrieved the soap he'd flung there earlier. Case watched her tippy-toe back to him, mesmerized by the pale skin revealed by her wet, clinging underwear.

She stopped just in front of him. "Turn around so I can wash your back." Her voice was that of a woman who would brook no resistance to her wishes.

He did as he was told and luxuriated in the feel of her hands lathering his skin. He turned and would have taken her in his arms, but she backed away, laughing, determined to have things her way.

"Behave yourself." She soaped his shoulders, scrubbing down the length of his arms, then back again to his muscular chest. The scrubbing had turned to stroking by the time she ran teasing, soapy fingertips over his hard male nipples.

"I can't stand any more of this, January." He grabbed her roughly around the waist and pulled her into his arms until her feet no longer touched bottom.

When his mouth came down on hers, she wrapped her arms tightly around his neck and gave herself up to his magical, earth-tilting kiss. She melted against him, already yearning for the feel of him inside her. When he tore his lips from hers, she threatened him with a smile. "That had better not be all, Case."

"It isn't, my little spitfire, not by a long shot." A sly smile flirted on his lips. Setting her away from him, he dove under the surface to rinse off the soap, then came up for air with a whooping splash. Grabbing her hand, he pulled her to the water's edge.

She laughed at his haste. "You act like the very devil's on your heels. Where're we headed in such an all-fired hurry?"

"We are going to bed," he told her when they reached the spot where their clothing lay forgotten. Lifting her face up to his, he kissed the tip of her nose. "You got anything to say about that?"

"Nary a word."

"You do want me," he said softly, his gaze searching.

She wanted to tell him just how much, but the words

wouldn't come. Taking matters into her own hands, January grabbed his wrist and began dragging him toward the house.

"Now, what's your all-fired hurry?" he teased with a laugh. He pulled her to a stop and wrapped his arms around her, sliding her up the hard length of his naked body until she could feel his warm breath on her lips. "Answcr me, January. It's time we talked."

"I'm afraid of talkin', Case. Ever'time we do, one of us ends up madder than a sore-tailed bear. Can't the talkin' wait?" She kissed him quick and hard. "Until after . . . ?" she asked suggestively.

She had a point and Case knew it. He'd thought to explain his theory about why the sparks flew between them so thick and fast, but what the hell. There would be plenty of time for talking later. "Why do I get the feeling you're about to set off a bigger explosion than the one you created in Joplin?"

Brazenly, she pushed out of his arms and stood back, inviting him to take a good look at her. "Don't be silly, Case. As you can plainly see, I ain't wearin' enough clothes to be concealin' any dynamite on my person this time."

A brow arched and one side of his mustache lifted in that hot grin of his. "Honey," he drawled, "you aren't even wearing enough clothes to conceal your person."

Her gaze dropped to follow his and January gasped when she realized her wet underwear was practically transparent. She took off running, but he caught her easily, sweeping her up in his arms.

"Don't, Case. What if neighbors were to ride past? What on earth would they think?"

"They'd think Case Latimer was about to make love with his beautiful wife." With that he flung her over his shoulder and paced off the steps toward the house.

He carried her inside and tossed her, wet and shivering, onto his bed. She reached for a quilt, but he pushed it away and joined her on the mattress.

"I'll warn you," he said huskily. He proceeded to dry every inch of her skin with the white-hot warmth of his lips. He rolled her onto her stomach and trailed his fingertips down her spine. His touch brought delicious shivers, but following in their wake was a blood-deep warmth that spread outward and downward until she felt the tingling deep inside her. It was as though her body was half ice and half flame.

When his tongue followed the path his fingers had traced, January gasped. His laugh was low and intimate. "It's all right, honey. I'm your lover. I'd never do anything to hurt you, so don't be afraid of my touch. I know the fiery passion you hide so well is there. It's time to let go the reins, January. Just let go."

She'd never thought she could be so excited by words and soon her need consumed her. No longer able to remain passive, she twisted around and over him, allowing her own lips to trail down his chest until they encountered his flat belly. As her hand inched daringly down to the juncture of his thighs and closed around him, it was Case's turn to gasp.

"I can't hide a thing from you, Case, any more than you can hide *this* when I'm near you. I feel like I'm fixin' to bust right out of my skin. Is that how it's supposed to feel?"

"Oh, yes," he rasped as he tucked her beneath him.

Her flimsy drawers and camisole fell away beneath his questing hands. When she felt his fevered flesh against her own, she opened her mouth to his in a fierce and wildly arousing kiss. Like wildfire, the flames leaped between them, threatening to consume them in their intensity.

Lovingly, he gathered her close and murmured, "You're so beautiful, January. I love you so much it hurts."

"Oh, Case." She melted into him, urging him to touch her, to taste her, to know her most intimate self. He caressed her nipples as his tongue slipped across her lips in a torturously sensual dance. January drew his tongue into her mouth and wrapped her arms tightly around his neck.

Her breasts quickened at his touch, jutting with plump lushness against his palm. His mouth slid downward and a small sigh of satisfaction escaped her when he drew the pebbly bead between his lips.

Her senses careened in the face of his incredibly erotic onslaught. She writhed in pleasure when his hand slid downward across her silken belly. He touched her moistness and she quivered against him. The pure pleasure she found in his urgency dispelled all doubts and she gave herself up to his masterful touch. As he kissed her, the languid in and out motion of his tongue matched the tempo of his intimate caresses.

His body imprisoned hers in a web of growing arousal. Soon January was lost to everything save the ecstasy and sweet madness that was Case.

"Love me," she commanded and, unable to wait any longer, eagerly guided him inside her.

"I do love you," he whispered softly as their bodies became one. He plunged deeper with each thrust, her hips rising to meet him, until his full length was sheathed in her warmth. Beads of perspiration dotted his forehead as he fought against the demands of his own body. As his momentum built, his gaze never faltered from her face.

January's head tossed on the pillows and she strained toward him as she was drawn to a height of passion she had not known before. Her need was profound as she pressed her hips hard against his pulsing thighs. Though she wasn't sure what she hungered for, didn't really understand the hysteria of delight held captive inside her, January fought for the release of that burning sweetness.

Case held back for her, thusting back and forth, faster and faster until finally, at long last, their restraint was shattered. Shuddering waves of pleasure washed over them, each more intense than the last, and they clung to each other against the turbulence of their passion.

For long moments, January lay in Case's arms, her head cradled on his shoulder, replete beyond words. His fingers played along her spine, brushing her love-burnished skin with feathery strokes. She turned her face into his shoulder and kissed away the dampness their loving had wrought.

Entwined in a lover's tangle, each was seemingly reluctant to move and break the spell between them. At last January's breath slowed to an even tempo that told Case she had fallen asleep.

He eased from the bed and went to work to correct a situation that had plagued him for weeks. By the time she roused, he'd made several forays from her room and back and had crammed most of her wispy underthings into the bureau drawer.

"What are you doing with my unmentionables, Mr. Latimer?" she sassed, stretching.

"I'm putting them where they belong."

She savored the words as she'd savored the wonderful feeling of satisfaction he'd given her. Clearly, the man had no shame for he hadn't bothered to get dressed. She watched in admiring silence, marveling at his potency and audacity, as he left the room only to return with yet another armload of her belongings.

"From now on, this is *our* room," he announced. "As it should have been from the beginning." Case slammed the drawer closed with a bang of finality. He faced her, his hands on his hips. "Now, what do you have to say about that, *Mrs.* Latimer?"

"Nothin'," she replied innocently.

"Nothing?" he asked incredulously. "No argument at all?"

"I ain't unreasonable, Case. I'm perfectly willin' to abide by any decision you care to make." She grinned. "As long as I agree with it."

"I don't believe it," he said, imploring the heavens. "I had everything all worked out, had thought up at least a dozen good reasons why we should share this room. I was all primed for a fight."

"Looks like you got yourself all worked up for nothin' then, don't it?" she asked, gazing pointedly at the part of his anatomy that looked most primed. "If you've got some excess energy to burn off, the henhouse roof needs fixin'."

Case smiled, striding toward the bed. "There's plenty of time for that."

"Oh, I don't know," she evaded. "It might rain and you know what they say about wet hens."

He snuggled up beside her. "No, tell me."

January was pleasantly surprised when her body began to vibrate with liquid fire all over again. "I can't worry about the hens now. I got my hands full with a rooster." She pulled the quilt to her neck, pretending her thoughts weren't headed recklessly in the same direction as his own.

"It's nearly suppertime, Case," she protested half-heartedly. "Decent folks would be out doing chores . . ." Her words were lost as his mouth claimed hers with unabashed possessiveness. Tasting the sweet surrender of her lips, his tongue met hers with a demand that left her breathless and shaken.

When he pulled back, she asked groggily, "Where do you think you're goin'?"

"If I'm going to keep you happy, I guess I'd best go out and fix that roof." He drew away from her in mock resignation.

January bounced onto her knees and clamped her arms around his neck. "What roof would that be?" she asked before she kissed him.

Supper was late that day, the completion of the chores even later. While she was waiting for Case to return, January worried about the best way to spend the rest of the evening. She'd been loved so long and so hard, she needed some time to ruminate on her new experiences.

Deciding that busy hands wouldn't be tempted to stray where they shouldn't, she plopped into the rocker on the front porch and took up the knitting Aunt Sarah had tried patiently to teach her. After pouring the milk into a jug in the spring house, Case joined her. He lounged on the top step, his head reclining against the porch post, his eyes taking in her every movement.

"Why don't you put that down and play me a song on the dulcimer? I'd fancy hearing you sing one of those sad love songs of yours."

"Can't waste time like that. I've got to stick to this job till I get the hang of it." She swore under her breath when she dropped yet another stitch. She knew she should be paying more attention to the tangle of blue yarn and less to the way Case's hair curled over his collar. "Hell's fuzzy!" she cried in frustration. "Knitting ain't fit for a loon."

"Then why bother with it?"

She looked at him in surprise. "Every woman has to know how to knit. We need socks and mittens and shawls and such for the winter. I don't intend to let this cursed yarn best me!"

"We can buy all that stuff," he said reasonably. "We can order it from the mail-order catalogue and have it delivered right to the door."

She frowned at him. "That'd be a foolish waste of money that's too hard to come by in the first place. Besides, what kind of wife don't knit her own family's things?"

"One who's all thumbs?" he suggested with a broad grin. She made a face and returned to her handiwork. Case sighed, knowing that come winter, he'd be wearing lopsided socks with tucked-under toes and mittens with the thumb on the wrong side, all in the interest of saving a few dollars. Funny how that thought warmed his heart more than any woolen garment could.

When it came to housewifely duties, January made up in enthusiasm and determination what she lacked in natural talent. He'd choked down some pretty horrendous dishes during her experimental cooking phase and still worried each time she opened a jar of food she'd put by. But Aunt Sarah had supervised her efforts and so far no one had expired. What better recommendation could a cook ask for?

And what better woman could a man ask for? Their lovemaking had been almost frightening in its beauty and Case longed to talk about it, to share his feelings, to plan the future. But throughout supper, January had chattered about chicks and pumps and speculated whether the fishing would be good tomorrow down at the stream.

He knew she wasn't trying to lock him out of her heart. She just didn't know how to welcome him into it.

Although he hadn't twitched a muscle, it seemed to January that Case had drifted away from her. He was lost in one of those thoughts of his, as unreachable as if he'd climbed on Shadow and ridden far away. That thought clutched at her insides and made her blurt out the first thing that popped into her head. "Are you thinkin' about Alaska?"

"Are you so eager to be rid of me?"

The wounded look on his face made her feel as if she should cut out her tongue with a dull knife. "It ain't that," she allowed. "But didn't you say you had to leave before the fall otherwise it'd be too late?"

"It's already too late."

"Oh." She dropped several stitches trying to figure that one out.

"It's too late because I no longer have a hankering to go. I want to stay here with you."

"I can't believe you mean that. What about your dreams?"

Ignoring her question, he asked, "What would you say if I told you I didn't want to go at all? That I want to stay and make a home here with you?"

"I'd say you've been working too hard or been out in the sun too long." She put her palm on his forehead in a mock test for fever.

"I've changed, January, and you know it. But more that that, *you've* changed. Don't you know how much I want you?"

"I think so," she admitted softly. "But loving and wanting are two different things. I worry that Alaska would always be there between us. What about your precious freedom?"

"I don't care about that anymore," he said as honestly as he knew how. "I love you. I want to stay."

January leaned back, tipping the rocker into action. She wanted to believe him, needed to, but somehow she just couldn't allow herself that luxury. She didn't dare hope he could be happy with someone like herself. "You'll change your mind when boredom sets in and there's nothing to do on long winter nights but chuck wood on the fire."

He leered at her playfully. "That's where you come in. I thought we might help each other while away those long evenings."

He tempted her, but what about the next big gold strike he heard about up north? Wouldn't he get itchy feet and want to see it for himself? "If you stayed on account of me, you might grow to hate me for it later."

"Never."

"You can say that now, but how do you know what you'll feel a few years from now? I don't want to be the one holdin' you back, tyin' you down." Her throat constricted and she momentarily feared she couldn't scrape her next words past its rawness. "I think you should go and get it out of your system."

"Dammit to hell, I'm your husband! I love you. Doesn't that stand for anything?"

"A gal's pa is supposed to love her, too, but I wrote to mine as soon as I learned how and I never heard a word from him. Love's an iffy thing that only serves itself. It has a way of disappearin' when it's convenient."

"Don't compare me to your father," Case said, tamping down his bitter anger. Knowing her as he did, and knowing how she'd grown up without a shred of affection or tenderness, he could understand her self-doubts. But understanding didn't make dealing with her fears any less frustrating.

He'd tried wooing her, had worked his ass off to show her he'd changed. He'd sworn his love and still she shut him out. She'd given him access to her body, but she wouldn't let him into her heart. "If I do hang around, how many years do you think it'll take to convince you I mean what I say?"

"Hellfire!" January, who had been knitting and rocking furiously, dropped another stitch.

Case took the knitting needles from her and pulled her to her feet. "Come on, let's go inside. It's getting dark and you've cussed enough for one day."

"I ain't sleepy," she said, suddenly overcome by his sweet concern and trembling with need and doubt.

"Good," he said, understanding her shyness. "We'll play cards."

January followed reluctantly, protesting, "I don't know how."

"I'll teach you." He grinned rakishly. "It'll give us something to do with our hands."

Cheeks burning, she flopped into a kitchen chair and waited while Case fetched a leather case. "Cards are the devil's play-pretties," she said.

"Says who?" Case divided the cards, then flipped them together again with one-handed ease.

"Me." At his encouragement, she picked up the five cards he dealt her. She went along, listening as he revealed the rules of the game. She didn't balk until he laid his money on the table. "I refuse to gamble for money," she said self-righteously. "It ain't seemly."

He swept the money carelessly onto the floor. "Fine. We'll play for kisses."

"No."

"Well, what then?"

"For fun?" she suggested.

"It isn't much fun if the winner doesn't gain something from the loser. You lose the competitive edge that way." When she hesitated, he prodded, "Afraid you'll lose, January?"

"Of course not," she replied too quickly. "Once I learn how, I'll beat the pants off you."

"That's just what I had in mind. You've got yourself a deal." Case reached across the table and shook her hand. "The loser of each hand will have to forfeit an article of his or her clothing," he said with the feigned air of one who has resigned himself to his fate.

January scrutinized him warily. She couldn't back down from his challenge; it wasn't in her nature. And she'd watched him get dressed this afternoon, not even bothering to pull on his drawers. He had a lot less to lose than she did.

"You hold the advantage over me," he added persuasively. "You pinned up your hair."

"Do hairpins count?"

Smug in his ability, he could afford to be generous. "Sure."

She rubbed her hands together. "It might be fun to best you at your own game."

By the time Case had won all her hairpins, she wasn't feeling quite so cocky. She glared at him across the table. "I thought jacks were higher than the numbered cards."

"Yes," he agreed, "but I had three sevens and you only had two jacks."

"Right." January handed over her last hairpin and dealt the cards as he'd taught her. Looking at hers, she couldn't help cursing herself for running around barefoot. She didn't have shoes or stockings to forfeit and, if she lost again, she'd have to move on to the big stuff.

"Two cards, please." Case grinned amiably.

She laid her king to one side, gave Case his two cards and herself four. Lifting them, she slowly fanned them out; a nine, a queen, and two more kings. She squealed delightedly and squirmed on her chair. Three kings could beat just about anything Case could come up with.

Watching her, Case arched one brow. "One thing you obviously haven't learned, Mrs. Latimer, and that's how to maintain a poker face."

"What's that?"

"All that gloating just tipped your hand. Play it a little closer to the . . . uh . . . vest."

After that, Case's fortunes took a downward turn. The next few hands saw the loss of his shoes, then his socks and shirt. Before long, it was a standoff. Case had lost everything but his trousers; January had a slight edge with her drawers and dress.

"How many, January?" He stretched and tipped back in his chair.

January couldn't help noticing the muscles ripple smoothly across his chest as he laced his fingers behind his head. The sight made her heart set to pounding with a vengeance and conjured up memories of an afternoon whiled away so delightfully. Unable to tear her gaze away because of such libidinous thoughts, she accidentally asked for three cards instead of two, which meant she was forced to throw away one of her queens. There went her unbeatable hand.

Case spread his cards on the table with a flourish, three fours. "Your loss, my gain."

January stood up, turned her back, and skinned out of her bloomers. "Here." She threw them at him with all the hauteur she could manage.

Laughing, Case caught them easily. "Well, this makes things about even. The way I figure it, the next hand will be the decisive one. What do you say we sweeten the pot a bit?"

She eyed him skeptically. "Just exactly what do you have in mind, Mr. Latimer?"

"Oh, I don't know." He glanced casually around the room, then with a sudden inspiration that was clearly well-thought-out, he suggested, "Why don't we say the winner gets to have his or her way with the loser?"

January pretended to consider. The way she figured it, win or lose, she would enjoy settling the score. Maybe she'd just throw the game. She knew from experience that when it came to having his way with a body, Case was a much better hand at it than she was. "You're on!"

As the game unfolded, she couldn't figure out how, after throwing away her good cards, she still ended up with a royal flush. Hellfire, she was in serious jeopardy of winning the dadblamed thing. Disappointment drew down her features.

Across the table, Case watched her carefully. Why did she look so woebegone? He'd been away from the tables so long, he must have slipped up somehow on that first deal. But he'd made up for it later and there was no way she wasn't holding a royal flush. He glanced at his own hand. No matter what she held, it was sure to beat him.

"Dealer has only a pair of deuces," he said with a resigned sigh, already anticipating the forfeiture.

January scooped up the remaining cards and pushed hers into the middle of the deck. "Could be the old Latimer luck just made poker history. I fold."

Case knew she'd held a winning hand. Why had she pretended to lose? He eyed her suspiciously and a sly grin tipped up the corner of her mouth. The little minx knew exactly what she was doing. Kicking back his chair, he extended his hand. "You really should work on that poker face of yours, Mrs. Latimer."

Chapter 22

At breakfast the next morning January felt so ill she could make only the barest pretense of picking at her food. Her normally ravenous appetite had deserted her of late. Earlier, as she'd prepared the meal, the smell of frying ham had sent her rushing out the back door, praying to reach the necessary before her heaving stomach gave up its contents.

While trying to freshen her face with a damp cloth, she thought about the last twenty-four hours. Just recalling the abandon she'd displayed made her blush. The things she and Case had done to and for each other had seemed so right and precious in the dimly lit bedroom, so why did she feel so poorly this morning? Maybe this was what people meant when they said a body was "lovesick." Maybe too much loving wasn't good for the system. How in tarnation was she to know?

Case came in from milking and wolfed down the food she'd had so much trouble preparing. If his appetite was any indication, lovesickness was not a communicable disease. Still weak and worried, all January could do was push an unappetizing piece of fried egg around on her plate and avoid Case's pointed glances.

"What's the matter?" Case could conceal his concern no longer. A well-loved woman with no second thoughts about her man shouldn't look so pale and pindly. "Aren't you hungry?"

"Guess not," she allowed as she scraped her plate into

the slop bucket. "You know what they say about living on love." Her laugh was thin and nervous, her face pinched.

Case would have questioned her further, but the sounds of a heavy wagon rolling into the yard interrupted him. He pushed back his chair and stepped outside, January right behind him.

A tall, familiar figure was already climbing down from the high seat of the wagon and January cried out when she recognized him. "Dr. Clarence Goodnews? Is it really you?"

"It's me all right," he boomed. "Mind if my family lights and stays awhile?"

Surprised by his words, January caught the older man in a welcoming hug. "I didn't know you had a family, Clarence. When did all this happen?"

"It's a long story, but one I'd be proud to tell you." He swept off his hat with one hand and helped a small woman down from the wagon with the other. Three silent children, two girls and a freckle-faced boy, huddled behind the woman, who was regarding January with an expression of glowing intensity.

"No need to stand around out here. Let's all go in and have some coffee," Case invited.

Once the adults were settled in kitchen chairs with cups of steaming coffee, while the children ate jam-filled biscuits, Clarence cleared his throat.

"January, this is my wife, the only woman I ever loved." His craggy features beamed as the two women shook hands politely. "It took a while to find her, but now that I have, I'm not lettin' her go." He paused, obviously hoping to lend dramatic effect to his next announcement. "It's Daisy, honey, your mammy."

"My mama?" January stared at the tiny woman, whose upswept hair was just a shade darker than her own russet curls. Her eyes were swimming with unshed tears, but they were the same wide brown eyes as January's. The woman's nose was slightly more uptilted, but her tremulous smile was a reflection of January's own.

January's heart raced as she tried to take in the words. Her mama! The woman she'd yearned after for so many long years was actually sitting at her table. She was so surprised she couldn't even speak.

"January?" Daisy's voice cracked and tears flowed down her face, unchecked and unashamed. "My God, baby, it really is you. You're so beautiful."

Thc ycars fell away and were consumed in the beat of silent seconds. Overcome with happiness, January rushed into her mother's outstretched arms. "I never thought I'd see you again," she confessed with a sob.

"Nor I you," Daisy admitted. "Clarence told me all about how he met you and we've been looking for you ever since. There's so much I want to tell you, so much that must be said. But for the moment, can you ever find it in your heart to forgive me?"

January drew back and stared into her mother's face. Daisy was approaching forty, her skin peach-soft and etched with fine lines. But she was still as lovely as January remembered. "Forgive you? There's nothing to forgive. You're here and we're together at last. That's all that matters."

"Oh, my dear, sweet girl." They hugged and cried and laughed all over again and soon everyone was talking at once. The children were introduced—first, January's sister, thirteen-year-old Elizabeth, or Lizzie as she was called. Lizzie was a bright-eyed girl with a soft voice and refined manners. She seemed only too willing to be crushed in her newfound sister's embrace.

January could scarcely take her eyes off her mother and sister long enough to meet Clarence's orphaned niece and nephew, whom he and Daisy had recently adopted. Ten-year-old Ray and seven-year-old Carrie were quiet, well-behaved children who needed only slight urging to have a second biscuit.

It didn't take long for January and her mother to feel comfortable in each other's company. In no time at all, it was as though they'd never been separated. There were things they needed to discuss, but those could wait until they had uninterrupted privacy. In the meantime, talking didn't seem so important. It was enough that they were together.

Before he went out to help Case with the morning chores, Clarence explained how he'd fetched the children after dropping January and Case off in Branson. Once he'd settled his business there, he'd decided it was time to disregard Daisy's request that he not look for her and he and the children had returned to Springfield in an effort to pick up her years-cold trail. Daisy's former employer sympathized with his quest and gave him some startling information about her apparent disappearance years before. After that, it hadn't taken long for Clarence to find her.

Ironically, Daisy and Lizzie had never left Springfield. She'd taken a job as housekeeper for a wealthy family and was living a mere three miles away. After their reunion, it took a lot of talking, but Clarence finally convinced her that she'd denied herself happiness for too long.

Overjoyed to see Clarence after such a long time, Daisy agreed to marry him provided she could be freed by obtaining a divorce from Jubal. To that end, they wrote a judge in Butler County requesting him to grant one. Within weeks, they'd received word of Jubal's death.

At January's stricken look, Daisy pulled her into her arms. "You poor little thing—you didn't know, did you?"

"N-no," she whispered. "I wrote him a letter, but he never answered it." January knew she should be feeling grief for her lost father, but it was all tangled up in her joy at being unexpectedly reunited with her mother.

Clarence spoke up. "According to the judge's letter, he was killed in May."

"Killed? You mean he didn't die of natural causes?"

"No, dear." Daisy drew January into her arms and patted her consolingly. "A man named Mose Cleek murdered your father over a poker game and was duly hanged for the offense."

"Mose killed Pa?" January tried to marshal the appropriate outrage, but she wasn't really surprised by the news of Jubal's violent demise, or by Mose's part in it. Her father had lived a dissolute life, one that tempted fate's ire at every turn. All she could feel was pity and sorrow for both men. Releasing a shuddering breath, January found comfort in her mother's long-denied embrace.

Clarence picked up the threads of the story. Following their marriage, he and Daisy had tried to find January. Since he believed she was homesteading in the Territory, they'd written the Land Bureau offices there, requesting a search of records for a deed filed in her name. When those efforts proved a dead end, Daisy had been heartbroken, but they hadn't given up.

Quite by accident, Clarence had run into an old gambler he'd known in Hot Springs who told him he'd heard Case Latimer had taken a wife and settled on a farm near Gainesville. Apparently, the news had shaken the gambling community to its very foundations.

"I reckon we was taking a chance that his wife would be you," Clarence told January with a broad wink in Case's direction. "But we had to come and see for ourselves."

"I'm glad you did. It feels so good to have all of you here." January felt the tears well up again. She was sorry Pa was dead, but his passing had meant overdue happiness for her mother. It was true what the Bible said about the Lord giving and taking away. "I don't mean to cry. I'm just so happy."

Case was pleased for January. Although he knew how much it meant to her to see her mother and sister, he regretted not being responsible for her joy. They owed Clarence a lifelong debt of gratitude for reuniting the family. "What are your plans now?"

Clarence glanced at Daisy. "She's got a hankering to move back to the hills. I sold my sister's place and we banked that money for Ray and Carrie. But I've got a little nest egg saved up and we were kind of hopin' to buy a farm near here. We brought a wagonload of house plunder along, in case we could find a likely place. That is if you young folks don't mind having your kinfolks move in on you."

January laughed. "Mind? I'd be right put out if you didn't! It's going to take us at least ten years just to catch up. Case, tell them about the Patterson place."

Case related what he knew of an untenanted farm for sale a few miles to the west and promised Clarence he'd go with him to check on it after the chores were done.

"So you've given up the road for good, have you, Clarence?" January prodded.

"Yep. No more Dr. Goodnews. It'll be plain old Mr. Riley from here on out. Not that farmin' will be any kind of new experience for me. I grew up on one and I reckon I still know a thing or two."

Late in the day, after Case and Clarence left to see about the property and the children were sent outdoors to explore, Daisy and January went into the quiet bedroom to talk.

They sat side by side on the bed and Daisy admired the pieced butterfly quilt January used as a counterpane. "It was a housewarming gift from one of my neighbors. Sarah Wilcox and her husband, Henry, have been good friends to us."

She told Daisy about their early days on the farm, about the difficulties she'd had adjusting to the community and how she'd come to rely on Case's superior knowledge of all things social. She related their hardships and triumphs, always speaking of her husband in the most tender terms.

Daisy squeezed her daughter's hand. "I'm so happy for you, Jannie. Do you mind if I call you that old pet name?"

"Not at all. You're the only one who ever did. I kind of missed it."

"Jannie, I have to explain why I left you. Why I never came back to Possum Holler."

"Mama, it doesn't matter anymore."

"It matters to me. I don't want you ever to think I

abandoned you because I didn't love you. I always loved you."

"I know that. Sometimes I got terrible lonely. Pa was always off somewhere drinking and gambling with his friends and I was alone a lot. I played a game and pretended you were there. I'd close my eyes and conjure up your violet scent, then I'd imagine your soft hands stroking my hair, your sweet voice singing me lullabies. I always knew that wherever you were, you were loving me. Sometimes the memories were the only good things in my life."

Daisy sobbed into her hands. "Oh, baby, I'm so sorry. I don't regret the years Clarence and I were kept apart because now we have each other and we have the children. Most of all we have a chance to start all over again. Not many get that out of life. My only regret is for the years you and I lost."

"Don't cry, Mama." January pulled her mother into her arms and now it was she who did the comforting.

"When Jubal made me leave, I didn't know what to do," Daisy confessed. "I wanted to take you with me, but he wouldn't let me. He threatened to . . . hurt you if I didn't leave. I was big with Lizzie, tired and sick, too weak to fight him. I always planned to come back when I was able, but I never did. That's what I want to explain."

"You had your reasons. You don't owe me an explanation," January insisted.

"Oh, but I do. When I went to work in the Hollisters' big, happy house, Lizzie and I finally found some security. At first I told myself I didn't have the resources to go back to Possum Holler, but as the years got away from me, I finally realized that what I lacked was the courage."

"I don't blame you, Mama, for not wanting to let that dark meanness back in yours and Lizzie's lives."

"As much as I loved you, I was too cowardly to face Jubal again. Can you forgive me for not coming back?"

"I was just a little girl when you left, but I knew you didn't leave because you wanted to. I hated Pa for making you go and for taking all the beauty and joy from my life and I wished for some way to punish him. I think he hated me for looking so much like you and for reminding him of what he'd done. For a long time the hating lay between us like a deep black pit.

"As I grew older, hating him just seemed too much trouble and I started feeling sorry for him. Pa was a sad and lonely man who died without a soul to mourn him. I guess that was his punishment. I don't hate him anymore, but I'll never forgive him."

Daisy sighed. "The saddest thing of all is that Jubal did love me. He just never believed I loved him. People said I married beneath myself, but I was a young girl who'd lost her parents and was blind to everything but the way he made me feel. Your pa was quite the dashing young man, Jannie."

"Pa?"

"He was different before he took to drinking, before he gave up on us. He was uneducated and hard-turned sometimes, but I think deep down he had a good heart."

"Why'd he change, Mama?"

"I don't know for sure, but I think he felt he couldn't give me the things I was accustomed to. He never accepted that I didn't care about that. He wasn't the type to look inward, so he blamed me for everything. It seemed the more doubts he had, the more he drank. Finally, he lost all reason. I take comfort in knowing I never gave him cause to doubt me."

January looked up, surprised. "Pa treated you so bad and accused you wrongly of so many things, why did you feel you owed him your loyalty?"

Daisy smiled sadly. "I felt I owed it to myself and to my daughters not to become what he accused me of being."

January's resentment toward her father found new fuel. "If only he'd believed in himself and in you, things would have been so different for all of us."

"That's true enough, dear. But God works in mysterious ways. If things had been different, you might never have found Case and the happiness you were meant to have."

As January listened to her mother, a frightening thought chilled her. Like Jubal, she was guilty of doubting her own worthiness to be loved. It was hard to accept that a polished, educated man like Case could ever truly love an ignorant nobody like herself. "Things are still shaky between Case and me," she admitted. "He says he wants to stay here, but I'm afraid I can't hold him. What do I have to offer a man like Case?"

Daisy grasped January's shoulders and forced her to meet her gaze. "I don't ever want to hear you say another word against yourself. Any man would count himself lucky to have a wife even half as good and kind and beautiful as you. I know you're strong and determined or you never would have survived. Case knows that, too."

January was about to interrupt when her mother went on. "My biggest fear for you over the years was that living with Jubal would shrivel up your heart like a frost-killed rose. Don't let him have that final triumph, Jannie. Beat him by accepting the love Case is offering you."

January's mind worried her mother's words like a tongue worrying a sore tooth. It was all true, only she'd been too blind to realize it. "Thank you, Mama."

Daisy swiped her tearstained cheeks. "For what?"

"For coming back when I needed you most, for showing me the truth, for preventing me from making a terrible mistake. And most of all, for helping me understand that I have something to offer Case."

Daisy pulled her close and they held each other for a few long moments. Setting her daughter away from her, she said, "I'd say you have the most important thing in the world to offer him."

"What's that?"

Daisy smiled knowingly. "His baby."

"Baby? What baby?"

"Don't try to keep your happy secret from your own

mother, girl. It's plain you're carrying Case's child. About three months gone, I'd say."

January was staggered by this revelation. "Are you sure?"

"Aren't the signs all there?" Daisy detailed the early symptoms of pregnancy and a wide-eyed January recognized them at once.

It had to be true. She was pregnant. How ironic that all the time she'd been plotting to get in the family way, she already was.

"I take it Case doesn't know, either."

January gasped. Case! Lord a-mercy, how would she tell him? She was thrilled, but how would he take such surprising news? Would he feel some of his choices were gone forever? Could she gamble her pride and risk his rejection after this new development? Her new understanding gave her the strength to decide to do just that. "No, he doesn't. I reckon I'll have to lay my cards on the table and tell him."

"That's the way things are usually done, dear."

"Then that's what I'll do. I know I ain't—I mean, I'm not a cultured lady like his mother was, but I'm trying. Aunt Sarah has been teaching me cooking and sewing and such, and even if I don't seem to have any aptitude for it, I'm not about to give up. I'm a fair hand at farming and I plan to be a good mother if it kills me. Hellfire, put like that, I'd say he was getting a right fair bargain."

Daisy laughed with her daughter. "Maybe Case was a gambler, but he wasn't risking much when he tied up with you. Obviously, he was smart enough to recognize a sure thing. You have a good heart, Jannie. And you found a good man. Case Latimer is as fine a husband as a woman could hope for."

January got up and twirled around the room, filled with giddy happiness. "Ain't he, though? He's fine and I'm dandy. What a matched pair we make. Our offspring ought to be a humdinger."

"I can't believe I'm about to be a grandmother. When will the happy event take place?"

"Hellfire!" January stopped dancing around and chewed a nail thoughtfully. "I don't know. How does a woman figure out these things?"

Daisy rolled her eyes dramatically. "Part of your education as a woman has been completely neglected. I'm sorry I wasn't around to enlighten you about such things, but come sit down and I'll remedy that."

Between them they calculated the baby's arrival for early February.

Case was as excited as Clarence when they left town with a signed deed in the older man's pocket. It would be good for January to have kin close by. Not only that, but the thought of having the family all together for Sunday suppers and such gave Case a sense of belonging that he hadn't felt for years. Banished forever were those old feelings of rootlessness. It was a big responsibility to tie your life to that of another, but it was a responsibility he welcomed. The future seemed so bright, he found himself whistling on the drive home.

"You're mighty chipper," Clarence observed dryly.

"And why shouldn't I be? I've got a good woman, fertile ground, and fair weather."

Clarence slapped his thigh. "Danged if you don't sound just like a farmer."

Case grinned sheepishly. "I guess I do."

"You know, when I heard you'd settled down, I had myself a good laugh. I never figured you'd amount to a hill of beans as a farmer. I reckon you fooled me."

"I even fooled myself. But to be honest, most of this"—his sweeping gesture took in the verdant fields on both sides of the road—"is January's doing. She told me when and where to plant what. Hell, I was so ignorant, she had to teach me to plow. But she never made me feel half as useless as I was."

"It's a good woman who's wise enough to coddle her

man's pride,'' Clarence observed. ''Either she's a smart teacher or you're an apt pupil because you've got some mighty fine crops. You'll get a good price for the corn and the money will come in handy. It promises to be a hard winter.''

''January says the same thing. How is it you Ozarkers know so much about predicting the weather?''

Clarence scratched his head thoughtfully. ''There's lots of signs. All you got to do is keep a sharp eye out. I recollect a beaver dam on a stream we crossed on the way here. It had more sticks on the north side than on the south. That's a sign of a bad winter, for sure. The crows have been flocking together, too.''

''January says she can tell because the carrots grew deeper than usual this year and the onions grew more layers.''

''Those are good signs. Your gal knows her weather.''

''My gal knows just about everything,'' Case said proudly. It was too bad she didn't know his heart as well.

Later, when everyone was seated around the supper table, January asked the blessing. She thanked God for delivering her family to her and expressed gratitude that everyone she loved was together at last. When the prayer was over, she looked up and caught Case's keen, tender look. It filled her with nervous anticipation.

As Clarence relayed his good news, sad memories of the past were all but forgotten in a flurry of plans for the future. ''The place is vacant and if it's all right with Daisy, we'll go on over there tonight and start settling in.''

Daisy's eyes, and those of the children, lit up excitedly at the prospect of spending the night in their new home.

''What's your hurry?'' January wanted to know. ''Can't you stay with us a little longer?'' She had mixed feelings about being left alone with Case again. Hard as she tried, she had yet to find the necessary words to tell him about the baby.

Clarence smiled. ''Maybe you two are old married folk,

but Daisy and me are still newlyweds. I'm hankering to tote my bride over the threshold."

Later, January and Case watched the Rileys' wagon pull away and stood for long moments in the gathering dusk. He put his arm around her and tugged her close. "Happy?"

"Very." She thought of the baby swimming in the dark depths of her and smiled. Surely Case would be as happy as she was. Wondering what his fellow knights of the green cloth would say if they knew old Hard Case Latimer was in serious danger of settling down to domestic bliss made January erupt in a fit of giggles.

"What's so funny?" he demanded.

"Nothing." She squirmed from his grasp. "Imagine Clarence calling us old married folks. Ever hear such sheepdip in your life?" She darted playfully away, challengingly, and dashed up the steps into the house.

"Imagine that." Case sprinted after her. He caught her on the porch and kissed her so stirringly that January feared her legs would fail her. Somewhat belatedly, Case scooped her up into his arms and carried *his* bride over the threshold.

Inside the house, noting her wayward grin, he demanded, "What's gotten into you, woman? Don't say 'nothing' because I know better. I've played cards with you, remember? You can't hide a thing behind that pretty face."

"Who, me?" January batted her eyelashes dramatically and clung to him fiercely.

One dark brow arched suspiciously. "Yeah, you. If I didn't know better, I'd say you were holding four aces."

She shook her head in denial. Just before his mouth closed over hers, she whispered, "More like a full house."

Case meant to question that smug little remark, but in his fervor to lay claim to her body and heart, it slipped his mind.

Chapter 23

Case drifted up from a deep and satisfying sleep. Though the bedroom was quiet and the world beyond the window dark, he sensed the nearness of dawn. Before long the rooster would crow, the sky would brighten to pink, and the farm would demand his attention once again. If anyone had told him six months ago that he'd be up at first light milking cows and worrying about the egg count, he would have dismissed them as mad.

He smiled wryly when he thought of the surprises life could spring on a man while he was busy making other plans. And the gifts it could bestow. The most precious gift of all stirred beside him and he reached for January's softness and warmth. In her sleep she cuddled into his arms and his heart expanded to accommodate the profound love he felt for her.

Case wanted to waken her, to demonstrate with words and kisses how much he cared. But he didn't. With a certainty he'd never felt about another thing, he knew there would be plenty of time to tell her of his love. They had a whole lifetime to share. His only regret was that he'd clung to such an ill-fitting dream as Alaska for so long. Or maybe it hadn't been a dream at all, just an illusion. He'd thought to find freedom in solitude, but it had proved just the opposite. His winter-hearted reluctance to give of himself had become the very prison walls he'd sought to escape and had made him unable to accept the love January had offered from the very beginning.

Gently, he traced the beloved planes of her face and marveled at her tender beauty. She was not the same wild young girl he'd met only a few short months before; she'd changed. There was a womanliness to her now, a fullness, a ripe promise. His hand slipped down to her breast and he thoughtfully caressed her sleep-warmed skin. He recalled her remark about holding a full house and, as he waited for dawn, Case tried to scrape fragmented observations into full-fledged understanding.

He had little experience with the travails of women, but there had to be an explanation for January's recent qualminess. She was as healthy as anyone he knew, but lately he'd seen her make stumbling retreats to the necessary with her hand clamped over her mouth. She'd excused the nausea as "something she'd eaten," but since they partook of the same food, he suspected there was more to her uncharacteristic squeamishness than she was letting on.

Also, for someone with her vitality and energy, it didn't seem right for her to be as tired and sleepy as she'd been of late. She tried to hide it, but Case had grown increasingly concerned about the dark smudges of fatigue under her eyes.

He panicked at the thought of January becoming ill, of her falling prey to some dire malady. The knowledge that he couldn't bear life without her pointed out to him just how much he had changed as well. No longer was he the same self-interested young fool he'd been before. Now he had someone to love and his life had meaning.

As he held her possessively and vowed to keep her from harm's way, his mind relinquished the final puzzle piece and he gasped in realization—since their arrival at the farm, January had not once been visited by her monthly courses. When he put it all together, there could be only one answer. She was expecting his child.

He caressed her abdomen in wonder. Was it possible a babe was already growing in the shelter of her small, sturdy body? With all his being, Case hoped it was true. A baby would be a blood bond between them that could never be broken.

He tried to recall just when he'd made the decision to stay with her, to make her his own. Most likely the idea had been planted the first night when he'd saved her from drowning, and nurtured throughout the weeks they'd spent together. Only he'd been too damned ornery to admit that what he felt was more than unrequited lust.

All their fights, verbal and otherwise, had been no more than a futile attempt on both their parts to deny a frighteningly powerful attraction. He sighed in relief that neither of them had succeeded at the denial.

The rooster announced the new day with noisy abandon and still January did not awaken. Surely he was to blame for her unusual sluggishness. He'd kept her up most of the night, but at the time, she'd lodged no objections. In fact, she'd been eager to forego the pointlessness of sleep for the excitement of extended lovemaking. In that regard she was, indeed, a changed woman.

But one thing hadn't changed. All her newly acquired maturity, wisdom, and domesticity hadn't altered the fact that she was still as literal-minded as ever. He could talk until judgment day and never truly convince her of his love or his good intentions. Maybe if he hung around for twenty or thirty years she'd begin to believe he'd outgrown the wanderlust forever, but he knew a quicker way to prove the depth of his commitment.

Reluctant to leave the love-tangled bed, Case kissed the tip of January's nose and swung his legs over the side. Luminous summer sunshine slanted through the windows as he dressed. Once outside, he went to the workshed and gathered up the tools he'd need to put his plan into action. The cows heard him and, rebuking him for his inattention, lowed to be fed and milked.

"Sorry, girls," he told them with a jaunty wave. "You'll just have to be patient until I finish a building job so important it can't wait a minute longer." January would be mad enough to eat clay when she found out he wasn't tending to business, but gambler that he was, Case was inclined to bet she'd forgive him.

Waking to the steady ring of a hammer, January reached for Case. He was gone. A desolate chill swept through her before she realized he was most likely the one creating all the commotion outside.

She rolled over and stretched, luxuriating in the remembered delight she'd found in his arms. Never had she expected to know even one jot of the earth-rattling joy they'd shared. Truly, if this was what being in love meant, she never wanted to be out of it.

The hammering persisted and she smiled lazily. Danged if Case wasn't finally showing a little gumption by getting out so early to fix the henhouse roof. Most likely, this was his way of showing her he wanted to stay and make the farm his home.

After slipping on her wrapper, January stepped over to the window and breathed deeply of the dew-damp air. As she surveyed their snug holdings, her heart quickened with an intense pride of ownership, with a feeling of belonging. She belonged not only to the land but to the man who'd become a part of it.

He'd fought it every step, but there was no way around it. It was no longer just her farm. It was theirs.

"The Latimer place," she said aloud. The words sounded good together; they spoke to her very spirit. In them she sensed not only the steadfastness of the present but the whispered insistence of the future. It was a fine place for a child to grow up.

Lovingly, she stroked her abdomen in an effort to communicate her happiness and assurance to the life growing within. Then she hugged herself and the secret she would soon share. She'd meant to tell Case last night, but the way things had worked out, she'd never had the chance.

Glancing toward the henhouse, January realized he wasn't there. Yet the clamor of his hammering was steady and persistent above the reproachful bawling of the cows.

If he wasn't fixing the roof, what in tarnation was all the ruckus about? What was so danged important it couldn't wait until the cows were milked?

Tugging her wrapper tight, January padded through the house and stepped out onto the front porch. The dooryard was drenched in golden light and she shaded her eyes with one hand. When she saw what her husband was building, all practical matters fled her mind and she didn't know whether to laugh or to cry.

A picket fence!

''Latimer,'' she called jubilantly, ''you're crazy!''

He looked up and removed a clutch of nails from his mouth before answering. ''I know. You're the one I'm crazy about.''

''It's too early to be out here hammerin'.'' Surprised at her own audacity, she added, ''Come back to bed.''

''Nope. I have to finish this.'' Case bent to his task, nailing pickets to the uprights he'd already positioned in the ground.

January was delighted by his absurd determination and by the method he'd chosen to prove his devotion. But she couldn't resist teasing him. ''I hope you aren't building that fence to keep my family out.''

''Nope.'' He flashed her a knowing smile. ''I'm building it to keep mine in. Can't have the baby toddling off.''

The baby! January couldn't guess how he'd figured it out but she didn't care. He knew and darned if he didn't seem as happy about it as she was.

Case swung his leg over the fence-in-progress and, with a devilish gleam in his eyes, strode to her side.

''Does this mean what I think it means?'' she asked breathlessly.

''It means you didn't marry an idiot after all.''

''What about Alaska?'' she had to ask, needing to hear the words.

''Hell, who needs Alaska? I've heard Ozark winters are bad enough.''

''But what about freedom?''

He took her into his arms and pulled her close. ''I am free. Free to grow old with the woman I love.''

''What about gambling?'' she whispered, afraid she would melt under his gaze like a puddle of sunshine.

''You should know. Farming is the biggest gamble of all.''

January's love for him was so grand, she feared her heart could ill contain it. Unable to resist one last question, she whispered, ''What about adventure?''

Case claimed her with a long, promise-filled kiss. Holding her fast in the shelter of his arms, he whispered back, ''Darlin', loving you is all the adventure this man can stand.''

JOANNA JORDAN

JOANNA JORDAN is a pseudonym for the writing team of Pat Shaver and Debrah Morris who live in Norman, Oklahoma. They choose to collaborate because there is safety in numbers and two heads are better than one. With their busy schedules, having four hands and forty-eight hours in the day is a distinct advantage.

With dogged determination they faithfully juggle their roles as writers, wives, and mothers, along with just about any other role that requires their reluctant attention.

They lace their romances with humor because they feel love and laughter are essential for a happy life, and entertaining the reader is what it's all about. They enjoy matchmaking on paper, but the best part is helping fictional couples find their happily-ever-afters.